ONLY AS A STRANGER

RAY CHAPMAN

ANTRA PUBLICATION

To

Valerie and Alisa

Also in print by the same author:

We'll Meet Again

Order on the internet
www.antra.co.uk
or buy in bookshops

Antra Publishing

ANTRA PUBLISHERS

33 Oakdene Park
Finchley

London N3 1EU

A CIP catalogue record for this book is available from the British Library.

IBSN: 0-9545899-1-2

Cover by Novel Graphic

Printed by Biddles Ltd,
King's Lynn, Norfolk,
England

ONE

The small group of people gathered by the green Jaguar car parked in the suburban tree lined road were saying their goodbyes, the men and women comfortably dressed in lightweight summer clothes. Music from a nearby open window whispered gently in the balmy early evening air, the sun still bright in a clear blue sky.

Tom Fisher gripped Dixie's arms and smiled.

'It's a lovely flat,' he said, and raised a hand to shield his eyes as he looked once again at the large Victorian property cleverly converted into four homes.

'Thank you, Daddy,' she said, and gave him a peck on the cheek. Her parents and boyfriend, Nick, had arrived four hours earlier. A corny Sunday first time visit for her mother and father since Dixie had bought the flat in Woodside Park, north London, a month ago.

It was her very first home that wasn't rented since she'd left her family's protection two years before, just after her twenty first birthday.

Her parents got in the car and the window whirred down on her mother's side.

'You should have let me give you a hand with the washing up before we left.'

'That's okay, Mother,' Dixie smiled, her deep blue eyes twinkling. 'I'll leave it until tomorrow,' then quickly added, as she saw the older woman frown, 'only joking. I'll do it as soon as I go back in.'

She bent, gently kissed her mother, and whispered, 'Maybe a dishwasher for Christmas?'

Her mother laughed.

'I'll see what your Father says.'

'What's that, dear?' Tom asked, as he switched on the engine.

'Nothing, darling,' his wife replied. 'I'll have a word with you later.'

Dixie gave her tousle haired boyfriend a kiss and he slid into the back seat. Her parents were giving him a lift back to the flat he shared with his divorced mother near Marylebone High Street. Nick had an early plane to catch to Rome the following morning and still had to pack.

'We'll give you a ring when we get home,' her mother said, waving from the window as the car moved off.

*

Fifty yards behind where the Jaguar had been parked a black Cherokee Jeep suddenly burst into life. The driver glanced in his rear view mirror then eased away from the kerb and began following the green saloon car.

When Tom Fisher reached the end of the road and swung right at the T-junction the Jeep took the same direction, allowing one vehicle between them. The driver adjusted the air conditioning and turned on the radio. It was the third weekend in a row he'd tailed the Fisher's, each time in a different car, hoping for the right opportunity.

Maybe it would come today.

*

Tom Fisher slowed for the lights and glanced sideways at his wife as the vehicle stopped. A smile played across his face as he admired her pert and pretty profile, her dark hair in contrast to his silvery white thatch. He loved Margo as much now as he did all those years ago when they'd married.

Tom pressed gently on the accelerator as the lights changed to green and the powerful car crept forward. After he'd left Dixie's street he'd driven in the direction of Nick's mother's home in central London. The young man had been going out with their daughter for about six months and, although Dixie told them it wasn't serious, he had lasted longer than the norm.

*

The three punks sat on a low brick wall in a side street in West Kilburn. The two youths were dressed in sweaty black T-shirts, jeans and heavy boots, the girl, no more than seventeen, wore a dirty white shirt, black fishnet tights and a short black leather skirt. Her straw blonde hair stood out in all directions, and light glinted off silver rings and studs pierced through her ears, with several more stuck through her nose.

The three had been popping pills and smoking for the last forty eight hours, but had finished their last spliff an hour ago. They desperately needed more gear - but were broke.

'So what we gonna do?' the youth with an acne cratered face like the far side of the Moon impatiently asked his friend, whose long black hair was plastered back with a ton of oil. At nineteen he was the leader.

'Wait,' Greasy replied, then stiffened and started to walk as he saw a dark blue Ford Focus, with elderly occupants inside, carefully park about twenty yards away. 'Come on, Poxy,' he said, and quickened his stride towards the target.

The other two followed and as they reached the car Greasy walked into the road and wrenched open the driver's door.

'What do you think you're doing?' the old man gasped, his eyes wide with shock.

The oily haired lout gave a leer, reached inside and yanked the man out. He grabbed the car keys from the driver and shoved him hard away from the Focus, sending him sprawling on the pavement.

Poxy following his leader yanked open the passenger door and dragged the elderly woman straight onto the hard concrete. The blonde girl grabbed the old lady's black leather handbag and tried to twist it from her, but a gnarled fist hung on grimly.

'Let go of it, you dozy old cow,' the girl said, and punched the pensioner hard in the face. The woman's gold frame glasses flew off and her hands instinctively went to her bloody nose.

The tatty blonde shouted with delight as the bag came free and she opened the car rear door and jumped in. The old man tried gamely to get to his feet to help his wife but stopped when a knife blade flashed in front of his eyes.

'Get in the car,' Greasy barked out the words, and the other youth jumped obediently into the front passenger seat, his head jerking back as the dark blue car accelerated away from the kerb.

'Hey, stop,' a young man shouted as he ran down the front steps of a nearby house. He'd seen what had happened to his elderly neighbours but it was over so quickly he'd been unable to help. By the time he reached the old couple other people were giving assistance so he rushed back indoors and called for an ambulance and the police.

*

The Ford screeched around the corner into the mainstream traffic, its driver ignoring the frantic horns, as he weaved dangerously in between the orderly vehicles.

'Did the old bird have much bread in her bag?' Greasy shouted into the back as he took one hand off the steering wheel to give another driver the V sign.

'Thirty five quid, that's all,' the girl replied.

'That's enough to score,' Poxy said, his red rimmed eyes showing some sign of life at the thought.

'Yeah, and then we can go for a ride in the country,' Greasy gave a crazy chuckle and wrenched the wheel hard over, just missing the front of a red bus. Poxy punched the roof of the Focus and whooped, then turned his head and looked out the rear window as he heard the piercing sound of a police siren.

The pock marked punk grinned and slapped the driver on his shoulder.

'The old bill...but I bet you can lose 'em.'

Greasy grinned back.

'Don't worry about that,' he said,

*

The number of the stolen Ford Focus came over the car radio just about the same time as the policemen spotted the car weaving dangerously in and out of the traffic. They would have chased the vehicle anyway.

PC Alan Shaw immediately switched on the siren of the white police car and his foot pushed harder on the accelerator. His partner confirmed the car number with their control room and said they were in pursuit.

'We're heading towards Kilburn High Road,' he said, then added, as the Focus mounted the pavement at a busy intersection, luckily missing a couple of pedestrians, 'the crazy buggers. We've got some right nutters here.'

Both white shirted policemen stared intently through the windscreen saying silent prayers they came through the chase without injury.

*

Greasy was enjoying himself and loved the feeling of power as he overtook the slower cars. Typical Sunday drivers, he grinned. He'd show 'em.

Traffic lights ahead changed to red as he approached but he didn't care and picked up speed.

'Get out the fuckin' way,' he shouted, and went through the crossroads at eighty miles an hour with cars honking furiously.

'Did yer see that?' Poxy, one arm casually dangling over his seat, looked behind him. 'Amazin', two bloody cars smashed right into each other. Must be lousy drivers,' he laughed.

Greasy shouted out loud as the car hit the kerb of a white bollard and the Ford leapt several feet in the air. Then he shouted louder as he sideswiped a parked vehicle. By now there were two police cars in the chase as they headed towards West Hampstead.

*

The green Jaguar cruised effortlessly along the Finchley Road, the motor purring like a contented cat in Tom Fisher's safe hands. They passed through Temple Fortune and Golders Green heading in the direction of the West End.

Dropping off Nick wasn't too much out of their way, even though Tom and Margo lived on the other side of the river in Richmond. Just a different route, that was all.

The road ahead widened just before a set of traffic lights. They had been green for some time and Tom pressed slightly harder on the foot pedal so he'd get safely across before they started to change. Then he suddenly heard a siren and automatically began to slow down trying to establish which direction the noise was coming from.

*

The driver of the Cherokee Jeep, now directly behind the Jaguar, immediately realized this was the chance he'd been waiting for. In a split second he took in the situation as he saw the blue Focus hurtling along the other road chased by a police car and knew the Ford was going to jump the lights. So he gripped tight the steering wheel with his gloved hands, pressed hard on the accelerator and tensed himself as the heavy vehicle slammed forcefully into the green car in front of him.

Tom Fisher felt the impact of the crash in his rear and was pushed forward, but was powerless to do anything. Then the Jeep once again cannoned into the back of the Jaguar propelling it into the path of the Focus. Tom briefly glimpsed the blue car out of the corner of one eye and his body felt the tremendous impact as the Ford smashed into him, the air bag ballooning in his face, the sound of tearing metal a hideous sound in his ears as he spun across the intersection.

Several workmen, earning weekend overtime unloading scaffolding from a lorry, jumped for safety as the large saloon car hurtled towards them. There was another loud collision as the car shunted into the back of the lorry and metal poles flew through the air, several piercing the Jaguar's windscreen.

Then deathly silence as the police sirens were switched off.

*

Dixie looked at her watch. Her parents should have reached home by now and phoned, but she wasn't too worried, they could have stopped off to see some friends. They had many.

It was still hot and humid so Dixie had a shower and washed her long black hair, put on a short white nightie and switched on the television.

An hour later she tried her parents home number but only got the answer machine. She left a brief message then phoned her father's mobile, but a voice informed her it was switched off.

She'd hung back from phoning Nick because she knew he was going to have an early night and had a minicab booked for six am to take him to Heathrow Airport. Another hour went by and her uneasy thoughts had become a nagging worry. Finally, she could contain herself no longer, and made the call to her boyfriend. She had her apologies ready for Nick's mother, but there was no reply, so Dixie kept the phone ringing until the answer machine turned itself on and left a message.

It was nearly midnight when Dixie's front doorbell rang and the suddenness of it made her heart jump. It was still thudding as she opened the door and saw the two uniformed police officers standing there. A man and a woman.

One of them started to speak and, as she heard the words, pressure in Dixie's ears built up as though they'd explode. Instead, a wave of dizziness swept over her, tossing her into a pit of darkness.

The policeman caught her before she hit the floor.

TWO

Her mother was killed outright in the crash and her father died three hours later in hospital. Nick fought on for longer, and at one stage his young strong body seemed to rally, but his injuries were too severe, and he also lost his fight for life.

The days passed - but the daze didn't. An awful pun but it stuck in Dixie's mind. Her thoughts were a kaleidoscope of shattered pieces and nothing fitted together. She was given sedatives and took more than the prescribed dosage. Not that she ever once thought of taking her own life. She was already dead. But she wanted to forget...forget. The word hammered in her brain. Forget...and the pain will go away.

It gave her no satisfaction whatsoever when she'd been told that the two punks in the other car had also been killed and the third occupant, a young girl, was in a coma, only kept alive by a life support machine.

However, the driver of the Cherokee Jeep remained a mystery. Witnesses were a bit hazy. Everything had happened so quickly. Some said he was driving too fast, too close to the Jaguar and couldn't stop in time. But it didn't look like it was his fault. He didn't appear to have much of a chance once the Jaguar slammed on its brakes.

Some said the man had a moustache, others said he was clean shaven. He could have been tall and slim, or medium height and weight. The usual conflicting eye witness accounts.

But all agreed he was in his fifties, with grey curly hair.

One other thing was certain. The abandoned Jeep had been stolen a couple of days before the accident and had false number plates. And the driver just seemed to vanish in the confusion, which was understandable in the circumstances. The forces of law and order were the last people a car thief would want to see, even though he was unwittingly involved.

The final conclusion reached by the police was that the occupants of the blue Ford Focus were solely responsible for the fatal crash.

*

Dixie tried to distance herself from the events around her and was only dimly aware of arrangements being made that needed doing immediately. Even death had a procedure to follow.

People tried to comfort her, but their sympathy, well meaning as it was, just washed over her. She smiled blandly and thanked them. But she didn't want relatives or friends. She wanted her mother and father.

However, there was *one* person who seemed to connect with Dixie in her grief. Linda Brooks, the daughter of one of her mother's closest friends, a pretty young woman with short dark curly hair, and a knack for listening. Not that Dixie was saying much, but Linda's caring and easy going nature, brought a certain comfort to her. The proverbial shoulder to cry on.

*

The day of the funeral was bright and sunny, just like that Sunday, the last time she'd seen her parents alive.

The service was held in a small 19th century church in Surrey, and the only reason she was able to cope was because of the physical strength her father's younger brother, Robert, gave her. His was the firm, strong hand that supported her arm, steadying her through the simple, dignified ceremony.

The only other close relative still living was her father's sister who'd travelled down from Nottinghamshire. Dixie's

Aunt Lucy was the eldest in the family, a frail, but cheerful spinster who walked with the aid of a walking stick. Unfortunately, illness had aged her ten years.

But the rest of the somberly dressed congregation just blurred into an anonymous collection of faces.

And the sight of the two polished wooden coffins being slowly lowered into the ground, one on top of the other, was just too much for her, and she broke down completely at the finality of it all.

Her mother and father – gone for ever.

*

Kate Smith stood in the crowd of people gathered around the grave, every now and again removing her rimless glasses and dabbing her eyes with a small white handkerchief. Kate had been Tom Fisher's private secretary for the last five years. An efficient, neatly dressed unmarried woman in her late thirties she'd taken a lot of pressure off his back and was privy to all his files. There'd been no secrets between them and Tom had trusted her implicitly. Especially in the last month before the car crash.

Kate had been deeply shocked by the sudden death of her boss. He'd been a wonderful man to work for and in all the time of their working relationship never known him lose his temper once.

When the service had finished and people started to disperse Kate walked slowly towards Dixie and Robert Fisher.

She smiled at the young woman and kissed her gently on the cheek.

'I'm so sorry,' she said, and nodded silently at Robert before walking away.

This wasn't the time to say what was really in her thoughts. The family was grieving and she'd wait a decent period before making her information public.

Or would she?

Because, deep inside her Kate knew she was only making excuses to herself by putting things off. If she was going to tell the truth - then now was the time to speak up - not wait.

But Kate had a lot of thinking to do before she made a decision. Maybe it was time she thought of herself and her future. She wasn't getting any younger.

As Kate hurried to her small Ford Fiesta she knew her first priority was to find a safe place for the papers her employer had insisted she copy in case something happened to the originals. Then she could decide what to do because Kate had serious doubts about the deaths of Tom Fisher and his wife.

She didn't think it *was* an accident.

*

Linda moved into Dixie's flat in Woodside Park. It was to be a provisional arrangement, just until Dixie felt she could manage by herself, then Linda would move back with her parents. She worked in their family business so a temporary leave of absence was no problem.

Dixie quit her job. She had been the personal assistant to the managing director of a large property company but couldn't face the prospect of going back to her old job.

Anyway, she was now a very wealthy young woman, and didn't need to work.

Dixie's father had been a director of a firm of chartered accountants, a business he'd started twenty years ago with his only brother, and three weeks after the funeral Robert asked her to come to his office.

'We've got to get those financial details we spoke about last week sorted out,' he said.

*

Dixie entered through the plate glass doors and walked across the marble and thickly carpeted entrance lobby of the tall block in High Holborn, the air conditioning a welcome relief. It was the middle of August and the weather was blistering hot. Dixie took a lift to the fifth floor.

In the last ten years the business had expanded and Fisher, Peterson and Partners occupied all of the office space on this large floor.

Dixie was dressed in a dark blue cotton shirt and skirt. Her long hair hung loosely about her attractive face, but lacked its usual lustre, and the dark bags under her eyes now seemed a permanent feature.

Her uncle ushered her into his bright, airy office, sat her in a comfortable chair, then returned to his large green leather topped desk. There was no need for small talk enquiring how she was because Robert had been in contact every day. He was five years younger than her father, with a slim athletic build gained from squash and swimming. His hair had turned silver which suited him and it was obvious he had looked after himself. And Robert, whose wife had died years ago and never had children, maintained an old fashioned sense of family responsibility. He knew he could never fill Tom's place but told his niece he'd always be there for her, if she needed him.

'You've only to ask,' he said.

The previous week Dixie had visited her father's solicitor's office for the reading of the will. Everything, except for a few small bequests, had been left to her and Robert had been named as the chief executor. But the exact amount hadn't been worked out until now.

Over the next half an hour Robert carefully explained his niece's financial affairs, which had taken a dramatic change since the death of her parents.

'I think you'll be surprised to find out just how much money you're worth,' he said in his kind voice.

'Your parents house has been valued at a million and a quarter pounds and you can add another sixty to seventy thousand for the contents. Your mother had a good eye for antiques and there are some valuable pieces there. Then there are insurance policies and your father had a healthy portfolio of stocks and shares. We accountants tend to be careful with our money.' Robert gave a small laugh and turned a few more pages of the thick file in front of him.

'Your father owned nearly a third of this company,' he continued. 'Tom and I were the founder members, but ten years ago Wyatt Peterson bought into the firm, and that's when we began to grow. We also have a few other partners in the company, who have been given a small amount of shares for their loyalty, but that was to make sure we kept them. They're good men and we are one of the biggest firm of chartered accountants in the country, plus we have a subsidiary company which handles investments for some of our clients.'

Robert picked up a gilt paper knife and turned it idly in his fingers.

'And we intend getting bigger. We've got a lot of plans...Tom and I talked so much about the future...it's so sad...,' his voice tailed off, his thoughts elsewhere. 'But I can still talk about the future. *Your future*,' he said, bringing himself back to the present. 'Even after death duties, I should imagine you'll have close to one and three quarter million pounds. And don't forget, that's not including your father's shares in this company, which now belong to you. They're worth quite a bit.'

Dixie was surprised at the amount but waited patiently for her uncle to continue.

'There are two things you can do,' he said. 'We can either buy you out or you can keep your shares and we will pay you a monthly wage as a silent partner. You wouldn't have any dealings in the day to day running of the company but you would retain your right to vote at any board meeting.'

Dixie nodded her head understandingly.

'How much would I get if you bought me out?'

'Peterson and I have discussed this and we are prepared to offer you two million pounds,' Robert answered.

The young woman sat looking at her uncle and slowly became aware of the silence in the room as she tried to calmly digest his words.

'This money is on top of what you say I'm already worth?' Dixie couldn't keep the amazement out of her voice.

'That's right.'

'And if I don't want to sell?'

'You keep your shares and the company pays you ten thousand pounds a month.'

More silence as the man and woman sat looking at each other. Then Dixie spoke.

'I'd like your advice, Uncle. What do you suggest is the best for me?'

'Keep the shares and accept the ten thousand a month. I can arrange for you to sign all the necessary papers some time next week. You see, this company is expanding and in five or ten years time,' Robert shrugged his shoulders, 'who knows, you'll probably double your money. I think it'll be worth your while.'

'Then that's what I'll do.'

'You sure you don't want time to think it over?'

Dixie shook her head.

'No, my mind's made up. The monthly money is something I never expected anyway, so I'll settle for that. But there is one question.'

'Yes?'

'What happens if I do want to sell my shares sometime in the future?'

'No problem. You would have to give the company three months notice of intention, that's all.'

Dixie had listened carefully to everything her uncle told her but somehow couldn't help thinking how ghoulish it all seemed. She was now rich because her mother and father were dead. She felt like a grave robber.

Robert's voice broke into her thoughts.

'Your parents house was put on the market, like you wanted, but *you* will have to sell the contents...or put them in storage.'

'I've made arrangements to go to the house the day after tomorrow where I'm meeting someone from a removal company,' Dixie said. 'I want all my parents personal possessions, and there are also a few pieces of furniture and some paintings I want to keep. Those I'll put in storage and the rest can be sold. Don't worry, I'll see to it.'

'What will you do with the money from the sale of the house?' her uncle asked.

'I'd like you to invest it for me. In fact, I'd like you to look after all my finances, be my accountant.'

'Keep it in the family, eh,' and Robert allowed a slight smile to cross his face. Surprisingly, he saw his niece briefly return the smile. Encouraged by this sudden show of normality he smiled again. Dixie had been such a wonderfully warm person before the tragedy. She was a good looking woman, beautiful in fact, but now looked drawn and had lost a lot of weight.

'And how are you getting on with Linda?' Robert asked.

'We get on fine, she's a nice woman.'

'Are you going to stay in Woodside Park, or will you be moving?'

Dixie looked thoughtful. She'd always known her parents had money but never thought of them as *rich*. Her private schools and comfortable home life had made her realize she was better off than a lot of people, she only had to read the papers or watch television to understand that, but Tom and Margo had never spoilt her.

'I don't know. Being left all this money is a bit hard to take in at the moment. I'm not sure what my plans will be now.'

THREE

Joey Judd stood waiting for the lift to arrive, his baggy denim shirt hanging out over his trousers, and his shortish dark straight hair with dyed blonde streaks carefully combed to look as though it wasn't. He wasn't particularly good looking except when he smiled and his dimples stood out, which made him look cheeky more than anything else. In his late twenties his clothes were in contrast to the smart busy people who moved from office to office.

Several times he smiled at the young mini skirted women as they passed. They smiled back, flattered, and no doubt would have immediately said yes if he'd asked them for a date. For Joey Judd was a pop superstar and his meteoric career over the last five years had been well documented, his photo a regular feature in all the newspapers and magazines. His latest single was riding high in the charts - his third number one in a row - all of them holding the top slot for more than three weeks.

The star had just spent an hour with his accountant checking his money was working well for him. Too many people in the music business had been ripped off in the past and Joey was making sure it didn't happen to him. No way would he ever end up skint. He'd already been there - and didn't fancy a return journey.

Everybody who worked for him had their own little slot. His manager managed for him and all his other employees did whatever they were supposed to do.

But when it came to his money there was only one person in charge. And that was Joey. He was worth twenty five million pounds and his accountant had assured him he would never have to worry about his future as long as he was careful with his investments. It wasn't worth taking unnecessary chances because he already had more money than most people dreamed of. That's why Joey had chosen this firm of accountants. They were solid. They had a good name in the City and, although the advice on their investment side wasn't as adventurous as some, Joey knew his money was safe. And that's all that mattered.

Not bad for a bloke who'd been brought up on a grotty council estate in London's East End.

He'd been advised he could become a tax-exile and increase his fortune but that would mean being able to live in England for only so many months of the year. Maybe he'd consider it later, when he was older, but he was too busy enjoying life at the moment to think that far ahead. Maybe in a few years.

He turned his head and saw an attractive young woman dressed in dark blue walk towards the lift. She was accompanied by an older, distinguished looking man who Joey knew was one of the firm's partners and stood talking a few feet from him. From the odd bits of overheard conversation he gathered the man was her uncle. She was certainly a looker - but her eyes seemed sad.

The lift arrived and Joey politely let the young lady enter before him, then other people pushed between them, and the lift began to descend, picking up more people on the way.

As the crowd surged from the lift Joey looked at his watch. He had to meet someone. Pity. He would have liked to have chatted up that dark haired bird who was now in front of him. She was first to get a taxi in the street and Joey wondered where she was going.

*

Joey spent the next two hours in a pub not far from the London Palladium with his record producer, Henry Smythe. Joey was a regular and nobody bothered him. Some tourists looked but the guv'nor of the pub made sure the pop star enjoyed a few pints in peace.

Joey had made a promise to himself that he was going to spend the next six months, or even longer, making a new album. In the last three years he'd done two world tours and countless gigs in the UK. Now he wanted time off to make some good music.

The next stop was a restaurant just off Berkeley Square but at nine thirty the record producer announced he was going home to his wife and kids. Henry was a good family man so Joey didn't push him to stay.

As Joey sat by himself drinking the last of the champagne, and doodling with the fluted glass over the thick white linen tablecloth, he wondered if he'd ever settle down. He knew he should, even if only to give his body a rest. He was just twenty eight but at times felt eighty eight. He didn't do much drugs now. Two years ago he spent six months zonked out of his mind on cocaine and had a bad experience when he collapsed on stage during a gig at the Wembley Arena. The tabloids had it right when they said it was drugs but his management insisted it was exhaustion and Joey got away with it.

At the same time a good friend of the pop star, roadie, Zak Shannon, died of an overdose and the harsh reality of that made Joey stop shoving junk up his nose.

He decided he wanted to live.

So he only did a bit of pot now and again, and although he loved a drink, knew he was in control.

But he was addicted to women. He couldn't help himself. He had all this crumpet throwing themselves at him and he couldn't say no.

*

Joey left the restaurant and walked in the direction of Regent Street. It was a beautiful warm evening, still only ten o'clock, and Joey knew where his footsteps were subconsciously taking him. He was going to one of Terry Hayman's clubs. A hostess club.

His feet turned into a side street towards a dark red scalloped canopy overhanging the pavement. A scar faced doorman dressed in black dinner jacket and bow tie stood outside. Alex, the guardian of the Tailgate Club, whose shoulders were nearly as wide as he was tall, smiled broadly as Joey approached and opened the door.

'Evening, Mr Judd,' he said.

'Is Terry in the club?'

'Not yet, but as soon as he knows you're here, I'm sure he'll be straight over. I'll get him on the blower.'

'Thanks,' Joey said, and as he entered the doorway Alex took a mobile phone from his inside pocket.

Joey went down the red carpeted stairs which led into a small bar area and stood looking around. It was dimly lit and only about half the tables in the main part of the club were doing any business. But it was still early. The club wouldn't liven up until after midnight.

There were about twenty hostesses scattered around the tables and bar. Young, scantily dressed and all on the lookout for punters, usually out of town businessmen on expense accounts. The girls got paid commission on how much drink and food they persuaded the customers to buy, but made their real money arranging to see a punter after they'd finished work.

However, Terry Hayman insisted this was their personal business and nothing to do with him. He didn't want to get nicked for living off immoral earnings. He was happy with the lucrative profit from the booze that was drunk every night.

But every time Joey had visited the club Terry made sure one or more of the hostesses were available to him, who jumped at the chance of having a quickie with the pop star. No charge, of course.

Terry's office in the rear of the club had a large couch which was well used.

Joey walked to the bar. Tilly, the usual barmaid was on duty and she leaned over showing ample cleavage in a low cut shirt.

'Champagne, Joey?'

'Yeah, thanks,' and Tilly went to the fridge behind the bar and took out a bottle of Moet & Chandon.

Joey was on his second glass when he felt a friendly arm on his shoulder. He turned and saw Terry Hayman's grinning face.

'How's the serial shagger, then?'

'Why do you think I'm 'ere?' Joey grinned back.

Terry was classically tall, dark and handsome, and so laid back you'd think he'd fall over any minute. Nothing bothered him and everyone liked him. Still only in his mid-thirties his business was a great success, with four clubs operating in Soho and the West End. He drove a Bentley and, as well as a flat in town, had a large country house in Oxfordshire, where he did a lot of entertaining. Joey had been to a couple of his weekend parties, which had turned into mind blowing orgies. There was never a shortage of women when Terry was around.

The two men had met at a showbiz dinner held at the Hilton Hotel in Park Lane two years ago and clicked immediately. Then Terry had invited the pop star to the Tailgate Club as his guest and Joey had sent Terry a few VIP tickets for a couple of his gigs.

After finishing the bottle of champagne they went to a corner circular booth and as they sat down Terry beckoned to a tall slim blonde woman standing by herself near the small stage. Sharon, the lady in charge of the girls and running of the club walked towards them, one long leg tantalizingly showing through the high cut slit in her black dress. She bent down and Terry whispered in her ear.

Sharon walked away and returned a few minutes later holding the hand of a big, blonde girl about nineteen who simply oozed fitness and energy. She was beautiful and perfectly proportioned, but must have been over six feet tall. Joey looked up at her. She was a fuckin' Amazon.

'Tammy, this is Joey.' Terry did the introduction as the girl sat down next to the singer.

'I know, I've got lots of your CD's,' she smiled, and turned her body towards Joey who got a close-up of one of the biggest pair of knockers he'd ever seen. Tammy was dressed like a cheerleader, in a short red mini skirt and tight red sweater which ended just under her bust, leaving her midriff bare.

'Tammy's new here, in fact, this is her first night,' Terry said, as he rose grinning and moved away from the booth. 'Maybe you'd like to take her to my office and interview her...see if she's suited for the job.'

Joey nodded and looked once again at the curvaceous young woman. *Interview* her - that was a novel way of putting it.

Slapping skin with this beauty would take more than one session. He'd probably end up in the morgue.

FOUR

Dixie packed all her parents personal possessions into wood storage chests except for the jewellery which she'd take with her. Gathering together *their* intimate mementos in their home was heart breaking. Albums of photographs were bad enough but when Dixie found a bundle of love letters written by her mother and father before they were married she couldn't handle it.

She felt like an intruder and started filling up the chests quickly, hardly bothering to look anymore. She'd do that at a later date when she took them out of storage. She would be able to handle it then.

Dixie and Linda stayed just over a week in the large house in Richmond organizing the sale of the rest of the contents. It was more sensible than driving from one side of London to the other.

Dixie picked out the furniture and paintings she wanted to keep and the rest of the more valuable items were sent to Sotheby's to be auctioned.

Several lots were sold on the spot to antique dealers who came to the house and the cheaper stuff was sold to a second hand dealer.

But Dixie got the best price for everything. Uncle Robert saw to that. One of his clients was big in the antiques business and spent a couple of days at the house helping out, much to Dixie's relief.

*

The second week in September Dixie knew she had to change her attitude. She was depressing everyone with her tearful, miserable expression and lack of communication. The realization came when two old friends unexpectedly paid a visit to her flat one afternoon.

But once their words of sympathy had been said the pauses became embarrassingly long and Linda had to keep the conversation going. Finally, after making lame excuses, the two friends left.

'You're going to have to snap out of it.'

The bluntness of the words surprised Dixie.

'You can't keep behaving like this,' Linda continued. 'I feel sorry for you, your relatives and friends feel sorry for you, but you can't keep wallowing in self pity,'

The words were harsh and, coming from anyone else other than Linda, would have caused a swift and angry response because Dixie wasn't just hurting, she had a deep anger inside her against the world. She wanted to strike out and make people suffer, like she was. But Dixie didn't lash out. She listened instead to the woman who had been so kind and caring to her since the death of her parents.

'I know it's only been a couple of months, and I know it's so easy for me and others to say the words everyone uses in difficult times like this, but people do care about you.'

Linda got up from her easy chair and knelt on the carpet in front of Dixie, taking her hands in her own.

'I know nobody can feel exactly what you're going through right now and it will probably take a long time for the pain to go. But the choice is yours, and yours alone about what you want to do in the future.' Linda looked deep into her friend's dark blue eyes. 'You can either shut yourself off from the rest of the world, and if that's the case then you don't need me around, or you can start living again. Make a life that your parents would have been proud of.'

'But I feel so unhappy,' Dixie said.

'I know, but time is a great healer, and you'll have to be patient. Slowly, you'll get better.' As Linda said the cliché she couldn't help thinking the times it must have been used by countless people. But it *was* true.

'Then put me to sleep and wake me in ten years.'

'No Dixie, there's no easy way out.'

The two women held each other's gaze for a long time.

'Okay, I'll try,' Dixie finally said, 'I really will. But I'll need your help, for a while at least.'

'You've got it,' her friend replied.

*

The next morning Dixie waited until they'd finished breakfast and were dawdling over coffee before announcing her plans.

'We're going travelling,' she said.

Linda looked at her in surprise.

'We are?'

'Yes, you're right, it's time to start building a new life, and I reckon on being away a month, if that's okay with you. But there is one condition to this holiday, I pay for everything.'

'There's no need to, I do have money of my own.'

Dixie knew her friend's parents were comfortably off, her mother had told her so.

'I know, but I'd appreciate it if you let me do something for you. God knows, you've helped me enough. And, as you know, I can easily afford it.'

'That's right, you're a rich bitch now,' Linda teased.

Dixie nodded her head slightly and gave a smile.

'Yes, I suppose I am,' she said.

FIVE

The first stop was John F. Kennedy Airport in New York where the two women checked into The Plaza Hotel opposite Central Park.

Dixie immediately loved the vibrancy of the bustling city and wanted to visit all the glamorous places she'd read about or seen in the movies. Although the Empire State Building was no longer the highest in the world it still had the most magic attached to its name and, visited on their second night, it was almost fairylike to see the city's illuminations twinkling so far beneath them.

They spent five wonderful days in New York, took in the obligatory tourist attractions and weren't one bit disappointed. In fact, they enjoyed every minute they were in America, even though their feet hardly seemed to touch the ground in their rush to see as much as possible. Their next stop was Niagara Falls, then on to Boston and Chicago, before journeying to the west coast. But Dixie and Linda spent longer in Los Angeles and San Francisco than they anticipated and by the time they flew to Miami a month had already elapsed.

'So, we'll extend our holiday,' Dixie declared. The breakneck speed of their trip had suited her. The more she saw, the more her mind had to think about, and not dwell on her grief. Slowly she began to lose the feeling of guilt that she shouldn't *look* as though she was enjoying herself and should be clothed in black, beating her breast in anguish.

'All you're doing is trying to live a normal life,' Linda told her. 'Something *everyone* wants you to do.'

'It's still not easy,' Dixie said.

'I know,' her friend said understandingly.

Although the two women had been friends since they were teenagers they hadn't seen that much of each other. Their mothers had been closer and it had been Dixie's tragedy that had changed their lives.

But by now the two women had developed a close, relaxed relationship. A bond, and when they checked into hotels it was a double rather than two single rooms and spent most nights talking until the early hours of the next day.

Linda was very pretty with a head turning figure. She had a good sense of fun, an impish smile and it had puzzled Dixie that Linda wasn't married or going out with a regular boyfriend. Then one night she learnt the reason why. For two years Linda had been the mistress of a wealthy married man - and just two months before Dixie's parents accident he'd ditched her.

'During the second year he kept saying he was going to divorce his wife and we'd get married,' Linda recounted in a cold matter of fact tone. 'Then I got pregnant, an accident, and he persuaded me to have an abortion. That's when he told me it was all over. He said it had made him realize how much he loved his two children by his wife, and he couldn't leave his family after all.' Linda gave a harsh laugh. 'It's strange how men can change after they get what they want. When we first started going out together it wasn't too serious and we had a lot of fun. Then I fell in love and I believed him when he told me his feelings were the same.'

Linda explained that after about twelve months, the man, a stockbroker in the City, had installed her in a luxury apartment just off Baker Street.

'I gave up work and became a kept woman,' she continued, 'so I suppose I've only myself to blame ending up as somebody's whore. We were good in bed and he said sex with me was the best he'd ever had.' Linda paused and shook her head. 'But being good between the sheets doesn't guarantee lasting happiness, as I discovered.'

Slowly it became clear how hurt Linda had been, and still was, which made Dixie appreciate even more her friend's tolerance and understanding towards her.

Also, it made her realize that, although Linda was only two years older than her, how much more worldly she was.

Dixie had started to regain lost weight, bringing back her shapely curves and once again began to take care with her makeup. Several times the two women accepted dinner dates but with their rapid progress around the States could hardly remember the men's faces a few days later.

After a couple of days in Florida the weather gave Dixie a taste for the sun. It was winter in London and it didn't take much thought to stay an extra week before heading back home.

*

They flew into Heathrow at the beginning of November, tanned, relaxed and with a pile of luggage. A couple of days ago Dixie had phoned her uncle and he'd confirmed the sale of her parent's house had gone through. Also, someone had put in an offer for her flat in Woodside Park.

Before Dixie had left for the States she'd decided to move. An idea which Uncle Robert had agreed with and while she'd been away had found several flats for her to look at. Apartments which were good investments, as well as somewhere to live.

Within a week Dixie made her choice. A large flat, with enormous potential, in a red brick mansion block in South Kensington. It was expensive but the long lease could only increase in value, her uncle assured Dixie. There was twenty four hour porterage and a big bonus was underground parking.

At first she thought she'd delay the sale of her flat in Woodside Park while the workmen and decorators started in her new place. It would be more convenient, but a recently wed young couple wanted to move in as soon as possible, and the festive season was only just over a month away.

So a few days later Dixie had a removal company transfer her furniture and belongings to her new home.

SIX

Kate Smith double locked the front door of her small terrace house and a few minutes later was driving her white Fiesta through the busy traffic. It was the last week in November, the weather chilly with a dampness in the air.

She lived in South Woodford and travelled by tube train to her place of work at Fisher, Peterson and Partners, but today was Saturday and Kate was on her way to visit her mother in Leytonstone. They were going on holiday together to Barbados in a week's time and she wanted to make sure her mother had everything prepared. Kate was fussy like that, but that's what made her a good secretary. In fact, since the death of her boss she had been given a promotion and was now the head of the company's Personnel Department. A promotion which, for a time, played on her conscience.

After Tom Fisher's funeral Kate had thought long and hard about what to do. At first, as a normally law abiding citizen with a sense of duty, she considered going to the police but then quickly changed her mind. It wouldn't bring back her boss's life, she reasoned, and would definitely give extra heartache to Dixie, which was of no use to anybody.

Besides, this was probably the only golden opportunity she'd ever have in her life to make a lot of money.

So Kate decided to confront the guilty person and lay her cards on the table. She knew she had a winning hand and her only problem had been working out how much money she should ask for. She didn't want to be greedy and ask for a huge amount in one lump sum. An initial payment of ten thousand pounds and then two thousand a month for the next five years would suit her. Kate had worked it out that by then she would have enough to retire on.

And, much to her surprise, her deal was immediately accepted. But the cash would be paid to her by a third party, delivered to her home.

The only warning Kate received was that it would be better if she kept the money somewhere safe and not put it into her bank or building society. Many banks these days reported to the police any amounts of cash over five thousand going into somebody's account. Could be drug money or something criminal like that.

Whether or not this was true Kate wasn't sure but she didn't want to risk involving herself in an embarrassing situation. She couldn't very well explain it was blackmail money, so she listened as her victim explained it would be sensible to open several more bank accounts and spread the money around in small amounts. Or, keep it in a safe place, somewhere like that place she'd hidden those papers.

And that's how Kate could afford to take her mother on a luxury trip to the Caribbean. An exotic holiday in winter had always been one of her dreams, now going to come true, but they'd be back for Christmas. Kate's mother had insisted on that.

Twenty minutes later the Fiesta parked outside a semi-detached house with a small front garden and Kate opened the front door with her own key. Her father had died three years ago and her mother now lived alone.

As she closed the door Kate didn't notice the old, dirty blue Mercedes slow down and then speed off down the road. It was a month since the driver had started following her, on the underground train during her working days, and sitting in his car the rest of the time keeping her house under observation. Kate Smith didn't go out much, didn't appear to have a boyfriend, but it was the third time he'd tailed her to this address. His partner had made enquiries and established the owner of the house was Kate's mother.

There was no need for the driver of the Mercedes to hang around. His plans were already made.

*

A week later mother and daughter were followed to Heathrow Airport and their observer didn't leave until their plane took off with them safely on board.

At two am the next morning a figure dressed in thermal underwear, black tracksuit and carrying a large black bag, expertly, and silently, entered through a window at the rear of Kate's end terrace house. Using a shaded torch the man went up the stairs into one of the bedrooms, pulled out a sleeping bag from the holdall, and slithered into it. No need to begin searching straight away, it would be easier during the daylight hours. Besides, the intruder knew the two women wouldn't be returning for two weeks, so there was plenty of time.

Several miles away, at exactly the same hour, another black clad man had entered Kate's mother's house and gone through the same procedure.

They were professionals.

During the next day both houses were searched with a fine toothcomb. Every room and stick of furniture was thoroughly gone over and at least three hours spent rummaging amongst the collected bric-a-brac in the lofts - but no trace of any blackmail papers was found.

Only the mother's house had a garage, with no car, but a thorough probe into every nook and cranny also drew a blank.

In the course of the day the men had eaten packed sandwiches and drank water from the taps with plastic cups brought with them. Every precaution was taken to see that everything was put back just the same as when they'd first entered. They weren't worried about finger prints because they wore skin tight plastic gloves most of the time.

Anyway, when they left through the front entrances in the dead of night, carefully stepping over the mail and double locking the doors with their special tools of the trade, nobody would have known they'd been there.

But the men were frustrated with their feeling of failure and, as the grey curly haired man reached his car, knew his employer wasn't going to be happy either.

The next day at noon, as arranged, the man made a call from a phone box and reported the bad news. As expected, his words were given a cold reception, but after the initial disappointment the two men discussed their next move.

A new plan of action was needed and the employer said he thought his caller should take over delivery of the monthly payments to Miss Smith. He probably had a better way with women than the man already doing the job, and should get to know her better.

'What, chat her up and sleep with her? She's not the best looking woman I've seen.'

Maybe not, the other man agreed, but that should make it easier for him. Besides, what was the alternative?

'I could beat the shit out of her. I know methods to make her talk.'

But then the woman would have to be killed. The employer admitted that course of action might have to take place in the future but he would prefer to try the soft approach first. And if the grey haired man took over the payments from January and succeeded then he would get a bonus.

'Yes?' interest showing in the man's voice. 'How much?'

When he received the answer the man gave a broad grin and laughed.

'For that kind of money I'd sleep with a bloody kangaroo...so don't worry, I'll get your information.'

But he was instructed not to push too hard because Miss Smith wouldn't do anything as long as she thought she was safe and getting her money. Also, she might have made arrangements to have those papers sent to the police if anything happened to her. And that must never take place.

'I understand,' the grey haired man said, then added, 'fortunately, you can keep an eye on her too.'

SEVEN

It was cold and Dixie pulled her coat collar high over her ears. The gusting snow stung her eyes as she walked along the pavement trying to spot a vacant taxi and was careful to avoid the bustling people, their arms laden with parcels, as they barged past the brightly lit shops. The next day was Christmas Eve and last minute shopping was a priority.

Her high heeled boots sank into three inches of snow as she stepped off the kerb and frantically waved an arm at the black cab. She swung open the door and welcomed the blast of warm air from the interior heater switched on high as she settled in the back seat.

As the vehicle moved carefully away, the street lights gleaming on icy roads, Dixie stared out at the flickering illuminations of the festive window displays. Then the inside of the cab got dimmer as they swung off the main road and weaved through the narrow residential streets of South Kensington. Five minutes later Dixie pressed her mouth close to the open glass panel behind the driver's head and told him to stop outside a red brick apartment block.

She paid the driver and hurried through the thick glass plate doors, smiling at the uniformed porter as he gave her a cheerful greeting, then took the lift to the second floor.

The temporary arrangement of Linda's stay had been lengthened for a while longer and she'd moved with Dixie to her new flat. The one difference was that Linda had gone back to work as a secretary in her father's catalogue shopping business. But Dixie hadn't thought much about her future because she was so busy organizing the renovation of her flat and ordering new carpets, curtains and furniture.

Dixie had just finished a mug of coffee when her front doorbell rang. It was Carla Evans, her neighbour who lived opposite. Carla was the partner of Joshua Rodriquez, a swarthy South American, who was a director of a Swiss pharmaceutical company.

Carla had introduced herself just a few days after Dixie moved in and she was the kind of open woman you couldn't help liking straight away.

Carla had explained Rodriquez spent a lot of time travelling and because she wasn't very keen on flying didn't mind staying behind.

'Besides, I prefer the London shops,' she'd said.

And Carla, a bottle blonde, certainly had an expensive wardrobe, even if her clothes did seem to cling extra tight to her voluptuous figure.

Carla also had another reason for staying at home. She was crazy over her dog, Mikey, a King Charles Spaniel.

'Just checking everything's okay for tomorrow,' she smiled, her red lipstick accentuating her brilliant white capped teeth.

'Yes, everything's fine,' Dixie replied.

Carla and Rodriquez were flying to Switzerland the next day for a week and Dixie had offered to look after her dog. On the odd occasion Carla did go away she usually put Mikey in kennels but Dixie assured her neighbour it would be a pleasure to help out.

Carla looked around Dixie's lounge, with it's decorators ladders, tins of paint and brushes stacked on a wooden trestle.

'Well, Mikey can't do much damage in here,' she laughed out loud.

'No,' Dixie agreed, 'it is a bit of a mess. But I'm hoping the builders will be finished in this room by tomorrow,' she paused, and gave a slight grimace. 'Only another three rooms to do.'

*

Christmas Day dawned bright and clear but with a biting wind. Dixie had bought a new red Mazda sports car and by mid-morning was carefully driving over the crisp white snow towards Linda's parents home, a large detached house in Hampstead Garden Suburb. Mikey was happily wrapped up in a plaid rug on Linda's lap.

As soon as they arrived at their destination, presents were exchanged, then everyone pitched in helping prepare lunch. Linda's parents, John and Eve, had invited friends to eat with them and by two pm there were ten people seated around the large dining table scoffing turkey, mounds of vegetables and knocking back glasses of wine. Crackers were pulled, party poppers let off and soon everyone was wearing brightly coloured silly paper hats, giggling self-consciously.

The rest of the day passed pleasantly – then it was time for bed.

It had been a good old fashioned traditional Christmas but, as Dixie turned off her bedside light and pulled the duvet up to her chin, a thought crossed her mind.

It had been the first Christmas she could remember not spent with her parents.

*

Dixie and Linda were late getting up Boxing Day. Another inch of snow had fallen overnight and a quick look out the window was enough to make them doze off again.

When they finally went into the kitchen Linda's mother, already preparing vegetables for lunch, insisted they have breakfast, even if it was only toast and coffee.

'Do you fancy taking Mikey over the heath this morning?' Linda asked, in between mouthfuls.

'That's fine with me,' was Dixie's immediate reply. 'I wouldn't mind a walk in the snow.'

They decided to go in Linda's father's Volvo estate which everyone agreed would be safer than the sports car in this weather. The part of Hampstead Heath they drove to was off Wildwood Road, a quieter part of the heath, much preferred by the locals.

Yellowy sun filtered through heavy grey clouds as Linda parked the car, carefully nudging the wheels against the kerb, which was completely covered by snow.

As soon as Dixie released Mikey he was running down a slope leading away from the road towards a group of children building a snowman. King Charles Spaniels aren't big dogs and Mikey was finding the deep snow hard going in places, but he was enjoying it, and kept on running and barking. The kids threw a couple of snowballs and Mikey went chasing as fast as he could.

Then he took off towards a line of tall hedging and trees, ran across a small footbridge over a wide ditch, and disappeared from view. Dixie started to follow but felt a snowball hit her in the middle of her back. She turned and saw Linda grinning at her. Then both women bent down and started scooping snow into their hands and hurling it at each other.

Suddenly Dixie looked around her.

'Mikey...Mikey,' she called. 'Come on, Linda, let's find the dog.'

They walked towards the footbridge shouting the dog's name. Mikey came into view barking loudly then turned and went back behind the foliage enjoying the game of hide and seek.

'Mikey...Mikey,' Dixie shouted as she got to the other side of the hedge and saw the spaniel take off towards a group of people also engaged in a friendly snow fight. One of the men, wearing a dark blue jacket, turned and gave an inquisitive look.

'Mikey...Mikey,' Dixie called again.

The man started to walk towards her as Dixie struggled to catch up to the dog in the deep snow.

'Can I help you?' he asked, his intense brown eyes locked on to hers.

A sudden gust of wind whipped Dixie's long hair across her face as she looked at him...his strong jaw, dark hair and easy going smile. She felt something. A feeling stir inside her, like nothing she'd ever felt before.

'You called my name. Do I know you?'

'Pardon?' she was lost for words, but smiled back at him.

'My name's Mike,' he said.

'Oh no, I was calling my dog, Mikey. His name's Mikey,' Dixie was flustered in her explanation.

'Oh, your dog,' and he smiled again. 'I've never been mistaken for a dog before.' He turned and shouted, 'Mikey, come on, boy.'

The spaniel, hearing his name called by a different voice, spun around and scampered towards them, loving the excitement.

'That's a good boy,' Mike said, and bent down. He ruffled the dog's ears. 'We've got the same name, eh.'

He straightened and looked at Dixie.

'He's a lucky dog, to have you as his mistress.'

'Well, he's not mine exactly, he's a friend's...'

Dixie's voice tailed off as another broke across hers.

'Mike, we've got to get a move on.'

Dixie looked over at the rest of the group. Three more men and two young women.

'Don't forget we're having an early lunch,' the oldest of the men called.

'I'm coming,' Mike shouted, and turned back to Dixie.

'I've got to go.'

They stood staring at each other, the smiles gone, gentle white flakes settling on their hair. The sun had disappeared and it had started snowing again.

'What's your name?' he asked so softly it was almost a whisper.

'Dixie,' she replied.

'Dixie,' he repeated, and nodded his head slightly as though in approval. 'Bye, Dixie.'

'Bye,' she said and turned and followed the King Charles Spaniel, now ploughing his way to Linda, who'd discreetly kept her distance.

'Who was that?' Linda asked as they started walking up the slope past the playing children, their large snowman now finished.

'I don't know,' Dixie replied, and didn't say another word.

Linda gave her friend a puzzled look, but she too kept quiet. Linda looked again at Dixie's face as they neared the car. Her friend seemed different somehow. Linda shrugged her shoulders as she unlocked the driver's door. What kind of crazy thought was that?

Dixie picked up the dog, opened the passenger side but before slipping into the car, looked back towards the footbridge.

The figure in the distance stood still, the collar of his dark blue reefer jacket turned up, his hands shoved deep in the side pockets, looking in her direction.

The flakes were now pelting down from the overcast sky and his friends were blurry dots as they slogged through the snow away from him.

But Mike hadn't moved.

EIGHT

Mike Saxby waited until Dixie got in the car before turning and following his friends. There was something about the woman he'd just met. Something special. He'd felt it and he knew she had when they'd looked at each other. Something had passed between them and Mike wondered if he'd ever see her again.

He lengthened his stride and caught up with his friends ten minutes later, just as they left the heath.

'Who was that?' one of the young women, Cherie, asked, and linked her arm through Mike's.

'She got me mixed up with someone else,' he replied.

'Yeah, who?'

'Her dog.'

'Her *dog*?' Cherie swivelled her face in front of Mike's in surprise, then smiled. 'Are you a dirty dog?'

'No,' Mike smiled back.

'Would you like to be?'

He didn't answer.

'I'm a bitch, you know.'

'That's for sure.'

'Do you *really* think so?' and Cherie sounded hurt that he'd so readily agreed.

They'd slept together a few times over the last couple of months, but then, Cherie had slept with a lot of people over that period of time. She was a groupie. A rich groupie, daughter and heir of Lord Madison, the publishing magnate, and rumour had it she was compiling a list of all the pop stars she'd slept with. Then she'd write a book.

The trouble was - she didn't stop at the lead singer - she had to bed the rest of the band too. It would be a massive tome.

The house they were walking back to belonged to Joey Judd where Mike was spending Christmas and New Year. They were close, like brothers, and their memories went back to when their mothers were pushing them around the streets in prams.

'You 'elp me keep my feet on the ground,' the pop star repeatedly told him. 'Most of the people I know these days are a load of wankers, only interested in my money.'

*

From the very beginning Mike and Joey had a lot in common. They were both born in London's East End and neither of their mothers were married at the time. In later years being a couple of bastards became a private joke between them - and strong bond.

Their mothers, Doreen Saxby and Patty Bell were friends and just turned eighteen when the boys were born, Mike a month older. Then five years later Patty married Joseph Judd, Joey's father, a month after he got his divorce.

But Mike never knew who his father was, in fact, his mother wasn't sure either. An attractive woman, she always had a string of boyfriends on the go. But nevertheless, she was a good mother, and never neglected her son. He came first.

Mike and Joey had gone to the same schools, shared their first hangover together, and done their best to deflower as many teenage girls in Wapping as they could.

'If it moves - shag it. If it doesn't - drink it,' became their motto.

Money was only important to them because they didn't have any. Jeans, black T-shirts and cheap black leather jackets became their uniform, the reason being they were hard wearing and lasted longer. Certainly not for any trendy reason.

Designer clothes were day dreams.

They were inseparable. Mike was taller, bigger built and better looking but Joey had the cheekiest grin imaginable. Everybody liked him immediately they met him - especially the women - and he got away with murder.

They left school at sixteen and by then both teenage boys had decided what they wanted in life.

Mike wanted to be an interior decorator and designer. But that would only be the first step because he wanted to plan and build houses too, from the foundation stones to the last lick of paint. He wanted to become an expert at colour schemes and lighting; be able to choose the right carpets and curtains; pick the correct furniture and make sure kitchens and bathrooms weren't just pretty - but functional too.

Mike wanted to make everything he touched a work of art. Something people would appreciate.

Glossy magazines had sparked off his ambition from when he was a kid. He'd look at them in the newsagents and then go home to his crummy two bedroom council flat. It wasn't his mum's fault - she just didn't have the money. She kept her home clean and tidy but everything always seemed worn and threadbare.

Mike's mother worked hard, usually in shops or cafes as a waitress, but she never wanted to get married, or hook a man just for the sake of getting someone to pay the bills. She enjoyed playing the field too much.

And now Mike was old enough to work he felt it was his responsibility to help out with the family budget. There was no way Mike could afford to train as an architect, or interior designer, so he'd have to do it his way.

It would be hard graft - but Mike had a plan.

*

Joey also had a plan.

He wanted to be a pop star and make buckets of money. It was as simple as that. Except, as he found out, it *wasn't* that simple.

Joey was lucky in the fact that he had a natural ear for music and by the time he was fourteen had graduated from an acoustic guitar to an electric model. He was good, even though he was literally self-taught, and could also pick out tunes on the piano, which helped him write songs. However, his main asset was his voice, gravelly, but with a fair range of high notes and a knack of sounding breathless whenever he wanted to. Very sexy, the girls told him.

But Joey was intelligent enough to know that he had to get a band around him. Singing by himself in local pubs and at a few weddings was better than nothing, but it wasn't going to propel his career into orbit.

He tried recruiting musicians but most of them were lousy and the others more interested in making a few quid as street buskers. They thought it a safer career and said overnight sensations didn't happen any more. Bands these days were put together by managers and sold as a package deal to the public. It was not what you knew - it was *who* you knew. Luck, really.

Well, if that was the case then Joey would have to make his own luck.

There was a local band that weren't half bad. *Fitz and The Freemen* had met in their last year of school and formed a group. Then, when they left the comprehensive decided to keep their band together, part-time, and see what happened. Dave Fitzroy and Frank Gibbs were the lead guitars, with John Duncan as the keyboard player and a dynamic drummer called Omar Jones.

A couple of years later they had made a bit of a name for themselves, but still only locally, and were no nearer success then when they'd left school. And their enthusiasm was waning.

Joey was nineteen when he took an interest in the band and decided they were for him. Dave Fitzroy - Fitz - was also the singer and Joey knew he was a lot better than him. So he thought it would be a doddle once they heard him and couldn't believe it when they said they weren't interested. Not at all.

But Joey persisted and when the group did listen to him weeks later they were impressed. However, Fitz wasn't going to give up his position in the band that easily, after all, he'd started it. But they did compromise. If Fitz was ever sick and couldn't perform then Joey could take his place. The trouble was, Fitz was as healthy as a horse.

Then fate stepped in three months later. Fitz's parents decided to emigrate to Australia and Fitz couldn't wait to go. Sun, sandy beaches, barbecues and beautiful girls was all he could think about and couldn't stop counting the days until departure.

And when he left - *Joey Judd and Company* were born - the new name of the group.

But the cockney singer still had a long way to go before he'd make it to the top and a year later the band split convinced they'd never make it. Then after two years spent, either on the dole or in a variety of jobs, Joey persuaded the others to give it one more try.

He'd be twenty three next birthday. Over the hill, even at that age, judging by the youngsters appearing on television pop shows.

*

Joey looked out the frosty window and saw his friends walking along the snow covered private road, their heads bent down against the driving blizzard. There were only five houses in this road. Two on either side and his situated at the end. Two million he'd paid for it and spent another half a million doing it up. Well, Mike had done it up. He'd just footed the bill.

He loved his home and everyone said what good taste he had. But Joey knew the only real taste he had was being able to tell the difference between a fillet steak and a hamburger. So he made sure everyone knew it was his best mate who was the genius, not him.

Georgian style windows and meandering ivy on the outside brickwork gave the house a warm and welcoming feeling. There were six bedrooms, four bathrooms and a games room which would have had any pub goer drooling with its own bar and snooker table. A sound proof extension built at the rear housed a fully equipped recording studio and a two bedroom staff flat over the double garage made up the rest of the property.

Joey was standing in one of the front bedrooms and heard the door open and close behind him. He turned and saw Shirley standing there, long blonde hair touching her shoulders, a tight black sweater over her big bust, but minus her skirt. The rest of her was clad in black thong knickers, black holdup stockings and high heeled boots. Joey inwardly groaned and turned back to the window. He'd left Shirley in his massive four poster bed in the back of the house hoping she'd fall asleep. He should have gone for a lovely refreshing walk with his friends but, as usual, his cock made up his mind for him. It usually did.

Shirley moved in front of Joey and knelt on the thick pile carpet. Her hand went to his fly, pulled down the zip and expertly pulled his erection from his underpants. Joey stared out of the window panes at the snow as he felt the warmth of her mouth enclose him. Then he started to relax and smiled. He wondered if he'd get a blowjob in Heaven. He felt himself shudder as he came and held on to Shirley's head for support.

Bloody knee tremblers.

NINE

The snow lasted throughout January into the first week of February, a constant reminder of Dixie's meeting with Mike on Hampstead Heath. This had made her feel guilty because she hadn't given a lot of thought lately to her boyfriend Nick who'd been killed in the crash with her parents. Of course she'd been sorry he'd died because he'd been such a lovely man, but she hadn't been in love with him, even though they had shared the same bed on several occasions.

They'd never had that magic between them. That gut feeling two people get when they know they've met the right person.

In fact, ever since Dixie had entered her teenage years and taken an interest in the male population she knew she'd never been in love. Not the kind she'd read about or seen in the movies. Yes, she'd whispered her love to men when she'd enjoyed sex, but that was only because of the feeling at the time.

But maybe there had been *one* moment.

Dixie had driven back to the heath a few times on her own and gone for walks hoping to see her mysterious stranger again but he'd never materialized. She didn't tell Linda because she felt foolish and silly, behaving like a schoolgirl with a stupid crush.

Her flat was nearing completion and she was pleased with the result. Chintzy and comfy, with lots of pictures on the walls, it reminded her of her parents home, which it was meant to. She felt secure and safe. Her new roots mingling with memories of the past.

Yesterday she'd taken delivery of her parents possessions she'd put into storage. The furniture and paintings were now in their right places and Dixie was sitting on the carpet in her lounge going through the remaining cardboard cartons marked personal. Cartons containing the odds and sods Tom and Margo had collected over the years which meant so much to them at the time. Cuttings from newspapers, maps, coins, keys, photographs and those love letters Dixie couldn't bear to read when she'd first discovered them. She still couldn't because she felt she was prying, but she couldn't throw them away either.

As Dixie went through the boxes she remembered there was a lot of stuff she hadn't looked at. She took out a buff coloured folder and opened it, pulling out a sheaf of documents. There were birth and marriage certificates, solicitors letters and, as she began to read through them, distant recollections started to come back.

Fisher wasn't the name she'd been born with. Margo was her mother but she'd been married before and after she'd remarried Dixie's surname had been changed by deed poll.

This was no secret and Dixie couldn't even remember her real father, who'd left before Dixie's first birthday. Her mother had explained this to her when she was about seven or eight but as far as Dixie was concerned Tom was her *father*...her *dad*. And that was how she'd loved him. She'd never been adopted by Tom but that had never bothered her. Grown-ups had their own way of doing things and as the years went by all this background just faded into nothing.

Danny James Buckley was the name of her real father on her birth certificate and she'd been born Dixie Buckley. She looked at her mother's first marriage certificate, then at her second to Tom six years later. Dixie found the divorce papers which stated her mother had divorced Danny on the grounds of adultery and named some woman as the co-respondent. Then she found her deed poll document which had been registered at the High Court in London.

She'd had to produce her original birth certificate when applying for a passport but to her it had been just another document. So she had another name...so what?

Dixie put all the papers back into the buff folder and sat there thinking...and wondering. What was her real father like? Did he know about her mother's death? Should she try and find him and tell him?

The accident had been reported in the national press. Then again, maybe he hadn't seen it.

Dixie stood and walked to the window staring out into space. But what if he didn't care and accused her of interfering? Margo was just an ex-wife and he was probably married again with a different family now. He'd never tried to contact her, so why should she bother? She couldn't ever remember thinking about her real father before. Besides, after all she'd gone through, did she need any more complications in her life?

No, probably best to forget it. Every family had skeletons in the cupboard...still, it was an intriguing thought. Maybe she'd have a word with Linda. Dixie had finally persuaded her to stay permanently with the strict understanding that she treat the flat as though it was her own. And Linda had agreed with the strict understanding that she shared the day to day running expenses.

They'd review the agreement only if one of them wanted to get married, although neither of them thought that would be for quite some time yet. But you never know, they laughed.

Dixie went through all the boxes carefully separating the stuff she'd throw out and what she would keep. From the cartons she discarded the contents of two. Even the remainder some people would have thrown out but Dixie decided to keep them. A hoarder, Margo would have called her.

Linda arrived home just after six and the two women started organizing their dinner.

Another agreement was that they both shared the cooking. Just because Dixie wasn't working didn't mean she had to get stuck with preparing everything.

Dixie had just finished peeling potatoes when she had a sudden whim to confide in her friend.

'Did you know I had another father?'

The question came out of the blue and Linda looked at her friend in amazement.

'Pardon?'

'I said, did you know I had another father?'

Linda wiped her hands on some kitchen paper and stared at Dixie.

'No, I didn't,' and an inquisitive smile played across her face. 'Tell me more, I don't understand.'

'Oh, it's no secret,' Dixie said, 'I've known for years. Margo is my Mother but she was married before she met Tom. After they got married my surname was changed by deed poll to Fisher.'

'Well, *I* never knew,' Linda said. 'So who is your mystery father?'

'His name is Danny Buckley.'

Linda waited for her friend to continue - but she didn't.

'And that's it? That's all you know about him?'

'Yes, that's about it. You see, he left my Mother and me before I was a year old.'

'And you've never seen him since?'

'No.'

'This *is* interesting,' Linda said. 'But what made you bring it up now?'

'That stuff of my parents which was delivered yesterday. I found some papers this afternoon and everything came back to me.' Dixie shook her head. 'But it doesn't change things really.'

'Oh, you've got to find out more,' Linda grinned conspiratorially. 'Why don't you phone your Uncle Robert or Aunt Lucy, they must know something.'

'Do you think I should? I mean, there might be some dark family secret that they don't want anyone to know.' Dixie's voice sounded apprehensive.

'Let's hope there is,' Linda said. 'You've really got me interested now.'

They opted to eat first and during the meal discussed who to phone. They decided to call Dixie's Aunt Lucy rather than her Uncle Robert because they thought a woman to woman chat a better idea.

Besides, she was a great lady and Dixie got on well with her. Since her parents funeral Dixie had kept in regular contact by phone and her aunt had given her an open invitation to visit her in the country any time she wanted.

'I won't last forever,' she'd told her niece, 'and the only close relatives you've got left now are Robert and me.'

Although Aunt Lucy had a frail old body her mind was still sharp and alert. And the only reason she'd remained a spinster was because her fiancé, a Royal Air Force pilot, had been killed in a crash during NATO manoeuvres in Germany forty years ago and she'd remained steadfastly faithful to his memory over the years.

All very romantic.

As soon the two women had finished eating Dixie went straight to the phone and called her aunt. They exchanged pleasantries then Dixie got straight to the point.

'What do you know about Danny Buckley? My real Father.'

Over the next couple of minutes Dixie tried to break into her aunt's reply, but Lucy was having none of it, and just carried on. Finally, there was silence.

'Aunt Lucy, I take it you don't like Danny Buckley.'

Then Dixie had to listen for another minute before she got a chance to speak again.

'I never knew nice little old ladies could swear like that,' she chuckled.

'It's not a laughing matter,' Lucy said. 'There was a lot of bad blood between Danny Buckley and my brothers.'

'Okay, I get the message. But it was such a long time ago I wouldn't have thought it mattered now.'

'Maybe it doesn't now, but...anyway, why this sudden interest? You're not thinking of contacting him, are you?'

'I'm not sure. Why?'

'Because I don't think it's a good idea.'

'Yes, maybe you're right. Thanks anyway, Aunt Lucy. Goodbye and I'll speak to you again soon.'

'Goodbye, Dixie, and don't forget to come and see me.'

Dixie put down the phone and turned to Linda.

'Wow, my Father has certainly got a reputation.'

'What did your aunt say?'

'I'll leave out all the swear words, but it appears Danny Buckley is quite a ladies man. He's bedded and screwed his way all over the country and leading my Mother up the garden path was bad enough, but he led her up to the altar as well. And that nearly ruined her life. He's a flash, conceited man who thinks he's God's gift to women, but couldn't be faithful to a woman if he tried. He's always short of money and I should have nothing to do with him. He drinks too much and Aunt Lucy thinks the world would be a better place if he was dead.'

Dixie stopped and the two women stared at each other.

'After a build-up like that you've definitely got to find him,' Linda said, positively beaming.

TEN

Once Dixie decided to track down her father she and Linda suddenly realized it wasn't as easy as that, and they didn't have the slightest idea how to go about it.

Dixie waited until Linda came home from work the next day and they sat curled up in comfortable chairs in the lounge discussing what to do.

An advert in a national newspaper?

'No,' Linda said. 'I would have thought the best bet is a private detective, don't you?'

'That sounds a bit dramatic,' Dixie replied. 'Anyway, where do we get one? The Yellow Pages?'

'As good a place as any.' And sure enough when they looked they found what they wanted listed under, Detective Agencies.

But which one to choose?

That decision was made for them when the telephone rang. It was Uncle Robert.

'My sister's just called me,' he said. 'She's not been telling tales, it's just that she's worried about you. She said you were on the phone to her last night asking about Danny Buckley. Is that correct?'

'Yes, that's right,' Dixie said apprehensively, not sure of her uncle's reaction.

'Why didn't you phone me?'

'You wouldn't have minded?'

'Of course not,' Robert replied pleasantly.

'Aunt Lucy said there was bad blood between you and my real Father.'

'That was years ago, Dixie. That's all forgotten now.'

'Well, I am thinking of trying to find him.'

'Any particular reason, if you don't mind me asking?'

Dixie paused for a long moment.

'Curiosity, I suppose more than anything,' she replied.

'And how do you intend to go about it?'

'I was thinking of hiring a private detective.'

'Do you know any?'

'No. Linda and I were just looking through the Yellow Pages, but there are so many to choose from.'

'I might be able to help you there.'

'Do you know one?'

'No, but our solicitors probably do.'

'That's a good idea, Uncle. I've read that solicitors often use private detectives in shady divorce cases.'

Robert laughed.

'I'm sure our solicitors don't do that sort of work but I'm pretty certain they'll know of someone. I'll phone you tomorrow and let you know.'

'Thanks.'

'There is one thing more...' and Robert paused. 'This is why Lucy phoned me, something she didn't know how to tell you herself.'

'Yes, what's that?'

'Your father has been in prison. It was after he was divorced from your mother...it's just that I thought you should know,' and Robert's voice sounded apologetic.'

There was silence then Dixie spoke.

'What did he do?'

'He killed someone.'

'I see...yes, it *is* something I should know. Thanks.'

Dixie sat staring into space long after her uncle had hung up until Linda interrupted her thoughts.

'Is there something wrong, Dixie?'

'My Father is a murderer and went to prison,' she replied in a dull, flat voice.

Linda looked shocked, stunned herself.

'I'm sorry,' she said, unable to think of anything else to say, then quickly added. 'Would you like a drink?'

Linda got up from her armchair as her friend nodded her head, went to the drinks cabinet and poured two large brandies.

'Thanks,' Dixie said and took a gulp.

'Do you still want to find this man now?'

Dixie hesitated then shrugged her shoulders.

'Yes, I think so. Why?'

'Well, you could be opening a can of worms. You've been through enough heartache already and this might be something you could regret later. Don't you think it best to leave things as they are? This man, your father, supposing he doesn't want to know you. He sounds like a right bastard, and I'd hate to see you get hurt.'

Dixie was touched by Linda's thoughtfulness but her mind was made up.

'As far as I'm concerned Tom Fisher was my Father and that's how I loved him. Danny Buckley is just a name to me and if we ever do meet I will think of him, *only as a stranger*.'

'So you're determined to go ahead and find him?'

'Yes. As a matter of fact, more than ever. I must know more about this man. After all,' and Dixie stared at her friend, 'it's his genes...his blood that flows through me.'

*

Uncle Robert called mid-morning the following day, bright and breezy as usual.

'Our solicitors came up with a private detective for you,' he said. 'He's busy at the moment but I'm assured he'll contact you within a couple of days. He's got your number and his name is John Fallows.'

'Thanks Uncle, I appreciate it. There is something else though.'

'Yes, what's that?'

'Last night, what you said about Danny Buckley killing someone...do you know what happened?'

'Yes. He killed a man in a fight and got five years for manslaughter.'

'So it wasn't murder, then?'

'Well, technically no. I suppose it depends on which way you look at it, but a man still died.'

'Okay Uncle, thanks once again. I'll let you know how I get on with Mr Fallows.'

*

The private investigator rang on the third day full of apologies.

'Sorry I couldn't get to you sooner,' John Fallows said, 'but a couple of my operatives are off sick, as well as my secretary, and I had to go out of town to finish a job.'

Dixie assured him she understood and arranged to be at his office two hours later.

Fallows operated from a large Victorian house in Wandsworth, south west London, which had been converted into office accommodation. A small notice board in the entrance hall displayed various business names, and it showed that Fallows Investigations was on the second floor. The carpet on the stairs was well worn and the walls looked as though they could do with a lick of paint. But the slightly rundown appearance fitted in with Dixie's idea of what a private detective's office would be like.

The young woman felt a tingle of excitement.

She saw the metal nameplate on the door she was looking for and entered into a small room with a desk and filing cabinets. Another door opened and John Fallows appeared and introduced himself. A medium size man about forty, of medium build with shortish mousy brown hair and an average face, his appearance could only be described as nondescript. Perfect for an investigator, Dixie thought.

'I'm sorry, but my secretary is still off sick,' he said, and Dixie followed the man into the other, bigger room, containing a larger desk and more filing cabinets.

When they'd spoken on the phone this morning he'd told Dixie to bring along as much information as she had about Danny Buckley with her.

'This is everything,' she said, and passed over a buff folder.

Fallows shuffled through the contents and picked out the green marriage certificate of Margo's marriage to Danny, then put all the other documents back in the folder and handed it to Dixie.

'This is all I need,' he said.

'That's all?'

'Yes, it's got his full name, his father's name and his age at the time of the marriage. I'll get someone to pull his birth certificate then once we get that I'll have no trouble finding him. Now,' and Fallows looked serious, 'do you just want me to find out where he is living at the moment? Or do you want copies of his bank statements and credit card and medical records as well? Oh, and a copy of his criminal record, if he's got one?'

'You can get all that?' Dixie was amazed.

'Yes,' Fallows replied in a matter of fact voice.

'No. Thanks, but no. Just let me know where he's living. That'll be enough.'

'You didn't give me a photograph of Buckley, so I take it you don't have one.'

'Correct.'

'Do you know what he looks like?'

'No, I've never seen him,' Dixie admitted. 'Well, not that I can remember.'

'Would you like me to get an up to date photo for you?'

'Yes, yes that would help, thank you.'

'The information's no trouble, that will only take a couple of days, but getting the photograph might take a bit longer.'

'That's okay.'

'Right you are, Miss Fisher. I'll be in touch with you in a week to ten days at the most.'

*

Eight days later a motorcycle courier delivered a foolscap size brown envelope to Dixie's flat. Inside were two sheets of paper, seven six by four colour photographs with captions written neatly on the back, and the returned marriage certificate. She spread them over the large coffee table in her lounge and gazed at them. Two immediately took her attention. Close-ups of Danny Buckley, taken in a street, obviously without his knowledge.

Her father.

It seemed strange to think, as she looked at his face, that she was the product of this person. A man she didn't know.

He was fifty two, it said so on one of the sheets of paper, and was born in Camden, north London. Dixie picked up the clearest photo and studied it. Danny had grey curly hair and his nose seemed ordinary but it was difficult to tell the colour of his eyes. Were they blue, like hers? Would people recognize them as father and daughter if they were seen together?

But he had a hard, mean look and could do with losing some weight. Probably the booze. Aunt Lucy had said he was a heavy drinker. Her aunt didn't like Danny and Dixie wondered how her mother had felt. Margo must have loved him, or she wouldn't have married him. What had gone wrong? There were always two sides to every story.

Dixie felt a bit disappointed that Buckley wasn't a handsome man, a dashing rogue, but quickly pushed aside any romantic thoughts like that. He was a convicted criminal and had killed another human being. That was what she had to keep in mind.

In the letter from the private investigator Fallows explained that he'd supplied two addresses Danny Buckley lived at and his place of business, which is all she'd asked for. However, he had added that Buckley drank nearly every day in a pub called, The Grapes, and gave the address which was near his business premises.

The photographs were captioned on the back with extra information relating to them on the second sheet of paper.

One pictured a small terraced house in Holloway, north London. This was Buckley's London home and another showed a picturesque detached cottage near Potter Heigham, on the Norfolk Broads. This house was owned by a woman called Jessie Baker, a widow, and Danny Buckley's name appeared as well on the local electoral role. He also owned a four berth cabin cruiser which was moored in a small boatyard on the river Thurne.

The young woman furrowed her brow then felt a shudder go through her as she brought the photograph closer to her eye and read the name written in bold letters on the bow of the boat. *Dixie.*

The breath caught in her throat. A moment later she got up and crossed to the drinks cabinet, poured a brandy and took a large sip before sitting down again. After all these years he still thought of her. He must do, otherwise why would he name his boat after her?

Dixie picked up another photograph. It was of a row of lockup warehouses in Kings Cross. Her father's was number four and showed clearly the name of his business, Buckley Trading Company.

The last photo was of the car he drove, a three year old black VW Golf.

Dixie raised the brandy glass to her lips and took another sip. Seeing her name on the boat had thrown her.

However, she'd got all the information she'd requested, now all she had to do was call on her father.

But could she? Was it as simple as that? The more she thought about it the more confused she became.

Tom and her mother hadn't been dead very long and here she was meddling in their past. She felt guilty as though she was betraying them.

Her uncertainty stayed with her the remainder of the afternoon until Linda came home from work and Dixie showed her the contents of the brown envelope.

After they'd discussed it Linda could see her friend was clearly upset.

'Maybe I was right after all,' Linda said. 'I said you might be opening a can of worms.'

Linda experienced a sense of guilt because she felt she'd pushed Dixie into finding Danny Buckley. What had then seemed like a harmless idea had now turned serious and maybe she should do something about it.

'Forget it,' was her advice. 'You're just starting to enjoy life again and I think it would be foolish to change anything,' she paused. 'On reflection, I don't think it was such a good idea after all.'

But Dixie couldn't forget it and next morning she thought about what she should do so much it started to give her a headache. She sat at the dark wooden kitchen table drinking coffee for hours before getting dressed. The weather was still cold and she tucked her tight black jeans into knee high boots, put on a heavy sweater and three quarter length black coat. She wore no makeup and tied her hair back in a ponytail.

Her decision to go for a drive to clear her head was just an excuse, she knew that as soon as she slipped behind the wheel of her sports car, and started driving towards the Kings Cross area.

Her curiosity had got the better of her.

Lost in thought she didn't notice she'd been followed since she'd left the apartment block's underground car park, a black Volkswagen tailing her through the traffic.

Dixie drove past the main line station and found a vacant parking meter in a side street. She fished out of her pocket the sheet of paper with Buckley's addresses typed on it and took her A to Z street guide from the glove compartment.

The VW Golf parked on a yellow line some distance behind her.

Ten minutes later, and after asking directions, Dixie stood in the street on the opposite side of The Grapes pub. It was chilly and she shivered despite her warm clothes. She crossed the road and pushed open the saloon bar door. It was crowded and noisy with a heavy haze of smoke in the air, and she hesitated, not moving.

'Close the door, luv,' a young man sitting near the entrance said. 'It's bloody freezin'.'

The young man's comment instantly made up Dixie's mind for her and she stepped back outside.

She felt foolish. To come this far and not even have a proper look inside the pub was silly. Her heart was beating faster and she was nervous, but of what she wasn't sure.

However, Dixie didn't immediately walk back to her car, and five minutes later stood at the beginning of a short street which led to a wide cobble stoned yard in front of some warehouses.

As soon as the man following on the other side of the road saw where she was headed he pulled a silver flask from his overcoat and took several large swigs of whisky.

Dixie checked the address on the paper against the street sign. It was the same. Slowly she walked forward, around the corner until she came to the open space, her eyes searching until she saw a sign, Buckley Trading Company. She stood there looking, but once again her confidence let her down, and began to retrace her steps.

Dixie quickened her pace, her eyes fixed downwards, and didn't see the man as she hurried back around the corner until she bumped into him.

'Sorry, young lady,' he said in a slurred voice. She raised her eyes, looked at his face, and her heart missed a beat.

It was the face in the photograph.

'Can I help you?' the man asked, and Dixie instinctively pulled her face away from him. He stank of booze.

The suddenness of the unexpected meeting left Dixie flummoxed and she stood staring at the man. Her mind wanted to say one thing but her lips blurted out something entirely different.

'No, I took the wrong turning,' she mumbled, and went to walk away but felt herself grabbed by both arms.

'What about if you came to my office and we had a little drink together?'

'No thank you,' Dixie replied, and tried to struggle loose, but the man's grip was too strong.

'Well give me a kiss, then. A good looking woman like you shouldn't be by herself,' and he pushed his face close to her.

Dixie pushed hard with both hands against his chest, her face contorted with repulsion and anger.

'You're Danny Buckley, aren't you?'

The man grinned.

'Yeah, that's right, darling. Don't tell me you've heard of my reputation. Come on, let's have a drink together, and then I'll show you what a good time is.'

'Let go of me,' Dixie shouted, and lashed out with her boot hard against Buckley's shin. He immediately let go of her and Dixie turned and sprinted back the way she'd come.

'Piss off, you silly young bitch,' echoed after her.

Tears ran down Dixie's cheeks as she ran into the street away from her father.

Linda had been right - she should have left things the way they were.

ELEVEN

'Mind you don't trip on that timber,' Mike Saxby said to his colleague as they walked from the stairs into a large room. A workman in paint speckled white overalls raised his hand in greeting as they entered.

Mike smiled back, then turned as he heard footsteps behind him. It was one of the two carpenters working on the job and after a few minutes conversation Mike promised to get an extra sanding machine hired as soon as possible.

Then Mike and his colleague, both in suits, went into an adjoining room, carefully stepping over various lengths of wood and piles of new floorboards. Interior doors, stripped back to their natural pine, rested against the walls.

'I think it would be best if there were bookshelves on both sides of the fireplace,' Mike said.

'But don't you think there are enough shelves in the room he wants as a study?' the other man asked.

'Yes, maybe for an average person, but Mr Spencer is passionate about books,' and Mike went on to explain the conversations he'd had with best selling author, Roger Spencer.

This property was the last of seven large terrace houses Mike had completely renovated over the last eighteen months. Each interior had been personally designed in co-operation with the buyer.

And they were pleased.

*

As soon as Mike left school he began working on a building site because he desperately wanted to start the practical side of his plan.

At school he'd been a natural at art and design so he continued his studies by going to night school. And as the years went by he lost count of the hours he spent in the local library absorbed in books. But as well as interior design and architecture Mike was determined to be more than just a labourer on the different building sites he was employed. He was determined to learn the basics. Brick laying, carpentry, plumbing, electricity, painting and wall papering.

Mike wanted to have a fair knowledge of them all.

It was hard work, but the young man didn't mind, and took as much overtime as possible. He was learning his business – and thinking of the future.

The manual toil had an added benefit. It did wonders for his physique and by the time he was twenty two his body was hard sinewy muscle.

Joey was still performing in local pubs, still waiting for that big break - and always short of money, as were the rest of his backing group. So Mike paid for their nights out, with Joey vowing to make it up to him when he was rich and famous.

Then Mike got the opportunity of working on a building project about a mile outside Stevenage in Hertfordshire. It was a development for exclusive detached houses on a small estate.

It was during the building of these houses in the country that Mike met Gerry Dolan, an architect who'd helped design the estate. He impressed Mike with his ideas and whenever the two men got into conversation Dolan was flattered that the bricklayer took such an interest in his work. He was also surprised with Mike's knowledge of architecture and the studying behind it.

Mike explained his ambition was to start his own company and design and build houses, but also be an interior designer.

He wanted to be able to sell his ideas to a client and do it all, inside and out.

Dolan had wished him the very best, and every time he visited the site always took time to stop and chat with Mike.

The two men got on well.

There were only five houses on the development, but they were large, and every one in the millionaire class. They were all a different design and each one had high surrounding walls and hi-tech security systems.

Two houses were finished to the satisfaction of the buyers, who wanted to move in as soon as possible. Then the wife of one of them decided she didn't like the kitchen cabinets and wanted them changed. But two of the chippies had already left the site, so Mike was taken off bricklaying and put on carpentry, which he was very good at.

Mrs Ruebens was in her early thirties with a nine year old son and a daughter two years younger, who had sensibly stayed behind in London with her husband until she got the house sorted out. A good looking, cheerful Jewish woman she was easy to get on with.

It wasn't until days later that Mike found out what her husband did for a living, and when he did, could hardly believe it.

Vic Ruebens and his brother, Alan, were in the music business. They managed several groups and had their own record company, one of the most successful of the smaller labels.

As soon as Mike heard this he immediately thought of Joey. But what could he say? My mate's a great singer - and all he needs is a break. No. Anyway, it was the husband he needed to speak to, not the wife. Mike would have to bide his time...and hope the right opportunity came along.

On the day Mike was due to be finished in the kitchen he arrived to find Mrs Ruebens having a screaming match on the telephone with, Robin, her interior designer. She finished the conversation in no uncertain terms and told him not to come back.

When Mike asked her how she was going to manage, the woman had shrugged her shoulders, and said she'd try and handle the job herself. She'd tell the painters and decorators what to do.

It was then Mike offered his services and told Mrs Ruebens in detail about his studies, his future ambition and the reason for working on this site.

However, Mike had to reluctantly admit he didn't have any practical experience of interior designing, in answer to the woman's questions, but quickly assured her he was certain he could do it.

Maybe it was the young man's honesty or the fact that she was in a spot, but Mrs Ruebens decided to give Mike a chance, and after a few days knew she'd backed a winner because Mike had real talent. So she didn't interfere and let him get on with it. He worked hard, had a natural way with the workers, now taking his instructions, and the job went smoothly.

During their conversations Mrs Ruebens discovered that Mike's twenty third birthday was just a month away and decided to give him a party.

Mrs Ruebens was very impressed with his work - and grateful.

Mike was flattered and flabbergasted. Nobody had ever done anything like this for him before. There was only one disappointment, Mrs Ruebens told him. She had been hoping to get one of her husband's groups to perform live but none were available, so they'd have to make do with a disc jockey instead.

When Mrs Ruebens said her husband would be there Mike told her about Joey and said he was sure he could get him to come along.

'Is he any good?'

Mike had given Mrs Ruebens a confident look.

'As a matter of fact, he's *bloody terrific.*'

*

Mike stood with his colleague outside the terrace of houses and admired the restoration work. The stone and brickwork looked as good as when it was built in the early eighteen hundreds. Now that the last house was nearing completion inside Mike was looking forward to his next project, completely refurbishing a Victorian mansion in Highgate.

And he'd just put in a bid to buy some land in Yorkshire. But the deal was in its early stages yet, and could go either way. Mike hoped it went his.

A Mercedes drew up silently at the kerb and Mike saw Roger Spencer get out. The author was ecstatic about his new home and couldn't wait to move in.

'How's it going, Mike?' he asked, as they shook hands.

'Everything should be finished in about three weeks.'

'Great, I can't wait.'

Mike turned to his colleague.

'I don't believe you've met Roger Spencer, have you?'

'No, we've only spoken on the phone.'

'Roger, this is Gerry Dolan,' Mike continued. 'He's usually back at the office slaving over his drawing board.'

It had taken some persuasion but eighteen months ago Gerry had finally agreed to join Mike as a director in his new company.

TWELVE

The doorbell chimed at eight thirty. It was expected and Kate Smith hurried from her small lounge to the front door. The weather was foul, the rain pouring down in torrents, and the man on the doorstep was soaked, his grey curly hair plastered over his forehead. There was no porch over the front entrance and Kate immediately felt sorry for her caller as he held out a large brown envelope.

'Would it be possible to use your bathroom for a moment?' he asked as she took the money, the sixth monthly payment of two thousand pounds, since her initial ten. The only difference was that the person delivering the cash had changed, from a nondescript sort of man to the character now standing in front of her.

Kate hesitated for a moment, adjusted her glasses, then replied, 'Of course,' and stepped to one side.

'Thank you, Miss Smith,' the man said, his lips parting in a smile, which did little to soften his hard looking face. 'I should have gone before I left the pub.'

'Go to the top of the stairs and it's the first door on the right.'

The man nodded and started his climb. Little did she know, but he was as familiar with her house as she was.

Kate went into her kitchen and switched on the electric kettle.

'Would you like a cup of tea or coffee before you go?' she asked, as the man reappeared in the small downstairs hall.

'Yes, thanks, coffee would be nice,' he replied gratefully. 'It's a lousy night outside.'

The man took off his raincoat and Kate hung it on a hook on the back of the kitchen door. Then she showed him into the lounge, switched on the television, and went back to preparing a couple of hot drinks.

'Thanks,' the man said, when she returned to the room carrying a tray with two cups and saucers and a plate of assorted biscuits.

Kate was curious about the person sitting on the chair in front of her, and just a bit nervous.

'Who do you work for?' she asked, after she took a sip of her coffee.

'I'm in the security business,' the man lied, with a smile. Lies dripped easily off his tongue, they had for most of his adult life.

'What's your name?' Kate asked.

'Eddie,' he replied.

'Well, Eddie, do you know what's in those envelopes you've been delivering to me the last few months?'

'No, Miss Smith, none of my business. Your envelope, with your name and address, is posted to me inside a larger one, and the date I'm supposed to deliver.'

'Oh, I see,' she smiled, 'and by the way, call me Kate. Everybody at work calls me Miss Smith.'

'Okay Kate,' he smiled back. It was going better than he'd hoped, quite expecting to have the door slammed in his face when he'd requested to come inside. But the woman was *nice*, just as he'd been told. Not the most attractive, in fact, she was on the plain side, but she dressed well and her figure was passable.

It was the third time he'd delivered the envelope to the house and thought enough time had elapsed for him to make his move. He had to find those papers the woman had hidden somewhere. He'd been promised an extra five grand if he did.

However, the man had a feeling it wouldn't be an instant result, so after finishing his drink didn't outstay his welcome, and said goodbye. But he left an opening for the future.

'Would it be all right if I phoned you sometime?'

'Why, yes...yes, of course,' was the woman's slightly flustered reply. She wasn't used to attention from the opposite sex.

*

A week later Kate received a call from her new found friend asking to take her out to dinner, which she accepted, but with a slight feeling of nervousness. She was on uncertain ground. Most of her evenings she spent by herself and could hardly remember the last time she'd been on a date with a man. *It had been a long time.*

Eddie picked her up in a black VW Golf car and took her to a small French restaurant not far from where she lived. He was a perfect gentleman and the conversation during the meal was mostly small talk. She learnt that he was divorced, lived by himself and owned a third share of his security company. And when they returned to her home about eleven pm he said goodnight on the doorstep without the slightest hint of a pass.

It seemed her misgivings were groundless.

Kate had enjoyed herself and when he phoned the next week to say he'd booked theatre seats for a popular play, much acclaimed by the critics, she once again said yes, and found herself looking forward to the meeting.

She'd never married, although she thought she'd been close to it one time, but that had been fifteen years ago. Neil...she often thought about him, even though she did have difficulty remembering what he looked like.

He'd broken it off after they'd been going out together for two years just when she was certain they had a future together. Maybe it was talking about marriage that changed his mind...but she'd been positive he felt the same way too. Obviously not, as it turned out in the end.

She'd given herself to him as though they were a married couple and Neil had been her only lover. She often stayed overnight at his small flat and liked the feeling of sleeping with a man. But that seemed such a long time ago.

Kate was realistic enough to know she was a plain woman, not particularly attractive to the other sex, but she did try to make the most of herself, and her shape wasn't too bad. However, men didn't ask her for dates and she resigned herself to staying single...she hated the word *spinster*. Reminded her of Lucy Fisher, but maybe that's why she got on so well with her. When her boss had been alive he'd taken her several times to visit his sister. Tom had been close to Lucy, seemingly a lot more than his brother, Robert. But she was a sweet old lady.

And Kate was still only thirty nine. Still young enough to find a partner, so she hoped.

But she did have a secret.

Ten years ago when she'd put a deposit on her small house she decided to experiment with her loneliness. She might not be a good looking woman but she had a strong sexual urge, and never had a problem reaching an orgasm using her finger in the privacy of her bed. But she felt she needed more and six months after moving to her new home visited Soho and browsed nervously in the sex shops, notorious to the area. Too shy at first, it took several visits before she plucked up the courage to purchase anything. Two pornographic videos were her first buy which really excited her and gave her more ideas. A few months later she had enlarged her sex collection with a vibrator and several dildos of different size and colour, plus more blue movies. She even bought an extra television and video recorder for her bedroom, much preferring her bed to the couch in the lounge.

Sometimes she made love to herself in front of a large mirror using the artificial penises on her body, while watching the people in the films, often engaged in group sex. She also practiced with her mouth, wishing it was a real warm cock ready to ejaculate down her throat and not a lifeless object.

And she invested money in sexy lingerie which gave her great delight to wear under her clothes, which although smart and *sensible*, were so different to her flimsy panties, and suspenders and stockings or holdups. She often wondered what people would think if she suddenly whipped off her top clothes.

So she had her dreams and fantasies, and now that she had plenty of money she'd often thought about hiring a male escort and paying for sex to satisfy her craving. But day dreaming such things was totally different from doing them, and always backed away from actually following her desire. She just didn't have the confidence.

But now she'd met a man who was interested enough to take her out, despite her prim and proper looks. At first she'd felt cautious knowing the circumstances under which they'd met, but was glad she didn't feel that way now. Maybe she would soon know what it was like again to have a man inside her. But she wouldn't be pushy or talk about anything permanent in case it put him off, like it had Neil. Anyway, it was early days yet.

However, one thing was sure - she wouldn't say no - to whatever he wanted.

THIRTEEN

The telephone rang just after Dixie stepped from the shower and put on a white towelling robe. It was Linda.

'Have you thought about tonight?' she asked

'Yes, but I think I'll give it a miss,' Dixie replied.

There was an awkward pause before Linda spoke again.

'He's a nice man, Dixie.'

'I know. But I just don't feel like going out for dinner this evening.'

'Why not? You've been out with Trevor before...and I know he likes you a lot.'

'Yes, and I like him. But I don't want him to get the idea that he's my boyfriend. I'll probably see him again sometime, but I don't want to see him tonight.'

'Okay, I'll tell him you've got the flu.'

'Thanks, Linda,' and Dixie replaced the receiver.

She'd been out with her flatmate double dating several times and, although she'd enjoyed herself, wasn't looking for a lasting relationship. In fact, she didn't think much about men these days, even that good looking stranger she'd met on Hampstead Heath was becoming a distant memory. That was months ago. It was Easter this weekend.

Dixie opened her wardrobe door and stood there wondering what to wear...Mike, she still remembered his name. Yes, he *was* different...

Dixie took a hanger from the rail trying to concentrate. She was meeting her uncle for lunch so she should wear something smart, not too casual. She replaced the hanger and selected another. She'd wear a dark blue two piece suit and navy cashmere sweater.

She looked at the bedroom clock. Ten past ten. She had plenty of time and wandered into the kitchen to make another cup of coffee. She wasn't seeing Uncle Robert until one o'clock.

*

There was a distinct knock and the lounge door opened.

'Your minicab's here, Mr Judd,' the man dressed in a short grey jacket and crisply pressed black trousers said.

'Thanks, Stan,' and Joey eased himself off the large five seater settee.

Stan and Marie Pearce looked after the pop star and the running of his house. A childless, middle aged couple, they had been recommended by Terry Hayman and Joey soon realized what a good choice they were. Hard working, discreet, and with some of the people who came to this house they needed to be, and both had a wonderful pleasant nature.

'Their previous employer moved to Italy and they didn't want to leave England,' the club owner had told him. 'Mark my words, you're lucky to get them.'

A sentiment Joey now wholeheartedly agreed with.

Joey left his house and got in the minicab. He had a Rolls Royce and Aston Martin in his garage, and Stan doubled as a chauffeur when necessary, but Joey travelled a lot by cabs.

He was meeting Mike for lunch and then they were going to see their accountant. Two years ago they'd started a company together. Joey put up the money, and Mike the expertise. But Mike was touchy about money. Right from the first moment Joey started to make it big he wanted to shower gifts on his mate. But Mike refused to accept the presents. It was his pride. In fact, it was the only time they'd ever had an argument, so they compromised. Small gifts such as shirts and sweaters were okay, and nights out in restaurants were acceptable. But Mike didn't want a Ferrari or the deposit on a flat or house. He appreciated the thought, but no thanks. Joey offered to put Mike on his payroll as a special consultant with a whopping salary but still the answer was no.

By then Mike had started his own business, small, but he was determined to fulfill his ambition. Joey said he'd pump some money into it, and Mike said maybe sometime in the future, but not yet.

Then Joey became a millionaire - and the next year a multi-millionaire - so the pop star put his foot down.

And after Mike saw the size of his friend's bank balance he finally relented. They would go into business together.

Joey smiled to himself as the cab slowed down for traffic lights. He owed so much to Mike.

*

The minicab dropped off Joey outside the restaurant in the Covent Garden area. Mike was already sitting at a table, drinking scotch and ice.

'Wearing a suit and a collar and tie,' Mike commented, as Joey sat down, a trace of amusement in his voice.

'Well, seein' as you're gettin' to be such a smart bugger these days, and we are goin' to see our accountant, I thought I'd better look the part. After all, I am a fuckin' millionaire.' Joey paused. 'Besides, you'd only nag me if I didn't.'

'It's the people I mix with these days, I have to make an impression,' Mike said. 'Not like you scruffy pop stars.' But he was inwardly pleased. There weren't many people Joey would dress up for.

The meal was pleasant and unhurried as they discussed business. There were several details Mike wanted to clarify with his friend about the land he wanted to buy in Yorkshire. Building permission had been granted, subject to plans, and the overall cost was very reasonable, so long as everything went according to budget. But, this was Mike's first venture at building houses from scratch, so far his company had only been involved in conversions and interior decorating. Profitable, and the accountant was pleased, but today's meeting was called because the company was taking a large step forward.

'The accountant's only bein' cautious,' Joey said. 'But, at the end of the day, it's our money, and if you say it's a good deal then that's okay with me.'

Joey knew this development of houses was Mike's ultimate ambition, so Mike was going to get his wish, no matter what. Joey would see to that.

After the meal they got a taxi to their accountant's tall office block in High Holborn, but had to stop some distance from the entrance because of busy roadworks. As Mike paid the cab driver, hardly able to hear him because of pneumatic drills tearing up the road, another black cab drew up behind them. A well dressed distinguished looking man got out and waved goodbye to another passenger inside the cab before turning and walking briskly towards the office building.

As the other taxi tried to ease out into the flowing traffic Mike felt his heart quicken as he glanced inside. It was *her*, he was sure of it. That long black hair framing her hauntingly, attractive face. Dixie. He had a clear view as she looked in the direction the silver haired man had taken.

'Dixie,' he shouted. 'Dixie,' but the sound of the drilling drowned out his voice. Then the taxi found an opening in the stream of traffic and was gone.

'Shit,' Mike cursed, and looked around for the elderly man. But he too had disappeared.

'What's the matter?' Joey asked.

'That girl in the cab. Did you see her?'

'Yeah, a real cracker. Why?'

'I met her once,' Mike muttered. 'And I'd like to see her again. But I don't know how to get hold of her.'

'I met 'er once too,' Joey said.

Mike stared at his friend.

'You did? Where?'

'Well, I didn't actually *meet* 'er, but we shared the same lift together.'

'I don't understand,' Mike said.

'It was sometime last summer.'

'Do you know her name?'

'No, but you do. I just 'eard you call 'er name. Dixie, wasn't it?'

'Her *last* name.' Mike sounded impatient. 'Have you any idea what it is?'

'No, but I can easily find out. Anyway, why all the interest? You don't usually react this way over a bird.'

'Joey,' Mike took a deep breath and smiled. 'Don't let's play silly buggers.'

'Right, let's go and I'll fill you in,' and Joey began walking. "er uncle is one of our accountants...it must be Fisher...ours is Wyatt Peterson...so yes, it must be Fisher.'

'You think her name's Dixie Fisher?'

Joey shrugged his shoulders as they reached the lifts.

'We're seein' Wyatt now,' Joey continued, 'so let me do the talkin'.'

A secretary showed them straight into Wyatt Peterson's office. He was a big man with short blonde hair and wore gold rimmed glasses. He was American, from Boston, and his face beamed as the two men were shown in.

'Take a seat gentlemen,' he said in his clipped Ivy League accent. 'I take it everything is well?'

'Yeah, fine thanks,' Joey replied.

'Good,' Wyatt said, and opened a stiff black plastic folder on his desk.

'Wyatt, I'd like to ask you a favour,' the pop star said.

'Sure, what is it?'

'Do you know a young woman called Dixie?'

'Dixie?' Wyatt thought for a moment then started to shake his head. 'I don't think so...'

"er last name could be Fisher...Dixie Fisher,' Joey interjected. "er uncle is one of the partners 'ere.'

'Ah yes, of course, Robert's niece. That was a tragedy.'

Wyatt Peterson stopped speaking.

'What was?' Mike asked.

'Dixie's father was Tom Fisher, Robert's brother. Tom was also an equal partner in the firm.' Wyatt rested his elbows on his desk and joined the tips of his fingers together. 'Yes, a great tragedy. Such a good man.'

Mike and Joey remained silent and waited patiently for the accountant to continue.

'Tom Fisher and his wife were killed in a terrible car crash. It happened last summer. Terrible,' he repeated. 'Margo, his wife, she was a lovely woman...such a loss.'

'I'm sorry to hear that,' Mike said.

'Do you know where Dixie Fisher lives?' Joey asked.

Wyatt placed his arms flat on the desk and gave Joey a puzzled look.

'Lives? No, I've got no idea where the young lady lives.'

'Could you please find out for me?'

'Do you mind telling me why?'

'It's personal.'

'I'm sorry Mr Judd but that's family business. I'm sure Robert Fisher wouldn't like strangers prying into his private affairs.'

Joey got up from his chair, walked to the large window and stood looking out. Then he turned and faced the accountant.

'Do you think we're a couple of fuckin' perverts? Do you, Wyatt? Do you think we want to meet this young lady for some perverted reason?'

'No, no, of course not,' came the flustered reply.

'I'm glad you think that way, Wyatt, because I wouldn't like to 'ave an accountant who thought I was a pervert.' Joey paused then said slowly, 'Otherwise I'd 'ave to take my business somewhere else.' He paused again. 'So, I'll spell it out for you. Mike wants to meet Dixie again. They 'ave met before but she's moved and Mike doesn't know where to. So I would be very *grateful* if you could get Dixie's address and phone number before we leave after our business meetin'. Okay?'

Wyatt Peterson stood up.

'Of course, Mr Judd,' he said. 'I didn't realize Mr Saxby and Miss Fisher were old friends. Just excuse me for a moment and I'll go and speak to someone.'

As the accountant left the room Joey turned to his friend and winked.

FOURTEEN

After they left the large concrete and glass building Mike and Joey split. Joey was meeting drummer, Omar Jones, the only remaining member of the original group at the office of their manager, Vic Ruebens.

Mike got a cab and gave the driver an address in Notting Hill. It had once been a small factory producing metal tubing but had closed down years ago. However, the shell of the building was solid and Mike's company had bought the freehold and converted the inside into offices and a variety of showrooms. Bedrooms, bathrooms, kitchens, lounges, dining rooms and kids nurseries, each one in a different style. As well as showing clients photographs in books it gave them a better idea of the real thing.

Gerry Dolan was talking to Josie, their secretary, and they waved to each other as Mike walked through the main office into a smaller glass sided one. He sat at his desk thinking, then looked up as the door opened and a fresh faced teenager stuck his head around.

'Coffee?' Jeffrey asked. He was seventeen, and the general dogsbody.

'Okay,' Mike replied, 'make it a large mug,' then smiled as an auburn haired, pretty woman pushed past the young man.

'I want to leave on time today,' she said, looking at her wristwatch, 'in about twenty minutes, if that's okay with you. It is important.'

Mike also looked at his watch. It was nearly five thirty.

'Sure,' he replied, ' you work too hard as it is.' And that was true. Laura was a bachelor girl in her thirties and worked double the hours Mike paid her for. She didn't have to but she loved her job. She was an interior designer and her ideas were exactly in the same mould as Mike's. They agreed on most things and any problems that did arise were amicably thrashed out with the end result usually better than the original idea. Laura had a young girl, Emma, in her early twenties under her wing who was a wonder at choosing fabrics and matching up colours. Another secretary and teenage office girl made up the rest of the staff.

All the building and decorating work was sub-contracted out on a job-by-job basis.

At six o'clock the rest of the staff left and Gerry checked that Mike was locking up before saying goodnight.

*

Mike had changed over the years. Even Joey said so. His voice had softened, lost its sharp cockney tone, and he didn't use slang words or swear as much as he used to. He seemed quieter in his manner, more interested in listening and learning from people, rather than thinking up smart answers. But the biggest change over the last year had been his attitude to women. He was fed-up trying to prove he was a superstud in bed and had slowly eased out of Joey's groupie scene. There had been the odd girlfriend, one even lasted a few months, but nobody meant anything special.

Until he'd met Dixie in the snow on Hampstead Heath.

And why he'd never asked to see her again or taken her phone number was beyond him. Maybe because it was the first time a woman had ever made such an immediate impression on him. But he *knew* she'd felt something too in that look that passed between them.

Or had it just been his imagination?

Anyway, after all this time she'd probably forgotten about him by now. And it was that thought which had been putting him off lifting up the handset and calling the number his accountant had given him.

A smile crossed Mike's face. He was behaving like a wimp...and he grabbed the phone and began pressing the buttons.

*

Dixie put the plate of smoked salmon on a tray, poured herself a glass of white wine from an already opened bottle in the fridge, and carried the tray into the lounge. Linda was going out straight from work and Dixie was looking forward to an evening by herself in front of the television. There was a movie on later she wanted to see.

She was chewing on a mouthful of salmon and brown bread when the cordless phone rang on the coffee table in front of her.

'Hello,' she said, then added, 'I'm sorry, but I'm eating,' and covered the mouthpiece with her hand as she swallowed her food. She took a quick sip of her wine and then began speaking again. 'Sorry about that, but I had a mouthful.'

'Could I speak to Dixie Fisher, please?'

It was a man's voice. A voice that sounded vaguely familiar.

'Hello, can you hear me?' the man asked.

'Yes,' she replied. 'I'm Dixie.'

'Look, this is a bit awkward. We have met, but I'm not sure if you remember me...'

Dixie felt her heart quicken.

'...my name's Mike. We met at Christmas on Hampstead Heath...remember? You had a dog with you called Mikey.'

'Yes, I remember,' Dixie replied. Very much so, she added silently to herself.

'How did you get my number?' she asked.

'We share the same accountants,' he replied. 'I saw you earlier today with your uncle, but your taxi took off before I could speak to you.'

'I never saw you,' she said.

There was silence then Mike asked, 'What are you doing this evening?'

'Staying in, there's a film on TV I want to see.'

'You said you were eating. I hope I'm not interrupting you.'

'No, it's just a snack.'

'Would you like to have dinner with me this evening?'

Dixie was glad her caller couldn't see the delight on her face.

'Well, I was looking forward to seeing this film.'

'Record it,' Mike said.

'Yes, I suppose I could do that.'

'So you'll have dinner with me?'

'Umm, okay then. What time?'

'Eight thirty.'

'Where?'

'I'll pick you up at your place.'

'You have my address too?'

'Of course.'

'I'll see you in the lobby on the ground floor,' Dixie said, and as soon as she clicked off the phone headed for the bathroom, all the time quickly going over in her head what she should wear.

She wanted to make an impression.

*

Mike was waiting in the brightly lit green carpeted foyer when Dixie stepped out of the lift. She was wearing a black wool mini-dress with a lightweight black coat draped over her shoulders. She looked gorgeous, her long black hair brushed straight back from her face and gleaming in the light. He smiled admiringly as she walked towards him.

'No dog tonight?'

'No,' Dixie replied, returning the smile. 'He's upstairs with his proper owner.' She tucked her arm into Mike's and looked up into his face. 'Where are we going to eat?'

As soon as Dixie touched him she felt a tingle go through her body and was conscious of Mike pressing his arm against hers.

'I've got a cab waiting outside,' he said, and a minute later they were both sitting in the taxi.

'Have you been a client of my Uncle Robert for long?' Dixie asked as they sat close together.

'About two years, and Wyatt Peterson is our accountant, not your uncle.'

'*Our* accountant?'

'Yes, I've got a business partner, an old friend of mine.'

'And what kind of business are you in?'

During the next five minutes Mike explained the workings of his company and before Dixie could ask any more questions they arrived at their destination.

*

The restaurant was small and intimate, with a single red rose in a slim crystal holder on each table. A waiter in a crisp blue shirt and bowtie showed them to a corner table and left them to read through the menu.

They ordered, neither wanted starters, and Mike told the waiter to bring a bottle of white wine before the meal.

As they sipped the chilled dry wine Mike continued talking about his plans for the future building development in Yorkshire.

Then he paused.

'What about you?' he asked. 'What kind of work do you do?'

'I haven't worked for some time,' Dixie replied. 'Not since my parents died...last year,' and her voice lowered.

'Yes, Wyatt told me about it. A car accident,' Mike's tone was gentle.

'And my boyfriend too.'

'I see,' Mike said. 'I'm sorry.'

'That's okay.'

'So, there's no one special in your life now?'

Dixie shook her head.

'No,' she replied.

At that moment the waiter arrived with their food and as they started to eat it gave Dixie an opportunity to study the man sitting opposite her.

He was just as she'd remembered him. His dark medium length, slightly wavy hair, and his relaxed mouth which readily broke into a smile. But there was a strength of character and energy in his good looking face which gave Dixie the impression that he wasn't the kind of man who could be taken advantage of. His hands looked strong and his aura was definitely very masculine.

Mike wore his clothes well and the dark blue single breasted suit, blue button down shirt and tie matched perfectly.

'Is there anyone in *your* life?' she asked.

'No, nobody *special*.'

The two of them stared at each other as they chewed their food.

*

When they left the restaurant they walked arm in arm towards the Thames embankment. It was a clear night and a myriad of stars stretched across the sky. They reached Cheyne Walk and headed east, the bulbous streetlights casting long shadows. A breeze blew off the river ruffling their hair.

'Are you cold?' Mike asked. 'Shall we get a taxi?'

'No, I'm fine,' Dixie replied. 'It's a lovely evening.'

They walked in silence for a while, content with the feeling of being together.

The conversation during dinner had been relaxed as they slowly discovered each other. Dixie had laughed a lot too, more than she could remember for a long time. Especially when Mike talked about his childhood.

Joey Judd.

Dixie couldn't get over the way Mike talked so casually about the pop superstar and their years of growing up together. More like brothers, was how Mike put it.

Mike said he never knew his father but talked warmly about his mother.

'And, it looks as though she might have finally settled down. Two months ago she went to live with a man in Scotland, in Edinburgh, and for my Mother to leave London means he must be somebody special.'

Comparing their backgrounds Dixie realized how different they'd been. The luxuries she'd taken for granted were only pipe dreams as far as Mike was concerned when he was young, and this had fuelled his ambition to succeed. Dixie was impressed by the matter of fact way Mike spoke. No complaints - he just accepted life as it was.

'It's Easter this weekend,' Mike said, breaking their silence. 'Are you doing anything tomorrow?'

'No,' Dixie replied, and walked to the stone embankment wall. She rested her arms on the top and stood looking at the reflected lights on the rippling water. Mike joined her and she turned her face to him.

'Do you have anything in mind?' she asked.

'Lunch...to start with.'

'Then?'

Mike smiled.

'What about dinner?'

FIFTEEN

Good Friday. A Bank Holiday, and as Dixie got out of bed and put on her dressing gown the telephone rang.

'Good morning,' Linda said.

'Good morning,' Dixie echoed.

'And where were you last night? I phoned to tell you I wouldn't be home but you weren't there. I thought you said you were staying in.'

'I changed my mind,' Dixie said.

'Oh yes?'

'Yes.'

'Come on Dixie, don't just say, yes. There's more to it than that. Was it a man?'

'Yes.'

'Dixie, if you keep on saying yes, I'll scream. And then my Mother will want to know what's going on.'

'You're at your mother's?'

'Yes.'

'Now *you're* saying it,' Dixie laughed. 'What happened? You said you were having dinner with Stuart.'

'It was a disaster. I won't bore you with the details but I got a cab to my parents. I was nearer their place than ours. Anyway, I want to know about your night. Who is the man?'

'His name's Mike.'

'Mike? Who's he?'

'You've seen him.'

'I have? When?'

'At Christmas. Remember we took the dog for a walk? You saw me talking to him.'

'Yes...I remember,' Linda said slowly. 'You mean, he phoned out of the blue, just like that?'

'I'll tell you about it later.'

'Are you seeing him again?'

'Lunch-time.'

'I'm on my way,' Linda said. 'See you soon.'

Dixie replaced the receiver

*

Mike picked her up in his dark green Range Rover dead on noon, drove in the direction of Shepherds Bush, then cut onto the A40 and headed out of London. During the morning the weather had steadily got warmer with the sun bright in a clear blue sky and the traffic flowed in a steady stream out of the capital.

The couple were perfectly at ease with each other. Only their second date but there wasn't the slightest awkwardness between them. They made small talk about the sudden change in the weather and what a wonderful spring day it was. But their idle conversation was unimportant because their eyes said everything.

And once when Mike changed gear, Dixie lowered her hand and gently squeezed his, the touch sending her nervous system haywire.

They had lunch in a beautiful old pub near Gerrards Cross in Buckinghamshire. Then two hours later drove through the country roads, stopping to walk hand-in-hand through a grassy field to explore the ruins of an ancient church, before carrying on to Windsor. There they wandered through the town dominated by its great royal castle. In a narrow alley they discovered a quaint bow fronted tearoom and ventured inside to taste its strong brew and wolf down scones with jam and clotted cream.

'No diet?' Mike asked.

Dixie shook her head and grinned, her lips milky white with cream.

'It's lovely,' she said, and crammed more into her mouth.

They drove leisurely back to London and arrived in South Kensington just after eight pm where Mike parked close to Dixie's apartment block.

'Are you hungry?' he asked.

'No, but I wouldn't mind a drink,' Dixie replied.

They only had to walk for about five minutes before they came to a pub where they spent the next two hours. Dixie slowly began to talk more about her parents, then discovered it wasn't as painful as she'd expected. Mike was an understanding listener and didn't ask too many questions, letting her guide the conversation.

'They'd have liked you,' she said.

'Thanks,' Mike said, and felt sorry he'd never have the opportunity to meet them.

'But I do have another Father,' and Dixie gave a small smile as she saw the puzzled look appear on his face. Dixie went on to explain about Danny Buckley, the findings of the private detective and then suddenly stopped speaking.

Mike sensed there was more.

'Is there something else?' he asked.

'Yes, there is,' and Dixie slowly related the horrible experience she'd had when she met her father.

'He sounds like a right bastard,' Mike said, 'but, did he know you were his daughter?'

'No, and I'm glad, because I think I saw the true side of him, what he's really like. Linda told me it's best if I forget him.'

'Maybe she's right,' Mike shrugged. He'd briefly met Linda when he'd picked up Dixie from her flat and liked her straight away. 'But if you do ever think of trying to see him again I think it would be a good idea if I came with you.'

*

The next couple of weeks were a whirlwind of dates for Dixie with nearly every evening spent with Mike. They went to the cinema, theatre, a variety of restaurants and enjoyed hours walking. Mike was a regular visitor to her home but she had yet to see where he lived.

On the Saturday of their third weekend together they went to an Italian restaurant in Queensway where Mike was greeted by several waiters over the hub-bub of noise. The place was busy but the couple were shown to a reserved table for two in one corner of the room.

'I often eat here,' he explained. 'It's convenient...not far from where I live.'

'It's nice,' Dixie said, looking around the dining area with its wood panelled walls and low lights. 'It's got a nice atmosphere.'

A well rounded man in his forties with black tight curly hair pushed through the doors leading from the kitchen, stopped briefly to speak to the young man behind the small bar, then looked around before moving towards them. His face broke into a smile.

'Ah, Mr Mike,' he said in a slight Italian accent, as he arrived at their table, 'good to see you.'

'Hello, Dino,' Mike said, then introduced his companion. 'Dixie, this is Dino, the owner of this establishment.'

Dino gave a slight bow and beamed.

'She is truly a beautiful young lady, Mr Mike. Much better than any you've brought here before.'

Dixie wasn't sure how to take the remark as Mike exploded into laughter. Then he leant across the table and held her hand.

'You're the *only* woman I've ever brought here,' he told her. 'This man has been nagging me for ages to meet my girlfriend.'

'Yes, Miss Dixie, you're the first lady to come here with Mr Mike. Mr Joey comes here with many ladies, but not Mr

Mike.' Dino leant slightly towards Dixie. 'You must be somebody special.'

Mike winked at her and silently mouthed, '*You are*.'

'He's nice,' Dixie said, as the Italian moved away cheerfully talking to his other diners.

'It's a family business,' Mike said. 'Everyone who works here is related in some way. I love this place.'

The meal was excellent with the added bonus of a bottle of champagne on the house.

'And make sure you come here again with Mr Mike,' Dino insisted as they left the restaurant two hours later.

'That's a promise,' Dixie smiled, as she tucked her companion's arm into hers. 'No other woman but me.'

'Sounds like I don't get much say in the matter,' Mike grinned at the proprietor.

The couple moved into the street walking past the brightly lit shop fronts. Queensway had always been a busy area with its cosmopolitan population and late night shopping. It was a lovely pleasant evening and Mike guided them through several residential streets before stopping outside a large house in the middle of a terrace.

'I have a flat in the basement,' he said, and opened the heavy black iron gate.

Dixie kissed Mike on the cheek. 'About time,' she said and followed him down the wrought iron stairs.

The inside was nice but nothing special, which surprised Dixie. Mike was quick to sense her feeling as they took off their coats.

'It's a furnished flat,' he said. 'I've been here nearly a year and it'll have to do until I buy a place of my own. To me it's just a place where I can put my head down. I've been too busy building and designing other peoples homes to worry about myself.'

Dixie moved against Mike and as she looked upwards into his face he placed his arms around her.

'How many bedrooms have you got?' she asked, and gently nuzzled his mouth with her lips, then looped both arms around his neck.

'Two,' Mike replied. 'Why?'

'Because I want to stay the night.'

Mike slightly parted his mouth and felt hers open wider as their kiss lingered, her body pressed tight against him.

'In that case,' he said, breaking away and looking into her eyes, 'I've only got one.'

'I'm glad,' Dixie said, and took hold of his hand, 'because that's all we'll need.'

In the bedroom they slowly undressed each other but couldn't contain themselves as their hands aroused their passion. They made love still partially clothed, each marvelling at the sensation they felt.

'I love you, Dixie.'

'And I love you, Mike. So very much.'

SIXTEEN

It was inevitable that Dixie should ask Mike to bring Joey along to her flat for dinner.

By now Dixie had heard so much about the pop star she was dying to meet him. And, of course, so was Linda.

'I love his voice,' she said. 'And I want to find out if he's as bad as the tabloids make him out to be. They say he's a real bastard with the women.'

'Mike says a lot of that is just media hype, and he's really a nice person,' Dixie said.

'Anyway, I might not meet him.'

'Why's that?'

'He might want to bring along one of his girlfriends.'

'Don't worry, I'll make sure it'll be a dinner for the four of us.'

It was a month since Mike and Dixie had first slept together and now they couldn't seem to get enough of each other, spending most of their spare time in bed, sometimes staying overnight at Dixie's, sometimes at Mike's.

Linda asked Dixie if she should move out but her friend said there was ample room and wouldn't hear of it.

'I *am* in love,' Dixie confided to Linda, 'and Mike feels the same about me. But we're not pushing it. We just want to let things happen naturally.'

'Would you marry him, if he asked?'

'Yes, I would,' Dixie replied without hesitation, 'but Mike's got a lot on at the moment. He's negotiating a deal in

Yorkshire and he'll have to go there soon. Besides, he's a very single minded person and I know he'd never think of asking me until his business is sorted.'

*

Mike had told Joey a week after his first date with Dixie that they were seeing each other, but it didn't mean much to the pop star. He had a stable of girls who changed every few weeks and being serious about just one female didn't enter his mind.

He was enjoying life too much.

So it came as a surprise when Mike phoned and invited him to Dixie's for dinner.

'Some nice home cooking,' Mike said.

'What's wrong with restaurants?' Joey asked.

'This is different.'

'Different?'

'Yes, I want you to get to know Dixie.'

'Why?'

'Because she's someone special.'

'You're not in fuckin' love, are you?'

There was silence before Mike answered.

'Yes, I am.'

A sudden chortle of laughter came from Joey.

'I don't fuckin' believe it. My best mate's in love. Not thinkin' of gettin' married are you?'

'No, not yet. But it will happen some time in the future.'

'Bloody 'ell, Mike. That means responsibility, kids, shitty nappies and all that. Think of all the shaggin' you'll miss out on.'

'Time to grow up, Joey.'

'Not for me it ain't. Anyway, what's this dinner thing you're talkin' about?'

Mike told him when and where he was expected and added Dixie's flatmate, Linda, would also be there.

'What's she like?' interest appearing in Joey's voice.

'She's good looking with a great figure...but keep your hands off. She's not that sort...she's a nice girl.'

'But she might fancy me.'

'Joey, I want you to behave yourself. Oh, and there's one other thing.'

'Yes?'

'I'd appreciate it if you really tried hard not to swear. You do eff and blind a lot.'

'Mike, you're invitin' me to dinner where there's going to be a good looking woman I mustn't touch, and now you're telling me I've got to watch my language. Shall I bring some knittin' along?'

'Joey, I really do want you to be on your best behavior.'

'Okay Mike, I promise I won't touch the bird and I won't swear.' There was another burst of laughter from Joey. 'I can't believe it, my best mate's in love. It's fan-fuckin'-tastic.'

*

And Joey did behave himself that evening but it took some time for Mike to relax before he realized his friend wasn't going to let him down.

The pop star was polite, listened interestedly and let Mike take the lead when they talked about their past. Even so, Joey couldn't resist winding up his friend, and several times when the women weren't looking, grinned and silently mouthed *fuck, fuck, fuck*, in Mike's direction.

And Mike didn't have to worry about Joey's attitude towards Linda either. In fact, he wasn't sure if his friend was purposely being reserved in his manner, or if he was really interested in Linda. Either way, they hit it off immediately, and spent a lot of the evening laughing together, much to Mike's relief.

Joey had arrived in his Rolls Royce, and Stan, in chauffeur's uniform, had carried up a case of champagne to Dixie's flat, where several bottles were put in the fridge to be chilled in time for dinner.

'Is your chauffeur going to have to wait downstairs in the car until you're ready to go home?' Linda asked, with some concern in her voice.

'No,' Joey smiled, and Linda noticed how attractive his dimples were. 'I told 'im to leave. I'll get a taxi 'ome.'

'How thoughtful,' and Linda returned the smile.

The dining room in the apartment was green with subdued lighting, and the yew table was laid with Dixie's parents finest crystal glasses and silver cutlery.

The meal was a great success with the women praising each other's earlier joint efforts in the kitchen, which the men used as an excuse to drink more champagne in toasts to their beautiful hosts. The four enjoyed themselves so much they agreed to do the same next week, but have a buffet instead, and Dixie said she'd invite her neighbours, Carla and Joshua Rodriquez.

'Don't forget,' Dixie reminded Mike, 'it was Carla's dog who brought us together.'

The following week was just as enjoyable, but this time Joey was badgered into bringing along a guitar. His new album, *Freezing Fire,* was being released in a week's time and the pop star gave his audience a preview of some of the songs. Mike had heard Joey sing without a backing group many times before, but the others were impressed.

'Your voice is fantastic,' Linda said. 'Not many people can sing live like that.'

Dixie was happy seeing her friends laughing and drinking together. Since she'd met Mike the painful loss of her parents had lessened somewhat and she didn't feel the slightest bit guilty because she knew Tom and Margo would have approved of her choice.

Carla Evans had arrived in one of her skintight mini dresses which left nothing to the imagination, but Dixie knew her neighbour well enough by now to know she wasn't a flirt. She wasn't interested in other men, only Joshua.

Towards the end of the evening Joey pulled Mike to one side.

'Three gorgeous women 'ere and I'm behavin' like a fuckin' saint,' he said.

'Joey, just keep remembering that one day one of these women will be my wife, and the others are her friends.'

'Well, I 'ave asked Linda for a date.'

Mike looked quizzically at his friend.

'And what did she say?'

'She'd love to go out with me.'

'Be nice to her Joey. Dixie told me she's still getting over an affair that went wrong.'

'For chrisake, Mike, I'm only goin' to take 'er out to dinner, or somethin' like that.' Joey grinned and indicated towards Carla. 'But I could certainly give 'er one.'

Mike grinned back.

'Behave,' he said.

'Mike, you know when you die, your body goes 'ard and stiff.'

'Yeah, it's called rigor mortis.'

'I think my dick just died.'

SEVENTEEN

Kate was infatuated with the new man in her life. After so many years of loneliness and lacking a bedmate she was now experiencing happiness.

Making love again was wonderful, even though Eddie was rough with her at times. Not that he deliberately tried to hurt her, it was just that, well, he was a rough type of person. A hard man.

It was a little over two months since he'd asked to use her bathroom and during that time they'd seen each other once a week. But they'd only been to bed together half a dozen times, and Eddie had never stayed the night, always leaving as soon as they were both satisfied.

At first Kate had thought he might be married, and not divorced as he'd originally said, but Eddie assured her he wasn't - he just liked to wake up in his own place in the morning.

However, that was about to change. He'd promised to stay overnight and all day Sunday with her.

By seven o'clock Kate was ready to go out for dinner. She'd been using some of her blackmail money lately to buy a few new clothes. Nothing too flashy, but she bought some very expensive underwear which Eddie loved. The briefer the better was his opinion.

*

The black VW drew to a halt not far from Kate's house and the driver sat staring deep in thought.

The reason he'd decided to stay the night was because he knew it was time to start pushing for the information he needed. Eddie figured he was now liked enough by the woman for her to begin trusting him, but was still apprehensive about something going wrong. Nevertheless, ever since he'd got to know Kate intimately another idea began forming in his mind. And the more he thought about it - the better he liked it.

At worst it was a safeguard, but it did give him a second option.

Either way he'd make money.

Eddie got out of the car and walked towards Kate's house. The job he'd been given was turning out more pleasurable than expected, although at the outset he'd wondered if he could pull it off because when he'd broken into her home last year, before Christmas, one thing had puzzled him during the search.

The collection of dildos, vibrators and video cassettes had seemed out of character to what he'd been told about the woman. He'd never viewed the videos but the other sexual aids gave the indication she might be a lesbian. There was nothing to suggest there was a man in her life, privately, or at work. And that had been the main reason he'd been slow during the build-up getting her to bed.

But now he understood.

Kate was just a lonely woman who'd been starved of affection from a male partner and had found her own means of satisfaction. In fact, she was highly sexed and willing to do anything he suggested. She enjoyed everything - and loved him to talk dirty to her. So different from her usual staid life.

She'd brought up the subject after they'd made love for the first time and told him she was so happy to have a real man after all these years.

Kate confided she'd been a bit worried about telling him her secret and was pleased when he said he liked porn films too. And it excited him when she demonstrated on the bed how she made love to herself.

Eddie classed himself as an ordinary, normal man who liked women, but when it came to sex - he usually paid for it. He used prostitutes simply because he didn't want any involvement other than a quick lay.

Women were too nosy as he'd found out when he'd been married for a few short years. It was much less hassle to pay for it when the need arose.

But Kate was different. She didn't want anything other than his company and his body in bed. Whenever she asked about his background she didn't probe too much if he changed the subject. Kate took him at face value.

And the fact she was a blackmailer appealed to his own character, made him feel more comfortable.

He had to admit, he was getting quite fond of Kate. It seemed almost a pity he'd probably have to kill her.

*

Their dinner date was enjoyable and both were quite tipsy when their minicab picked them up from the restaurant and took them home.

They hadn't been in the house more than five minutes when they made love in the lounge, still with most of their clothes on, and Kate in a chair with her legs spread wide apart over the arms and Eddie kneeling on the floor.

Then they took a bottle of wine upstairs, undressed completely, and watched a film until they became aroused again.

Twice more they made love until finally exhausted they lay back against the pillows, sweat pouring from their bodies. They were quiet, each waiting for their heartbeat to return to normal.

'Would you like something to eat?' Kate asked, rolling over on her side and resting her chin on Eddie's chest. The smell of sex strong in her nostrils.

'That's sounds a good idea,' he replied. It was now two am and the fullness of their dinner eaten hours ago had long disappeared.

Kate got off the bed, slipped on a dressing gown and picked up her rimless glasses from the bedside table. She had tried contact lenses years ago but found them too uncomfortable.

'Sandwiches or bacon and eggs?' she asked.

'Bacon and eggs,' Eddie smiled. He quickly put on his underpants and trousers and followed Kate downstairs but didn't bother with a shirt. It was the first week in June and the weather was warm.

'This is nice,' Kate said, as they sat eating at the small kitchen table.

Eddie just nodded his head, took a large swig from the can of lager in his hand, then continued tucking into his food.

'That was great,' he said minutes later, wiping the remains of the egg yolks on a piece of bread before putting it into his mouth. Eddie got another can of beer from the fridge and stood with his back against the porcelain sink. He smiled amiably at the woman.

'I'm so glad you're staying the weekend,' Kate said.

'Yes, and it's something I intend doing more often.'

Kate felt a tingle run through her at the welcome news.

'That'll be lovely,' she said.

Eddie put down his beer, removed the dirty plates from the table and sat down again, taking the woman's hands into his own and gently squeezing.

'But there are some things I would like to know about you.'

'Yes? Like what?' Kate's voice sounded puzzled.

'Are you in any trouble?'

'Trouble? I don't understand.'

Eddie stared at the woman seated opposite him and hoped his voice and expression seemed understanding and sympathetic.

'Well...' he hesitated...'it's about those packages I've been delivering to you...'

'Yes, what about them?'

'You're...you're not involved in drugs, are you?'

'Drugs?' Kate's eyes opened wide. 'What makes you think anything like that?'

'Well,' and Eddie shrugged his shoulders, 'I thought maybe someone was using you. You're a respectable woman, just the sort the police would never suspect. If anyone's forcing you to do anything against your will...then I'd like to help.'

Kate slipped one hand free, placed it on top of Eddie's knuckles and squeezed.

'No, I'm not involved in drugs.'

'Are you sure? You can tell me the truth...I thought maybe someone was making you pass them on to someone else. The packets were too big to be for your personal use...so I thought somebody was using you.'

'No, I promise you, there are no drugs in those packages.'

'Well, that's a relief,' and Eddie visibly relaxed. He sat staring at the woman, started to speak, but then stopped himself.

'Yes?' Kate smiled. 'What is it?'

'Oh, I don't suppose it's really any of my business...' and Eddie paused, 'but what is in those packets?'

Kate didn't reply straight away but sat thinking. Did she trust Eddie enough to tell him the truth? He certainly seemed a man of the world, not a weak namby-pamby person. But what would his reaction be if she confessed she was a blackmailer? Also, he would have a hold over her…a strong hold.

However, she knew she wanted to keep this man in her life and couldn't bear the thought of losing him, destroying her newfound happiness.

Then she had a thought. Eddie didn't seem to have much money and if he knew she was on her way to being a wealthy woman he might be more interested in her. So Kate made an instant decision and reckoned it was worth taking a chance.

'It's money...cash.'

'Money?' and it was Eddie's turn to look surprised.

'Yes.'

'I don't understand.'

The two sat looking at each for a long time in silence.

'It's awkward to explain,' Kate finally said.

'Try me...take your time,' and Eddie paused as he sensed his partner's embarrassment. 'Look, I think a lot of you,' he continued slowly, 'and it would probably be better if you told me.' Eddie shrugged his shoulders. 'Who knows, you might need some help in the future, and I'd like to know what I'm getting into.'

'My boss was killed last year. A so-called accident but I think he was murdered. And I know the reason why.'

'And you know who did it?'

Kate nodded her head.

'Yes...yes I do.'

'And he's paying you to keep quiet?'

'Yes.'

'I take it you have proof?'

'Yes, I have some papers.'

'Papers?'

'Yes.'

'Where are they?'

Kate looked long at Eddie before replying.

'They're safely put away.'

'Not here?'

'No.'

Eddie was disappointed she hadn't revealed her hiding place straight away but was frightened he might alarm her so quickly changed tack. He'd done the hardest part getting her to talk and knew he could always come back to it. Most probably in bed.

'How much money do I deliver each month?' he grinned.

'A couple of thousand,' and Kate smiled back, breaking the tension.

Eddie had always known what was in the envelopes and had racked his brains trying to work out a strategy to find out where Kate had hidden the papers. That's why he'd used the drug angle. He figured she was naive enough to fall for it. And he'd been right. The main thing was, her secret was now out in the open, and he knew he had to build on it.

'You're not in any danger, are you?' he asked.

'No, I don't think so. Why?'

'This person you're getting the money from...maybe he might turn nasty.'

'No, he'd never harm me.'

'You sound confident,' and Eddie paused. 'Who is he?'

'I'm sorry,' Kate replied, 'but that's something I can't tell you. I'm sorry,' she repeated.

'I understand,' Eddie said, picking up his lager and draining the liquid. 'Come on,' and he rose from his chair and took another bottle of white wine from the fridge. 'Let's go back upstairs.'

*

It was while they were making love and Eddie was moving slowly in and out of her when he started talking again.

'You will promise me you'll tell me if things begin to get a bit heavy for you...if things start to go wrong and you need some help.'

Eddie started to thrust himself harder and faster into Kate, beads of sweat forming on his face.

'You promise?'

Kate gasped, her breathing quickening in pleasure.

'Yes, yes,' she replied.

'Are you sure?'

'Yes...oh, don't stop, it's beautiful,' she panted, as Eddie slowed his rhythm.

'Are you sure the papers are safe?' and he speeded up his movement again.

'Yes, yes, I'm sure.' Kate's face was covered in perspiration and her breathing was short and noisy as she started to climb to an orgasm.

'Do you like me fucking you?' Eddie whispered in her ear.

'Yes, yes I love you fucking me.'

'Where are the papers, Kate? Where are they?'

'They're in the country,' she replied, her hands tight on Eddie's buttocks, pulling him deeper inside her. 'An old lady's looking after them for me...oh, fuck me harder.'

'Do I know her?'

'No.'

'What's her name? What's her name?' and Eddie started to grunt in excitement, pushing stronger. 'I want to come Kate...right into your pussy…do you want me to?'

'Oh yes, come...come inside me.'

'What's her name?'

'Lucy,' Kate gasped in reply, and thrust herself firmly against him, breathing loudly as a wave of ecstasy swept through her body. 'Oh, it's beautiful...wonderful...I can't stop coming,' she moaned.

Eddie collapsed with a deep groan on top of the woman then rolled over on the bed as he slipped out of her.

'That was so lovely,' Kate said and put her smiling, sweaty face close to her man.

Eddie was smiling too - but for a totally different reason.

EIGHTEEN

Linda liked Joey but was determined not to be one of his easy conquests. He *was* a lot different from his reputation she'd read about in the papers but Linda knew all of it couldn't be hype and that a great deal of it was probably true.

Also, Joey was very rich, and after her unhappy affair with another wealthy man Linda was being cautious.

However, she and Joey *had* hit it off from the moment they met. They shared the same sense of humour, were quick to laugh at each other's remarks, and felt comfortable together. Joey's cheeky grin was infectious and he was so down to earth. Even the blonde streaks in his hair suited him and didn't make him look the slightest bit theatrical. Not like some of the show-offs on television.

After Linda had several dates with Joey, Dixie suggested the four of them should go out for a meal at a restaurant. Make a special night of it.

'And I think I'll invite Uncle Robert,' Dixie said. 'He and Aunt Lucy are the closest family I've got now, and I'd like him to get to know Mike.'

Mike and Joey thought it a great idea when they were told and the pop star had a further suggestion.

'Let's invite Wyatt as well,' he said, 'I was a bit 'ard on 'im the last time I was in 'is office.'

'Has he got a wife?' Linda asked.

'I'm not sure,' Mike replied. He's our accountant, and that's all we know about him.'

'I'll phone Uncle Robert and find out, and if he has, we'll invite her too,' Dixie said.

*

'Well, he does have a wife,' her uncle informed her the next day, 'but she's in the States with their two children. Personally, I don't think they have much of a marriage and I wouldn't be surprised if they split. That's if Wyatt can afford it. You know what these American lawyers are like when it comes to divorce. Anyway, I'll ask him and see what he says.'

Robert called back later and said Wyatt thanked her for the invitation and would love to join the party for dinner.

'Okay, I'll make the arrangements and let you know,' Dixie said.

She wasn't sure if her uncle had a girlfriend or not but had been too embarrassed to ask. Dixie hoped to find out more about his personal life when they all met. She'd known him all her life but now realized she didn't know that much about him.

Dixie would have liked to have had Aunt Lucy join them as well, but that was out of the question. She was too frail and suffered from osteoporosis, amongst other serious illnesses she'd had over the years.

'But we can go and see her,' Dixie told Mike. 'She's got a beautiful house in the country.'

*

The restaurant they chose was a newly opened one in Knightsbridge and its theme was 1930's Hollywood. Large and brightly lit with a split level floor the entertainment was big band music, crooners and sexy sultry singers on a semi-circular stage. The food and drink was excellent and the decor lavish.

And on Saturday nights there was a strict dress rule. Men had to wear dinner jackets and bow ties and the women evening dress. And if you weren't attired like that then you weren't welcome - no matter who you were.

Gimmicky maybe, but the restaurant had been packed since its opening, especially on Saturdays, which was the night Dixie booked for.

The six were seated at a large round table on the slightly raised floor part of the restaurant overlooking the stage. They had finished their first and main courses washed down with several bottles of champagne and the conversation was light and easy, although Dixie hadn't managed to discover much about her uncle's private life that she didn't already know.

He had a lovely penthouse flat that overlooked the River Thames which Dixie had been to a couple of times when her parents were alive, and Robert said he did go out with women but didn't have anyone special.

His favourite pastime was horse riding and he also enjoyed going to a health club.

'Why the interest?' he smiled.

'Just wondered why you've never married again.'

'My wife died when you were very young,' and her uncle's eyes took on a faraway look. 'But, she was the only woman for me. Nobody else has ever come close to her.' Robert shrugged his shoulders. 'However, who knows, maybe one day I'll meet someone else and change my mind. I'm still not too old, you know.'

'No, you're certainly not,' Dixie laughed. 'And you look very healthy and fit.'

'Ah, flattery, that's what I like to hear,' and her uncle smiled again. 'Makes all those hours in the gym worthwhile. Mind you, it's getting harder.'

Robert poured some more champagne and Dixie took a sip.

'Do you get to see your sister very often?' she asked.

'No, and believe me, she's often on my conscience. I phone her at least once a week but I haven't been to see her for a couple of months. I know I should go more often but somehow I never seem to make the time. We're always so busy at the office.'

'I'm going to visit her next weekend with Mike,' Dixie said. 'Aunt Lucy is always asking me to go. She keeps reminding me that you two are the only relatives I've got now.'

'What about Danny Buckley?'

The smile dropped from Dixie's face and she looked seriously at her uncle.

'I decided not to bother...no point raking up the past.'

Robert nodded his head solemnly.

'Probably for the best.'

'Aunt Lucy isn't very well, is she?' Dixie said, quickly changing the subject.

'No, but she's a tough old bird, and I don't think she's on her last legs yet,' Robert replied, a smile back on his face. 'She should be good for quite a few years yet.'

'Hey, you two, this is supposed to be a party,' Linda interrupted.

'Sorry,' Dixie laughed, 'I was just trying to find out about Uncle Robert's love life,' and she held out her glass for some more wine.

The restaurant had a resident photographer going from table to table taking pictures and Dixie ordered her dinner companions to smile and say *cheese* as the man snapped away. She told the photographer to pick out half a dozen of the best and send them to her. Dixie gave the man her address and he said he would put the charge on the dinner bill.

'Thanks,' the young woman said.

After a couple of singers had finished their stint on the stage conversation came around to the beginning of Joey's career.

'Yes,' Linda said, 'tell us the full story how you started.' She'd heard snippets on their dates and read some in the newspapers, but knew there must be a lot more.

Joey looked at Mike and winked.

'I think I'd better leave out the bits about all the women.'

'Yes, you do that' Mike laughed.

Joey relaxed in his chair, surprisingly comfortable in his black double breasted dinner suit, white wing collar and bow tie.

'Well, this is when you'll find out 'ow much I owe to my friend Mike. If it wasn't for 'im, I might not 'ave made it,' the pop star said.

'Joey, cut out all the crap,' and Mike was clearly embarrassed, much to Dixie's amusement. 'Just get on with it.'

Joey quickly recounted the forming of his group, their disappointments and how they'd split up, and their decision to give it one more try.

Then Mike had got the job which had taken him to Vic Ruebens country house. A job that was to change everyone's lives.

Mrs Ruebens was so pleased with Mike's work she decided to put on a birthday party for him and agreed that Joey and his band could provide the live music. It was on a Saturday, when they usually had a booking, but fate seemed to be lending a hand because the gig had been cancelled due to a fire in the pub they were due to appear at.

'So everything turned out all right for you on that night,' Linda said.

'Did it 'ell,' Joey grinned, then stopped speaking as dessert was served and a couple more bottles of champagne placed on the table.

Fifteen minutes later the group had finished eating and Joey informed them it was time to get down to some serious drinking.

'The night is still young,' he said.

'I'll go along with that,' Wyatt agreed, and took a deep sip of the bubbly liquid in his glass, obviously enjoying himself.

Then something caught the pop star's eye and he stood, wiping his mouth with a white cloth napkin. 'I'll be back in a minute,' and he began moving through the crowded tables towards the entrance.

Linda watched him until he disappeared from view behind a large pillar and didn't see him stop and talk to a man, club owner, Terry Hayman.

'I thought it was you,' Joey smiled.

'Yes, I saw you sitting with your friends,' Terry said, 'but I didn't want to disturb you.'

'Weren't you with a woman?'

'That's right,' Terry replied. 'She's in the loo.'

'Well, come over and meet them before you go.'

'I'm in a bit of a hurry, Joey, maybe some other time. Besides, I know Mike and one of the other men.'

'Yeah?' and the pop star raised his eyes quizzically.

'Yes, he comes to my club in Jermyn Street, loves the women. And I sometimes see him at a casino in Kensington, bit of a lunatic gambler...must have a lot of money.'

'Which one you talkin' about?' Joey asked, intrigued.

Terry lifted an arm and started to point.

'The one sitting next to...' and stopped as a beautiful young woman, wearing a dark green off-the-shoulder dress, appeared by his side '...this is Marietta,' he added.

'Hello,' Joey said.

'Hello,' and the young woman returned the greeting with a wide smile, obviously recognizing the famous singer.

'Joey, sorry to rush, but we really are in a hurry,' Terry said. 'Got to drive to the country, we're staying with Marietta's parents for the rest of the weekend.'

Blimey, everyone's gettin' serious these days, Joey thought.

'Okay, see you soon,' he said, and started back to his friends.

'Everything all right?' Linda asked as Joey sat back in his seat.

'Yes, fine,' he replied, 'just saw an old mate. Now, where was I?'

'You were just on your way to my birthday party,' Mike said.

'Oh yes,' and the pop star paused, 'you sure you want to 'ear this? I don't want to bore you.'

'Come on Joey,' Dixie said. 'I'm sure my Uncle wants to know how you started on the road to making your fortune, after all, he and Wyatt now look after your money.'

'Okay then, if you insist,' and Joey's eyes took on a distant look, 'we'd packed our old transit van with music gear and started off just before six thirty. We didn't 'ave to be at Mike's party until eight o'clock, so we 'ad plenty of time, or, so we thought. But then we 'adn't been drivin' more than five minutes when the radiator blew up. So me and one of the band, John Duncan, got a cab to Freddie Walker's place. He'd sold us the van in the first place...'

NINETEEN

Freddie's garage, just off Cable Street, was nothing more than a couple of lockups with a bit of space at the front for a few second hand cars.

The owner was in one of the lockups tinkering with the engine of an old Vauxhall. In his early fifties with a boozy red face and large beer gut Freddie looked up and smiled when he saw the two young men. He wiped his greasy hands on dirty blue overalls then picked up a lager can and took a long swig.

'That's better,' he belched, and wiped his mouth with the back of his hand. 'Now, what can I do for you?'

Joey quickly explained about their breakdown and their urgent need to get to Mike's birthday party.

'How much money you got?' Freddie asked.

'Petrol money, that's all,' Joey replied.

Freddie thought.

'I could let you have a couple of cars, I suppose.'

'No, we need a van or somethin' like that because of our equipment.'

Freddie thought longer.

'Well, I've got something which might help you out, but it doesn't belong to me.'

'What's that?' Joey asked eagerly.

'Come on, follow me,' and Freddie walked outside, the young men trailing after him. He walked about a hundred yards then stopped in front of another single lockup, heavily padlocked. Freddie dug into his overalls, produced a large bunch of keys and carefully opened the three locks. He went inside and a minute later an engine whined into life and Freddie slowly reversed into the sunshine then stopped.

'Bloody 'ell,' John Duncan said, a look of awe on his face.

'What do you think?' Freddie asked, grinning widely, as he opened the driver's door and jumped down.

The vehicle was another transit van but there any comparison to any other on the road ended. The shiny black body was covered in a mass of gold and white. A large golden halo painted on each side contained the words, *God Loves You*, also in metallic gold. Surrounding the halos were white painted clouds with golden cherubs floating amongst them, with more angels on the bonnet and side doors. Another two halos painted on the rear doors, like bull's-eyes, one saying, *Go To Heaven*, and the other, *Not To Hell*, were guaranteed to keep following motorists at a distance. And on top of the van were two large, horn shaped loudspeakers, gleaming golden in the sun.

'What the f...,' then Joey stopped himself swearing as though out of reverence, and finished in a croak, 'is it?'

'It's a *godvan*,' Freddie answered.'

'A *godvan*? What's that, and who does it belong to?'

Freddie explained the owner of the van was a religious nut who'd spent two years painting and doing up the van. His intention was to drive around and spread the good word, having got fed up with standing on street corners.

'Where is 'e now?' Joey asked.

'In the nick.'

'What for?'

'Fraud. He was done for running a bogus charity. He got weighed off last week...got eighteen months.'

'So 'ow come you've got the keys?'

'I'd done bits and pieces on the motor and he bunged me a few hundred to look after it for him. The garage rent's paid in advance for a year so it's no problem. And it's a good runner.

It'll get you where you want to go, but you'll need to put some more petrol in it.'

'What's with the speakers on top?'

'Get in.'

John sat in the driver's seat and Joey got in the other side. Freddie leaned inside, unhooked a hand microphone on a long lead from the dashboard, and gave it to Joey.

'Just click that knob on and speak. The other knob is the volume control.'

'Testing, testing,' Joey gave a start as his voice boomed out clearly in the still air. 'Blimey, that's great, I'll give a sermon as we go through town.'

'It's not taxed, Joey.'

'We'll take the tax disc off our van and stick it on this. And let's 'ope nobody looks too closely.'

'Don't worry about the insurance,' Freddie said, 'if there's any problem I can always get you a back dated cover note.'

Fifteen minutes later they arrived back at their broken down van and Frank and Omar fell about laughing when they saw their new transport. Joey gave a hurried explanation and the four of them quickly transferred their equipment before heading for north London where they stopped for petrol, then carried on to the motorway.

The van ran smoothly and they kept well within the speed limit but plenty of cars couldn't help slowing down out of curiosity as they passed the *godvan* before hooting their horns and speeding off.

Joey sat in the front passenger seat with a pious look on his face and his hands clasped in front of him as though in prayer. A white police patrol car drew up and the coppers gave the front occupants a funny stare but shot off as Joey raised one hand towards them and made the sign of the cross.

*

The birthday party was going great and Mike felt flattered by all the attention, but still couldn't get over what Mrs Ruebens had done for him. Nearly all of the workers from the building company, and a few of their wives and girlfriends, were there.

And he'd finally met Mrs Ruebens husband, Vic, a short stocky man with black curly hair ringing his nearly bald head. A dynamic man usually chomping on a cigar.

'My wife tells me that a friend of yours, and his band, are going to play here tonight,' Vic said.

'That's right,' Mike replied, and looked at his watch. It was eight thirty, and somehow didn't think it a good idea to give Joey a big build up, just in case he didn't show. 'They're a bit late but should be here very soon.' Mike drained the last of his pint of beer and put down the glass on a nearby table. 'I think I'll take a walk to the front gate and see what's happening.'

'Yes, this house isn't easy to find unless you've been here before,' Mrs Ruebens said, 'but I'm sure your friend will arrive soon.'

It was a wonderfully warm evening and the loud music coming from the open fronted marquee had a lot of the guests dancing. The DJ had good equipment with a wide enough choice of records to keep everyone happy. There was plenty of drink and Mrs Ruebens had even gone to the trouble of hiring outside caterers to supply the food, which was constantly being offered around by several waitresses holding silver trays, as well as a buffet table.

But where was Joey?

Mike walked from the back of the house to the front where half a dozen cars were parked, with another dozen at least stretching down the gravel driveway leading to the front gates. And because of the crowding it had been decided that latecomers would have to leave their vehicles on the grass verge outside on the road.

Normally there wasn't a guard on duty and anyone trying to gain entry to the grounds would be scrutinized by a security camera and the gates opened electronically from the house. But because of the number of people invited two uniformed guards had been hired for the evening to monitor the large black and gold wrought iron gates. It was an easy enough job and the men had decided to work an hour on, hour off system for as long as the party lasted.

After checking with the security guard on the gate that Joey's name was on the list of guests and would be let through as soon as he arrived, Mike walked back to the marquee, passing the other, older guard holding a plastic carrier bag, returning to relieve his partner.

Mr Ruebens had kindly told the security men that they too could help themselves to refreshments, for which she was gratefully thanked. The trouble was, the older one had helped himself a bit too much to the booze.

When the guards swapped over the older man moved a beige canvas chair from by the gate and placed it out of view under a large tree. Then he sat down, pulled a nearly full bottle of whisky from the carrier bag, and took a long swig. He settled back with a happy smile on his face, his pot belly straining at his shirt buttons.

The guard wished every job was as cushy as this.

*

They were making good time, but still running late. Joey looked at his watch. It was eight forty five already, and it wasn't as though they knew the area. He peered at the crumpled bit of paper with the address written on it. Mike said the private estate was between Stevenage and Baldock, not far from a place called Weston.

Fifteen minutes later they cut off the motorway onto a minor road, headed further into the countryside, and promptly got lost.

A further ten minutes and a small village came into view, then a few shops, and a pub. Joey breathed a sigh of relief and leapt from the van. He was told to head for the next village pub and ask directions from there, which he did, and finally they arrived at their destination.

Not that there were any streets, just large gates spaced about five hundred yards apart leading to private estates.

The *godvan* slowly eased forward to the set of double wrought iron gates with bright domed lights perched on top of concrete pillars. Gold initials, VR, stood out on the black gates. Vic Ruebens. They were at the right place.

There were cars parked outside on the grass verge and as Joey stuck his head out of the window he could hear music in the distance.

Joey got out of the vehicle, walked to the gates, and looked through the bars, but nobody was in sight.

'Anyone about?' he yelled several times. No reply and his view was obstructed so he couldn't see the drunken guard now passed out and snoring his head off.

As he looked around Joey saw a press button on a metal grill intercom, but after keeping his thumb pushed hard on it for over a minute, moved away.

The others joined him and Omar said, 'Are you sure they're expecting us?'

'Of course, but we're over a fuckin' hour late. Still, I would have thought there would be somebody on the front here,' Joey replied. 'We've got to get word to Mike.'

'Well, one of us could climb over,' Frank said, looking nervously at the eight foot high gates with spikes on the top.

'No, I've got a better idea,' Joey grinned, and went back to the *godvan*. A minute later his voice boomed out from the two large golden horn shaped speakers on top, 'Testing, testing, testing,' and Joey's voice got louder and louder as he turned the volume to full, making the others put their hands over their ears.

Then the cockney began to sing.

'*Amazing grace,*
How sweet the sound,
That saved a wretch like me,
I once was lost...'

The amplified words seemed to float up to the starlit heavens and swell the surrounding dark countryside with Joey's voice, and the others took their hands away and listened.

No doubt about it. Joey *was* someone special.

'*...but now am found,*
Was blind, but now I see...'

Mike was standing talking to Mr and Mrs Ruebens when he thought he heard something and moved his head as though trying to listen to another sound not coming from the marquee.

'Excuse me,' he said, and rushed towards the disc jockey. 'Stop the music,' he shouted, and drew his hand across his throat in a cutting motion as the guests looked at him in amazement. 'Cut it, cut it.' Which the DJ did and immediately a voice seemingly coming from nowhere was heard as clear as a bell in the sudden silent night air.

'*Through many dangers, toils and snares,*
I have already come,
'Tis grace hath brought me thus far,
And grace will lead me home...'

Mike grinned with genuine pleasure and smacked his right fist into his left hand. *Amazing Grace*, his favourite song, from when they were kids.

Joey had arrived.

TWENTY

'What a lovely story,' Dixie said. 'I don't think I've ever read that in the papers.'

'No, neither have I,' Linda agreed. 'From what I can remember the press said you used to sing in pubs and then your manager discovered you at a birthday party. Mind you, that's near enough right, but yours is a much more interesting version.'

'One question,' Uncle Robert said as he emptied the last drops of a bottle of champagne into his glass. 'Why Amazing Grace? It's not your type of song. You've never recorded it, have you?'

'No,' Joey replied, 'but both our Mums loved it. The song was popular the year Mike and I were born, and they were always singin' it. As a matter of fact, it was the first song I can ever remember learnin' all the words.'

'It will always remind us of our misspent youth,' Mike grinned, 'and it's still one of my favourite songs. I suppose it identifies me and Joey somehow.'

The pop star caught one of the waiters eye and ordered another three bottles of Krug. Then the second cabaret entertainment of the evening started and by the time that had finished and they'd all had several sessions on the small dance floor it was nearly midnight.

'I think it's about time we moved on,' Joey said, as he gave one of the waiters his American Express card, insisting on paying for the evening against protests from Dixie and Linda who said it was their idea in the first place. 'Us men can't have women payin',' the pop star grinned. 'Anyway, Wyatt, you're my accountant, get it off my income tax.'

The younger men and women decided to go to a night club but Robert and Wyatt opted to go home to their beds. It was a warm July night and the six stood outside the restaurant saying their goodbyes. There was no hurry, they were too relaxed after the good food and drink, and there were plenty of passing taxis due to the establishment's popularity.

They were so taken with each other's company they didn't notice the black Volkswagen parked on the other side of the road nearly opposite the restaurant's entrance. Nor did they spot the two men sitting in the front seats who were closely scrutinizing their every move. Every now and again a passing car's headlights highlighted the colour of the men's hair. One grey, the other red. The watchers continued to stare, burning the faces of the four young people into their minds.

*

When they'd had enough clubbing they decided to stay at Joey's mansion in Hampstead, and arrived at three am, where the pop star insisted they all have a nightcap before going to bed. The *one drink* turned into several and it was a good hour before they went upstairs to the bedrooms.

Mike and Dixie were up by ten o'clock and fifteen minutes later Linda joined them in the kitchen, having spent the night by herself in one of the guest rooms. Mike couldn't believe it. A woman as beautiful as Linda and Joey was behaving like a perfect gentleman. A miracle.

Mike was casually dressed in jeans and a short sleeved shirt. He'd stayed at Joey's so many times he always kept some spare clothes in the house. But Dixie and Linda were still in their long evening dresses from the previous night.

It was the first time Dixie had been to Joey's home and was impressed, but none of the rooms looked so grand that she felt unwelcome, in fact, the house oozed comfort with a happy lived in feeling. There was an elegant mix of Regency and Georgian furniture plus a smattering of Victoriana. Genuine antiques blended well with expensive reproductions, and oil paintings, good water colours and glass framed prints adorned the walls. Thick pile fitted and Chinese carpets gave a person the feeling of walking on air.

Mike had done a great job creating such a lovely home for his friend,

The kitchen was enormous and stocked with enough food to feed a small hotel and Marie, the housekeeper, quickly made a huge pot of coffee and was soon preparing a fry-up. As she cooked, Marie chattered on in her homely manner about the wonderful musical she and her husband, Stan, had seen the previous evening. Joey had managed somehow to get them a couple of theatre tickets for the show which everybody wanted to see.

Just as they started eating Joey walked into the kitchen looking bleary eyed.

'I shouldn't 'ave gone on to the brandy,' he groaned.

'Have some breakfast,' Mike said, 'help get rid of the hangover.'

Joey made a face as he looked at the fried sausages, eggs, mushrooms and tomatoes on his friend's plate, then went and poured himself a mug of coffee.

'Leave it out, I don't fancy food,' he said, taking a large gulp of the hot liquid he was holding.

The weather through the open kitchen windows was bright and sunny, a beautiful summer morning.

'What shall we do today?' Linda asked, her teeth flashing in a big smile.

"ow can you be so full of energy?'

'Because I wasn't such a pig with the booze last night,' Linda replied.

'Well, I'm goin' to take it easy today,' Joey said. 'I think I'll do some sunbathin' in the garden.'

'Actually, that's not a bad idea,' Dixie agreed, 'but I do feel a bit overdressed.'

'Yeah, you two are a bit tarted up for breakfast,' Joey grinned.

Linda clenched her fist and raised her middle finger towards the singer.

Joey stuck out his tongue in retaliation.

'But the clothes shouldn't be a problem,' he said. 'Marie,' and he looked at his housekeeper, 'take these two ladies up to my room. I've got plenty of jeans and shirts...or try on my swimmin' trunks, I'm not that big around the waist.'

Half an hour later the women were back in the kitchen both wearing elasticated bathing trunks and denim shirts tied at the waist.

'Certainly look better on you than me,' Joey grinned, his eyes drooling.

Ten minutes later the four of them were stretched out on sun beds on a marble stone raised terrace at the back of the house overlooking the landscaped garden, sipping cool drinks. Joey and Mike were on lager.

'You've not had anything to eat yet,' Linda said.

'Don't nag,' Joey groaned, 'I must 'ave somethin' to get me goin'. I'll 'ave somethin' to eat later.'

'I'm surprised you don't have a swimming pool, Joey.'

'No thanks, I'd probably drown myself,' he said, and stripped off his shirt before lying back again.

Mike also took off his shirt.

'Got any sun lotion, Joey?' Dixie asked. 'It's getting hot.'

'Go and find Marie,' he replied. 'She knows where everythin' is.'

'I'll come with you,' and Linda swung her legs off the sunbed as her friend stood. 'I fancy some ice cream.'

'There's plenty in the freezer,' Joey said.

'And bring a couple more lagers,' Mike called out, as the two women started to descend the green tiled steps, then turned to his friend. 'You've certainly changed since you met Linda.'

'Yeah? 'ow?'

'You hardly ever swear these days, Joey.'

'Well, Linda is the nicest bird I've ever met in my life. She's a real lady, not like some of those stupid young girls I've been screwin'. And we got on well.'

'How does she feel?'

'I'm not sure.'

'Are you in love with her?' Mike asked, a wide smile on his face.

Joey ignored the question, instead asking one of his own. His face serious.

'Do I sound rough when I speak?'

'What do you mean?'

'Well, *you* speak better than when we were kids. As a matter of fact, you've sounded different from when we left school, and I've been thinkin' maybe it was about time I did. So...,' and Joey's voice tailed off.

'So, what? Come on, what are you thinking?'

'Promise you won't laugh if I tell you.'

'Of course I won't, Joey...on my honour.'

'You sure?'

'Positive,' Mike replied with a straight face.

Joey looked hard at his friend as he hesitated, then blurted out, 'I'm thinkin' of takin' elocution lessons.'

Mike immediately burst out laughing and doubled over.

'You bastard, you said you wouldn't laugh.'

Mike could hardly speak he was laughing so much and pointed a finger at his friend before managing, 'Elocution lessons...*you*...,' and doubled up again.

'Oh piss off. See, you've started me swearin' again.'

Mike straightened and drained his can of lager.

'Joey, I'd say you were in love,' and he chuckled. 'I don't fuckin' believe it, my best mate's in love. Not thinkin' of gettin' married are you? Now, where have I heard that before?'

'Mike, you are definitely takin' the piss.'

'No I'm not,' his friend grinned, and then added, 'I can't believe it, my best mate's in love. It's fan-fuckin'-tastic.'

Mike was still laughing when the women returned.

'What's funny?' Dixie asked, as she handed him a can of lager.

'Oh, nothing,' Mike replied. 'A joke Joey just told me. Too dirty to repeat to you ladies.'

Mike noticed the look of relief on his friend's face and lay back, enjoying the warmth of the sun. And that's how the four of them spent the rest of the afternoon, relaxing and sunbathing. They were becoming very close to each other.

'What about a barbecue later?' Joey suddenly asked, now feeling much better after several cans of beer.

The rest of them agreed it was a good idea, but didn't move. They were too comfortable.

It was a tranquil, peaceful day. Almost like the lull before a violent storm.

TWENTY ONE

The elderly lady, her white hair drawn back in a bun, stirred as the ornate gilt clock on the stone mantelpiece chimed ten times. Lucy Fisher slowly opened her eyes and felt the welcome cool breeze from the open window on her face. She yawned and sat up in the comfortable gold brocade wing chair, the book in her lap slipping on to the carpet.

'Time for bed,' and she yawned again, stretching out her arms, trying to ease the ache in her shoulders.

'Shall I get you a drink?' her companion asked, blinking her eyes behind tortoise shell glasses and starting to rise from the large sofa. She too had dozed off. 'Something hot or cold?' she added, and picked up Lucy's book.

Mary Hayes was in her early fifties, about ten years younger than her employer. She was a widow and had worked for Miss Fisher for the last eight years. Her duties were housekeeper, nurse and cook, although Lucy kept reminding her that she thought of her more as a friend, and not an employee.

'I think a glass of orange juice would be rather nice,' Lucy replied, then put her weight on her carved walking stick before carefully making her way from the drawing room.

'As soon as I've locked up and checked everything I'll bring some to your room,' Mrs Hayes said, and crossed to where Lucy had been sitting and closed the leaded glass window.

Elm Hall was a country house, not far from Southwell in Nottinghamshire, and over two hundred years old. It was really much too large for just two women but Lucy wouldn't have dreamt of living anywhere else. When her fiancé had been tragically killed in the plane crash his parents had invited Lucy to live with them. Their son had been an only child and when they died left the house to Lucy, whom they'd grown to love as their own daughter, plus a fortune which would enable her to have a wealthy lifestyle for as long as she lived.

As well as Mrs Hayes working full-time there was also a permanent gardener and odd job man who lived in a village a couple of miles away. Plus, Mrs Barlow, another villager, or one of her daughters, came to the house three times a week and did all the cleaning and dusting.

Mrs Hayes went round the ground floor of the house checking the doors and windows then went into the kitchen, but before getting orange juice from the fridge, opened the back door and shouted into the darkness.

'Blackie, come on boy, Blackie...Blackie.'

By the time she'd poured the drink the aptly name black Labrador had padded slowly through the kitchen and into a small room where coats and Wellington boots were kept. The old dog, with failing eyesight, lay down on the blanket in his basket and in a matter of moments was fast asleep.

The housekeeper opened a cupboard and switched on the burglar alarm before leaving the kitchen and going upstairs.

*

The black VW drove slowly along the quiet country road, pulled up outside the open entrance to Elm Hall then reversed carefully about twenty yards on the loose gravel driveway, trying to make as little noise as possible. The car when it stopped was hidden by some conifer trees from the house which was another seventy five yards away.

Two men dressed in black, one carrying a small dark leather bag, got out and sprinted over the neatly trimmed lawns at the front, their shadows from the bright half moon trailing behind them. Then they silently made their way along a flagstone path at the side of the property until they reached a large wooden shed at the rear of the house. The man carrying the bag took out a small pair of bolt cutters and a few seconds later the heavy padlock was laying on the ground. Opening the door the men removed a long adjustable metal ladder, cautiously propped it up against the brickwork of the house and disabled the burglar alarm, which, by the age of it, might not have been that effective anyway. Next, the telephone wires were cut and the ladder returned to the shed.

Standing outside the double glass doors of the drawing room the men slipped black woollen masks over their heads and smoothed the tight plastic gloves they were wearing over their hands.

The doors were no problem and once inside the house the intruders switched on slimline torches and made straight for the small room off the kitchen. They had been supplied with a rough plan of the premises.

The Labrador stirred as they entered and the shorter of the men knelt down and gently stroked the dog. 'That's a good boy, Blackie. We're friends...you just go back to sleep.' The man reached into the bag and took out a handful of dog biscuits and put them by the large wicker basket. Then the men closed the door behind them, went into the wood panelled hall leading to the stairs, and began climbing silently on rubber soled shoes.

They went into the housekeeper's room first and the taller of the men shoved one hand over the sleeping woman's mouth and grabbed both her wrists with his other. Mrs Hayes suddenly came awake and her eyes opened wide then turned to fear as she saw the two masked men standing over her. She started to struggle and the man whispered in a hard tone. 'We're not going to harm you, understand? If I take my hand off your face, I don't want you to scream...you got that? You understand?'

The woman nodded her head which was pressed hard against the pillow and the gloved hand was slowly removed from her mouth. Mrs Hayes immediately gasped in lungfuls of air.

'We're going to tie you up but we've no intention of hurting you,' the man continued, 'that is, unless you play me up,' and his voice became threatening.

The woman nodded her head again.

'Okay,' she replied in a weak voice, 'okay, I promise I won't be any trouble, but please be careful with Miss Fisher, she's not a well woman.'

The men pulled back the bedcovers, revealing the housekeeper's paisley patterned pyjamas, then a ball of thin, strong cord was produced from the bag and in minutes Mrs Hayes was bound hand and foot. More cord was looped around her body and under and over the bed, securing her tightly.

A piece of surgical tape was clamped firmly over the housekeeper's mouth, then the two men left.

Lucy Fisher's bedroom was at the end of the corridor and she must have been a very light sleeper because as soon as the men entered the old lady spoke out in a loud voice.

'Who's that? Who's there?' she demanded.

The men quickly closed the gap and shone their torches on the figure propped up against a couple of large fluffy pillows.

'Don't worry, we're not going to harm you,' one of the men growled.

'Oh, I'm too old to worry,' Lucy said, giving a nervous laugh, 'but take those lights out of my eyes,' and she stretched out an arm and switched on a bedside lamp.

'Ah, burglars,' she said, when she saw the black clad masked men. 'How is Mrs Hayes? Is she all right?'

'Yes, she's fine...there's no need to worry about her. We've just tied her up, that's all. Which we're going to do to you. So move yourself and get up.'

The shorter of the men pulled a heavy chair with wooden arms closer to the bed.

'Sit in this,' he commanded.

Lucy slowly got out of bed and put on her pink dressing gown over her cotton nightie, her long white hair now released from its bun, straggling over her shoulders.

'Be quick,' the taller man hissed impatiently as the old lady lowered herself into the seat. The two men bound her tightly, then fastened her ankles to the carved wood chair legs, but when they'd finished didn't put tape over her mouth.

They were under strict instructions not to hurt Lucy Fisher in any way which annoyed the taller man.

'We're not going to gag you,' he said, 'unless you make any noise...which will upset me.' and he gripped Lucy's chin in his right hand forcing her head back. 'And I wouldn't like it if you upset me...nor would you.'

Lucy could see the glint of the man's eyes through the holes in his mask and knew he meant every word.

'I understand,' she said in a subdued voice, but stared defiantly at him, determined not to show her fear.

When the men left the room they went back downstairs, drew all the curtains on the ground floor, switched on the lights and began their search. They went through every room methodically, looking in every drawer, cupboard, behind pictures, under carpets and shoved their hands down the backs of all the upholstered furniture.

At one point they discovered a big old fashioned safe in the book lined study and the adrenalin pumped through them as they tried the handle on the front, only to find it wasn't locked. The door swung open easily - and it was empty.

Cursing, the men returned upstairs, but again, despite painstakingly going over all the bedrooms and two bathrooms, drew a blank. They found the stairs to the attic, but when they turned on the light and saw the area it covered, and the amount of accumulated old furniture and rubbish, knew a search would take more time than they had. Besides, what they were looking for was hardly likely to be in the attic.

'So what are we going to do?' the smaller man asked.

'There must be another safe in the house, the old lady's got some valuable jewellery, but we haven't come across it yet,' his companion replied.

'It must be in her bedroom, we haven't searched that.'

'So let's do it, and we'd better find what we're looking for...' The words trailed off almost as a snarl which bothered the smaller man because he knew how vicious his partner could be.

'Ah, the burglars return,' Lucy said with a brave smile when the masked men appeared and turned on the bedroom lights. 'Have you robbed me of all my treasure?'

'Shut it,' was the blunt reply she got as the men began their search.

'Here's some stuff,' one of them said, emptying the contents of a red leather jewellery box on to the dressing table. Rings, earrings and a pearl necklace glinted in the light.

'And this is where the rest of it will be,' the other said, excitement in his tone. 'At last,' and he swung back a large gilt framed picture on its hinges to reveal a wall safe. Modern with a combination lock.

The taller man stood in front of Lucy and, although she couldn't see his facial expression, sensed he was dangerous.

But Lucy was angry that her home had been invaded.

'What's the combination?' he said in a low, menacing voice.

'Aren't you a safecracker? Don't you use a stethoscope? That's what they do in the films,' the old woman replied with a show of bravado, and immediately regretted it.

The man's reaction was instant and the back of his hand caught Lucy's face with force, causing her to cry out as her head was whipped sideways.

'Don't,' and the other man grabbed his companion's wrist, 'you said you were told we mustn't hurt her.'

The bigger man shook himself free, pulled a flick knife from his tracksuit trousers, pressed a button and released the blade.

'That wasn't the fucking answer I wanted,' he said, and held the weapon in front of the old lady's eyes. A small trickle of blood seeped from one corner of her mouth.

'Don't,' the other man repeated, pleading in his voice, 'we're going to blow it if you cut her.'

The blade was slowly lowered and the man silently nodded his head.

'Yes, you're right...but that doesn't apply to the other woman,' he said, and started towards the open door. He stopped and turned, looking at the old lady tied to the chair. 'I'm sure you'll be able to hear the screams of your friend from here.'

'What do you mean?' Lucy asked in a croak, afraid of what the answer would be.

'If you won't talk then I'll make your friend tell me the combination.' He waved the shiny blade in front of him. 'Believe me, after I've cut off several of her fingers, she'll soon start talking.'

'But she doesn't know the combination.' There was panic in Lucy's voice.

'I'll believe that when I've finished with her. As a matter of fact, I think I might cut off her nipples first.'

His words seemed to hang in the silence of the room.

'All right,' the old woman said resignedly, 'I'll tell you what you want to know. That oil lamp over there...on that small table.'

The man followed her eyes, crossed the room and picked up the antique brass lamp.

'Yes?'

'The bottom unscrews.'

The man turned the lamp upside down, causing the glass top to fall off and smash on the floor as he turned the bottom anti-clockwise. A section smoothly unscrewed and in the base plate there was a neatly folded piece of white paper.

The man quickly went to the wall safe, began turning the small round knob, following the written numbers, and a minute later the door swung open. There was one metal shelf dividing the safe and eagerly the man inserted a hand pulling out two slim grey velvet boxes. He lifted the lids and silently whistled as he saw the diamond necklace, rings and bracelet.

'Here, catch,' he said, tossing the boxes to his partner, who shoved them into their small leather bag, and then did the same with the jewellery on the dressing table. There was also a small pile of silver downstairs they'd take with them when they left. The burglary had to look as though they were after valuables.

'What's this then?' the man by the safe said, and began shuffling through the papers he'd retrieved from the safe. Stocks, shares, bank statements, a copy of a will, all of which he dropped to the floor. He pulled out a bundle of letters held together by a large elastic band, the envelopes yellowing with age, but it still wasn't what he was looking for.

'Be careful with those,' Lucy said, which made the man look up, then peer closer at the letters.

'Why's that?' and he moved nearer to the old lady.

She didn't reply but looked anxious as the man slipped off the elastic band, opened one of the letters and began reading.

'A love letter...from someone special, eh?'

Suddenly the man stopped reading and sat on the edge of the double bed, one gloved hand tapping his knee as though trying to make up his mind about something. He stayed where he was for a full minute before raising himself to stand menacingly in front of Lucy.

'I want some information from you,' he said, slowly tearing the pages in half.

'No, no, please don't do that,' Lucy pleaded, struggling to free herself, then stared aghast as she saw the pages torn again. The letters were from her fiancé before he was killed. She valued them more than anything else in the world. 'Please, please stop, what is it you want?'

'You have some papers, some papers that were left with you to look after.'

'What are you saying?' the other man shouted. 'Do you know what you're doing?'

But his outburst was ignored.

'You were left some papers to look after by a woman, and I want to know where they are.' The man crumpled the ripped pages in his hand, threw them away and stooped down to pick up another love letter. He slowly extracted another two pages from the envelope and stood looking down at Lucy.

'No, please, no more,' her words sounded desperate, and her brain was spinning. So that is what this is all about. 'I presume you're talking about Kate Smith, aren't you?'

'Could be.'

'Yes, she did give me something to look after...a big brown envelope...foolscap size.'

'Where is it?'

'It's not here anymore,' and Lucy paused anxiously as she saw his fingers tighten on the pages, then hurriedly raised her voice. 'She took the envelope back.'

'She took it back?' the man said incredulously. 'When?'

'About a month ago. She came for lunch, told me she'd taken the day off work, and said there was no need for me to look after the envelope anymore.'

'Do you know what was in it?'

'No...just felt like papers...that's all.'

'Was there any writing on the envelope?'

'No.'

'Did Miss Smith give you any instructions? Suppose she didn't come back...suppose something happened to her...did she tell you what to do with the envelope?'

'No, she never said anything like that.'

'Fuck,' the man swore out loud. It was now five weeks since Kate had told him where the papers were and was surprised his employer hadn't told him to try and find the documents sooner.

But his instructions had been explicit. He was told to plan carefully and take his time. Reconnoiter the country house to make sure he wasn't caught. His boss had said as long as Kate got her monthly money there wasn't any hurry. A few more weeks, or a month weren't going to make much difference. So he did exactly as he was told.

But that had suddenly changed three days ago when he'd been told to get inside Elm Hall before the coming weekend and make sure he found the blackmail papers.

However, that hadn't happened and the man he took his orders from wasn't going to be very pleased.

'Come on, let's get out of here,' he barked at his partner and walked towards the door, yanking the woollen covering off his head.

His grey curly hair glinted in the light as he left the room, slapping the black mask against his leg.

TWENTY TWO

As soon as the two men reached the VW they changed the tops of their all black outfits into something more colourful then started on their return journey to London. They drove well within the speed limit and after an hour stopped at a telephone box. Holding a handkerchief over the mouthpiece one of them called 999 and informed the police that two old ladies needed help and gave the address of Elm Hall.

Dawn had broken by the time they reached the outskirts of the capital and stopped at a service station for petrol and an early breakfast. It was already warm and the forecast on the car radio had said it was going to be another bright sunny day. Which was the exact opposite to the gloomy expressions on the men's faces as they slowly ate their meal.

'I don't think our news is going to go down too well,' the smaller man, nicknamed Red because of his close cropped hair of that colour, mumbled.

'Personally, I think we left it too late,' the other man said. 'We should have tried weeks ago...it's not our fault.'

'What we going to do with the jewellery? After you asked about the papers I thought you might leave it behind.'

'Sell it. You've got better contacts in that line so I'll leave it to you,' and the grey haired man took a sip of his hot coffee. 'That way the whole thing won't be a complete disaster. Not for us, anyway.'

Red nodded his head. He'd been the other person who'd broken into Kate Smith's mother's house before last

Christmas. Burglary was his trade and disposing of stolen goods, especially jewellery of this high quality, presented no problem.

'Why'd you do it?' he asked. 'Why'd you ask the old lady about the papers? I thought we were supposed to make it look like a straightforward burglary and taking the papers, if we found them, wouldn't have been much of an issue. After all, they didn't belong to Lucy Fisher. But now she'll tell the police what we were really after, and they will most likely go and see Kate Smith.'

The bigger man took another drink of coffee, nearly draining the cup.

'I'm not so sure the old lady will talk about that envelope she was looking after. I've got a feeling she might let the police think that it was just an ordinary burglary.'

'Why's that?'

'Because Kate Smith worked for her brother before he died, and still works for the company. Her other brother's still there and I'm sure she won't want the name of the family business involved with the police. No doubt she'll contact Kate and tell her what happened...but I think that'll be it. I don't think she'll take it any further.'

'Suppose you're wrong.'

'Well, suppose I am, what's Kate going to say? *I'm a blackmailer*. Hardly. She'll think of something. She's not going to want her money to stop, so she definitely won't tell the cops the truth. She's not stupid.'

'But what will the Smith woman do now? You've got pretty friendly with her but won't she figure it was you? I mean, she did tell you where she'd hidden the documents.'

'Yeah, that might be a problem,' and the grey haired man shrugged his shoulders. 'But I'm going to tell her I didn't have anything to do with the break-in. She hasn't got a clue that I know the man she's blackmailing. She thinks the money is sent to me through the post and I pass it on to her. I just hope

I can persuade her I'm telling the truth...that it's all some strange coincidence.'

'Do you think she'll buy that?'

'I hope so, and she has trusted me so far.'

'Umm, maybe you're right,' Red said. 'You're screwing her, and from what you've told me, she's in love with your cock. So maybe she will believe you.'

'Even so, that still doesn't help us find out where she's now hidden that fucking envelope. I think my first idea was the best.'

'What was that?'

'Get her to talk...*my way*. Then get rid of her.'

The taller man pushed his empty cup and saucer across the shiny Formica table top and stood.

'Get some more coffee in, I'm going to make a phone call ...and pass on the bad news.'

Red didn't know the identity of the man who was employing him for the job. He just followed instructions. The money was good and that's all he was interested in.

Eddie was in charge - let him have the worry.

The curly haired man walked through the restaurant, which was now starting to get busy, and into a corridor leading to a bank of phones. He picked the end one, near a wall, slipped some coins in the metal box and his fingers hit the buttons. He thought it safer to use a landline rather than his mobile.

The voice that answered was sleepy but immediately came wide awake when he realized who the caller was. His first question was to ask if the papers had been found.

'Unfortunately, no,' and the man who'd broken into the country house quickly explained the events of the night. Surprisingly, the person on the other end of the phone didn't lose his temper as had been expected and listened carefully to every word. He understood the situation was serious but kept his voice calm, knowing that ranting and raving wouldn't serve any purpose. It was time to use his brain, not his mouth, and wondered what had made Kate Smith take back her envelope a month ago?

After all this time, why now?

'I've got no idea at all. She didn't say anything to me. It was a complete surprise,' Eddie replied, then paused before continuing, 'did I do the right thing by asking the old lady about the envelope? I couldn't think of any other alternative.'

The employer assured Eddie he had been correct otherwise they wouldn't have been any further ahead. It *was* a chance - but one that had to be taken.

However, the employer knew that if the Smith woman did go to the police he would be in grave trouble. But the chances were she wouldn't because she had a lot to lose as well. She'd have to admit she'd been blackmailing him all these months. And he thought her main motive for keeping quiet would be the cash. Plain old fashioned greed.

But he did think she'd have something up her sleeve... probably want more money.

As soon as she found out what had happened she'd be straight on to him. Even if Lucy Fisher didn't call her the burglary would probably be reported in the newspapers, maybe on television. Two old ladies tied up and robbed in a secluded house...bound to get some coverage. But maybe there was something that could be done.

'I have made arrangements to see her this Saturday,' Eddie replied in answer to the question. 'I was going to stay the weekend.' Then he listened carefully to his new instructions.

He was to phone Kate Smith early this evening. She'd been off work this week, with some stomach bug, or something like that, but not to call during the day because he wasn't supposed to know she was ill, and that might look suspicious.

'I'm a bit worried about what her reaction will be.'

His employer told him to charm her...convince her he had nothing to do with Lucy Fisher's burglary, that's if she knew about it by then.

He was assured he wasn't to blame for what happened - and he'd still get his bonus.

'Thanks,' the man talking into the pay phone said and smiled to himself, 'I'll let you know later this evening what the score is. Don't worry, I won't let you down, but I'm not sure whether she'll believe me.'

Eddie hung up the receiver and walked back to the restaurant, the smile still on his face.

His plan seemed to be working. He was a good actor.

*

Dixie was sitting at the kitchen table drinking coffee and wondering what to make for lunch when a ringing sound interrupted her thoughts.

'Hello,' she answered, picking up the white cordless phone.

'Dixie, this is Robert.'

'Hello, Uncle, what can I do for you?'

There was a pause.

'It's Lucy, there's been a burglary at her house.'

'She's not been hurt, has she?' concern in Dixie's voice.

'No, not too badly. Shook up more than anything else.'

'What happened?'

'Two masked men broke in sometime after midnight, tied up Lucy and her housekeeper, and ransacked the place. I would have known earlier but the telephone wires had been cut and the engineers had to fix them.'

'How dreadful...are you sure she's all right?'

'Yes, positive, and she said I wasn't to worry. Lucy asked me to call you and wants you to phone her.'

'I was going to go and see her this weekend, remember I told you the other evening. I was going to take Mike with me.'

'Well, I'm sure Lucy will still want you to visit her.'

'Okay Uncle, thanks for letting me know, and I'll call her straight away.'

Dixie clicked the off switch and went into the lounge to find her handbag. Fishing in it she pulled out her small black address book, found her aunt's number, and pressed the numbered buttons on the phone. She should put it on memory.

'Hello, this is Elm Hall.' The voice was hesitant and sounded young.

'This is Dixie Fisher, is my Aunt Lucy there, please?'

'She's in bed, but she is expecting your call. I'll go upstairs and tell her you're on the phone. Please hang on for a minute, if you don't mind.'

Silence, then the sound of an extension being picked up.

'Dixie, I'm glad you rang.'

'Aunt Lucy, are you okay? Uncle Robert phoned me and told me what happened. It sounds dreadful.'

The older woman gave a small chuckle.

'They didn't really hurt me, scared me a bit...but it was all right in the end.'

'And how's your housekeeper?'

'She's okay too, but the doctor said we've both to stay in bed for at least today, to get over the shock.'

'Who answered the phone?'

'Oh, that was Julia, one of Mrs Barlow's daughters. Mrs Barlow does all the cleaning and her daughter is staying here for a few days to help out.'

'Aunt Lucy, I was going to visit you tomorrow, stay for the weekend, remember? I wanted you to meet Mike, but...' Dixie's voice tailed off.

'I still want you to come. That's why I wanted you to phone me, to make sure you *were* still coming.'

'Will that be okay? Don't you need more rest...peace and quiet?'

'No, Dixie, I assure you I feel much better. You know I suffer from osteoporosis, and my bones are very brittle, but fortunately nothing got broken. And I do so much want to meet your young man.'

'Well, we'd love to come. Will lunch-time be all right with you?'

'That will be fine. Oh, and one other thing, before you go. How well do you know Kate Smith?'

'Kate Smith?' Dixie's voice sounded puzzled. 'Who's she? The name sounds familiar but I can't quite...'

'She was your father's personal assistant,' her aunt interrupted.

'Oh, yes, of course. How stupid of me to forget...but why do you ask?'

'I just wondered if you'd seen her lately. I know Tom thought a lot of her.'

'No, Aunt Lucy, I haven't seen her since the day of the funeral. Is there something I should know?'

'No, no...I'll see you tomorrow. Until then, goodbye.'

After her aunt broke the connection Dixie sat staring at the silent phone in her hand, a mystified expression on her face. What was that about?

*

At seven o'clock Eddie tried phoning for the first time and kept repeating the process for the next hour, but there was no answer. Then he went outside to where his black car was parked and a few minutes later was driving in the direction of Kate's address. The traffic wasn't too bad and it only took just over half an hour.

He'd had a bath a couple of hours ago and felt fresh and relaxed as he got out the car, the evening sun still bright in the sky. Eddie walked up the path of Kate's house and stood with his finger on the doorbell for a good thirty seconds, then banged hard on the chrome knocker. He looked through the letter box and the windows of the front room but couldn't see very much. Kate was one of those women who hung net curtains everywhere.

But he had a spare set of keys Kate had cut for him and unlocked the front door. Swiftly he went through the rooms and found the house empty. He went back to the ground floor, once again looking in the rooms, but this time taking it slowly. And then he saw a piece of white paper on the kitchen table. Picking it up he read the words printed in large capitals.

EDDIE YOU'RE A BASTARD

He folded the paper, put it in the top pocket of his khaki sports shirt, and made his way back upstairs to Kate's bedroom. He opened the fluted doors to Kate's fitted wardrobe and saw large gaps on the hanging rails. He searched the drawers where Kate kept her sexy lingerie and found them nearly empty. Then he looked where she kept her sexual aids and collection of porn videos. But everything was gone.

Eddie left the house, double locked the front door as he'd found it, then went next door and rang the doorbell. Mrs Powis was Kate's neighbour and they'd spoken several times over the last couple of months. He'd made sure of that.

Mrs Powis was in her eighties and had lived with her husband in the house for over fifty years. She answered the door because Mr Powis was a bit weak on his legs and spent most of his time in a wheelchair.

'Sorry to bother you, but have you seen Kate?'

The old woman peered closer at the man on her doorstep. She'd left her glasses in the lounge and her eyes weren't what they'd used to be. Then she smiled, crows feet appearing on either side of her watery eyes, and parted lips revealing shiny white dentures which moved as she spoke.

'Oh yes, I recognize you. You're Miss Smith's friend. Yes, yes, I did see her. She's gone away...on holiday, I think she said. Yes, she asked me to keep an eye on the place.'

'Do you know when she went.'

'Today, before lunch, because I was going to cook some haddock. My Ron loves his fish.'

'Did she say when she'd be coming back?'

'Oh no, she didn't say...or did she? I can't remember,' and the old woman ran a bony hand through her wispy white hair. 'No, it's gone...silly me,' she smiled again.

'Not to worry,' the man said, 'no doubt she'll send me a postcard and I'll see her when she gets back. Thank you, anyway.' Then he turned and walked back to his car.'

Twenty minutes later Eddie stopped by a public telephone box.

'She's not at home,' he informed his employer. 'Gone away, according to a neighbour, maybe on holiday. I had a look around her house and she's taken a lot of clothes. Her car's gone too.'

Once again it was unexpected news but the man on the other end of the line kept his composure. What was Kate Smith up to?

'She has my home number,' Eddie said. 'I live by myself so I didn't think there was any harm in giving it to her. But somehow I don't think I'll be hearing from her,' and he explained about the note he'd found on the kitchen table. 'I took it, and I'll show it to you the next time we meet.' He paused. 'She left today, at lunch-time, so she must have heard about the burglary and put two and two together.'

The news wasn't getting any better and it didn't seem there was much either of them could do for the moment. The trouble was, which the employer was only too aware of, the ball wasn't in his court anymore.

TWENTY THREE

Mike had been in Yorkshire most of the week and arrived back in London early Friday evening. He'd finally been told that his building project had got the go-ahead and immediately finalized the purchase of the land, ten acres which lay between Wakefield and Hemsworth in West Yorkshire.

Dixie had phoned him earlier in the day and told him about the burglary, but said her aunt was insistent they still stay the weekend with her.

Mike stopped at Dixie's apartment first to pick her up, impatient to see her again, then carried on to his place.

'Four days without you,' he said.

'Did you miss me?' Dixie pouted.

'Only your body,' and he winked.

'That's good...but I do have a brain as well, in case you've forgotten.'

'I know, but that's not in the right place for what I have in mind for you later.'

'You sound like a dirty young man,' and Dixie snuggled against him.

'And I hope I grow into a dirty old man,' Mike said, as he nuzzled his mouth against her head. 'What about going to bed with a takeaway pizza and a couple of bottles of wine?'

'And what's for dessert?'

'You.'

'I'm glad you said that. Do you like seconds?'

'Of course,' Mike chuckled, 'I'm greedy.'

*

Just before noon the next day Mike's Range Rover turned into the entrance of Elm Hall and crunched up the gravel driveway. It was hot, the sun a yellow ball in the blue sky, and the young couple were dressed in lightweight clothes.

'This is a lovely old house, got a lot of character,' Mike observed, as he carried their two overnight bags to the front door. They walked up several concrete steps and Dixie rang the brass bell on the brickwork next to the large white painted panelled door.

Moments later they were warmly greeted by Mrs Hayes as the door swung open on well oiled hinges.

'Hello, Dixie,' the housekeeper smiled. They were on first name terms from the young woman's previous visits with her parents when they were alive.

Mike was introduced and then the three of them walked through the downstairs rooms out on to a large stone terrace at the rear of the kitchen cluttered with comfortable garden furniture. Well cut lawns, beds of flowers and shrubs running down to a line of conifer trees gave a beautiful scenic backdrop.

Aunt Lucy was lying on a padded sun lounger dressed in a short sleeved floral dress, a newspaper resting on her lap, and an old black Labrador stretched out nearby. A large green and white striped umbrella shaded them both. She smiled as she saw her guests.

'Hello, Dixie.'

Her niece went and kissed Lucy gently on her forehead.

'Hello, Auntie,' Dixie said, returning the smile, 'and this is Mike.'

The elderly lady offered her right hand which Mike gently shook.

'Pleased to meet you at last, young man. I've been asking my niece to bring you to my home for ages,' she said.

'I'm glad to meet you too, Miss Fisher. And you have a lovely home. The house is magnificent.'

Thank you,' and Dixie's aunt paused. 'One thing though, if we're going to get along. Not Miss Fisher, if you please. Reminds me too much that I'm an old spinster, so call me Lucy. Understand?'

'All right then...Lucy,' Mike smiled, and knew he was going to enjoy the weekend.

*

The three had lunch on the terrace, served by Mrs Hayes and the young Julia.

After they'd finished eating cold meats and salad, washed down with wine and beer, the conversation turned to the break-in the night before last.

'That's a nasty bruise on your cheek,' Dixie said, and her aunt's hand instinctively went to the side of her face.

'Yes, I'm afraid one of the burglars lost his temper with me because I wouldn't give him the combination of my safe to begin with.'

Then Lucy spent the next ten minutes telling her two young companions as much as she knew about the robbery.

'Do the police have any idea who it could be?' Mike asked.

'Professional criminals, is what they said. Probably had my house under observation for some time.' Lucy shrugged her shoulders. 'Two elderly women living alone...they most likely thought it would be easy.' She laughed. 'And it was.'

'Did you see their faces?' Dixie asked.

'No, they wore masks, those balaclava things with eyeholes. But right at the end, the taller man, took his off as he left my bedroom and I saw the back of his head. He had grey curly hair, so he couldn't have been a youngster.'

'But they did speak to you?'

'Yes and both of them had southern accents, from London I'd say, especially the bigger one. His voice was hard, and there was something about his eyes, something that gave me the impression he was a nasty piece of work.' Lucy gave an involuntary shudder. 'But let's forget about it now. I'm insured, so there's no real harm done. Let's talk about something else.'

'Well, I'd like to have a wander around your house, and also take at look at your gardens,' Mike said, rising from his chair. I've got a camera in my car...do you mind if I take some photographs?'

'No, of course not,' Lucy replied.

'This is how I get ideas for my projects,' and Mike went back into the house.

'You've got yourself a very nice young man there,' Lucy said, and took a sip of her wine.

'I know,' Dixie said.

'Is it serious?'

'Yes.'

'Good. So I can expect an invite to your wedding.'

'Aunt Lucy, it won't be for some time yet, Mike's got a company to run,' and Dixie explained about his new building scheme in Yorkshire. 'But I reckon you can count on about next Easter at the latest.'

'Ah, you're plotting already. Poor man doesn't stand a chance.'

Dixie gave an impish smile.

'Of course...so don't worry, he won't get away.'

Mrs Hayes and Julia appeared and started to clear the plates and empty bottles from the garden table. They had each brought a large tray and the procedure took only minutes, but Lucy waited until they'd finished before talking to Dixie about what had been on her mind since the burglary.

'Do you remember when we spoke on the phone yesterday I mentioned Kate Smith?'

'Yes, of course I do.'

'Well, there was something I didn't tell you. Something I thought best to talk to you about in person.'

Dixie gave her aunt a puzzled look.

'Sounds mysterious,' she said.

'The burglars weren't here to rob me of my jewels and silver...I think they just took them as something extra.'

'Then what were they after?' and Dixie's voice sounded more puzzled.

'An envelope Kate Smith left with me to look after. A large brown envelope with papers inside.' Lucy quickly explained what had happened after the burglars had opened the safe. 'And they weren't too happy when I told them that Miss Smith had been here about a month ago and taken the envelope back,' she continued.

'And *did* she come a month ago and take it back?' Dixie asked.

'Yes, yes she did...but I didn't tell those men about the conversation Miss Smith and I had before she left. You see, it was about you.'

'*Me*?' and Dixie couldn't keep the surprise from her voice.

'I'd better go back to the beginning,' the old lady said. 'About a month after your parents funeral Kate Smith phoned and said she'd like to come and see me. Of course, I said yes. I'd met her before and she'd been here several times with your father. And he had always spoken very highly of her in the past. Anyway, she arrived and after we had some lunch she produced this envelope and asked me if I could look after it for her. She wouldn't tell me what was in it but stressed I should keep it safe and give it to no-one...unless something happened to her. And then the only person I should give it to, *was you*.'

'I don't understand,' Dixie said.

'Nor do I,' Lucy continued, 'because when Miss Smith came back for the envelope I asked if the contents were important. She said they weren't and so I reminded her, if that was the case, why had she said the envelope had to be given to my niece, Dixie, if something had happened to her...and by that I suppose she meant an accident, or maybe even her death.'

'And what did she say?'

'Said I'd got the wrong end of the stick and she hadn't said anything like that at all. She admitted she had mentioned your name when she'd visited last year because it wasn't that long after Tom's death and she felt sorry for what had happened. But the papers in the envelope were nothing to do with you, in fact, they were personal papers to do with her and her mother and I must have been mistaken.'

'And were you?'

'No, she was lying, but I didn't want to embarrass her, so I let it pass. At the time I didn't think it was important because it wasn't really any of my business. But I was wrong. That burglary made it my business.'

'Have you told Uncle Robert?'

'No, and for the same reason I didn't tell the police. I thought I'd better speak to you first, and let you decide what you wanted to do.'

'Thanks,' and Dixie frowned in thought. 'No, I can't say I'd like to talk to the police myself. I don't know anything about that envelope, so I don't think I'd be of any help anyway. However, it might not be a bad idea if I went and saw Kate Smith.'

'Yes, but be careful,' Lucy said. 'If she's mixed up with the likes of those men who were here the other night then it could be a bit risky.'

Dixie looked at her aunt seriously and nodded her head slowly.

'I'll have a word with Mike and see what he says.'

'There is one more thing,' and the old lady paused. 'When one of the men hit me, the other one got very agitated and said they were told, *they mustn't hurt me*.'

'Whatever did that mean?' Dixie asked in a perplexed voice.

'I've got no idea,' her aunt replied. 'But somehow I got the feeling that they'd been sent by someone...someone who knew me.'

'That sounds ridiculous.'

'I know.'

'But if it is true,' Dixie said softly, 'then who is this someone?'

*

The rest of the day was as enjoyable for Mike and Dixie as from when they'd first arrived.

Mrs Hayes was an excellent cook and the dinner of poached fresh salmon, followed by home made apple pie went down a treat.

At nine thirty Lucy said she was going to retire to her room and left her niece and Mike on the terrace, where they'd moved to from the dining room to drink their coffee. It was a lovely warm summer evening and the fresh country air had made them sleepy too.

'I don't think it will be long before I hit the sack as well,' Mike said, giving a slight yawn.

'I feel the same,' Dixie said, also yawning. 'Must be catching,' she laughed. 'But there is something I want to tell you before we go to bed,' and Dixie related her conversation she'd had with her aunt earlier in the day about Kate Smith. 'Don't you think that's strange?'

Mike had listened intently to everything Dixie said and when she'd finished shook his head in bewilderment. 'I agree with you, it does seem strange. And you've no idea what could be in that envelope?'

'None whatsoever,' Dixie replied.

'So what do you intend doing about it?'

'Well, I'm definitely not going to the police, I can't see any point in it. I'd only get snowed under with officialdom, and I couldn't stand that.'

'Then that only leaves Miss Smith.'

'I know,' Dixie said. 'So I guess the thing to do is go and see her.'

'And you'd like me to come with you?'

'Yes, please, darling.'

'I wouldn't have let it be any other way,' Mike said, and reached over the garden table to hold Dixie's hand. 'When are you thinking of visiting this mysterious Miss Smith?'

'Monday evening, I thought, but I'll have to get her address first. She still works at my Father's company and I'll get it from someone there. Is that okay with you?'

'That's fine,' Mike replied. 'I won't be going back to Yorkshire until the week after next.'

TWENTY FOUR

Monday morning Dixie tried to get her uncle on the phone but was told he was in a business meeting and wouldn't be free for at least another two hours. So Dixie asked if she could be put through to Wyatt Peterson. He was available and Dixie told him what she wanted but stressed she didn't want Kate Smith to know about her request.

'Sounds a bit secretive,' Wyatt said, clearly puzzled. 'Is there something wrong?'

'There's no mystery,' Dixie assured him, 'it's just that I want to go and see her this evening and I want it to be a surprise. I've got a present for her.'

'Ah, I see,' Wyatt chuckled. 'You women are all the same. Okay, I'll call you back shortly.'

And ten minutes later he phoned with the address and phone number, plus some extra information.

'Miss Smith was off work all last week, apparently she's not been very well. So you'll be able to visit her earlier than this evening if you wish.'

'Thanks Wyatt...maybe I'll do that.'

Dixie clicked off her phone and wondered what could be the matter with Kate Smith, then called Mike.

'But I can't go any earlier,' he said, 'I've got too much on today.'

'That's all right, lover, I didn't expect you to. I just wanted to hear your voice...I wonder what illness Miss Smith has got?'

'That's what you really phoned up for,' Mike laughed. 'You're intrigued about what's going on and want someone to gossip to. Well, you'll have to wait until this evening to find out. You know your trouble Dixie, you're bored. You should get yourself a job. I'm going to have to spend a lot of time in Yorkshire in the near future. Why don't you be my secretary?'

'But that means sleeping with the boss.'

'That's right.'

'In that case I'll work for nothing.'

'Wow! Where can I get more staff like you?'

'Seriously, Mike, that's not a bad idea of yours. Going back to work might be just what I need.'

'We'll talk about it tonight.'

'Okay, see you later.'

*

They drew up outside Kate Smith's terrace house just after eight pm and Dixie had to persuade Mike to stay in the Range Rover.

'It might put her off if she spots the two of us. I know her and I think she'll feel more at ease if I'm by myself. She'll probably talk more freely.'

'Okay, my love, but if you're not out within half an hour I'll be banging on the door.'

Dixie gave him a peck on the cheek, got out the car and walked to Kate Smith's front door. She rang the bell and waited. No reply, so she rang again, this time longer. Still no reply, so she banged hard on the door knocker. Dixie stood patiently there but after a minute it became obvious no-one was going to answer.

Mike got out of the car as Dixie approached.

'Doesn't look as though there's anyone in,' she said, shaking her head.

'Let's take a look down here,' Mike said, and indicated towards an alleyway that ran by the side of the end terrace house.

They walked down the paved alley and Mike lifted Dixie high enough for her to look over the wood fence, but the small back garden was empty.

They retraced their steps and Dixie suggested they try the house next door.

A minute later an old woman with thinning white hair stood on her doorstep peering at the young couple. She had a pair of glasses in her hand which she slowly put on, enabling her watery eyes to focus properly.

'That's better, she said, and smiled. 'Can I help you?'

'I'm a friend of Kate Smith's,' Dixie replied. 'She doesn't appear to be in, which seems a bit strange because I thought she wasn't well. She hasn't been to work for a week and I thought I'd visit her, to see how she is.'

'Oh no, dear, you've got it wrong. She's gone on holiday.'

'On holiday? Are you sure?'

'Yes, dear. Quite sure. She asked me to keep an eye on her place while she's away.'

'When did she go?'

'Last week sometime,' the old woman said, her false teeth clicking as she spoke. 'I'm sorry, but I forget the exact day.'

'Did she say when she's coming back?'

'No.' and the old woman shook her head. 'No, she didn't say.'

Dixie opened her handbag, found a pen and tore off a blank page from her small address book. She quickly wrote down her name and telephone number and handed the piece of paper to Kate Smith's neighbour.

'Could you please call me on this number when Miss Smith returns,' Dixie said. 'It is important, and I would appreciate it...Mrs...I'm sorry, but I don't know your name.'

'Powis, Mrs Powis.'

'Okay, Mrs Powis, thank you for your help.'

The old lady peered closely at the piece of paper she'd been handed.

'And you're Dixie Fisher,' she said slowly. 'Nice name, Dixie.'

'Do you know if Miss Smith went on holiday with anyone?' Dixie added, as she started to turn away.

'I don't think so because her boyfriend knocked on my door asking if I knew where she'd gone.'

'Her boyfriend? Do you know his name or where he lives? It is important.'

'No, I'm sorry, I don't.' Mrs Powis replied.

'Okay, not to worry,' Dixie smiled. 'You've been a big help.'

'What does the boyfriend look like?' Mike asked, speaking for the first time.

'He's a nice man, with grey curly hair.'

'Thanks.' Mike also gave the old lady a big smile then turned and walked with Dixie back to the Range Rover. 'You look thoughtful,' he added, stroking the back of her long black hair.

'It's nothing,' Dixie said. But there *was* something. Mrs Powis's answer reminded her of something Aunt Lucy had said.

And a niggling suspicion was beginning to form in the back of her mind.

*

Kate Smith held the receiver to her ear and waited. She wasn't nervous because she knew she was in the driving seat. Besides, she'd rehearsed what she was going to say in her mind enough times during the day. The phone was ringing at the other end and Kate looked at her wristwatch. It was nine pm and the person should be at home. She was about to hang up when the line came alive and she heard a male voice say hello.

'This is Kate Smith,' she said.

There was a pause then the man apologized for not answering sooner, he'd been having a shower before going out. But he had been expecting her to call.

'I bet you have. And I bet you won't be surprised by what I have to say, either.'

There was silence in response to that statement and the woman continued.

'It looks as though I retrieved my envelope just in time. You were foolish to have sent those men because now I know I can't trust you. Which is a pity...not for me...but for you,' and Kate's voice took on a hard tone.

The man quickly agreed it was a mistake and was sorry.

'You will be...and I think you'll find it the most expensive mistake you've ever made.'

The man didn't speak, but Kate caught the sound of a deep sigh, and smiled.

'I have now made a copy of the documents,' she said. 'This set is lodged with a solicitor and the arrangement is that I phone him once a week, give him a code name so he knows it's me and not someone impersonating me, but if I don't contact him then he will follow my instructions.' Kate paused. 'If I don't contact him,' she repeated, 'he will deliver the envelope to the police in person. And, if you're wondering, the originals are also somewhere safe. So you'd better make sure nothing happens to me. And that also applies to my Mother. If you try to get to me by harming her then you'll have the police on your back straight away.'

The man congratulated her for being so well organized.

'Careful is more like it...and now we come to the money. I want two hundred thousand pounds in cash.'

There was a sharp intake of breath and then silence as the man digested her words. He was stunned by the amount and had to fight hard to keep his anger in check as he explained he didn't have that sort of money lying around.

'I'm sure you don't,' Kate said, 'but don't worry...we can come to an agreement. Fifty thousand pounds in two weeks ...another fifty thousand in the middle of October...and the final payment of one hundred thousand pounds a week before

Christmas. That gives you plenty of time. In fact, I think I'm being very reasonable.'

But the man didn't. Her demand was impossible, he said, in a raised voice, finally losing his calm.

'No it's not,' Kate said, 'you're a millionaire. You have plenty of money.'

But he was only a millionaire on paper, he tried to explain.

'Then de-paperise some of it, otherwise the police will get those papers sent anonymously to them in two weeks time.'

Then he would tell them she was blackmailing him. His voice sounded desperate.

'And I'll deny it, so how will you prove it?' Kate didn't bother to wait for an answer. 'You have no choice,' she added emphatically.

There was another long silence from him. Then he asked, in a deflated voice, how she wanted the money paid? His words dragged out slowly.

'I'll phone you again exactly a week from now on this number.' Kate looked at her watch. 'But I'll call earlier, dead on noon, to make arrangements for the first payment. And I warn you, neither of those two men you've used in the past had better come near me. As I said before, I don't trust you, and if I see either of those two characters then our business transaction is off.'

The victim said he understood.

Kate replaced the receiver, turned and smiled through the glass at the man standing outside the public telephone booth. She pushed open the door and kissed him lightly on his lips.

'It went just as you planned.'

Eddie smiled in return.

'I told you it would,' he said.

TWENTY FIVE

A couple of days later Dixie broke the news to Linda that she was going to join Mike in Yorkshire when his work took him there.

'But we will be returning to London most weekends,' she said.

'In that case, it would probably be better if I moved back with my parents,' Linda said thoughtfully. 'Or maybe I should look for a place of my own. The thing is, I've been too comfortable here, and I've let matters slide.'

'No, I want you to stay,' Dixie said. 'Don't forget we made a pact. Neither of us would move out until one of us gets married. Remember?'

'Well the way things are looking at the moment I shouldn't imagine it will be very long before you and Mike do just that,' Linda said.

'No, you're wrong, it won't be till next year at the earliest. Besides, you and Joey don't seem to be doing too bad.'

Linda shook her head.

'I'm treading careful on this one. Showbiz relationships can be very dicey and I don't want to end up just another statistic. I'm not sure if I can handle Joey's fame.'

Dixie understood what her friend was getting at. Linda and Joey had recently been snapped coming out of a restaurant and the photograph had appeared in several tabloids. First of all she'd been labeled as Joey's mystery date, then her identity had been discovered and reporters had got hold of the flat's phone number. Linda kept repeating they were just *good friends* and had nothing to say but knew once newspaper reporters started sniffing around they wouldn't give up that easy.

'In that case it would definitely be better if you stayed here,' Dixie said. 'Otherwise, your parents are going to get pestered.'

'That's true,' and after another ten minutes discussion Linda agreed it was more sensible to let their arrangement stay as it was.

*

The following Monday Mike and Dixie checked into a hotel on the outskirts of Wakefield. The previous time Mike had spent in the city he'd contacted various estate agents to find a large flat and this is what Dixie concentrated on while he met the builder and sub-contractors. He'd insisted he was only interested in the best craftsmen available and he wanted to make sure his instructions were being carried out.

Two days later Dixie found the perfect flat, large enough to be used as an office, as well as plenty of living space, and they could occupy it straight away. Mike signed a six month rental lease and as soon they got the keys moved most of the furniture from the lounge into one of the three bedrooms. The next day office furniture was installed, plus a new computer.

They were ready for business.

The plans and interior designs had already been completed in London and Gerry Dolan would spend some time, yet to be worked out, travelling to and from the capital. But Laura and Emma would only visit a couple of times in the beginning because their interior designing skills wouldn't be needed until the main structures were built, which would be some months yet, not until the new year. Besides, Mike had recently got a contract to completely refurbish the inside of a large house just off the Kings Road in Chelsea, and Laura would have to oversea a lot of that work. Still, it would give her a chance to show off her talent. The company was getting busy and Mike knew he would soon have to think seriously about taking on extra staff.

When Friday arrived Mike and Dixie were too tired to even think of heading back to London for the weekend.

'I'll see you next week,' Dixie told Linda over the phone, 'it's been hectic here and there's still a lot more organizing to do.'

'That's okay, I'm seeing Joey tomorrow night.'

'Give him our love,' Dixie said. 'Missing you, bye.'

'See you next week,' and Linda clicked off the phone.

She had felt lonely during the last few days, what with Dixie up north, and Joey busy promoting his new album around the country, including several appearances on TV.

And Linda was getting confused. She couldn't make out why the pop star was behaving like a perfect gentleman, so different from his newspaper reputation. The most he'd done was kiss her lightly on the lips, just a friendly peck, when he said goodnight to her. But Linda was beginning to get feelings towards Joey that were more than friendly. And more puzzling, she was sure he felt the same.

But he hadn't once tried to come on strong with her.

He was gentle and nice, didn't mention his female admirers anymore and even asked for her opinion on a couple of new songs he'd written - for which she felt really flattered.

Yes, confusing.

*

Kate Smith paid off the taxi and a minute later pulled open the door of one of London's familiar red telephone boxes. She inserted a pound coin, pressed the numbered buttons and held the receiver tight against her ear. There was no waiting this time and the phone was picked up straight away at his end. It was noon and exactly a week since they'd last spoken.

'I have my instructions for you,' Kate Smith said, 'so I suggest you get a pen and paper.' The man told her he already had them to hand, and she immediately carried on.

'I take it, you will have fifty thousand in cash ready for delivery in seven days time?' And Kate felt her heart quicken in excitement when she was assured she would get that amount. A fortune to her - and still more to come.

'Good. I'm not worried what denominations the notes are, the easiest it is for you will suit me.'

The man made a sarcastic remark which Kate ignored and continued speaking slowly for the next two minutes. 'You've got that?' she asked, and then it was her turn to listen. She gripped the black plastic receiver tight until her knuckles showed white as the angry words came over the line.

'I understand,' she said, and was surprised her voice sounded so calm, 'but I intend keeping my end of the deal too. I'll phone you in one month's time,' and Kate hung up just as the money ran out. She opened her handbag, pulled out her purse, and inserted another coin in the slot. A trickle of perspiration ran down her face. It was hot in the confined space.

'I've just finished speaking to him,' she said as soon as the phone was answered.

'Everything go okay?' Eddie asked.

'Yes, but he threatened me. He said he wasn't prepared to be bled dry for the rest of his life because if that was my intention then he would personally kill me, and take his chances.'

'Don't worry, he's bluffing. Anyway, you've got me.'

'I told him I'd keep my word, and we will, won't we? Two hundred thousand by Christmas will be enough. Plus I've got some savings and I can sell my house. Then we can start a new life somewhere else, like you said.'

'Of course, so there's no need to worry,' Eddie said in a soothing voice. 'But I'd better get off the phone because he should be calling any moment. See you soon.' Eddie replaced the receiver and took a swig from the can of lager he was holding in his other hand. His singlet vest stuck to his sweaty body. He was hot. But everything appeared to be going according to plan.

After he'd got Lucy's name from Kate he'd concentrated on getting her to reveal the identity of the man she was blackmailing. He wanted it to come from her because, at that time, he hadn't wanted her to know his full involvement. So he didn't hurry, and once again got his information from between the sheets. And then Kate told him everything.

As soon as that happened Eddie decided to tell Kate a bit more about his involvement. He had to if he was going to get her to co-operate. At first she was shocked but Eddie found it easy to persuade her to his way of thinking after promising they would go through with it together - and stay together.

However, unlike Kate, Eddie didn't divulge the complete details of what was going on. He couldn't take the chance of her accidentally blurting out something when she was talking to his employer on the phone. And obviously he omitted telling her he'd killed Tom and Margo Fisher. Eddie was upping the stakes and didn't want a blabbing woman fucking things up.

Maybe Kate suspected - but she never asked. Some things people didn't want to know.

Besides, there was now a newcomer on the scene. Eddie had seen it as an opportunity to make even more money. Possibly a lot more money. So could the other person he'd approached to make a deal.

He'd taken a gamble - which looked as though it was going to pay off. At worst he'd covered his back. And he'd found out more information about Dixie Fisher that was an eye opener.

Five minutes later the phone rang. It was his employer who quickly related the conversation with Kate Smith.

'Not wanting me anywhere near her shouldn't be a problem,' Eddie said, immediately thinking of Red. 'I can get hold of some people who'll be able to follow her. I think there should be two men in a car so that if she gets on a bus or tube train then one can get out and still keep tabs on her. The trouble is, we don't know if she'll be driving, in a taxi...or what.'

The other man agreed it was difficult.

'But there is one thing I'll have to do,' Eddie continued. 'I'll have to be with the two men to begin with, to identify Kate Smith, but as soon as they know what she looks like I'll disappear.'

His employer warned he'd better not be seen.

'Don't worry,' Eddie said,' but you know, that's a pretty clever plan she's worked out...having your package picked up by a bone fide carrier company...not a bad idea.'

The man at the other end became more intense as he said he hoped they didn't lose Miss Smith. But if they did, then, as an added precaution, it would be worthwhile keeping her house under surveillance because she'd have to go back there sometime.

It didn't make it any easier seeing as how she'd suddenly quit her job.

'No, I don't suppose it does,' Eddie said. 'I'll get someone to keep an eye on her house from tomorrow, and I'll speak to you in a week's time, after the pick-up.'

*

The Ford Fiesta came to a stop and Kate Smith got out. A few minutes later she was inside her home opening a couple of suitcases in the small bedroom at the back of the house. Eddie had told her that her place was being put under observation the next day and if she wanted anything then she'd better get it now. It would be her last opportunity.

Kate carefully went through the rooms gathering the rest of her clothes, shoes, make-up and anything else she might need. Soon both suitcases were full and she lugged them downstairs to the front door. Then Kate walked through all the rooms double checking she'd got everything she wanted. Finally she stood in her lounge looking around, reminiscing. The decorations she'd chosen, the carpets and curtains, the furniture she'd bought on hire purchase, now paid for.

She had a feeling she wouldn't be returning and felt sad. This had been her home for a long time.

Kate took the suitcases outside and was just turning the key in the mortice lock when she heard a noise, turned and saw Mrs Powis standing by the low separating hedge. The old lady had a flower patterned pinafore on over her dress.

'Going on another holiday?' she asked, with a smile.

Kate returned the smile. She liked her neighbour.

'No, as a matter of fact, I'm moving out.'

'Moving out? Have you sold your house?' Mrs Powis was obviously taken aback by the news.

'No, I haven't sold it yet,' Kate replied. 'But I will be putting it on the market soon. I'll be staying with friends for a while, until I get things sorted.'

'Ah, I see,' the old lady murmured, not exactly sure what to say, the announcement had been a surprise. And then she added, 'I'm going to miss you.'

'I'll miss you too,' and Kate leaned over the hedge and gave her neighbour a kiss on the cheek.

'Oh, there's something else,' Mrs Powis said, as Kate turned to move away. 'Someone was looking for you while you were on holiday.'

'Yes? Who was that?' Kate asked.

'A young lady...she was with her boyfriend. She said she was a friend of yours.'

The old woman was pleased with herself that she'd remembered to pass on the message. She was getting forgetful these days.

'What were their names, do you know?'

Mrs Powis looked thoughtful and clicked her teeth together.

'She had a nice name,' she replied. 'Now what was it? Ah, yes, I remember...Dixie...Dixie something or other.'

Kate couldn't stop the startled look that came over her face, but then forced a smile.

'I know who you mean,' she said, 'I'll phone her later,' and started down the short path.

'Have you got a new number I can get you on?' Mrs Powis called out.

Kate looked back and smiled again at the old lady.

'I'll write to you,' she replied, and quickly loaded the cases into the car and sped off, feeling nervous as she drove along, thinking about what the old woman had told her.

Dixie Fisher. Her aunt must have told her about the envelope. Kate thought she'd convinced the old spinster that leaving the letter for safe-keeping after Tom Fisher's death had nothing to do with Dixie. That Lucy was mistaken. After all, she was getting on. But Kate had been wrong.

However, Eddie had warned her that this might happen, and told her not to worry. But Kate *was* the worrying type and couldn't help wondering what she was getting into.

She took a couple of deep breaths to relax and loosened her grip on the steering wheel. It was a good job Eddie was thorough. He'd said it wouldn't be a good idea for him to go with her in case her neighbour spotted them together. Somebody else might talk to Mrs Powis and find out.

'Don't forget,' he'd reminded her, 'you're not supposed to want to have anything to do with me anymore.'

Eddie had said, with the amount of money involved, somebody might even start watching him, and he couldn't take that chance. But what he didn't say was that in the beginning it had been part of his employer's plan for him to be seen by Mrs Powis.

Playing a double-cross could be complicated. Or was it now a triple-cross?

He emphasized they both had to be very careful and tomorrow Kate was leaving Eddie's house and moving into a small furnished flat. She'd paid six month's rent in advance and tomorrow was also selling her car. She'd hire one if necessary.

Kate drew up outside her lover's house, her thoughts going back over how much her life had changed since the deaths of Tom and Margo Fisher.

She hoped her luck held out.

TWENTY SIX

Dixie liked Wakefield with its population of just over seventy six thousand inhabitants. And during her second week there realized how strange it was to think she'd so readily accepted living in London, sharing her daily life with eight million other people, and never given it a thought before.

She loved the space and appreciated the surrounding countryside. So did Mike - and that's what had helped him get his deal through.

If he'd wanted to build an estate of semi-detached houses or bungalows, then he wouldn't have got planning permission, but because he was building only three large country houses, and readily agreed to protect the local environment, his application met no obstacles.

Such was Mike's confidence that this would be the case he'd cannily sold all three properties before a stone had been laid.

His clients were a pop star friend of Joey's, a film actor and a stockbroker. And Mike made sure he gave each the special attention they deserved, after all, they were spending more than a million pounds individually.

*

They left Wakefield Friday afternoon, looking forward to their weekend in London. That evening they went to Dino's restaurant for dinner and Dixie stayed the night at Mike's. The following morning they went different ways. Mike to his office in Notting Hill, to work out some alterations to his original drawings, and Dixie got a taxi to her flat where Linda was waiting for her.

They had lunch at a bistro in Chelsea, lingering on over several coffees, then went shopping and eventually arrived home just before six pm. Mike had left a message on the telephone answering machine and Dixie immediately called back to his office, but he'd left, and she got him at his flat. He said he'd be at Dixie's in a couple of hours. She and Linda were cooking dinner and Mike agreed it would be best to stay in, watch television and get quietly plastered. Joey was away in Los Angeles, California, for a few weeks shooting a video for his new single.

It was after Dixie had replaced the telephone receiver that Linda remembered.

'You had a phone call a few days ago from a woman. She said you'd left your number with her to call if she saw her next door neighbour again...'Linda paused and gave a small grin...'well, something like that.'

'Did she leave her name?' Dixie asked.

'Yes, and her number.' Linda leaned over and flipped a couple of pages of the message pad. 'Here it is, Mrs Powis.'

Dixie smiled, looked at the number and pressed the buttons on the phone.

'Hello,' a voice said politely.

'Hello, Mrs Powis?'

'That's right,' the old lady answered, 'and who's that?'

'I'm Dixie Fisher, you left a message for me. You've seen Kate Smith, is that right?'

'Oh, yes. You're that nice young lady who was here a little while ago. Yes, I remember.'

'Kate Smith?' Dixie prompted,

'That's right, I saw her. It was at the beginning of the week, and I told her you'd tried to see her. She said she'd phone you. Did she?'

'No,' Dixie replied.

'She said she would.'

'Maybe she forgot...she'll probably phone me soon.'

'Well, she's moved out, said she was selling her house.'

'She did?' Dixie sounded surprised. 'Did she say where she's moving?'

'No, just said she'd be staying with friends, and she took a couple of big suitcases with her.'

'Did she tell you their names?'

'No, I'm sorry, but she didn't.' There was a brief silence then Mrs Powis chuckled, causing her dentures to click together. 'Maybe she's gone to her boyfriend's.'

'Yes, her boyfriend,' Dixie said interestedly, 'is that the one you told me about?'

'Did I?'

'You said you couldn't remember his name...'

'My memory's not so good these days,' the old lady said, 'but I do remember he's got lovely hair...just like my husband had before he went bald...lovely grey hair.'

'So you said.'

'Oh, and he's got a black car. That's right, Kate's got a white one, and his is black.'

'Do you know the make?' Dixie asked. The woman's remark had jogged something else in her mind. Something she couldn't quite place

'No, I'm sorry but I don't know much about cars.'

'And you're sure Kate didn't give you a number or address where to contact her?'

'No, but she did say she'd let me know. Would you like me to call you when she does?'

'Yes, please, Mrs Powis. And thanks for taking the trouble to keep me informed.'

The two women said their goodbyes and Dixie saw Linda staring at her after she replaced the receiver, a mystified look on her face.

'What was that about?' her friend asked.

Linda knew about Lucy Fisher's burglary but Dixie hadn't mentioned Kate Smith or the mysterious letter. With her move to Yorkshire, she'd had other things on her mind.

'Let's go into the kitchen and start getting dinner ready,' Dixie said, 'and I'll tell you about it.'

When Dixie finished relating what Lucy Fisher had told her and she'd explained about her fruitless visit to Kate Smith's house, Linda asked the obvious question.

'What could possibly be in that envelope?'

Dixie shrugged her shoulders.

'I don't know,' she replied, 'but Kate Smith should be back at work now, so I'll phone her there.'

TWENTY SEVEN

The black leather clad motorcycle courier, holding a large brown envelope, left the apartment block exactly seven minutes after he'd arrived. The man put the well sealed packet into the metal box behind his seat, slipped on his black crash helmet and roared into the traffic, the powerful Honda easily weaving between the cars. His delivery to the hotel had to be before three pm.

Plenty of time to get to Bayswater. The biker was the best courier in the company, as had been insisted upon.

Just over twenty minutes later he stopped outside the front entrance of his destination and, taking the packet from the box, entered through the double doors into a small lobby. After removing his helmet he had a brief word with the man behind the desk and waited patiently as the receptionist picked up the internal phone.

'She'll be down in a moment,' he said, and the courier nodded his head.

A couple of minutes later the doors of the small lift opened and Kate Smith stepped out. She walked over to the motorcyclist.

'Miss Smith?'

'That's right,' Kate replied, and took the held out brown envelope.

'Would you mind signing?' the man asked, unzipping his leather jacket and extracting a receipt pad and pen from an inside pocket.

Kate did as she was asked then returned to the lift. When she got back to her room she looked at her wristwatch. It was ten minutes to three.

She smiled then went to one of the large windows that overlooked the street and slightly moved the curtains. The white Citroen was still parked where it had been for the last hour and a half.

She picked up a bright yellow cardigan from the bed and slipped it on. Then she put the packet into a strong green plastic carrier bag, grabbed her handbag and hurried from the room. She left behind a cheap holdall containing a nightie and a few assorted toiletries. Let one of the maids have it. Kate had checked into the hotel yesterday, but wouldn't be returning, although she had paid to stay one more night.

*

Eddie was sitting in the back of the Citroen when he saw Kate emerge through the hotel's double doors, walk down mosaic tiled steps to the pavement and stop.

'That's her,' he said to the driver and Red, who was the other passenger sitting in the front.

'We've clocked her,' the driver said, a sharp featured man with short cut blonde hair and a small scar angled upwards from his mouth. 'Looks like she's going to get a cab.' And as he said that a black taxi stopped for the woman's outstretched arm.

'Right,' Eddie said, and opened the rear door, 'I'm out of here. Good luck.' He slammed the door shut, walked briskly away as the car started to move, and looked at his watch. Everything seemed to be going to plan.

His plan.

And there was one other person who would secretly play an important part in this afternoon's events, the only person Eddie trusted completely, leaving him free to go directly home in case his employer phoned him. Eddie couldn't be in two places at the same time.

Kate's taxi joined the traffic heading for Bayswater Road, the Citroen tucked in behind. They reached Lancaster Gate and the cab swung right at traffic lights into Hyde Park, then towards Knightsbridge, swinging around to Hyde Park Corner, up Mayfair's Park Lane, finally stopping the other side of Marble Arch in Edgware Road. The occupants of the Citroen closely watched as the woman paid off the taxi, the passenger ready with his hand on the door handle ready to leap out if necessary.

Kate Smith peered through her spectacles and looked around before walking twenty yards to traffic lights and crossing to the other side of the road. She immediately raised an arm, distinctive in her bright yellow cardigan, and another black cab put on its brakes, squealed to a stop, then quickly took off again with its passenger on board. The driver of the Citroen frantically stuck his arm out the window turning the steering wheel with his left hand and executed a hasty U-turn much to the irritation of other motorists who kept their hands heavy on the horn.

*

Kate sat in the back of the cab looking straight ahead as the taxi retraced her route along Park Lane leading to Hyde Park Corner. But this time the vehicle turned in the direction of Victoria heading towards the destination she'd given the driver. Kate knew the Citroen would be following but didn't turn her head to look out the rear window. She had changed cabs to give the impression that she was trying to elude any would-be-followers, but not clever enough to be any good at it.

Lull them into a false sense of security, Eddie had told her, and just follow his instructions.

Then they hit a traffic snarl-up and it took another ten minutes before the cab stopped to let off its passenger, the driver apologizing for the delay.

*

The Citroen drew to a halt fifty yards behind the taxi and the two men watched as Kate paid off the driver opposite the Army & Navy department store in Victoria Street. Once again she looked around before walking to the nearby traffic lights, patiently waiting for the pedestrian signal to turn green, before crossing.

As soon as the woman crossed the road and headed for the plate glass doors at the front of the store Red quickly got out of the Citroen.

'Stay where you are,' he said to the driver, 'and I'll contact you on your mobile.'

Red cursed as he waited for a gap in the busy traffic. Impatiently he held up an arm as a double-decker bus headed towards him, then dashed across the street, narrowly missing being hit by a white transit van as the driver was forced to stamp on his brakes.

Entering the store he breathed a sigh of relief as he caught a flash of yellow and saw the woman in the cardigan browsing in the perfumery department on the ground floor. He stopped and pretended to show interest in the brightly packaged goods displayed on the shelves of another counter close by, but told an attractive young assistant he was just looking when she offered help.

He watched as Kate made a purchase and put the small item into the green plastic bag. Then she walked through the menswear department towards the back of the store and a rear exit. Pushing open the doors Kate crossed the much quieter road and entered through more glass doors of the store's annex.

Red followed and as he entered the other part of the store stopped. There weren't many customers and he felt self-conscious at being the only male in the ladies clothes department. There was also a cafeteria with several women drinking coffee and as he passed it spotted the woman he was tailing on the escalator leading to the upper floor.

The moment Kate stepped off the escalator she quickened her pace through the lingerie department, then walked up a short flight of carpeted stairs leading to where nightwear was sold, which formed a bridge over the street below, and back into the main store. She shrugged off her distinctive cardigan, crammed it into the carrier bag, and smoothed the collar of her dark blue short sleeved blouse as she mingled with other shoppers.

Red bounded up the escalator as Kate disappeared from view and was slightly confused when confronted with rails of ladies lingerie then stairs and nightclothes. Then, as he walked down some more stairs, realized he was back in the main store.

But where the hell was the woman?

Red wrinkled his brow in frustration knowing he'd only been seconds behind his quarry. Widening his view he saw some other escalators and as he hurried towards them knew he had to decide whether to go up or down. Quickly making up his mind he took the escalator to the ground floor knowing she had to leave sometime or other. Fortunately the Army & Navy store wasn't as big as some of the other London department stores and he quickly reached one of the two front exits leading into Victoria Street. No sign of the woman in yellow so he literally ran back through the ground floor, pushing past startled customers, and barged open the rear exit doors he'd been through a short time before.

There was much less traffic in this street and Red turned right and then looked left down the next connecting road. He took his mobile phone from his jacket to phone his friend in the Citroen when he saw a woman straighten up beside a silver coloured Nissan Micra parked by a meter. She'd obviously dropped her car keys and, although he did notice from the side view she was wearing glasses, started to look away from the woman dressed in blue. Then his gaze suddenly riveted back to her as she opened the car door and tossed a green carrier bag on to the front passenger seat. But by the time he crossed the road and was only yards from the Nissan he heard the motor come to life as the ignition key was turned. Then the car drew swiftly away from the kerb and Red broke into a run, chasing for fifty yards before stopping as the vehicle turned a bend in the road and vanished from sight.

Red swore under his breath and began walking back the way he'd come.

'I've lost her,' he said disgustedly into his phone, when the driver of the white Citroen answered his call. Then added almost absent-mindedly, 'I'll be with you in few minutes,' as his eyes fastened on the parking bay now being occupied by the grateful driver of a grey Jaguar.

He moved closer and stared intently at the meter. The tariff written under the glass indicator stated it was one pound for every forty minutes, and there was still just over an hour's paid waiting time left on the clock. So the woman wasn't as naive as she'd first appeared to be. There were only three parking meters in this particular spot and to safely get one meant the car would have had to been there for some time. Someone else had parked the car and been feeding the meter.

Which meant the woman had an accomplice.

TWENTY EIGHT

It wasn't until the middle of the following week when she was back in Wakefield that Dixie got a chance to call Fisher, Peterson and Partners and asked to be put through to the Personnel Department. But then got a surprise. Kate Smith had suddenly quit her job.

No, she hadn't left a forwarding address, a secretary informed Dixie, but Miss Smith had said she'd let the company know at a later date how they could contact her. After all, she was in the company pension scheme, and there would be papers to sort out.

The secretary said she could try and find out more but Dixie told her not to worry about it.

Dixie thought the sudden departure strange but also decided against bothering her uncle to ask if he had any more information. It now looked as though Kate Smith was cutting free from her past, so why should Dixie bother, and the young woman put the matter from her mind. She had plenty of other things to occupy her thoughts.

August just seemed to flash by and Dixie realized Mike's intention of spending most weekends in London was a miscalculation as the inevitable building snags cropped up. So Dixie employed a secretary for three days a week, Monday, Wednesday and Friday. Sandra was a single parent and this arrangement suited her. It also suited Mike and Dixie because it enabled them to leave Wakefield earlier for the weekend and return later on Monday morning.

*

October brought the beautiful colours of Autumn, the leaves on the trees turning glorious shades of gold and brown. It also brought a written birthday invitation from Aunt Lucy with a message saying she wouldn't take no for an answer. So Dixie immediately phoned her elderly relative.

'Of course, we'd love to come,' she assured her aunt.

'Good,' Lucy said, 'and you'll bring that nice young man of yours?'

'I wouldn't think otherwise,' Dixie replied, and then added. 'When is the actual day of your birthday?'

'Sunday, so I'd like you to come for the weekend, that way there's no rush.'

'Agreed, Auntie. Mike and I will be looking forward to it.'

'That's good, Dixie, because there is something I want to discuss with you.'

'Yes?' Dixie queried.

'Don't fret,' and Lucy gave a short laugh, 'it's just something I want you to know.'

'Can't you tell me now?'

'No.'

'Okay then...you've got me intrigued, but I suppose I can wait until I see you...oh, and one other thing, I didn't know you had my address here in Wakefield.'

'I got it from Robert.'

'Of course,' Dixie said. Her uncle's company were Mike's accountants and they would know where to contact him.

The young woman said goodbye to her aunt, wondering what to buy for a birthday present, as she replaced the receiver.

*

There was a definite frosty chill in the air when they arrived just before one o'clock on Saturday outside the ivy clad country house.

Just in time for lunch.

The meal was simple and tasty and when they'd finished Mike decided to go for a walk.

'I'm stuffed,' he said, and offered to take Blackie, the aging Labrador, for some exercise.

'He's getting a bit slow these days,' Lucy said, as Mike started to leave the room. 'A bit like me, but he will enjoy it.' The frail woman waited until the young man had left before adding. 'Now we can have that talk,' she said smiling at her niece.

'After the burglary I realized I should put my affairs in order,' Lucy began. 'It made me think about what would happen to this house after I died.' She paused, her thoughts going back over the years. 'This is where Harry was brought up,' she said wistfully, referring to her long dead fiancé. 'His parents left the house to me knowing it would be in good hands and,' the elderly lady looked directly into her niece's eyes, 'that's why I'm leaving it to you.'

'That's wonderful,' Dixie finally said, her voice soft. 'I don't know what to say.'

'I had made out a will many years ago,' Lucy continued. 'I was going to leave everything to my brothers, my next of kin, as most people do. And as the years went by it's the kind of thing that slipped to the back of my mind. But then, after the robbery, it made me think. Your poor father had been killed and that meant everything would go to Robert. But what would he do with this house? I can't see him leaving London so he'd probably sell it. And that's why I've recently had a new will drawn up leaving the house to you. I'd like it to *stay* in our family.'

'But you've a long time to live yet,' Dixie said encouragingly.

'Hopefully so,' Lucy smiled, 'I've got to see you get married for a start. I must say, I like your Mike.'

'Yes, and he adores this house. Can I tell him?'

'Of course.'

'I'd never sell this house, Aunt Lucy.' Dixie looked sincerely at her elderly relative. 'I promise you that.'

'Thank you, my dear.'

Dixie was deeply touched by her aunt's kindness. Not by the thought of any monetary value attached to the house but knowing how much it meant to Lucy.

'Have you told Uncle Robert?'

'Yes,' Lucy replied, 'and he agrees with me that it would be more appropriate for you to have the house. I also have investments, enough to live off comfortably, and those I've left equally between you and my brother. Robert said he'd be here tomorrow for my birthday, so you can have a word with him then if you want. He is the executor of the will.'

Dixie expressed her gratitude again, but then added, 'My parents left me very well off. I have been fortunate in that respect.'

'I know, my brother told me Tom had been prudent with his money. A bit different to Robert, I fear. He's got an expensive hobby.'

'Yes, and what's that?' Dixie was intrigued by her aunt's remark.

Lucy grinned at her niece.

'None of your business, young lady. Now,' and she prodded Dixie with her walking stick, 'you can get me another sherry.'

*

Robert Fisher arrived for Sunday lunch and later in the afternoon friends from nearby villages joined the family to celebrate Lucy's sixty third birthday.

'Oh, I know I look a lot older,' she said, 'but my doctor says I'm lucky to be here at all. Must be all that sherry I drink,' she joked, and winked at her niece.

It was a hectic day and Dixie didn't get a chance to discuss Lucy's conversation with her uncle, even though he decided to stay overnight and not drive back to London that evening, as originally planned.

But Dixie had spoken to Mike the previous night in bed about her aunt's generosity.

'You're very lucky,' he told her. 'This is a magnificent house.'

'I know,' Dixie replied. 'A wonderful place to bring up a family.'

'That's right,' and Mike nuzzled her ear as he spoke. 'Are you getting ideas?' But covered her mouth with his before she had a chance to reply.

*

Monday morning and after breakfast it was time to say goodbye to Lucy.

'Thank you for the present,' she said to her niece. 'Exactly what I wanted, you must be a mind reader.'

Dixie hadn't let on, but she'd spoken to Mrs Hayes over the phone, and the housekeeper had advised in her choice. A dark blue cashmere scarf.

'Look after Dixie,' the elderly woman told Mike, as he bent and kissed her lightly on the cheek.

'Will do,' he replied, and smiled reassuringly at Lucy before turning away. 'Always.'

Uncle Robert had left half an hour before in his silver grey Bentley with the promise to his sister not to leave it so long before he visited again.

'And call me the next time you're in London,' he'd told the young couple, 'we can have lunch or dinner together.' And then he was off, wheels spinning on the gravel as he gunned the powerful motor.

'That was a very pleasant weekend,' Mike said, steering his Range Rover down the driveway at a slower speed.

'Yes, it was,' Dixie agreed, then they both settled into silence with their thoughts, hardly aware of the car radio pumping out music as the miles sped by.

It was a trouble free journey and they'd made good time by the time they entered Wakefield. Mike dropped off Dixie first with their bags at their flat, then continued driving to one of the building sites to check on a problem that had arisen the end of last week. Nothing serious but he wanted to make sure it was sorted out.

Neither had noticed the grey curly haired man sitting behind the wheel of a black Volkswagen Golf parked fifty yards away. He'd been sitting there for two hours, well wrapped up, with a half full thermos of coffee wedged between his legs.

Eddie had arrived in Wakefield the previous afternoon. He'd checked into a small hotel for a week but told the receptionist his stay might be longer.

Dixie Fisher had to be taken care of.

TWENTY NINE

Eddie sat with his eyes fixed on the entrance to Dixie's ground floor flat, situated in the middle house of a Georgian terrace, which he knew doubled as an office as well. The rest of the other large properties in the road had also been converted into flats, no doubt much more profitable for the landlords.

The same was happening all over the country.

There was private parking in front of the terrace, then a stretch of pavement and a busy street where Eddie had stationed himself. He'd chosen his place carefully, with a good view, but made sure he wasn't too obvious himself. He could also see the young woman's red Mazda sports car parked in the private road but Dixie didn't show at all during the rest of the day.

There were two other flats in the middle house and Eddie kept a mental note of all the people who came and went. Whether they were visitors or people who lived there he'd try to establish as soon as possible.

A youngish looking woman had arrived about nine thirty and then the lights in the ground floor flat had come on. He hadn't been able to get a very good look at her because she was well wrapped up against the cold with a scarf high around her neck and a wool hat pulled tight over her dark hair. But he had noticed she drove up in a brown ten year old Toyota saloon.

Maybe she worked for Mike Saxby.

Eddie used a local pub's toilet facilities and had a couple of whiskies to try and get warm but most of the time was spent in his car staring through the windscreen.

Dixie's boyfriend came home about five pm in his Range Rover and that was it for the duration of the evening. Eddie ate cheeseburger and chips, obtained from a nearby takeaway, drank cans of Coke, and by nine o'clock was thoroughly pissed off, cold and tired. So he went back to his hotel to think, stopping on the way at an off-licence to buy a bottle of whisky. There was a small bar at the hotel, which seemed a favourite stopover for travelling salesmen, but Eddie was in no mood to get involved in idle conversation.

Once in his room Eddie poured a large scotch, turned on the television, more for background company, then stretched out on the bed.

It didn't bother him that he had to get rid of Dixie, his conscience had vanished years ago, after the first time he'd killed.

His instructions were that the young lady had to be eliminated before the final payment to Kate Smith, which was just before Christmas. How she died was up to him, and if anyone else got hurt in the process, too bad.

The second payment of fifty grand had been paid to Kate last week. This time there had been no attempt to follow her and Eddie had been hoping for a quiet period leading up to the festive season and the final payment of one hundred thousand. Then it had been his intention to disappear, whether by himself or not, he hadn't yet made up his mind.

Kate was under control, although she wasn't very happy living in her temporary accommodation, and complained that she wasn't getting enough of Eddie's company. But, they had to be careful, he'd warned her. She'd only have to be patient until they had the money then things would change.

The problem was, now he had his own plan in operation, he had to juggle with the requirements of the man who was employing him. And Eddie realized to enable the situation to proceed smoothly he had to keep everyone happy. He needed Kate, because she was the only one who could get the money, and his employer needed to be kept sweet, otherwise he might not pay out.

He'd known for a while Dixie had to die, but it was sooner than he'd anticipated.

His employer's plans had changed dramatically since the deaths of Tom and Margo Fisher. Purely by coincidence, and that's why Eddie was being extra careful, you could never foresee what was going to happen next.

Eddie got off the bed and poured himself another drink. But first things first. He had to concentrate on the task in hand. However, this wasn't going to be a rush job, because one thing was for sure, he had no intention of getting caught. There was too much money at stake.

*

The following day, Tuesday, Eddie positioned himself in his stakeout spot early and saw Mike leave in his car just after eight am. Then the morning dragged slowly by until mid-day and Eddie was beginning to feel cramped. He'd just got out of the VW to stretch his legs and was turning over in his mind the idea of going to the nearby pub when he saw a woman in a hooded cream coloured coat get into the red sports car, so he quickly jumped back into his motor and switched on the engine.

The Mazda came out of the private road into the busy street and Eddie followed discreetly two cars behind. Dixie shopped at a supermarket, a chemist's, then a fashion boutique before returning home. But she didn't surface again during the day, nor did her boyfriend after he arrived home a little after six. So once again Eddie left at nine o'clock and returned to his hotel.

The next day he was back in his parking spot to see Mike leave, but this time Dixie appeared mid-morning and drove to the outskirts of the city where she stopped at a petrol station. After filling up she drove into the country for several miles then turned off the main road into a side road, then a few hundred yards along another, which was little more than a lane, before driving up a dirt track and finally stopping in a makeshift car park. There were a couple of lorries and vans stationary on the grass and Dixie drew up next to her boyfriend's Range Rover. She got out and trudged through a gap in a line of trees, beyond which were workmen and piles of building materials.

Eddie got out of his car but once he saw there was nowhere to park without being seen decided to go back to the flat and wait. That's all he could do for the moment. Besides, he was only trying to work out the young woman's routine, see if she had any set pattern.

*

The Monday morning of the following week found Eddie back on his vigil outside Dixie's flat. The rest of the day went much the same as it had the previous week, as did the following day, and he was beginning to think that a set plan was going to be out of the question. He'd probably stand more chance seizing a sudden, unexpected opportunity, like he had with Dixie's parents. So it was important he kept alert and on the ball.

But there was one thing he could do as soon as possible. He could get the young lady rattled and hopefully it would give her something to talk about with other people. All part of his employer's tactics, which Eddie was content to go along with, so long as it didn't interfere with his own scheme.

*

Dixie made coffee and a couple of thick slices of toast and butter for Mike before he left the flat.

'Are you coming out to the site today?' he asked, as he put on a heavy dark brown jacket over his sweater and jeans. He was wearing tough leather boots and tucked a pair of woollen gloves into his pockets. Mike would be out in the open a lot and it was cold.

'Probably,' Dixie replied. She usually did try and visit him every Wednesday, and also meet any new workmen, so they weren't just anonymous voices on the end of a telephone when she spoke to them.

They walked to the front door and Dixie gave Mike a brief kiss on his lips.

'I'll call you later this morning,' she said. 'There's some shopping I've got to get from the supermarket, but I'm sure I'll be able to see you. Maybe go to a pub for lunch.'

It was just turned eight o'clock and Dixie was still in her dressing gown. But, Sandra wasn't due to start work until nine thirty, so she had plenty of time to get dressed.

Sandra was only five years older than Dixie but already widowed and bringing up a seven year old boy by herself. She was an easy going sort of woman with long dark hair like Dixie's. And, most important, was a very good secretary.

Working only three days a week was convenient because she was determined her son, Connor, should have as normal a home life as possible. That was the reason she started work late in the morning. She drove her son to school although, in the afternoon he did leave with a classmate's mother, then Sandra picked him up after she finished work at five.

Dixie was on the phone when the secretary let herself into the flat. She had her own set of keys which she needed to open on Mondays and lock up most Fridays.

When Dixie got off the phone she handed several opened letters to Sandra.

'This is some stuff Mike needs ordering urgently,' she said. 'And I think it's time for our first cup of coffee, don't you?'

'Thanks, it's a cold one out there today, and coffee would go down a treat,' Sandra replied.

Two hours later Dixie said she was going shopping and asked Sandra if she wanted anything.

'No, I can't think of anything...but don't you usually see Mike on a Wednesday?'

'Yes, and I will, but I'm getting some frozen food and I'll need to bring it back here first.'

Dixie put on a three quarter length black coat and pulled a black wool ski hat over her head.

'Won't be long,' she said, and grabbed her leather shoulder bag as she left the flat. There was a biting wind but her sports car started first time and as she joined the steady stream of traffic turned up the heater.

Ten minutes later she found a space in the large open air car park and a few minutes after that was in the warmth of the supermarket. It didn't take more than half an hour to buy what she wanted and then she was heading back to her car with a carrier bag in each hand.

The exit barrier was out of order with the yellow crosspiece permanently stuck up in the air. But there were only a couple of cars ahead of her and Dixie patiently waited her turn. As she went through the exit there was ten yards to go before the main road and Dixie was just about to swing into a gap in the traffic when a parked car in the street suddenly moved in front of her. She swore under her breath and slammed hard on the brakes, managing to stop just feet away from the driver's side of the black car, which was facing against the oncoming traffic.

The driver didn't look toward Dixie and apologize for nearly causing an accident, instead he stared intently through his windscreen, then moved out, causing cars to slide to a stop or smash into him.

Dixie sat white faced and watched the Volkswagen Golf accelerate away from her amid much fist waving and honking of horns from irate drivers.

Then a loud blast from a car horn, this time directly behind her, jarred her back to normality, and she slowly moved forward.

The driver of that black car, even though she'd only seen his profile, was...she was sure she was right. His grey curly hair...the face of the man she'd met months ago.

Danny Buckley - her father.

THIRTY

The driver of the VW pulled into the small car park and turned off the ignition. He sat thinking for a short while then clicked his fingers as he made up his mind and hurried into the hotel where he informed reception he was checking out. But, he explained, a colleague would be arriving tomorrow to take his place and staying all next week.

Eddie hadn't intended being in Wakefield the following week anyway, and leaving immediately only slightly changed his plans. But now Dixie had seen him he thought it better not to take the risk of her finding him watching her flat. He'd wanted to be seen but daren't chance a confrontation at this stage. That would really screw things up.

Red was taking over and it just meant him starting a few days earlier. Red had been in the Volkswagen with him in the summer when Dixie and her friends left the London nightclub, so he knew what she and her boyfriend looked like.

On the drive back to London Eddie phoned Kate and told her he was returning earlier than expected. News she welcomed.

He stayed with Kate until the following Monday in her small rented flat just off Earl's Court which was now very special for them.

After Kate got her first big payment in cash Eddie knew he had to find somewhere safe to keep it. So he'd carefully lifted up one edge of fitted carpet in the bedroom and found the perfect place under the floorboards, where there were now two lots of fifty thousand pounds. And over that he'd moved a heavy chest of drawers.

A hidden fortune.

He'd originally offered to keep the money in his house but Kate had smiled at him and said she'd rather look after it herself. Eddie had smiled too. He didn't blame her.

The stakeout on Kate's house had been called off after a few weeks when it became obvious she wasn't going back. It was then Eddie told her it would be safe to sell.

The property market was booming and her house was snapped up straight away. The sale should be completed in about two or three weeks time and after the mortgage was paid off Kate would get a cheque for nearly one hundred and fifty grand. It was that extra money which might save her life, make it worth taking her with him.

She probably would have got more but Eddie urged her to sell to the first buyer, cut her links as soon as possible, and make it harder for anyone to track her. Her solicitor fixed everything and she didn't even meet the people who were taking over her home. Kate stayed out of sight in the background.

And, Eddie had to admit, there was one other reason for them to stay together. Sex with her was great. Simply because *anything* he wanted to do to her - she let him. She never complained and enjoyed everything.

On the Tuesday Eddie left Kate to go back to his place. He had a lot of phone calls to make. Everything had to be worked out for the next day. It was important. He had a special job on.

It took him nearly an hour of calls and he was almost at the end of the list on the table in front of him before he got the response he was hoping for.

'Thank you very much, Mrs St Clair,' he said into the phone, 'one of our representatives will visit you tomorrow morning at ten o'clock...yes, that's right...the Door To Door

Pottery Company...yes, it is a bit of a mouthful, Mrs St Clair, but I'm sure you'll find we give value for money.'

Later that day Eddie went to Selfridges Department Store and bought an expensive Wedgewood tea service, plus a cake stand of the same pattern and a few extra pieces. Yes, Mrs St Clair was going to get very good value indeed.

*

Joey picked up Linda in the dark blue Rolls but after Stan dropped them outside the restaurant in Knightsbridge he told his chauffeur to head home.

'We'll cab it the rest of the night,' he said.

Joey was wearing oatmeal coloured jeans with a baggy beige shirt hanging loose, and he'd asked Linda to also dress casual.

When they entered the restaurant and were shown to a reserved table for two the heads that turned and followed them weren't just for the recognition of Joey Judd, pop star, it was as much in admiration for Linda. She was dressed entirely in black. Skin tight leggings, stiletto heeled boots and a tight sweater which silhouetted the shape of her figure. Her elfin like face surrounded by a halo of short black curls gave the impression of a sweet, demure female - but her body said otherwise.

'You look fantastic,' Joey said, hoping his smile didn't come across as a leer. 'You've got a fabulous figure.'

'Thank you,' Linda replied. 'I don't usually put it on display like this,' and she leant forward and stroked his cheek, 'but I thought you deserved a treat.'

The food and wine were excellent. The service first-rate and the couple had no difficulty in finding things to talk about. And, of course, the conversation turned to their friends and Linda said how much happier Dixie was since meeting Mike.

'She went through a really bad time after her parents were killed.'

'I know, Mike told me,' Joey said. ''e's a top bloke, and 'e's 'elped me so much in my life I don't know if I'll ever be able to repay him completely.'

When Joey offered his credit card to pay for the meal the waiter whispered, 'I'm not supposed to ask, sir, but could I get your autograph for my little daughter?' and he produced a white card about four inches square.

'Sure,' the pop star smiled. 'What's 'er name?' and used the pen the waiter gave him to wish his daughter, Sophie, all the very best.

'What's it like being famous?' Linda asked, as the thankful waiter moved away. The question had crossed her mind earlier in the evening when she'd been getting ready and heard Joey's voice on the radio. Somehow it seemed strange to hear him singing, knowing that millions of people were also listening, and she would soon be having dinner with him.

'I love it,' and Joey's face beamed from ear to ear. 'It's fantastic to be recognized by so many people. And just think, I've got all my best years ahead of me.' He finished his drink and looked at his wristwatch. 'It's only just gone eleven, so what about a drink somewhere else?'

'Not for long though,' Linda replied, 'I've got work in the morning.'

They went to a club in Soho and it was nearly two am when they arrived by taxi outside the apartment block.

Joey gave his date a kiss on her cheek.

'Goodnight,' he said.

Linda was weary and had to put her hand over her mouth to stifle a yawn.

'Fed up with me already?'

'Of course not,' she replied, 'it's been wonderful, but I've had more than enough to drink and I feel tired. You can come up for coffee,' Linda added, as she saw a frown flicker across Joey's face.

The pop star smiled at her.

'No, you get a good night's kip, it's about time I went 'ome too.'

The two sat looking at each other in the back of the cab. They knew it was only a matter of time.

It would happen - but not tonight.

*

Linda was a bit hung-over the next morning as she rushed to get ready for work and was half an hour behind time as she hurried through the lobby, past the porter, and pushed open the plate glass doors leading to the street. It was chilly but the air helped freshen her up. Linda looked at her watch. Good job she worked in the family business. She quickened her pace and walked briskly around the corner into the road leading to the tube station.

Two men on the other side of the road stood watching as she left her building. They waited until she'd disappeared from sight then walked to the local McDonald's for breakfast and coffees. Over the next hour Eddie made several phone calls on his mobile to the same number. Each time the answering machine answered and Dixie Fisher's voice asked the caller to leave a message.

The flat was empty.

'Come on let's go,' Eddie said, and the two men left the restaurant.

Eddie was working with the one man he'd stake his life on. John didn't look much. In fact, he was a nondescript sort of person in his forties with shortish brown hair and an ordinary looking face. The type who blended into the background and easily forgettable. However, behind that innocuous facade was a vicious man, as several people in the past had found out to their cost.

The men had been friends for twenty years and knew they could rely on each other completely. They were professionals and had been involved in many jobs together.

Successfully.

And there was one thing that set Eddie and John apart from most other criminals. That bonded them together.

They were both killers.

Minutes later they reached a dirty blue transit van parked not far from where they'd been watching the apartment block and John opened the back with a key. Eddie got in, closed the door behind him, while John lit a cigarette and lounged against the side of the van staring idly at the passersby.

He'd nearly finished smoking when he heard a tap from inside and went back and opened the rear door. Eddie had changed his clothes. He'd taken off his topcoat and suit jacket and put on a thick patterned sweater, and three quarter length brown button up overall. He was also wearing black horn rimmed glasses, with plain lenses, and a light brown flat cap.

He jumped down from the van, turned and picked up a large cardboard box containing the individually wrapped Wedgewood china. John locked the back again and the two men began walking towards Dixie Fisher's apartment block.

John was wearing a blue suit, collar and tie, and dark blue raincoat. The salesman and his helper.

They reached the building, walked across the thick pile green carpet and stood in front of the porter's desk. It was a few minutes before ten o'clock.

The uniformed porter had watched as they entered through the glass doors and was now on his feet. A smile of greeting on his face. Although one of the men was just an ordinary workman like himself, carrying a large box, he was always polite and careful. A lot of rich people lived in these flats and it didn't pay to upset anyone, especially now. It might only be the beginning of November, but Christmas was looming, and he had to think of all those large seasonal tips he got.

'Yes, gentlemen, what can I do for you?'

John returned the smile.

'I've got an appointment with Mrs St Clair,' he replied. 'I'm from the Door To Door Pottery Company.'

'Okay, sir,' the porter said, and flipped open a book on the desk. He trailed his finger down a list of handwritten names until he found what he was looking for, then reached for the internal phone. 'I'll just check with Mrs St Clair.' A few brief words and he turned back to John and Eddie. 'The lift's over there, gentlemen,' and he pointed with his hand, 'it's the third floor. Mrs St Clair's expecting you.'

The two men got in the small lift, pressed a button and alighted on the third floor, where Eddie passed over the cardboard box.

'I'll call you as soon as I can,' Eddie said, then opened the fire exit door near the lift leading to the stairs and as he hurried down pulled on thin plastic surgical gloves. He opened the door on the second floor, walked quickly along the corridor and came to a halt outside Dixie's flat. Fishing in the right hand pocket of his overall he pulled out two keys on a ring, turned the larger one in the mortice lock then the other one in the Ingersoll, and the door swung open.

Once inside Eddie went straight to the lounge and began searching through every bit of furniture that had drawers. Then he did the same in the dining room, but didn't find what he was looking for. He ignored the bathroom and kitchen and one of the three bedrooms which didn't look as though it was used. That left two and he started searching the one that had a shower room en-suite, which turned out to be the right one.

He drew a blank in the two bedside tables but then started looking through a large mahogany bow-fronted chest of drawers. And, when he pulled on the brass handles of the bottom one, found the drawer crammed with papers, folders and envelopes. Eddie carefully took out the top layer, placed them on the carpet, knelt down, and began going through them. He was lucky, and the first foolscap envelope he opened contained what he was looking for.

He gently pulled out two sheets of typewritten paper and seven six by four colour photographs with captions printed neatly on the back, plus a marriage certificate. Eddie separated three of the photographs from the rest, then pulled a brown envelope from the left hand pocket of his overall, took out three photographs and swapped them over. He carefully replaced the large envelope and the rest of the stuff back in the drawer and stood.

Next he retraced his steps throughout the flat and made sure everything was just as it was before he began his search. Finally, convinced nobody would know he'd been there, he looked at his wristwatch. Nearly half past ten. Eddie pulled a mobile phone from his overall and called his friend on the floor above him.

John was standing by the table in the dining room with the contents of the cardboard box spread out. An old woman with blue rinsed hair in her seventies sat on one of the dining chairs. Mrs St Clair was well preserved, rich looking, with enough diamonds on her fingers to have kept John in luxury for a year. A small white poodle sat by her feet on the red carpet.

John had taken his time unwrapping the Wedgewood china and placing the porcelain carefully on the table, all the time waffling on about the fact that she didn't have to buy, only keep it for a month, but if she did like it, then it was half the price of what it cost in the shops.

Mrs St Clair had told him she was a widow and John used up time asking questions about her dead husband.

A subject she was only too happy to talk about.

'Excuse me,' he said, when his mobile rang. Turning away he listened, then muttered softly, 'Give me a few minutes.' The connection was broken but John kept talking into his phone and turned to face the old lady. 'Oh, that is good news...and Mrs St Clair qualifies for the special bonus?...yes, she will be pleased...I'll tell her straight away...yes, thanks.'

John put away his mobile, smiled at the woman and spread out his arms.

'That was our marketing director on the phone, and he said all this china is yours, for free.'

Mrs St Clair looked puzzled.

'I don't understand,' she said.

'Company policy,' John said. 'Every one thousandth customer gets a complimentary tea service.'

John started to edge towards the dining room door and the old lady stood.

'I still don't understand.'

'It's yours for free, no charge,' and John gave his big, giveaway porcelain smile. He was now in the hall.

'Don't I have to sign for anything?'

'We'll send the paperwork through the post. Sorry about leaving the box and wrapping paper.'

He was now opening the front door.

'Goodbye, and thanks,' he said.

'Well, *thank you*,' Mrs St Clair beamed.

John stepped outside, grabbed hold of the polished brass knob, and pulled the door shut behind him. He walked fast along the corridor and was nearly at the end when Eddie appeared and pressed the button summoning the lift.

The two men got in and stood impassively as the doors closed and they descended to the ground floor.

THIRTY ONE

Eddie returned to Wakefield Sunday afternoon but checked into a different hotel. He phoned Red and an hour later the two met in Eddie's room.

'I'm glad you're back,' Red said, placing a brown leather briefcase on the bed. 'It's been a bloody boring time. Cold too.'

Red opened the case and took out a large notepad where he'd meticulously written down the comings and goings of Dixie Fisher, her boyfriend and the woman who drove the old Toyota car. Who, Eddie had now found out, definitely worked for Mike Saxby. There was nothing surprising, and the results of Red's stakeout pretty much tallied with Eddie's previous stint.

Eddie didn't intend worrying about the job he had to do, that wouldn't solve anything. The right moment would come along. He knew it.

But it didn't happen on the Monday or the Tuesday.

*

Mike and Dixie were sitting at the small dining table in the flat finishing a Chinese takeaway and on their second bottle of wine. Half a dozen large candles their only light.

Mike was feeling relaxed. The laying of the site foundations were on schedule, there were no problems with delivery of materials, and the builder he'd employed had ironed out the last of the hitches with the sub-contractors. It seemed too good to be true.

'I like this town,' he said, and topped up their wine glasses.

'Certainly a different pace of life,' Dixie said.

'Yes, agreed, but I was talking about the style of the place. I love Georgian houses,' and Mike went on to explain that they reflected the prosperity of the days when, before the rise of Leeds and Bradford, Wakefield was the centre of the clothing trade.

'I see you've been studying the local history,' Dixie said.

'Just read a couple of brochures, that's all,' Mike replied. 'I like that style of architecture, a lot of old houses are still the best, built to last.'

The telephone rang and they looked at each other.

'Okay, I'll get it,' Mike grinned, and raised himself from his chair. 'You're getting lazy.'

'I'm full up, I ate more than you.'

Mike spoke into the telephone receiver then held it out towards Dixie.

'You'll have to move after all, it's for you.'

'Who is it?'

'Sandra.'

Mike went back and sat down, followed a couple of minutes later by Dixie.

'What was that about?' he asked.

'Sandra might be a bit late tomorrow. Her car's got problems, a friend's taking her and her son to school and then dropping her off here.'

'She ought to get a new car.'

'Yes, it is a bit of a banger, but I suppose it's hard bringing up a boy by herself.'

'Sandra's a good secretary,' Mike said.

'Yes she is,' Dixie agreed, and took a large sip of her wine. 'Talking about cars...'

Mike looked at Dixie as she stopped in mid-sentence.

'What were you going to say?' he asked.

'Oh, it's nothing.'

'Come on, what is it?' Mike prompted.

'I think I've seen my Father in Wakefield,' she blurted out in reply.

Mike looked puzzled.

'But he's dead.'

'No, not Tom Fisher, the other one I told you about. Danny Buckley.'

'When was this?'

'Just over a week ago. I was coming out of the car park at the supermarket and nearly ran into him.'

'Are you sure?'

'Yes...yes I am,' Dixie replied, her voice becoming firmer. 'Yes, I'd say it was Danny Buckley.'

'Why didn't you tell me before?'

'I suppose I didn't know how...or whether it was important or not.'

Mike smiled.

'You mean, you weren't really sure it was him.'

'Well, I am now.'

'Dixie, it was either a pure coincidence, or you were mistaken. Either way I don't think it matters.'

Dixie opened her mouth to say something but stopped.

'Don't let it bother you,' Mike continued.

'Yes, you're probably right,' Dixie agreed, and quickly changed the subject. 'Now, what were we talking about before the phone rang?'

'Architecture.'

'Umm, so we were,' and Dixie gave a coy smile, playing with her long black hair. 'What about *my* architecture, when *I* get old?'

Mike leaned back in his chair and appeared to think deep and hard before answering.

'Well, if you get too much subsidence you can always have plastic surgery, thick make-up will hide any cracks and a wig might come in handy if your thatch starts to thin.'

'Oh, thanks,' Dixie said. 'You make me sound like an old cottage which will soon be in need of renovation.'

'Not if you stick with me. My job is to create beauty, and make sure it lasts. So play your cards right and be nice to me. I assure you it will be worth it.'

They looked at each other, both grinning and a little tipsy.

'It sounds as though you're relating sex with your occupation,' Dixie said.

'Could be.'

'In that case it might have been better if you'd been a car mechanic.'

'Why?'

'Because then I'd know for sure I'd always be regularly serviced.'

Mike chuckled.

'Do you always talk this dirty?'

Dixie lowered her eyes seductively and put on an exaggerated sexy voice.

'Only when I'm with you, darling.'

Mike pushed back his chair then stood and pulled Dixie up towards him, their movement causing flickering shadows from the scented candles.

'How long have we known each other now?'

'Nearly a year.'

'I thought so,' and Mike picked her up in his arms and headed for the bedroom. 'I think it's about time you had an oil change.'

Dixie whispered something in Mike's ear as they went through the doorway which made him laugh.

'I don't know if that's in the car manual...so I might have to improvise.'

'That sounds interesting,' Dixie said, as she was lowered on the bed.

THIRTY TWO

Wednesday and Eddie was watching the flat. Not as cold as the previous two days but it was raining and windy. And the roads were dangerous with piles of fallen autumn leaves forming a slippery layer on the surface. Eddie had noticed that when he'd left his hotel in the suburbs and skidded slightly putting the brakes on going round a corner.

Mike Saxby left just before eight thirty, but an hour and a half later there was still no sign of the brown Toyota. Odd, because today was one of the days the part-time secretary worked. Maybe she was sick.

It was also the day when Dixie usually visited the building site in the country.

Several people had been in and out of the entrance since early this morning, and that was normal. But, because of the rain and umbrellas, it wasn't easy recognizing individuals. Much easier to identify cars.

And the red Mazda was still there.

Eddie sat huddled in the driver's seat. He had a thermos of coffee but didn't drink much, didn't want too much liquid in his bladder. The ever increasing rain would only remind him to go to the toilet, probably get drenched as well, on the walk to the local pub.

*

Sandra sat behind her PC busily hitting the keyboard. She'd finished three letters and had another two to write. Then there was some filing to do and a couple of phone calls to make.

Dixie was also behind her computer. She'd just e-mailed Gerry Dolan and was waiting for a reply when the phone on her desk rang. She picked it up on the third ring and was pleased to hear Mike's voice.

'Hello, darling,' she said, 'what can I do for you?'

'I think I must have left something behind this morning when I went to work. At least, I hope I did, I can't find it in my car.'

'What is it?'

'A large white envelope, it was delivered from London yesterday. Gerry did some alterations to the roof of one of the houses and the plans are in the envelope.'

'Any idea where it is?'

'Yes. I was looking at the plans last night, just before we had the takeaway...and then afterwards I got distracted. Remember?'

'Umm, yes I do,' Dixie gave a throaty chuckle. 'And you reckon the envelope is in the dining room?'

'Yes, I hope so.'

'Hang on, I'll look,' and Dixie left the lounge cum office and went into the separate room where they ate. As soon as she entered she saw the envelope on the table, picked it up and went back to the phone. 'Yes, I've found it. So what now?'

'I need it here,' Mike replied. 'But the weather is atrocious and I wasn't sure if you'd be coming to see me today. It's like a quagmire here.'

'No, I wasn't. As you say, the weather's lousy and I don't fancy traipsing all round your muddy building site. I thought I'd give today a miss.'

'I could meet you so you wouldn't have to get out of your car,' Mike said. 'And, I don't need it straight away. As long as I get it by four o'clock, that'll be fine. The person I want to discuss the change of plans with won't be here until then. So there's no rush.'

Dixie looked at her watch.

'It's only just coming up to noon, so there is plenty of time,' she agreed. 'Don't worry, I'll get it to you by four, and I'll phone you first. So make sure your mobile's switched on.'

'Thanks, see you later,' and Mike broke the connection. Dixie replaced the receiver and turned to Sandra.

'Are you going out for lunch today?'

'No, not in this weather,' Sandra replied. 'I brought a sandwich with me. I was going to have that and coffee.'

'Yes, I think that's what I'll have too.'

The two women had their break in the dining room then went back to work.

The phone call for Sandra came just after one o'clock. It was her friend, a woman neighbour, who'd given her a lift this morning and was supposed to pick up her son this afternoon then come for Sandra.

The friend's mother, who had heart problems, had been rushed into hospital.

'Sorry, but I won't be able to pick up Connor,' she apologized to Sandra.

'Don't be silly, you look after your mother, I'll make other arrangements,' Sandra assured her. 'Don't worry...and thanks for letting me know.'

'Something wrong?' Dixie asked, as she saw Sandra staring at the telephone.

'Yes, a bit,' Sandra replied, and went on to explain.

'So, what are you going to do?'

'I'll have to leave early, if that's okay with you...get a minicab, I suppose.'

Dixie looked thoughtful, then an idea came into her mind.

'Would you like to borrow my car?'

'Well...,' Sandra hesitated, unsure what to say.

'You know where Mike's working, don't you?'

'Yes.' Sandra was a local, lived in Wakefield all her life, and knew the city and surrounding countryside like the back of her hand.

'Mike needs something taken to him this afternoon, so why don't you take it in my car, then pick up your son from school. I'll phone Mike and let him know.'

'That sounds great, but when do you need your car back? Mine won't be fixed until some time tomorrow.'

'Whenever it's convenient for you,' Dixie replied.

'What about insurance?'

'What type have you got?'

'Only third party,' Sandra replied.

'Okay, I'll put you on my insurance as a named driver. Actually, it's not a bad idea because then you can use it at weekends, if you like, when Mike and I go to London. I'm sure Connor wouldn't mind riding around in a sports car. And it might help make yours last a bit longer.'

'Thanks, thanks a lot. I really appreciate it.'

'Okay, then that's settled,' Dixie said, genuinely glad she could do something to help. Sometimes she felt a bit guilty about her inherited wealth and sending a cheque to a charity wasn't the same as being able to personally help a friend. 'I'll phone my broker right now,' and a moment later Dixie was talking to her insurance broker, then she handed the phone to Sandra to pass on her details.

*

About two thirty Eddie saw a woman dressed in black leave the entrance to Dixie's property, run to the red sports car parked in the private road and get in. Eddie immediately switched on his motor and waited until the Mazda joined the traffic in the street then began to follow. If Dixie kept to her usual Wednesday routine then she should be heading out into the country, to her boyfriend. The only difference today was, she had left a couple of hours later than she normally did.

*

The young man sat with his feet up on the table, his chair leaning back on two legs. Carl was sheltering from the rain in the large porto-cabin used as a rest room by the builders.

There weren't many workers having a break today, most of them had already gone home early.

Carl took a swig of sweet tea from his chipped enamel beaker then a deep drag from the cigarette held in his other hand. He hadn't done much work himself but it wasn't his fault.

It was the weather. It was diabolical.

Carl drove a cement mixer truck and he'd only been able to deliver one load today because of the rain. Nobody was going to lay much cement in these conditions. He would have left the site earlier but promised to give his friend, Pete, a lift home to Wakefield. Pete, also in his middle twenties, was a labourer and bricklayer and they were going to a disco this evening, so they'd be able to make final plans on the drive back together.

It wasn't supposed to get dark until four thirty but the heavy rain clouds were speeding that up. Carl looked at his watch as the door opened and Pete appeared, drenched to the skin. Twenty minutes to three.

'Do you want to stay in here until the rain lets up?' Carl asked.

Pete grinned at him.

'I can't get wetter than wet,' he said. 'Besides, it ain't going stop. This is on for the rest of the day. So come on, let's get out of here.'

The two men left the porto-cabin and sprinted towards a gap in the trees that led into the field that was used as a car park. They reached the yellow painted heavy vehicle, opened the doors and jumped up inside.

'Phew, it's pissing down,' Carl grimaced, and swept his wet hair off his face. The rain had gone right through his worn anorak and he switched on the motor, revving hard, anxious to get the heater working.

'Take it easy,' Pete said, 'we don't want to get stuck in all this bloody mud.'

Carl nodded in agreement and slowly inched forward until it was safe to give the motor a bit more acceleration.

'Be all right, once we get on the road. Can't wait to get home and get these wet clothes off,' he said.

*

Eddie had his lights switched on. Not three o'clock yet, but the heavy rain and dark grey clouds made the visibility poor. The continual movement of the wipers didn't help.

The red sports car was about one hundred yards ahead of him, with no other cars in sight. He'd seen very few since he'd left the city's outskirts. Anyone with any sense wouldn't be out driving on a day like today.

Eddie had travelled these country roads enough times by now to know that in a few minutes the trees cleared and you could see the road twisting and winding steeply upwards for about half a mile. Then it dropped down out of sight over the other side of the hill. He pushed a bit harder on the pedal and the VW closed the gap on the sports car.

Then the road angled, the trees suddenly disappeared and Eddie saw lights of a vehicle come into view at the top of the incline winding downwards.

Eddie put further pressure on the accelerator and felt the motor respond.

*

Carl and Pete were now warm and drying off inside the truck. The radio was turned up loud and the two young men had to raise their voices to make themselves heard. The wind noise and rain outside making it worse.

'It should be good tonight,' Carl said.

'Yeah, I'm looking forward to it,' his friend said. 'If it's anything like last week I won't complain.'

'Yeah, we both pulled, but my one passed out on me when we got back to her place.'

'Mine didn't,' Pete laughed, and playfully punched Carl on his shoulder. 'Better luck tonight.'

'Let's hope so,' the driver said, and let the heavy truck pick up speed on its downward journey, not bothering to apply the brakes.

'Not too fast,' Pete said, checking his safety belt, 'not in this weather. I want to get home in one piece.'

Carl squinted through the rain lashed windscreen.

'Don't worry, there's not much on the road. Besides, people get out of the way when they see this coming towards them.'

*

Eddie was pushing hard on the tail of the sports car. He knew he'd only have one chance to pull it off and hoped to fuck he got the timing right. Beads of sweat showed on his forehead. Then he briefly saw lights in the distance heading towards him before they dipped out of sight, and trees again appeared on either side of the road, shutting off his view.

And then he was committed. Thrusting the accelerator to the floor he spun the steering wheel in his hands and shot past the red Mazda, then cut sharply in front. But, instead of speeding forward, Eddie hit the brakes, quickly eased off, praying not to skid, then changed down gear just as lights from the opposite direction hurtled towards him.

The driver of the sports car was startled as the Volkswagen suddenly appeared and slowed directly in her path. She immediately saw the danger, that she'd smash into the car unless she did something quick, and instinctively pressed as hard as she could on the brake pedal. But the wheels locked and the Mazda went into a skid. The driver looked frantically into the grey semi-darkness, the windscreen wipers working overtime, and tried to correct the slide. But the surface of the road was treacherous, with piles of wet leaves blown by the wind, and the driver wasn't used to the car.

The frightened face of Sandra stared helplessly, her heart thumping wildly, as the sports car spun sideways on to the opposite side of the road. She was vaguely aware of bright lights bearing down on her and the long, loud sound of a vehicle's horn blasting a desperate warning signal. But there was nothing she could do and the heavy concrete mixer truck smashed into the driver's side, pushing the Mazda along for a few yards before the sports car flipped over and impacted into the trees lining the road, finally coming to a stop.

What was left of it.

THIRTY THREE

Eddie drove around for an hour and stopped to fill up his petrol tank before driving back to where he'd overtaken the red Mazda. He was certain there had been a crash but the fleeting glimpse in his rear view mirror was too brief. And Eddie had to make sure.

It had now turned pitch black and the rain was heavier than earlier. Still not a lot of cars about but as he neared the spot saw flashing orange lights, two police cars, an ambulance and a low loader. A policeman in the middle of the road, wearing a bright yellow jacket, was directing traffic. He didn't look very happy as the rain lashed into his face.

As Eddie drove slowly past he saw police talking to two men by the side of a concrete mixer truck. Further along he viewed the remains of the sports car. Nobody could have got out of that alive.

Eddie drove carefully back to his hotel with the feeling of a job well done, and after making a phone call to his employer, checked out. He'd paid cash, given a false name and address, so that just left the car.

When Eddie arrived back in the capital he stayed at his own place and the next morning drove to a car breakers in west London. He knew the owner and they'd done business before.

Two hundred and fifty pounds cash and twenty minutes later the black Volkswagen Golf didn't exist. Just a block of compressed metal in its place.

Eddie walked to the nearest pub and had a few drinks before ordering a minicab, then phoned Kate to say he was on his way.

Eddie felt pleased, but all that evaporated after the weekend when he contacted his employer again, and got the bad news.

He'd killed the wrong woman.

*

The sight of the polished wood coffin being lowered into the hard, frosty ground brought memories of her parents flooding back. Dixie stood with Mike's arm around her amongst the group of a dozen people surrounding the graveside, her eyes riveted on the face of the seven year old boy clasping tight the hands of his elderly grandparents. Connor looked lost and bewildered, his pale face and fringe of black hair hanging over his forehead.

After the vicar finished speaking the grandmother took a flower from one of the bunches lying on the ground and handed it to the boy. She whispered to him and he threw the white carnation into the freshly dug grave on top of his mother's coffin.

Dixie moved towards him, bent down and looked into his sad eyes.

'How are you, Connor?' she asked in a gentle tone.

The boy stared back at her.

'I've lost my Mummy,' he replied in a pitiful voice, and held out his small arms in despair, then threw them around Dixie's neck, sobbing. Dixie held the boy close to her and felt his pain run through her body. She too couldn't stop the tears trickling down her face nor control her feeling of utter helplessness.

Finally, she straightened, fished a small packet of tissues from her handbag and dried the boy's eyes. She wanted to speak but didn't know what to say.

Dixie's eyes shifted to Mike and he gave her a comforting smile.

'Come on, Connor,' the grandfather said, a robust looking man with a red face and white hair. 'Say goodbye to Miss Fisher.'

The grandparents started to walk away, then the woman turned and looked at Dixie. 'Thank you,' she said.

It was over a week since the car crash. A shock that Dixie was still trying to come to terms with.

If Sandra's car hadn't broken down. If her friend's mother hadn't been taken to hospital. If she had delivered the plans to Mike instead of sending Sandra.

If only she could turn back the clock.

And then there was Connor. An innocent child, so young, but already a casualty of events in an adults world.

That's where Dixie could help. She wrote out a cheque for twenty five thousand pounds and a local solicitor was now making arrangements with the grandparents so that the money could be used for the child's upbringing and his future education. Dixie also made out a separate cheque for five thousand and gave it to Mr and Mrs Parry. They lived in a small semi-detached house and the grandfather made his living as a gardener. Not bad money in the summer but they had to tighten their belts in the winter. Now there were no immediate money worries and Dixie told them to keep in contact and let her know how Connor was getting on.

They were the good old fashioned sort of people who dearly loved their grandson and would give him a good home. All Connor needed was time - just like Dixie.

*

As Dixie and Mike started to leave the graveyard two young men stopped in front of them. Carl and Pete. They'd escaped injury in the crash, due to the unequal size of the vehicles but were devastated by the death of Sandra.

'I'm glad you came,' Mike said. 'Thanks.'

'It was the least we could do,' Carl said. 'We feel terrible about what happened.'

'I know,' Dixie said sympathetically. 'But try not to let it get you down. The family don't blame you at all, it was a tragic accident.'

There had been a post-mortem which had shown Sandra was not under the influence of drink or drugs. Not that there was any suggestion she should be, it was just a formality. The body had been released for burial and an inquest was scheduled for just over a week's time. But the police were satisfied it was an accident. The weather had been terrible, the road treacherous and Sandra wasn't used to driving the sports car. The two young men in the cement mixer truck didn't stand a chance of avoiding the crash. Sandra was on the wrong side of the road.

'We're just glad we didn't hit the other car as well,' Carl said.'

The crash had been in the local paper with a photo of the mangled Mazda. And there had been one thing in the report that had caught Dixie's attention.

'This other car that was mentioned, the newspaper article didn't make it clear if it was important or not,' she said. 'What do you think?'

'Well, it wasn't really. It was in front of the sports car and unless the driver had looked in his rear view mirror, wouldn't have seen anything. But the road dips and bends so much there it probably wouldn't have made much difference anyway. Mind you, it did look as though the Mazda was up the other car's tail. Your friend seemed to be driving too close.'

'You saw that?' Mike asked.

'It all happened so quick,' Pete replied. 'And it was very murky, what with the grey clouds, and it was nearly dusk. But I could see lights very close behind that black car which was in front.'

'*Black car*?' Dixie sounded puzzled. 'You could see the colour?'

'Yeah,' Pete replied. 'Carl was driving, trying to avoid the accident, so he didn't see as much as me. I was mesmerized...scared stiff...because I could see what was going to happen...and couldn't do anything about it.'

'The colour,' Dixie said.

'Oh, yeah, the colour...yeah, it was black or a very dark blue. Definitely a dark colour.'

'Did you notice the make?'

'The make? No, it all happened too quick. A saloon car of some description.'

'And the driver?' Dixie asked hopefully.

'No, I'm sorry,' Pete replied.

Mike looked curiously at Dixie then back at the two young men.

'Okay lads, once again, thanks for coming,' and Mike took hold of Dixie's arm and started to move. 'It's a bit cold out here, I think we should be going.'

'Yeah, sure,' Carl said, 'we should as well.'

The four walked out of the cemetery together then got in separate cars.

Mike switched on the ignition of his Range Rover but turned towards Dixie before putting the car in gear. He had a curious look on his face.

'Why the interest in that other car? Is there something I should know?'

'No, Mike, it's just that...well, I thought if the other driver had seen something...an animal in the road. Oh, forget it, it wouldn't help now anyway.'

Dixie had been fumbling for a reply because the words coming out of her mouth were not the thoughts in her mind.

A black car.

Dixie began piecing together the jumbled thoughts that had been gathering in the back of her mind for some time, not wanting to make a connection, scared she might be right.

But she had to face up to the facts.

Danny Buckley drove a black Volkswagen Golf. She had a photograph of it. Kate Smith's boyfriend had a black car. He also had grey curly hair like Buckley, as did the man who'd burgled Aunt Lucy's house.

And just weeks ago she'd seen Buckley here in Wakefield.

Now Sandra was dead. Killed while driving her car.

Danny Buckley - her father.

Dixie had to go back to London.

The answers were there.

THIRTY FOUR

Dixie spent several days after Sandra's funeral interviewing secretaries. She didn't want a temp or part-time employee, nor one that was married, had children or drove an old car. Finally she found the person she wanted and hired her on a full-time basis.

Miss Weller, a spinster in her early forties, wasn't the type of woman to be called by her christian name. She had excellent references and didn't mind the responsibility of having to open and lock up the flat. She looked a bit on the prim and proper side - and reminded Dixie of Kate Smith.

Dixie told Mike she needed to get away for a while, from the memory of Sandra, and the terrible accident. Also, she wanted to prepare for Christmas. Mike said he understood and drove Dixie to London on Saturday morning.

In the evening they went out for dinner with Linda and Joey, the first time the four of them had been together for some while. During the meal they discussed the fast approaching festive season and decided they would spend Christmas at Joey's mansion in Hampstead.

'And New Year,' the pop star insisted, to which the others readily agreed. 'A quiet Christmas, and a hell of a party on New Year's Eve.'

'Do you mean a piss-up?' Linda asked.

Joey raised his eyebrows.

'Did I hear you swear, young lady?' he grinned, and added. 'Yes, a good old fashioned piss-up.'

Joey had secretly started his elocution lessons and tried to get in an hour's practice every day in the privacy of his bedroom. He was talking slower, desperately trying to concentrate on pronouncing his aitches and the endings of his words. He was determined to keep at it even though at times he felt like Eliza Dolittle in My Fair Lady.

But, a few people were noticing, even if some were taking the mickey. However, his friends sitting at the table with him hadn't commented. He trusted he wasn't going to all this trouble for nothing and hoped they were just being polite.

When they left the restaurant they went back to Dixie's apartment for drinks, but Joey didn't stay the night, instead leaving by taxi about one in the morning.

On Sunday afternoon Mike had to leave for Wakefield so he'd be there the next day when Miss Weller started work.

'Going to miss you,' he said to Dixie when they kissed goodbye.

'Me too,' she said. 'But you'll be back next weekend, won't you?'

'Of course...Friday evening.'

During the drive Mike thought a lot about Dixie. He hadn't mentioned anything but he was worried about her. She seemed to have something on her mind though, what it was, he had no idea. It wasn't just the death of Sandra, he was sure of that. Although it had brought back memories of her parents crash, he was positive it was something else. Mike just hoped it wasn't serious.

No doubt she'd tell him in her own time.

*

Monday morning Dixie made several phone calls after Linda went to work, then left her apartment and walked to the nearest tube station. She'd thought about hiring a car but decided against it. Her Mazda was a write-off but she planned to wait until after the New Year celebrations before buying another motor. A Mercedes sports car this time.

Dixie changed trains at Kings Cross and took a Northern Line to Colindale station which was nearly opposite the British Newspaper Library. She showed her driving licence as proof of identity and signed in at reception near the front door. She then walked up a couple of flight of stairs to the first floor and asked at the enquiry desk for advice.

An hour later, after filling in request forms for the newspapers she wanted, she picked up the ordered boxes of microfilm and went to the machine she'd reserved.

She wound on spool after spool of film, every now and again adjusting the focus as she studied the newsprint on the large screen. She made notes on a pad she'd brought with her and two hours later was back on a tube train heading for home.

When her parents had died Dixie didn't look at the newspapers because she couldn't bring herself to read about the grisly details of the car crash. It would have been too upsetting.

In the library she'd ordered copies of all the local papers and national tabloids around the time of Tom and Margo's tragic death. And her findings were just as she'd suspected. She wasn't even surprised she was right. All along she'd had a feeling of dread that she would be.

As the train rattled along Dixie took out her pad and looked again through the notes. All the newspapers had reported much the same details and each gave the official conclusion reached by the police, that the punks driving a blue Ford Focus were solely to blame for the death crash.

But there was also one other item all the newspapers commented on. Something which still remained a mystery. What had happened to the driver of the stolen black Cherokee Jeep that slammed into the back of her parents Jaguar?

Witness reports were a bit hazy because everything happened so fast but the general consensus was that he couldn't stop in time. It didn't look as though it was his fault, even though he was close behind the Jaguar. He didn't appear to have much of a chance when Tom Fisher suddenly pulled up without warning.

The final detail every newspaper also agreed on was...*the mystery man was in his fifties with grey curly hair.*

*

It was when she arrived back at her flat that Dixie realized she hadn't eaten anything since breakfast. It was now the middle of the afternoon but she still didn't feel hungry. She wanted something stronger than coffee so Dixie went to the fridge, took out a bottle of white wine, opened it and took it into the lounge. She poured a glass, took a sip, and felt the wine hit her empty stomach.

Dixie sat in her favourite chair and read through her notes again as though looking at them might make a difference.

Then she got up, went into her bedroom, and opened the bottom drawer of the mahogany chest. She quickly found the large envelope she was looking for and went back into the lounge. She emptied the contents of the envelope on the coffee table and spread out the photographs, then stopped in amazement. Slowly she picked up the two photographs of Danny Buckley and gazed at them intently.

She was going mad. These weren't the same photographs. They were of a man with grey curly hair in his fifties, taken in the street, but it wasn't the same face. This man was much better looking, in a rugged sort of way. In fact, quite handsome. Nowhere as mean looking as the other photographs.

The other photographs?

What could she be thinking? They had to be the same. She turned them over and looked on the back. They were captioned in blue biro just like the others on the table in front of her. The writing was the same. She was going mad.

No she wasn't. These were not the same photographs or the same man. Then something else caught her eye and she picked up the picture of the black Volkswagen Golf. This was also different, she was sure of it. It was the same make of car but this one clearly showed the number plate. The other one hadn't.

Dixie put the photos back on the coffee table and took a drink of her wine.

They weren't the same pictures. She'd finally made up her mind on that. They'd been changed.

But who could have done that? And when?

It got dark and Dixie carried on drinking until she finished the bottle. A solitary table lamp, on a time switch, came on but she didn't move, just continued to sit there thinking. And that's how Linda found her, sitting in semi-darkness, when she came home from work at six thirty.

Linda immediately went to her friend and knelt on the carpet, holding Dixie's hands in hers, her eyes taking in the empty wine bottle and photographs strewn on the coffee table.

'What's wrong?'

Dixie looked at her friend.

'I honestly don't know,' she replied, in a strained voice, 'but I think someone's trying to kill me.'

'*Kill you*?'

'Yes.'

'Oh, Dixie, what on earth makes you think that?'

'I think Sandra, Mike's secretary, was murdered. I don't think it was an accident but a case of mistaken identity. I think someone thought it was me driving my sports car, and I was the one who should have died.' Dixie paused. 'I'm also pretty sure I know who was responsible.'

'What makes you think this?' Linda asked, her mind trying to make sense of what her friend was saying. It seemed too amazing for words. 'Have you got any proof?'

'No, but I just know I'm right,' Dixie replied, staring into Linda's eyes. 'And I don't think my parents car crash was an accident, either.'

'Of course it was, the police said so.' Linda let go of her friend's hand, took off her coat and turned more lights on. 'That's better,' she said, and looked once again at the empty bottle. 'Have you had anything to eat?

Dixie shook her head.

'No.'

'Then let me get something quick. Soup? Beans on toast?'

Dixie shook her head again.

'No, not yet, thanks,' and she picked up two of the photographs and offered them towards Linda. 'Do you recognize this man?'

Linda took the pictures and stared at the man's face in each. She shrugged her shoulders.

'No, I've never seen him before.'

'Look on the back.'

Linda did as she was told and turned the photos over. She read the name on the back then gazed incredulously at Dixie.

'It says Danny Buckley, but this isn't your father. This is a different man. Where are the other photographs?'

'Come and sit down, and let me try and explain what's going on. The trouble is I'm not all that sure myself.'

As soon as Linda sat in another chair Dixie slowly recounted everything she knew, finally pointing at the two pictures.

'I discovered those when I got back this afternoon.'

Linda was lost for words for a moment, then asked a question.

'When was the last time you saw the other photos?'

'The early part of this year. Remember the time I saw my Father when I went to Kings Cross?'

'Yes, yes I do,' and Linda remembered only too clearly the shock it had on Dixie.

'I put all those photographs in that envelope and put it in my chest of drawers. And I've not looked inside that envelope since then.'

'That means somebody must have got into this flat and switched them over,' Linda said slowly. 'But how? And when?'

THIRTY FIVE

They had gone out for a meal. Linda insisted on that. They went to a small Italian restaurant they'd been to before and thankfully Dixie got her appetite back once she saw the menu. She also got stuck into the wine and by the time they'd finished eating Dixie was slurring her words.

Dixie hadn't wanted to discuss the photographs or any of the other details she'd told her friend about over the meal, which suited Linda for the moment. Although, a few times she did catch Dixie staring into space, and it was easy to guess what was on her mind.

Dixie wasn't in the best of condition when they got back to their flat and all she wanted to do was go to bed. But Linda knew they *did* need to talk again soon because she was worried. No matter what else Dixie had spoken about, the fact was, somebody had been in their flat and swapped those photographs. And before Linda went to her bedroom made sure the chain was on the front door.

She wasn't taking any chances.

The next morning Dixie was up first and when Linda went into the kitchen coffee was waiting for her.

'Sorry about last night,' Dixie said a bit sheepishly. 'The demon drink.'

'Don't worry, I understand. You've got a lot on your mind and a lot of what you say makes sense. Have you any idea what we're going to do next.'

'*We*?'

'That's right, I'm going to take today off work, the rest of the week if necessary.'

'Thanks,' Dixie said. 'I've got a few ideas about what I'd like to do, and I'd certainly appreciate your company.'

'So what's first on the agenda?' Linda asked.

'John Fallows, he was the private detective I used to get those photographs and the information about Danny Buckley. I'm sure he'll be able to help.'

'Good thinking.'

'I've got a letter from him with the address and phone number on, so I'd thought I'd give him a call this morning.' Dixie looked at the kitchen clock which said it was just gone eight o'clock. 'Bit early yet but I thought I'd phone him about half nine. Give us time to get ready.'

*

When Dixie picked up the phone to speak to the private investigator she had pen and paper at the ready.

'Hello, can I help you?' a woman answered.

'Is that Fallows Investigations?' Dixie asked.

'Who is it you want?'

'John Fallows, he's a private detective.'

'Could you hold on a minute, please, I'll check,' the woman said. There was a momentary pause and then she came back on the line. 'No, we've nobody of that name listed here.'

'Excuse me,' Dixie sounded puzzled, 'but who are you?'

'This is an answering service,' the woman replied politely.

Dixie was confused.

'But I saw Mr Fallows at his office the early part of this year.'

'Well, I've checked, and that name definitely isn't on our current list.'

Dixie read out the address at the top of the letter she'd received. 'Is that your address?'

'No, all our clients live in different postal areas and use our telephone answering service because it saves them the cost of hiring a secretary. People phone here and then we contact our client and give him, or her, their messages.'

'So, have you got a number for John Fallows?'

'No, I'm sorry but I haven't. Besides, we don't pass on that sort of information. That's confidential.'

'I understand, thanks for your help,' Dixie said, and put down the phone.

'Is there a problem?' Linda asked.

Dixie quickly explained what she'd just been told. 'You see, I never had reason to call him before, so I never knew about this answering service,' she added. 'Strange that he's no longer using it.'

'He's probably got a new number now.'

'Yes, you're right,' and Dixie picked up the receiver again and got through to directory enquiries. But the operator told her there was no listing for Fallows Investigations at that address, nor under that name anywhere in London.

'There's only one thing to do,' Dixie said, 'let's put on our coats and get a taxi.'

'Where to?'

'I went to that address and saw John Fallows, so I know it exists. Let's see what we can find out there.'

Dressed in warm topcoats against the chill air, Linda, with a wool ski hat over her short curls and Dixie's long hair tied in a ponytail, they hailed a taxi and headed across the river Thames towards Wandsworth.

The taxi dropped them outside the large Victorian house which had been converted into office accommodation and the two women went through swing doors into the entrance hall, which Dixie remembered from her previous visit. She looked at the notice board which showed various business names but Fallows Investigations was no longer displayed, unlike the last time.

Dixie led the way up the worn carpeted stairs and noticed nobody had yet bothered to do any decorating. The place looked as rundown as before. She stopped outside a door on the second floor but the shiny nameplate now said, *Blazer Heating*.

Dixie looked at Linda, shrugged her shoulders, and pushed open the door to be immediately greeted by a babble of voices. There were plenty of telephones on the premises in here, four in the front small office and another eight in the larger back room. All on wood bench tables and manned by a mixture of young men and women reading from sheets of paper in front of them. Some of them were writing on pads of lined paper names addresses and other details obtained from the people they were talking to on the other end of the telephone.

From the gist of their conversations it appeared the people in the room were trying to sell central heating systems over the phone. Trying to get appointments for salesmen to pay the householders a visit.

One of the young women, a pretty teenager, replaced her telephone receiver and smiled at Dixie and Linda.

'Can I help you?' she asked pleasantly.

'The last time I was here this office was being run by a man called, John Fallows,' Dixie replied.

'Well, we've been here two months and I don't know anyone by that name.'

'Who's your boss?' Dixie asked. 'The person in charge. Maybe he will know.'

'Oh, that'll be Mr Norgate,' and the teenager pointed out into the corridor, 'go out this door, turn right and it's the next office. There's no name on the door, but just knock and go straight in.'

'Thanks,' Dixie smiled.

They went back outside, knocked on the first door on the right and entered. A sandy haired, well dressed man in his thirties, sitting behind a desk, held up his hand in acknowledgement to Dixie and Linda but carried on speaking into the phone. A minute later he finished and smiled at the two attractive women standing in front of him.

'Yes, ladies, what can I do for you? You're not here to complain about my central heating, are you? We're experiencing a few teething problems at the moment, that's all.'

'No, we're not here to complain,' Dixie assured him. 'I'd like some information, if possible.'

'Okay,' Mr Norgate said, obviously relieved with the answer. 'Fire away.'

'The early part of this year the office next door was run by a man called, John Fallows. He was a private detective and did some work for me. I visited him here and he posted some things to me, but now Mr Fallows seems to have disappeared.'

Mr Norgate shook his head slowly.

'Well, I took over these offices about two months ago and the people who were here before me were selling racing tips through the post. They went bust, I think.' Mr Norgate stared at the two women for a moment before continuing. 'Do you know what type of offices these are?'

'No,' Dixie replied.

'They're short-let offices. They're rented out on a monthly basis...one month, two months...depending on how long a person wants it for. If my business doesn't take off soon then I'll be leaving here in a month's time.'

'I see,' Dixie said. 'What about the landlord? Do you have a number where I could get hold of him?'

'Sure,' and the man opened a desk drawer, took out what looked like some headed notepaper, copied a name and number on to a sheet of paper and handed it to Dixie. 'But I'm not sure if you'll find the person you're after. There's no references needed when you want to rent space here. As long as you've got the cash up front there's no questions asked. By all means phone the landlord, but I don't think you'll get very far. A lot of dodgy people use this building. Me excluded, of course,' he laughed, then rose to his feet. 'If you don't mind ladies, I've got some work to do.'

Dixie and Linda took the hint and opened the door.

'Thanks for all your help,' Dixie said as they left.

Linda couldn't help chuckling as they walked back down the stairs.

'At least he was honest,' she said.

'Yes, but we're no further ahead,' Dixie said, deep in thought. By then the two women were standing outside on the pavement, feeling the cold on their faces, the sun feebly trying to penetrate the grey sky.

'What now?' Linda asked.

'Let's find somewhere to have a coffee,' Dixie replied.

They weren't too far from Wandsworth Common and after briskly walking for about seven or eight minutes saw a pub.

'An orange juice instead, eh?'

'Yes, that'll be fine' Dixie replied. 'I just want somewhere warm so I can make a phone call.'

The pub wasn't very busy, still a bit early, and when they'd been served and sitting at a table Dixie took out her mobile and called the number Norgate had given her.

But the response was as he'd forecast.

'I'm sorry, but we don't give out information about clients, past or present. That's confidential,' a brusque sounding man replied to her query.

'So what now?' Linda asked.

Dixie looked at the chalked menu above the food counter, then at her watch.

'Soon be lunch-time, so let's eat, then go back to the flat and work something out.'

THIRTY SIX

They'd discussed everything several times over by the time they got back to the flat and Dixie immediately opened up the envelope and laid out the contents on the coffee table.

'I wonder what all this means?' Dixie asked aloud.

'I still find it hard to believe that someone is trying to kill you,' Linda said.

Dixie frowned and looked at her friend.

'Okay, okay, let's assume what you say is right,' Linda continued quickly. 'What you've got to come up with is a reason.'

'I know, and I've been racking my brains, but I can't come up with anything. I really can't.'

'And you're positive you don't want to go to the police?'

'As I've already told you, Linda, I don't have any proof, so what could I say? That I think my Father, Danny Buckley, killed Tom and Margo. That he burgled Aunt Lucy's house and killed my boyfriend's secretary. That his girlfriend, Kate Smith, has disappeared along with a missing private detective. Oh, and by the way, there are now two Danny Buckley's. And the photographs I've got aren't of the man I think is behind this.' Dixie gave a small laugh. 'No, somehow I don't think the police would be very receptive.'

'Well, it's true,' Linda said.

'Yes, and I'm sure if anything happens to me then they'll believe it. But that will too late. Still, you'll be able to tell them.'

'Don't be silly, nothing will happen to you. We'll sort it out before anything like that takes place.' Linda tried to sound as convincing as she could.

Dixie didn't continue the conversation but pulled out her address book and picked up the cordless phone. She punched in some numbers and waited.

'Hello, Mrs Powis, this is Dixie Fisher, do you remember me? I'm a friend of Kate Smith, your next door neighbour.'

'Dixie Fisher,' the old lady repeated, 'yes, I remember you. But Kate never came back. She sold her house, you know, but the new people haven't moved in yet. The builders are doing some work next door.'

'And you're sure you haven't seen her, or her boyfriend?'

'No, definitely not, and if she had come back she'd have knocked on my door. I know she would.'

'Okay, Mrs Powis, you've still got my number?'

'Yes.'

'Well, if you should happen to see Kate Smith, please let me know straight away.'

'Yes, okay, Miss Fisher.'

'Goodbye, and thank you.'

'I don't see why you won't call your Uncle Robert,' Linda said, after Dixie had clicked off the phone. 'After all, it was through him you found this private detective.'

'I know, but something's bugging me at the back of my mind, and I don't think I should at the moment.'

'You don't think your uncle is mixed up in this, do you?' disbelief in Linda's voice.

'No, of course not,' was Dixie's emphatic reply. 'But there are two reasons why I don't want him to know right now. First, he'd worry about me, and second, he might mention this to someone else. Uncle Robert didn't actually find John Fallows for me. He spoke to his solicitors, and maybe other people as well, and then the private detective contacted me. Now, I've got a feeling someone is mixed up in this who knows me, and Uncle Robert might inadvertently voice my suspicions to the wrong person.' Dixie grimaced. 'I just hope I don't sound paranoid.'

'So what's next?' Linda asked.

'Two things,' Dixie replied. 'Tomorrow I'll have the locks changed, then I'm sure we'll both sleep better in our beds.' Linda seemed as though she was about to say something but held her tongue when Dixie picked up the two photos of Danny Buckley, looked at them, and passed them over. 'Then I must find him...and talk to him. I just hope the information that Fallows man sent me is correct.'

'You know,' Linda said, 'I think this is the real Danny Buckley. He's much better looking. You couldn't have got your looks from the other one. He looked a hard nut.' Linda put the photographs back on the coffee table. 'But it could still be a bit dangerous. When do you think you'll try and see him?'

'I'll speak to Mike first. I'd like him to be with me,' Dixie replied.

'Good idea.'

'I just wonder what his reaction will be when I tell him about this.'

'You mean you haven't told him yet?' Linda sounded astonished.

'No, I wanted to come back to London first and go to the newspaper library. And, don't forget, when I left Wakefield I didn't know about the photographs being switched. I had a feeling something was wrong, that's why I came back, but I wasn't certain. Besides, Mike's very busy at the moment.'

'Well, I think you should tell him,' Linda said.

'Yes, so do I now, but I don't want him haring back to London straight away just because of me. I'm going to ask him to make arrangements for Gerry Dolan to take his place for a few days.'

'What reason will you give?'

'That I need his help. That it's personal and I don't want to talk about it on the phone. I know Mike, he won't ask questions, he'll just come. But I don't want to worry him, Linda, so I'll say in a day or two's time will be okay.'

'I'll take time off work and stay with you until then.'

'Thanks,' Dixie said, and picked up the phone.

*

Eddie had been in a foul mood for a few days when he discovered the wrong woman had been in the sports car. He was a criminal, that's what he did for a living, and hated making mistakes.

Kate had noticed his sudden change and commented on it, but Eddie assured her she'd done nothing wrong. He'd let her know his recent periods of absence had been due to business trips up north and had just heard something had screwed up. He was sorry if he'd taken it out on her and said he only had their best interests at heart.

Eddie had told her as soon as they got the last payment of one hundred thousand pounds they would move abroad. Go to Spain or Portugal, or somewhere like that. Buy a house and start a new life together. But that was just to keep her happy. He *did* intend leaving the country, but whether or not he was going to take her, he still wasn't sure. It all depended upon circumstances. Eddie wasn't selfish, it was a matter of survival. He'd realized that when he was young and had his first tangle with the law.

He had to put himself first. A rule he'd stuck to ever since.

Then there was John to take into consideration. The man who'd posed as the boss of Fallows Investigations, the only other person who knew the full extent of what Eddie was up to. John, too, would like to move to a foreign country, preferably with a warm climate. He'd also been successful over the years and had quite a bit of money put away. Running a business together appealed to the two men.

Go straight. At least they could try it for a while.

Eddie left Kate in the flat, telling her he wasn't sure if he'd be back that night. She said she understood and told him to keep in touch by phone.

The small one bedroom apartment near Earl's Court was in a large block with long hard tiled corridors and Eddie's footsteps echoed as he walked to the stairs. He chose this route from the third floor because the porter on the desk didn't have such a clear view as he did with the lifts. Not that it really mattered because the men who took it in turn to do the eight hour duty shifts were usually reading a newspaper, or watching a small portable television, huddled close to a radiator.

Eddie went out into the street, walked to the tube station, and bought a ticket. He'd need other transport soon but hadn't yet decided what kind. He wasn't sure if it would be a car or motorcycle because that depended on what was going to be best for the job. Eddie was more determined than ever to make up for his mistake but, he realized, the young Fisher woman would probably be on her guard now. God knows, he'd left enough clues.

By now she should have figured things out, which was originally intended. It was hoped she'd tell people of her suspicions - and then she would die - with the finger of guilt focusing on someone else.

That's what his employer had planned on - but Eddie had screwed things up. And it wasn't going to be easy now.

Eddie got off the train at Whitechapel in the East End and walked ten minutes to his house. He'd paid key money to the previous tenant of the newly built two bedroom council house ten years ago, assumed his name, and nobody bothered him. All his bills were paid on time and he'd never mixed with the neighbours. Any who had tried to be friendly got a polite smile, and that was it. After a while people stopped trying and Eddie was left to himself. Except for Kate and John no-one else had ever been inside.

He took off his topcoat and walked up the stairs to the spare bedroom. He went to a chest of drawers against one wall, moved it into the centre, and pulled back the fitted carpet, just like he had done in Kate's flat. He took a large screwdriver from the bottom drawer, levered up a couple of floorboards, then pulled out a 9 millimetre automatic and a sawn off shotgun. Inserting his hand again he came up with a box of shotgun shells.

Eddie replaced the carpet and drawers as they were and went back downstairs into the lounge. He poured himself a generous whisky then set about cleaning and checking the two weapons. About an hour later he phoned John and asked him to come over. He'd worked out something but knew it needed talking through with his friend.

After all, they would both be putting their liberty on the line, possibly their lives.

*

When Dixie spoke to Mike that evening she found it hard to bring into the conversation what was really on her mind without sounding too serious. But Mike sensed there was something wrong and made it easy for her.

'Something's bothering you, Dixie. What is it?'

'No, no, I'm fine...everything's okay.'

There was silence as they both paused.

'I don't believe you,' Mike said. 'You've had something on your mind for some time. I know it.'

There was silence again.

'Yes, Mike, you're right,' Dixie finally admitted, 'but I'm not sure what, not exactly. I would like you here with me though. Could you get Gerry to take over from you in Wakefield for a few days?'

'Of course, I'll phone him immediately.'

'No, there's no rush. You don't have to come straight away...in a couple of days will be fine.'

'What's wrong, Dixie? Level with me.'

'I don't think Sandra's crash was an accident,' she replied in a subdued voice. 'I think someone drove her off the road because, I think, *that person*, thought *I* was in the car.'

Mike was stunned as Dixie's words sank in.

'You mean...what you're saying, is that somebody is trying to kill you. Is that right?'

'Yes.'

'What makes you think this?'

'Oh, Mike, I've got so much to tell you. But I don't want to go over it on the phone.'

'Okay, Dixie.'

Mike knew his woman well enough to know she was an incredibly sensible, level headed person and, amazing as her story sounded, believed her unquestioningly.

'Let me phone Gerry, and I'll call you back,' he said, and as soon as the connection was broken contacted his business colleague.

Mike didn't go into detail, but explained it was an urgent personal matter, and Gerry immediately agreed to his request, but said he'd have to go to their London office first and wouldn't be in Wakefield until about one o'clock.

'That's fine,' Mike said, 'but I might need you up here for as long as a week. I'm not sure.'

'That's okay,' Gerry said. 'Trisha might moan a bit but,' and he laughed, 'it'll give me a break from the kids.'

Gerry had only been married five years and already had three children. 'I'll phone the hotel I've stayed in before and book in for a week. You take your time. And don't worry. Laura is quite capable of running the London office.'

Gerry didn't ask questions because he knew it must be important for Mike to want a week off. He never took time off - not even for a holiday.

'Thanks,' Mike said. 'See you tomorrow.'

He called Dixie back and told her he'd be arriving at her flat sometime tomorrow afternoon.

'And I don't want you stepping outside your front door until I arrive. Is that understood?'

'Yes, I promise. Anyway, Linda isn't going to work. She's staying with me. So don't worry.'

*

Gerry arrived at the time he said he would and minutes later Mike was in his Range Rover heading for London. It was another cold winter day and Mike wondered if they'd have snow again this Christmas, like last year, when he'd first met Dixie.

He picked up his mobile phone.

'I'm on my way,' he said, after the woman he'd been thinking about answered.

'Good,' Dixie said. 'Make sure you drive carefully.'

'Yes, I will...but tell me, Dixie,...tell me more about what's happening.'

'No, Mike, I'll tell you everything when you get here.'

'Okay then...if you say so.'

Dixie heard the disappointment in his voice, so added, 'It's to do with Danny Buckley, my real Father, but I'm not saying anymore until I see you.'

'I understand...I'll be with you soon.'

Mike pressed his foot harder on the accelerator and the speedometer needle crept upwards.

THIRTY SEVEN

Danny Buckley got up from his cluttered desk, looked out the window and noticed the sun trying to break through the dull looking clouds. Not that it would do much to enhance the view over the back yards of the warehouses. His was one of six businesses situated not far from Kings Cross Station. The rent was cheap, but that wasn't much compensation for the neglected and rundown area.

The phone rang on his private line and Danny sat down again.

'Hi Ronnie,' he said, recognizing his friend's voice.

'Did you get the money?'

'No, not all of it. Not yet,' Danny replied

'Do you think you'll be able to raise it?'

'Probably, but I'm not sure if I'll be able to get all of it in time.'

'I can give you a week, but no longer, Danny. I've got at least two other people who want to come in on the deal.'

'Okay, I'll definitely let you have an answer in the next couple of days.'

Danny put down the phone and stared into space. He was past fifty and fed-up with always being short of ready money. It seemed to be the story of his life and he was no further ahead than he'd been in his twenties. Every time a deal came along it seemed he was always scrabbling to raise the capital. Yeah, he'd be able to live without this present one, but he'd still liked to have had a part of the action.

He ran a hand through his grey curly hair and sighed. He knew he'd never be able to raise the cash he needed but was too embarrassed to tell Ronnie that. Not yet, anyway. He'd call him the day after tomorrow and by then would have thought of some way to get out of it, without losing face. Oh well, he consoled himself, it was nice to have been thought of in the first place. But he didn't have a spare ten grand.

There was a soft knock and his door opened.

'You're a bit late today. What time are you going to lunch?' Mandy, his secretary, asked. She was an attractive, bubbly redhead of thirty and wore short mini skirts.

Danny looked at his watch, an expensive gold one. The same as his clothes, all expensive. Thank christ for credit cards.

'I'll go now,' he replied, rising from his chair and putting on his suit coat. 'It's nearly one thirty. I didn't realize it was this late. Mustn't miss my drinking time.'

'Make sure you don't spend the afternoon in the pub,' Mandy smiled.

'Yes ma'm.' He returned the smile and patted her cheek on his way out. 'Phone me if anything urgent comes up.'

The two of them took it in turns for lunch, making sure there was always one of them on the premises during office hours. Unless, of course, Danny was away on business, then Mandy stayed in for lunch. Which she moaned about, but only good-naturedly.

There was also another employee, Chris, a young man in his early twenties. Not the brightest of sparks but he was a strong, hard worker and enjoyed keeping himself busy downstairs amongst the racks and shelves, always tidying and checking the goods. And listening to his radio.

Danny had contacts up and down the country on the lookout for bankrupt stock and bulk buying of slightly damaged goods. He also had an in with some people who imported leather goods from eastern Europe at knockdown prices. Everything paid for in cash, of course, with only enough invoices to keep the taxman happy.

These items Danny then sold on to his customers, who were mainly market traders and cheap discount stores.

There wasn't a lot of profit in his business but it kept the bailiffs from the door and he made a reasonable living.

He arrived at The Grapes pub and opened the door to the saloon bar, glad to get in out of the cold. It was busier than usual and he had to push his way through the crowd to get to the counter.

'Wotcha want, Danny?' the barmaid shouted above the noise.

'Large gin and tonic,' he replied. 'You're busy today, someone win the lottery?'

'Naw, Jack Gee just got out the nick. The lads are giving him a bit of a do.'

Danny paid for his drink and took a sip before looking around. Jack Gee. He was about the same age as Danny and had just finished a ten stretch for armed robbery on a security van which had been carrying over a million pounds in cash. Jack had been unlucky to get caught but never grassed up his mates who were with him on the job.

He had just done his bird quietly, and word had it there was a nice wedge of money due to him when he got out. Jack was well respected in his own world. A man who could be trusted - but not to be crossed.

Danny finished his drink, bought another, and edged closer to the group surrounding Jack. Their eyes touched and both men smiled.

'Hello, Danny,' and Jack put down his pint glass and shook hands. Jack had a grip like steel. He was a hard man and had a ferocious reputation as a street fighter. 'Good to see you.'

'You too, Jack.'

They had met for the first time in Wormwood Scrubs prison a long time ago. Jack was doing three years for GBH and burglary, and Danny five years for manslaughter, which came as a big shock to his system. The only other brush he'd had with the law was when he'd been put on probation for receiving stolen goods. But that one prison sentence made Danny vow he'd never go back inside again. It wasn't that it was tough, it was his loss of freedom that really got to him. When his marriage had busted up he'd gone pretty wild for a few years, but he knew he could never handle being banged up again. He tried to be more careful these days.

But that didn't mean he'd ever let a good deal go by, even if it was a bit hooky.

Danny was pleased to see the recent years as a guest of Her Majesty's government didn't appear to have done his friend any harm.

'Thanks for going and seeing my Mother,' Jack said. 'I appreciate it.'

'She's a nice lady,' Danny said. A visit once a month and a bottle of gin and a box of chocolates at Christmas plus a present on her birthday was the least he could do. He'd never visited Jack in the nick but Jack understood Danny's aversion to prisons.

'Would you like to come to a party this evening?'

Danny looked questioningly at his friend.

'It's over at Micky Dawson's place in Kentish Town,' Jack continued. 'There should be some interesting people there. You could do yourself some good.'

'Is the party for you?'

Jack didn't answer but grinned broadly.

Micky Dawson was the head of a family of well known north London villains. A right tasty lot. Danny knew Micky, but not that well, so this would be a good opportunity to further that relationship. And a personal invite from Jack, the guest of honour, would help enormously.

Obviously, the party was a coming home present, and it didn't need a mind reader to work out why.

'I'll see you in here this evening,' Jack said, 'about seven thirty.'

THIRTY EIGHT

It was quarter to eight when Mike brought his Range Rover to a halt fifty yards from the Grapes pub. He'd driven past twice before picking his parking spot.

'You okay?'

'Yes, just a bit nervous, that's all,' Dixie replied.

'Don't worry, everything will be all right,' and Mike opened his door and walked round to Dixie's side. It was a cold, damp evening with spots of moisture settling on his hair. Rain or sleet? Hard to tell.

Dixie slipped out of the car and slung the black strap of her leather bag over her shoulder. The street looked dingier than she remembered, with a couple of street lights seemingly operating on half power. Still, the glow from behind the pub's frosted glass seemed inviting.

They entered and glanced around before moving to the bar. There were only about twenty people in the pub.

'There, in the corner,' Dixie whispered.

Mike looked, and sitting at a table were two men in their fifties. The one with grey curly hair he recognized from the photographs. The other man also had grey hair but it was straight and cut very short. His broken nose was obvious from his profile and Mike instinctively knew from his upbringing in the East End that he was a man to be respected.

The Grapes was a busy pub during the day and catered for local workers and passing trade, but business dropped off in the evening. With its brown nicotine stained walls and ceiling it wasn't trendy enough for the younger set, which suited the regulars.

Mike ordered a brandy and ginger for Dixie, and a bottle of lager for himself from the young blonde barmaid.

'Is that Danny Buckley sitting in the corner?' Mike asked, as the girl gave him his change.

'Yes, that's Danny,' she replied, and added, eager to help, 'he's sitting with Jack Gee.'

'Thanks,' Mike said.

'What now?' Dixie asked, when the barmaid moved away to serve another customer.

'There's no hurry,' and the young man and woman sipped their drinks where they stood.

Danny had noticed them walk in. A good looking couple, the woman an absolute stunner, and he couldn't help staring.

'The same again, Danny?' and he jerked his eyes back to Jack, who was holding up their empty glasses.

'Yeah, okay,' Danny replied, and his friend lifted himself off his chair and walked to the bar.

'Let's go,' Mike said, as the granite faced man reached the chipped wood counter a few feet from him. Dixie and Mike left their drinks on the bar and walked towards the table. They stopped and looked down at the grey haired man sitting by himself.

Danny had watched the two approach his table with interest and wondered what they could want when they stopped.

'Danny Buckley?' Mike asked.

'Yes, can I help you?'

'We're hoping you can,' but then Mike paused, knowing he was about to drop a bombshell. However, there was no other way to do it. 'This is Dixie Fisher.'

It was incredible the change that came over Danny's features as Mike's words sank in. Disbelief melted into shock and then changed to amazement as Danny started to rise from his chair.

'You mean, *my* Dixie?' he managed to get out as he stared hard at the beautiful young woman in front of him.

'You were married to my Mother, Margo, weren't you?'

'Yes...a long time ago,' Danny replied, pronouncing his words slowly, still in shock. 'I'm sorry about what happened...I read about the car accident in the papers.'

Dixie nodded but didn't say anything. Talking about meeting her father was one thing, but now he was standing just feet away from her, she was lost for words. If she'd met him with the intention of trying to be friends, a daughter and long lost father reunion, that would have been different.

If only it was that simple.

'*Are you trying to kill me, Danny Buckley*?' flashed through her mind. But how could she ask him that?

Nevertheless, that's why she was here.

Mike, sensing Dixie's discomfort, stepped in.

'We'd like to have a talk with you,' he said.

'Of course, anything you want,' Danny said, motioning with his hand. 'Take a seat,' and he lowered himself back down. 'Now, what is it?' he smiled and, as soon as he did that, all feeling of dread vanished from Dixie. He had a nice smile, a warm smile. A smile her mother must have loved. So different from the other man.

Dixie put her hand inside her shoulder bag, withdrew a large brown envelope and placed it on the circular Formica table top.

Danny stared at the envelope knowing it must have something to do with the young woman being here. He found it difficult to say in his mind, *his daughter*. But she was - and amazingly - sitting here in his local with him. His brain was overflowing with thoughts and everything jumbled up. Dixie must be twenty four now, but she'd been too young to walk the last time he'd seen her. He'd often thought of them meeting, but now it had happened, he didn't know how to handle it.

However, Dixie had made the first move so he had to leave it up to her.

'Excuse me.' Jack Gee had returned with a pint of beer and a large gin and tonic for his friend. Dixie moved the envelope as the drinks were placed on the table and then spoke.

'Mike, why don't you and this gentleman have a drink at the bar, and leave this to me.'

The young man looked surprised but stood up.

'Are you sure?'

'Yes,' Dixie replied, and turned her eyes toward Danny. 'I'm sure I'll be quite safe.'

'Of course you will,' Danny said, not sure what to make of her remark. 'Do you mind, Jack?' he asked his friend who was still standing. 'This is Dixie...I've told you about her.'

'Yes, no bother,' Jack said, just as surprised as his friend. He *did* know about the broken marriage and that Danny had a little girl somewhere. And here she was, all grown up. But what had made her suddenly turn up out of the blue? No doubt Danny was in the process of finding out. 'Come on, let's go to the bar,' he said to Mike, and they walked away from the table.

'I really am sorry about Margo,' Danny said. 'I did think about trying to contact you, but then, I thought you'd have enough on your mind without me suddenly appearing in your life. So I just left it.'

The two sat staring at each other. Their meeting was awkward - and they both knew it.

'The last time I saw you, you weren't even a year old,' Danny continued. 'So, young lady, what can I do for you? I think it must be pretty important for you to go to the trouble of tracking me down.'

'I don't think my Mother's death was an accident,' Dixie said.

'Not an accident? I don't understand.' Danny looked bewildered.

Dixie pulled the contents from the envelope and laid out the photographs, marriage certificate and two sheets of foolscap of information supplied by John Fallows.

'Have a look,' Dixie invited, and Danny slowly went through the contents on the table, his face becoming even more puzzled.

'After my Mother died I found this marriage certificate and your divorce papers...and I thought I'd try and find you...just in case you didn't know about Margo's death. So I went to a private detective for help.'

'Well, all this information about me is correct, so are the photos,' Danny said. 'But the date on this letter is in March. Why wait so long?'

'I didn't, I came to see you the day after I received that envelope.'

'You did?' and the confused expression was back on Danny's face.

'Yes, and that's one of the reasons why I'm here. I think I should explain what I know first, and then you may be able to help me.'

But before Dixie could begin her explanation Mike and Jack returned to the table.

'I'm going to have to leave,' Jack said. 'I know you're busy, but try and make it later. I'll be over at Mickey's place for the rest of the evening and I know you'll be welcome. You know the address, don't you?'

'Yes,' Danny replied. 'Don't worry, I'll be there, but I'm not sure when.'

'Okay, see you later,' Jack said. 'Nice to have met you,' he added, looking at the young man and woman.

'You too,' Dixie smiled, as Mike sat down beside her.

'That's the kind of man I'd rather have as a friend, and not an enemy,' Mike said, as Jack walked to the pub door.

Danny looked at Mike with a trace of amusement in his eyes.

'You're a good judge. Jack's a hard man, but he's a very fair man. He's never the first to start trouble but I've seen a few men try to take liberties with him, then wished they hadn't.' Danny shook his head. 'Everyone of them ended up in hospital.'

The three were so engrossed they didn't take any notice of the man who entered the pub as Jack left. The man, with close cropped red hair, scanned the room then walked to the bar and ordered a pint of bitter. Glass in hand he moved towards the three, sat at the next table, and pulled from his coat pocket a copy of the London Evening Standard.

He opened the newspaper - and pretended to read.

THIRTY NINE

The older man smiled at the young couple.

'We've not been introduced. Are you Dixie's boyfriend?'

'Oh, I am sorry,' Dixie said, feeling embarrassed. 'This is Mike, Mike Saxby. And yes, he is my boyfriend.'

Danny stuck out his right hand.

'Pleased to meet you,' he said, and the two men shook hands.

Danny picked up one of the pictures of himself and scrutinized it.

'I wonder when this was taken?'

'That wasn't the original photograph I had,' Dixie said. 'I met a different man who said his name was Danny Buckley.'

There was a brief silence.

'You're saying someone has been impersonating me?'

'It looks that way,' Dixie replied.

'You said you were going to explain something to me.'

Dixie nodded her head.

'That's right,' and slowly she related everything, with the odd bit of help from Mike, finishing with her recent fruitless visit to John Fallows office.

'That's certainly some story,' Danny said. It was a story that, at first, had been hard to believe but as he'd studied the faces of the young couple knew *they* believed every word. And as he'd listened their words had become more and more plausible. Also, it fitted in with a couple of things which had happened to him over the months.

Danny reached out and picked up the letter lying on the table, once again studying it. 'The date here...that just about fits...' and he lapsed into silence, a thoughtful expression on his face. 'Also about the time you say your Aunt Lucy was burgled. Ycs, that would fit as well. I thought there was something fishy at the time.'

The older man replaced the letter on the table.

'What are you talking about, Mr Buckley?' Mike asked. 'Do you know something we don't?'

The man sitting opposite took a sip of his drink and put the glass back on the table.

'Call me, Danny,' he said.

Mike nodded.

'Sure.'

'What I'm talking about,' Danny continued, 'is something that ties in perfectly with what you've been telling me. But let's take your story first, and I think there are several main points. If Margo and Tom were murdered, then I think this Kate Smith knew who was behind it, and is blackmailing him. The envelope she left with Lucy was meant for you in case something happened to her. Probably the name of the person behind this is written inside.'

'But she took it back,' Dixie said.

'Yes, so I think her plan must have changed. Now she's on the missing list, and you haven't had a letter sent to you, so I presume she's still alive. The other thing is, someone has gone to a lot of trouble to try and implicate me, even driving the same make and colour car.' Danny paused. 'This other man, did he look much like me?'

'Well,' Dixie replied, 'there is a similarity, he's about the same age as you, and about the same build. But it's the hair mainly. He's also got grey curly hair, and from a distance he could easily be mistaken for you.'

She wanted to add that Danny was much better looking but somehow thought it would sound too smarmy, so didn't.

'And don't forget,' Dixie added, 'I didn't know what you looked like. I'm sorry, but I couldn't remember you,' and her voice tailed off softly.

'No, of course not,' Danny said, his voice equally as soft. 'But,' and he raised his voice a pitch, 'the bottom line is, someone is trying to hurt you, and putting me in the frame. Any idea why?'

'No,' Dixie replied. 'Everyone's asked me that and I honestly can't think of a reason.'

'One thing I don't understand,' Mike said, 'is the chance that man took when he met Dixie outside your office. You might have come along any minute and spoilt everything.'

'That's right,' Danny said, 'and that's one of the things I was saying a minute ago that fits.' And over the next few minutes Danny explained what kind of business he was in, how it worked and the fact that he had contacts all over the country on the lookout for cheap goods he might be interested in.

'I'd have to double-check, but I'm certain a few days before the date on this letter, I got a phone call from a man I didn't know. He said he'd heard of me through the grapevine, and had some stuff going very cheap. It's not unusual for me to get phone calls like this so I went to Newcastle to meet this bloke where he showed me a lockup nearly full with stationery items. Paper, envelopes, pens, note pads, rubbers...that kind of thing...all easy to sell in my kind of business.'

Danny took another drink from his glass.

'I thought he was going to ask a couple of grand for the lot but all he wanted was five hundred,' he continued. 'This man assured me the stuff wasn't stolen but was bankrupt stock. However, there was one snag, I couldn't have the goods until I met the person who'd gone bust. And then it got very strange. This man checked me into a small bed and breakfast hotel, said it belonged a friend, so it wouldn't cost me anything, and there I waited. I stayed for three days and then it turned out I didn't have to see this person who'd gone bankrupt after all - and the gear was mine.

'I got Chris, he works for me, to drive and meet me in Newcastle and I paid out five hundred quid. I'd had three days eating and drinking, all on the house, and got a very good deal as well. I wasn't complaining but I thought it strange at the time, and now I think I know why. It looks as though someone was trying to get me out of the way,' Danny paused for a moment before continuing. 'And, about the time of your aunt's burglary, I met the same man, but in Birmingham this time. I was only there for one night, but again, it didn't cost me anything and I got another nice deal out of it.'

'What was this man's name?' Dixie asked.

'John...I only knew him by his first name, but then, I know a lot of people just by their first name. But I never had a phone number for him, not even a mobile. He said he preferred it that way. And I didn't push because, well, in my line of business some people are a bit cagey.'

'So you don't know how to get hold of him?' Mike asked.

'No, he said he'd contact me the next time some more gear came along. Though I doubt if that will happen now, not after what you've told me.'

'What did he look like?'

Danny shrugged his shoulders.

'Pretty ordinary, really. About forty, average build with short brownish hair. Nothing striking about him at all.'

'That description sounds just like John Fallows, the private detective I saw,' Dixie said. 'Fits him to a tee. Even his first name is the same.'

There was silence as the three sat there with their thoughts. Finally Dixie spoke.

'Have *you* any idea what this could be about?'

'No, no idea at all,' Danny replied. 'But it seems as though you could do with some help. Especially if someone is trying to...' His voice tailed off.

'Get rid of me?' Dixie asked.

'Well, yes...look, if you need some protection, I can arrange that for you. I have friends who would help me.'

I bet you have, Mike thought. And if they're anything like Jack, they'd be a right hard bunch.

'Thanks, but I'll make sure Dixie's safely looked after,' he said.

Danny nodded.

'Of course,' he said, then added. 'What does Robert Fisher think about this?'

'Why do you want to know?' Dixie asked. 'Aunt Lucy told me there was no love lost between you and her brothers.'

'Yes, that's true, and she would know,' Danny said, for the first time his voice hardening.

Dixie, realizing she'd struck a sore point, quickly added, 'Neither of them know. There's no point in me giving them unnecessary worry until I've sorted this out myself. Then I'll tell them.'

Danny nodded but didn't say anything.

'Okay then...' and Dixie stood, followed by the two men.

There was an awkward silence as the three looked at each other, then Danny put his hand in his back pocket and pulled out a wallet. He produced a business card and offered it to Dixie.

'All my telephone numbers, including my mobile are on this, just in case you want to talk to me. My mobile's switched on most of the time.'

'Thanks,' Dixie said, and put the card in her shoulder bag.

'Nice to have met you,' Danny said, and stuck out his right hand for Mike to shake. Then he leaned over the table, gently held Dixie by both shoulders and kissed her lightly on her cheek. 'Wonderful to see you,' he added, staring into her blue eyes. The same colour as his.

'You too,' she said.

'I hope you phone me.'

'I will,' she replied, then turned and walked to the door, Mike close behind.

Danny took his empty glass to the bar for a refill and asked the barmaid to order him a minicab.

He sipped his gin and tonic and stared at his reflection in the worn mirror behind the bar, conscious of one thing.

Whatever their thoughts might have been, neither he or Dixie, had spoken aloud the words, *Father* or *Daughter*.

FORTY

Red quickly downed the rest of his beer when he saw Dixie and Mike leave. Shoving the newspaper into his pocket he followed just seconds behind. But as soon as he got outside, lengthened his stride, and hurried in the opposite direction to the young couple.

Nearly a hundred yards away he opened the passenger door of a dark blue Volvo and got in. The driver knew exactly where Mike Saxby's Range Rover was parked and kept his eyes fixed straight in front of him. There weren't that many cars in the street.

'Did you get anything?' Eddie asked, not moving his head.

'I heard some bits and pieces. They sat with that bloke you described, Danny Buckley. The one with hair like yours.'

'And...?'

'They reckon somebody has been impersonating him. And Dixie Fisher, the one I had to keep tabs on in Wakefield, thinks someone is trying to kill her. Another woman was killed...should have been her...but I couldn't hear all of it. You're not trying to kill anyone, are you?'

'No,' Eddie replied, 'it's money I'm after, not murder. Ah, there they go, ' and Eddie quickly started the motor, put the car in gear and eased away from the kerb. 'What else?'

'They talked about some private detective or other,' Red replied, 'John, I think they called him. And they mentioned Kate Smith...that's your Kate isn't it? I heard her name clearly.'

'Anything else?' Eddie asked, as he closed on the Range Rover.

'Some uncle somebody or other of the Fisher girl was mentioned...and that was it.'

'Are they going to meet again?'

'Don't know...didn't hear.'

'Umm, thanks Red, you did well.'

Eddie noted with interest that Mike Saxby wasn't driving back into central London, towards Dixie's flat, but heading north. Then he realized where they must be going. Joey Judd lived not far from Hampstead Heath.

The traffic slackened as the Range Rover turned off a main road, into a side street, then swung in a sweeping curve around the heath. Eddie knew the address so hung well back until he saw the car lights ahead do a sudden right turn and disappear.

Eddie slowed down as he approached the pop star's private road, which was a dead end, then speeded up as he saw the flashing blue light of a police car. He had just enough time to take in Mike Saxby's stationary vehicle part way down the road and a policeman talking to the driver,

'Not the best place for a stakeout,' Eddie said out loud. He'd already driven down the private road last week and seen it was impossible. Security gates, closed circuit cameras and plenty of burglar alarms.

There wasn't a lot of time left to remedy the Dixie Fisher situation and Eddie made up his mind as he drove away. He'd stick to the plan he and John had originally discussed.

*

Mike and Dixie sank into one of the two five seater settees facing each other in front of the Adams style fireplace, Linda and Joey comfortably ensconced on the other.

'Got stopped by the police down the road,' Mike said. 'One of your neighbours had reported some prowlers. I hope it isn't anything to do with Dixie's present situation.'

'No,' Joey said, 'there are a couple of people in this road who are always calling the old bill. They think they see burglars behind every tree. No, this happens at least once a week. So don't worry. Anyway, why would anyone link Dixie with here?'

'Because whoever's behind this seems to know a lot about Dixie, that's why.'

'So how did it go?' Linda asked. 'Did you see him?' Linda had been fidgeting for the last hour waiting for Dixie to arrive.

'Yes, we saw him,' Dixie replied.

'And what is the real Danny Buckley like?'

'Completely different to the other man.' Dixie looked at Mike. They'd talked in the car and she knew how he felt. 'Mike liked him.'

'Yes, yes I did. And you'd like him too, Joey. He's our sort of bloke.'

'But what about you, Dixie?' Linda was insistent.

Dixie hesitated.

'Come on,' Mike said, 'you said you liked him as well.'

'I must admit he seems a nice person.'

'What else?'

'Well, he's got a nice smile, bit of a charmer I suppose.'

'What did you talk about?' Linda couldn't wait to hear everything.

But before Dixie had a chance to answer Marie came into the room carrying a large tray with coffee and biscuits.

'Thanks,' Joey said.

Linda poured the hot liquid into cups and Joey got a bottle of brandy from the drinks trolley and plonked it on the table between them.

'Give a bit of bite to the coffee,' he grinned, and began pouring.

'So, did you find out anything that might help?' Linda asked.

'Yes, as a matter of fact we did,' Dixie replied, and she and Mike went over the main points of the conversation they'd had earlier in the Grapes pub.

'The more I talk about this I can't help thinking everything has been well planned,' Mike said. 'But what was the idea in getting someone to impersonate Danny Buckley? So he'd get the blame?' Mike shrugged his shoulders. 'I can't think why, but it certainly looks that way, because why go to the trouble of getting him out of London?'

Mike paused and directed his gaze towards Dixie.

'However, I think I might have come up with the reason why those photographs were switched in your flat,' he said.

'And what's that?'

'If you'd been in that car instead of Sandra then you wouldn't have been alive to discover them,' Mike replied. 'And if the police had found them then it would have been another pointer to Danny.'

'But I would have known,' Linda said. 'Don't forget, I saw the originals.'

'Did anyone else?'

'No, I didn't show them to anyone else,' Dixie replied.

'I would have told the police,' Linda said.

'And they would have believed you? After all, your description of both sets of photos would have been pretty much the same, except that maybe Danny was better looking. Also, how could you prove the switch? No,' Mike said, 'somehow I don't think you would have convinced them.'

'I see your point,' Linda grudgingly agreed. 'So why don't we go back to when Tom and Margo were killed and take it from there,' Linda said.

The others agreed and Mike kicked off the conversation.

'Dixie, all the money, shares and house were left to you, is that right?' he asked. 'Nobody else got anything?'

'Well, except for a few small bequests' she replied, 'yes, everything came to me.'

'So that eliminates anyone else wanting Tom and Margo dead for financial reasons, simply because there weren't any other beneficiaries.'

'Maybe someone else thought they might be entitled to something.'

'Can you think of anyone?'

'No,' Dixie had to admit.

'Right, let's concentrate on you then. You're now a very wealthy woman, so who would benefit if you died?'

'I don't know,' she replied, and shrugged her shoulders. 'I haven't really thought about it.'

'What about a will? Have you made one?' Joey asked.

'No, of course not.' Dixie seemed amused by the idea. 'I'm too young.'

'Well, I have,' Joey said. 'Wyatt Peterson advised me to.'

'What relatives have you got left?' Mike asked.

Dixie shrugged her shoulders.

'As far as I know, Aunt Lucy and Uncle Robert are the closest. I remember Robert telling me that when my Mother and Tom were buried.'

'So who would get your money if you haven't made a will and you die?'

'I know a little about this,' Linda said. 'If a person dies without making a will it's called intestate and all their money and property goes to their next of kin,' Linda paused. 'But I think we're forgetting something here.'

'Yes, what's that?' Dixie asked.

'Danny Buckley...he's your next of kin. If Tom Fisher had adopted you then your real father would have relinquished any rights, but you weren't adopted. Your name was changed by deed poll, and that's all. Danny Buckley is still legally your father.'

There was silence in the room, finally broken by Mike. 'That puts him squarely in the frame,' he said slowly.

'Are you sure about this?' Dixie asked.

'Yes,' Linda replied, 'a friend of my Mother was in a similar situation a couple of years ago.'

Dixie stared at her friend.

'You mean, if I'd been killed in that car crash instead of Sandra, then everything I have would have gone to Danny Buckley?'

'That's correct,' Linda replied.

'I didn't realize,' Dixie muttered, her face serious.

There was another silence in the room.

Lucy Fisher had said her father was a liar and couldn't be trusted.

Maybe she was right, after all.

FORTY ONE

'Don't let's be too hasty judging anyone yet,' Linda said, as she saw the disappointment on Dixie's face. 'I think we should go back to the beginning if we're going to make any sense out of this because nothing so far explains why your mother and...,' she paused, suddenly realizing what she'd nearly said, 'why your mother and Tom were killed.'

'Maybe only one was meant to die,' Mike said, 'but it happened to both simply because they were in the same car.'

'But which one?' Dixie asked, knowing she couldn't have discussed this subject a year ago.

'Suppose one of them was having an affair with another married person and *their* partner found out. Jealously is a strong motive for murder.'

A look of disbelief appeared on Dixie's face as she took in her boyfriend's words.

'Mike, if you'd known my Mother and Tom, you wouldn't be saying that. They adored each other. No, either one of them having a lover is definitely out.'

Mike shrugged his shoulders.

'Well, let's look at it logically then,' he continued. 'The only other alternative I can think of is money. Maybe Tom had a business enemy.'

'Where does that get us?'

'Tom was an accountant,' Mike replied. 'He was in the money business, handling big accounts. So maybe some money went missing.'

'You think he stole money from his clients? But that's impossible,' Dixie said.

'Yes, I agree,' Linda said. 'More likely somebody would have wanted to expose him, rather than kill him.'

'I didn't say Tom stole any money. I said maybe some money went missing. So who are the other partners, or directors in the company?' Mike answered his own question immediately. 'There's Dixie, but only since she inherited Tom Fisher's shares. Then there's Wyatt Peterson and Robert Fisher, Dixie's uncle. So maybe it's one of them.'

'Blimey, you mean somebody could have nicked some of my money?' Joey sounded horrified and poured more brandy into his coffee cup. 'They better not had.'

'I think I see what you're getting at,' Linda said, her voice thoughtful. 'Supposing Wyatt or Dixie's uncle had mishandled some accounts and Tom found out...and then threatened to make it public knowledge. Yes, I can see someone wanting to kill him for that reason.'

'But making it public knowledge wouldn't have done the company image much good,' Dixie said.

'True,' Mike said, wrinkling his brow in concentration, then quickly continuing as another thought flashed into his mind. 'But supposing Tom wanted the guilty person to resign and pay back the money. He could have threatened to tell the other partner. That way it wouldn't have become public knowledge. And that's how Kate Smith fits in. Yes, that could be it...' and Mike's voice became more enthusiastic. 'Don't forget she was Tom's private secretary for years and he probably confided in her. And now she's blackmailing the killer.'

'That certainly sounds feasible,' Linda said. 'But which one could it be? Wyatt or Robert?'

'Dixie, you've got the authority to call in independent auditors to go over the books. That way we'd find out, one way or the other.'

Dixie pondered Mike's suggestion before speaking.

'Yes, I suppose I could do that,' she said.

'But surely that will make it more dangerous for Dixie,' Joey said. 'That will alert the person who's behind this. They'll know she suspects something.'

'He probably knows I suspect something already. I'd have to be pretty stupid not to. Somehow I get the impression I was supposed to find out.'

'So that Danny would get the blame,' Mike said. 'If Dixie had been killed in that crash it would only have taken a whisper to the police to make him suspect number one. And it would have worked if we're anything to go by. Only a few minutes ago we were ready to accuse him.'

'But if he'd been arrested, tried and convicted of murder then he wouldn't have got the money,' Linda said. 'The law wouldn't allow it.'

'I know,' Mike said, deflated. 'So that puts paid to that theory, doesn't it?' Then another thought sprang into his mind. 'But, on the other hand, he could have got off and then he'd get Dixie's money.'

'So then what would the person behind this gain?' Linda asked. 'He's got to be after something...make something out of it. It gets crazier the more we talk.'

'I bet there's a simple explanation somewhere,' Dixie said. 'If only we could see it.'

'You went to your uncle to find a private detective,' Mike said. 'And now it's odds on, after what Danny told us, that John Fallows, or whatever his name is, is involved in this. So, that's one link to Robert Fisher.'

'And he organized Aunt Lucy's burglary?' Dixie's voice was one of disbelief. 'His own sister? She might have got killed.'

'Dixie,' Mike prompted, 'remember what you told me your aunt had said? That when she got hit one of the men said they'd been told, *they mustn't hurt her*.'

Dixie hesitated before answering.

'Yes, that's true. Oh my God, do you really think it could be Uncle Robert?'

'There's something else,' Linda said. 'I was going to mention it to you earlier in the week, but we talked about so many things, I got sidetracked. And I must admit, I find it difficult to believe myself.' Linda paused. 'Robert found the apartment for you. And he'd looked at it before you ever saw it.'

'So? I don't see what you're getting at.'

'He could still have had a spare set of keys so that someone could get into your place and change the photographs over. There weren't any signs of a break-in, were there?'

A shocked expression spread across Dixie's face.

'Oh my God.' She spoke so softly the others only just caught her words.

'Can you think of anything else?' Linda asked.

There was a long pause before Dixie answered, the words coming out slowly, aware she might be condemning her uncle.

'Mike and I were at Aunt Lucy's birthday party. That's when she said she was leaving me her house in her will. She also said Robert had an expensive hobby. But when I asked what it was she told me it was none of my business.'

'I wonder what the hell that could be?' Mike asked out loud.

There was a long silence as they racked their brains, then Joey spoke.

'What about gambling?'

'What makes you say that?' Mike asked.

'Remember that Saturday evening in the summer when all of us went out for dinner? Including Wyatt and Robert.'

'Yeah, I remember,' Mike answered.

'Well, while we were there I saw a friend of mine in the restaurant and I left our table to speak to him.'

'I remember that, Joey,' Linda said, 'but I never knew who it was.'

'It was a club owner I know, Terry 'ayman...*Hayman.*' Joey flushed slightly as he made a point of pronouncing his friend's name correctly, before carefully continuing. 'And he said one of the men sitting at our table went to one of his clubs, and was also a big gambler. Sometimes saw him at a casino in Kensington. *A lunatic gambler*, was how Terry described him. Said he must have a lot of money. Terry knows Mike, so it must have been Wyatt or Robert.'

'So who was it?'

'I don't know. I asked him, but his girlfriend came out of the loo before he answered. And then they left.'

'And Terry could definitely identify him?' Mike asked.

'Sure,' Joey replied.

'Dixie, have you got a photograph of your uncle?'

'Yes, several...they were taken recently.'

'Of course,' and Linda smiled. 'Photographs were taken in that restaurant on the same night. We're all on them, Robert and Wyatt included.'

'Where are they?' Mike asked.

'In my flat,' Dixie replied.

'Then we'll have to get them,' Mike said, 'and then get Terry to show us who he was talking about.'

'Do you want to go now?'

'Let's all go,' Linda said.

'Yeah,' and Joey rose from the settee, 'I'll try and locate Terry so we can meet up with him.'

Joey crossed to a sofa table, opened the drawer and took out an address book, then picked up the phone. He spoke briefly, replaced the receiver, and returned to the settee.

'I spoke to one of his clubs...should get a call back pretty soon. So what time shall I say we want to meet him?'

Mike looked at his watch.

'By the time we get to Dixie's...and I suppose Terry will want to see us somewhere in the West End...about an hour and a half.'

Five minutes later the phone rang.

'Terry, thanks for calling me,' Joey said. 'I'd like to see you later...about midnight...at the Tailgate?...yeah, that's okay with me...no' and Joey laughed and looked over at Linda, 'no I don't want a woman, I'm bringing my own. And Mike will be with me, with his young lady...' Joey laughed again before hanging up.

'Are you taking me to some seedy dive?' Linda asked.

Joey grinned.

'No, Terry's clubs are the best. It's just that,' and he paused, 'some of the girls working there do sometimes look a bit underdressed.'

'We'll go in my car,' Mike said, and started to rise.

'No,' and Joey shook his head, 'I'll get Stan to drive us. That leaves both of us free just in case...' He didn't finish the sentence but the others knew what he meant.

'Isn't it a bit late?' Dixie asked.

'No' Joey replied. 'Stan will know it's important if I ask him to drive me at this time of night. I won't be a minute,' and Joey left the room.

*

The Rolls drew up outside Dixie's apartment block and the four got out, leaving Stan in the driving seat.

'Won't be long,' Joey promised, and then they headed through the lobby towards the lift, Mike stopping on the way to have a brief word with the duty porter.

There were four porters who shared the twenty four hour shift and Mike had given each one a hundred pounds to be on the lookout for anyone acting strangely or making inquiries about Dixie. He explained she was being pestered by a stalker but the police couldn't do much at this stage. So if they did see anything suspicious to let him know immediately. Mike had promised the porters another hundred pounds for Christmas.

'No, sir, everything's quiet,' the duty man informed Mike.

The four were only minutes in the flat. Dixie knew at once where to put her hands on the photographs and then they were back in the Rolls heading for the Tailgate Club.

They drew up outside the club and Joey told Stan to come back for them in an hour.

A biting wind made their ears tingle with cold and they hurried towards the glass fronted entrance under the dark red canopy. Alex, the bouncer, pulled open the door.

'Evening, Mr Judd,' he smiled. 'Mr Hayman's downstairs waiting for you.'

'Thanks,' and Joey led his friends down the red carpeted stairs into the dimly lit bar area. Scantily clad waitresses were giving orders over the counter.

'Hello, Joey,' Tilly, the barmaid shouted, as she busily mixed cocktails.

Joey smiled, waved and led his party through to the main part of the club. It was packed with middle aged businessmen chatting up the hostesses and Joey looked around. But almost immediately, Sharon, the club manageress, appeared.

'Terry's over there,' she said, and the others followed her, skirting the small dance floor, past the occupied tables, until they came to a large circular booth.

Terry got to his feet as they arrived. He shook hands with Joey and Mike then was introduced to Linda and Dixie. As soon as they were seated an attractive young waitress appeared with champagne in an ice bucket and glasses.

The four hadn't checked their coats on the way in and Terry told the waitress to take them to his private office.

'Good to see you, Joey,' Terry said. 'You haven't been around for a while.' He poured the chilled bubbly liquid into the glasses and held one up. 'Cheers,' he smiled, which the others repeated. 'Now, you and your friends must be here for a reason.'

'Yes,' Joey said. 'Remember the last time I saw you? In that restaurant in the summer.'

'Yes, I do, that was ages ago.'

'I'm a reformed character these days,' and Joey gave his cheeky grin. Slipping a hand under the table he gently squeezed Linda's thigh. 'But do you remember what we talked about?'

'No, not really,' Terry replied.

'You said one of the men sitting at my table was a heavy gambler...bit of a lunatic, you said.'

'Yes, that's right,' Terry said slowly and smiled, now recalling that evening. 'Why?'

'Dixie,' the pop star said, holding out his hand until she pulled a large white envelope from her shoulder bag. Then Joey took out the photographs and sorted through the half dozen, selecting two.

He laid them in front of Terry.

'Which one were you talking about?'

Without hesitation the club owner placed his index finger on one of the pictures.

'That's him,' he said.

The others craned their necks trying to get a better view and Dixie gave an inward sigh of relief as she saw the man Terry was pointing to.

It was Wyatt Peterson.

FORTY TWO

Following the club owner's identification of the accountant Joey asked his friend to find out as much as possible about Wyatt's gambling. How much did he lose, or win. And did he have any big debts at any of the casinos. Anything at all.

It was important,

Terry promised he'd do his best and when they left the Tailgate Club he said he'd go later to the casino in Kensington which Wyatt regularly frequented. He said he knew people who worked there and as soon as he had any worthwhile information he'd contact Joey or Mike.

The four went back to Joey's and stayed the night there. But early next morning Joey disappeared into his recording studio with the rest of the band. He said they'd be working on new songs all day so Mike and the two women returned to Dixie's flat.

There they spent the morning going over old ground - but failed to come up with anything new. It was all speculation and guesswork but nothing concrete.

Wyatt Peterson was the gambler.

But there were more links leading to Robert Fisher.

So what! Dixie felt like shouting. Because where was the proof that either of them was a man of violence?

And what was the motive?

'Maybe they're in it together,' Linda said, and the others weren't sure if she was joking, or not. After so many hours talking they were feeling frustrated, bored even, and the only thing that kept them going was the fact that Dixie's life could be at stake.

'I still think Danny is an important part in this,' Mike said. 'He was supposed to get the blame. But why?'

'You know, Dixie, there is one other person you could have a word with who might be able to throw some light on this,' Linda said.

'Yes, who's that?'

'Your Aunt Lucy. Talk to her.'

'Aunt Lucy?' Dixie sounded surprised. 'I don't know about that. Robert's her brother and I don't see how I could ask if he's capable of hurting me, or having me killed.'

'No, I suppose not,' and then Linda's face lit up as she had a sudden thought. 'But I bet Danny Buckley could help. Of course...Dixie, remember what your aunt said when you asked her about him.'

'What was that?'

'That there was a lot of bad blood between Danny Buckley and her brothers.'

'Yes, that's right, but when I spoke to Uncle Robert he said it was a long time ago, and all forgotten now.'

'That's what *he* said. But supposing that's not true. Anyway, I'm sure your father will tell us.'

'I agree with you,' Mike said. 'That might be just the point we've been missing all along. Dixie call Danny now and ask him to meet up with us. Don't say what it's about over the phone because I'd like to be able to see his reaction in person. Give him Joey's address and we'll all meet there. Today if possible, but if not, as soon as he can.'

*

The Norfolk Broads affected Jack Gee. After all the years spent banged up inside prison the space and beautiful scenery, even though it was winter, really got through to him.

'You should be here during the summer months,' Danny told his friend. 'I spend a lot of time on my boat.'

Danny had driven around for an hour showing Jack various places of interest before stopping at a pub in Ludham for lunch. The fresh air had blown away the last traces of their hangovers and given them an appetite. The night before had seen a lot of booze sunk at Jack's homecoming party hosted by Mickey Dawson, and this morning both men had been slow starters.

They gave their order over the bar and had just sat at a table near an imitation log gas fire when Danny's mobile phone rang.

'Hello,' he answered, then gave a broad smile. It was Dixie. 'Didn't expect to hear from you again so soon.'

'I phoned your office,' Dixie said, 'and a woman told me you were on your way to Norfolk.'

'That's right. I'm with Jack and we're in Norfolk now. Why, is there anything wrong?'

'No, it's just that I'd like to see you again as soon as possible. Will you be coming back to London today?'

'I didn't intend to,' and Danny paused. 'I suppose I could if it's really important, but I'd prefer to return tomorrow.'

'Oh, no, it's not that important,' Dixie quickly hurried to say, hiding her true feelings. 'Tomorrow will be okay. Have you got a pen and paper?'

Danny took a pen from his inside pocket and flipped over a beer mat to the blank side. 'Okay,' he said.

Dixie gave him an address and phone number and added, 'It's Joey Judd's house, you know, the pop star. He's a friend of Mike's, well, both of us.'

Danny had been impressed with the address and now he knew why. People had to have a lot of money to live in that part of Hampstead...people like rich pop stars.

'What time do you think you could make it?'

'About four o'clock,' Danny replied, 'if that's okay with you.'

'Yes, that'll be fine.'

'Dixie, is it anything to do with what we talked about yesterday?'

'Yes, yes it is.'

'Okay, see you tomorrow.'

Danny clicked off his mobile.

'Looks like I'm going to be seeing my daughter again sooner than I thought,' he said.

'Good,' Jack said.

After they'd eaten a home cooked lunch of steak and kidney pudding washed down with pints of the local beer the two men left the pub to find the weather changed. Snow flurries were pelting down in a high wind, which quickly turned to rain, and they were glad to arrive at the detached, thatched cottage near Potter Heigham, the home of Jessie Baker.

Danny Buckley and Jessie had met when she'd been in her mid-thirties five years ago and become lovers only weeks later. Jessie had been a striking looking woman with thick streaks of premature grey in her jet black hair which reached down to her shoulders. Not beautiful, but there was something attractively different about her. She had tremendous sex appeal. And she loved Danny, completely. She was that kind of woman. All or nothing.

But Jessie was dying.

A heavy smoker, ten months ago she'd been told by her doctor she had cancer of the lungs, *non-small-cell carcinoma*. It was terminal, non-operable, and she only had about a year to live, at the most. It had been diagnosed too late.

At first the physical appearance of the disease wasn't apparent and, except for getting tired more quickly, Jessie didn't look any different. But that had changed a month ago with a dramatic loss of weight.

Both knew it would be their last Christmas together.

FORTY THREE

Kate Smith sat in the back of the taxi as it drove through the East End on her way to meet Eddie. As she looked out the window at the bleak, dreary streets and the few people brave enough to battle the cold wind, she wondered where she would be this Christmas. Here in London, or somewhere in the sun? Soon she would get the final payment and then that would be the end of it.

Or rather, she hoped, the beginning. The beginning of a new life.

This evening she had to make the last phone call to arrange the handover of the hundred thousand. The only difference was that this time she would hand over both sets of documents, the originals and the copy, to the courier in exchange for the cash. Eddie had suggested she could make another copy, just as something extra for the future, but Kate had said no. She wanted to finish it once and for all. It was the first time Kate had gone against Eddie's way of thinking, and she surprised herself. But she stuck fast and in the end Eddie agreed with her. He didn't have much choice.

She hadn't seen Eddie since he'd left her flat in Earls Court two days ago. Then this afternoon he'd called and asked her to be at his house by seven and said they'd use a local phone box to pass on her final instructions.

His friend John would also be there. He'd been the person feeding the meter for her parked car when she'd dodged her way in and out of the Army and Navy department store in the summer. She'd been surprised when Eddie had introduced her to him because he was the man who'd been delivering her monthly money until Eddie took over.

'I've got my own agreement with John,' Eddie had assured her. 'The main thing is he's trustworthy, and will be of tremendous help to us.'

Kate hadn't questioned further, only too glad to have someone else on her side.

She reached her destination, paid the driver and pulled her coat tighter around her as she stood on the doorstep of Eddie's small house.

He opened the door and took her into the lounge where an open bottle of scotch and several glasses stood on a coffee table. John greeted her while Eddie poured a large measure of whisky into a clean glass.

'Get that down you,' he said, and looked at his watch. 'We'll be going out again in just a few minutes.'

Kate did as she was told and downed the drink in three swallows. She'd never really drunk much until she'd met Eddie but recently found she was drinking more, especially when she was by herself, sitting in her small apartment with only the television for company. There wasn't a video player so she couldn't watch her films, now packed in a suitcase.

Eddie poured himself another drink and sank it straight away. Then he put on a thick topcoat and smiled at Kate.

'Come on, one more call,' he said. 'Mustn't keep the man waiting.'

They left the house and started walking in the direction of a small parade of shops.

Nearly ten minutes later they approached a telephone box not far from a kebab shop. A group of youths standing outside talking in loud voices briefly stared as Kate went into the call box and Eddie stood by the door, but their attention was diverted as two teenage girls came out of the shop and joined them. Then the gang headed off into the night.

Kate's call was expected and the man patiently listened to his instructions. They were to meet on the Monday before Christmas, which fell on a Saturday this year, in the lobby of a large well known hotel. The time to be eight thirty in the evening. There would be plenty of people around and Kate would hand over her package to him personally in return for the money. No courier this time the man insisted, he wanted to check he was getting what he was paying for, and Kate agreed to his request, which she'd half expected anyway. It didn't bother her because she knew Eddie would be there somewhere in the background to protect her.

'Everything okay?' Eddie asked, when Kate stepped out of the box.

'Only a slight change in plan,' she replied, and explained about the swap of packages in person.

'I told you he might want to do it that way,' Eddie reminded her. 'It's understandable. I know I would if was parting with that kind of money.' Eddie squeezed her arm. 'Don't worry, I'll make sure nothing happens to you.'

The chill wind whipped at their faces and Kate began to think of the sun again. So she put her thoughts into words and on the walk back they chatted about different parts of Europe they liked. And by the time they reached Eddie's house they'd agreed to go to Spain first. In fact, Eddie said, he would book the flight tickets tomorrow. They wouldn't have to bother about booking a hotel because they'd have so much money they'd be able to get in anywhere. And Eddie meant what he said. He had to get Kate in the right mood tonight to agree with his next move. It was important.

He needed Kate to lure Dixie Fisher out into the open.

When they arrived at the house Eddie ordered over the phone an Indian meal for the three of them to be delivered from a nearby takeaway.

They ate off the small dining table in the corner of the lounge. Eddie made sure Kate's glass was topped up with wine but was careful not to let her drink too much. He didn't want her drunk - just in a happy frame of mind. John knew what was going on and smiled a lot, adding the right words every now and again to keep the conversation light.

They finished the meal, but kept sitting at the table, as Eddie opened another bottle of red wine. He poured and the three clinked glasses and toasted their future in the sun. Kate wasn't sure how John fitted in with this but she felt too relaxed to care. She was going and that was all that mattered.

'Kate, have you ever heard of a man called Danny Buckley?'

She looked at Eddie and wrinkled her face in thought.

'No, I don't think so,' she replied. 'Why, should I have?'

'It seems he's Dixie Fisher's father.'

Kate looked perplexed.

'But Tom Fisher was her father.'

'No, he wasn't,' Eddie said. 'Take my word for it. Danny Buckley was married to Margo first. They had a child, Dixie, and then they divorced. Margo married Tom Fisher and the kid's name was changed by deed poll.'

Kate shrugged her shoulders.

'It's just that, I worked for him for years and he never mentioned anything to me,' she said.

Eddie took a large swig from his glass, hoping he'd judged his moment right, and took the plunge.

'That's why I want you arrange a meeting with Dixie Fisher,' he said.

Kate looked even more bewildered.

'You what? You want me to meet her?' She paused. 'What for? Surely it would be too risky. Everything's going so well...so why...?' She was unable to finish the question, her mind totally confused.

'It will be all right Kate, just trust me. Let me explain.'

Kate stared at Eddie and listened carefully to what he had to say.

'I'm certain once you hand over your information and get the money,' he said, 'Danny Buckley is going to be blamed for Tom and Margo Fisher's deaths.'

'Did he do it?' she asked.

'No.'

Kate paused, but she had to ask a question that had been at the back of her mind for a long time. She had to know.

'Did *you* do it?' Her voice soft and faltering, scared of the reply.

'Yes,' Eddie replied in a firm voice, staring straight into her eyes. Kate's heart thudded and then seemed to miss a beat.

'It *was* me, but it *really* was an accident,' Eddie lied. 'I was just meant to frighten Tom Fisher, but those idiots being chased by the police rammed into him. I didn't see them. Honest I didn't. And those two people's deaths will be on my conscience for the rest of my life.'

Eddie reached over the table and held Kate's hands.

'That's why I can't let another man be blamed for what I did,' he said.

'But why will he?'

'Simply because we look a bit alike, especially from a distance, and are about the same age. But mainly because we both have grey curly hair. It wasn't originally planned this way. In fact, it was a coincidence, and it only happened after some photographs were taken of Danny Buckley and the similarity was noticed.'

'But who is going to blame him? The police?'

'Yes,' Eddie replied.

'But why now?' Kate asked. 'Why after all this time?'

'It's too complicated to explain but I really am being honest with you. That is what's going to happen.'

'It's so hard to believe,' Kate said.

'Well, *you* had a lot to do with the course of events.'

Kate looked puzzled.

'Me? How?'

'If you hadn't used those Tom Fisher documents for blackmail none of this would have happened. It made our friend desperate for more money. When the Fishers were accidentally killed - it should have been the end of it.'

'That makes me feel terrible,' Kate said.

'So that's why we should do something to rectify it.'

'But how will *me* meeting Dixie Fisher change all this?' Kate asked.

'Because I intend writing a letter which will explain everything, explain who is behind this. You see, I couldn't be happy living with you in Spain, and this guilt always bothering me. That poor Fisher girl has suffered enough without her father being blamed for something he didn't do. It just wouldn't be fair.'

'Eddie's telling the truth,' John said, breaking into the conversation, his words quiet and convincing. 'It's been on his conscience ever since it happened. And I know Eddie would like to get it off his chest...make his peace. So I think you should give him a chance.'

Lines wrinkled Kate's forehead as she thought.

'If I did meet her,' she finally said, 'when would you like this to happen?'

'Exactly a week before you pick up the money.'

'But surely you don't intend giving her a letter before I get the money. She could go to the police and we'd never get paid.'

'No, of course not,' Eddie smiled and squeezed her hand. 'I'm going to tell her that there was a reason behind Tom Fisher's death and that arrangements have been made for a letter to be delivered to her on Christmas Eve.' Eddie squeezed Kate's hand again. 'And by then you and I will enjoying ourselves in the sun. Besides, the bastard behind this needs to be taught a lesson. Because of him a man and his wife died.'

'You said, *you're* going to tell her.'

'Yes,' Eddie replied. 'I'd like to see her face to face. It'd make me feel better.' Eddie paused, and look of pleading came over his face. 'Please say you'll do this for me.'

Kate smiled.

'Of course, if that's what you want.' Eddie's admission to being involved in Tom Fisher's death had come as a shock but she believed him. It had been an accident after all, and that she could live with. She was also pleased with the fact that her lover now wanted to make amends.

Eddie returned her smile.

'Thanks.'

They cleared the table and turned on television. They had more to drink and Eddie said he'd bought a couple of porn videos yesterday. Specially for her, he told Kate.

'So let's see them,' he said, knowing she'd love to watch, but might feel a bit uneasy with his friend there. 'Don't be embarrassed,' he smiled. 'John's not shy. I bet you've seen a few in your time, haven't you?'

'Loads,' and John grinned.

During the second one, showing bodies locked together in group sex, Eddie kissed Kate and slipped his hand up her skirt.

'Not in front of John,' she whispered, but was already aroused.

'Don't be silly, let him watch.'

Eddie reached out and removed her glasses, pushed her flat on the couch and took off her shoes. Then he pulled up her skirt and slipped her white knickers down over her holdup stockings. Kneeling on the floor he opened her legs and pulled her towards him, one leg on the couch and the other trailing over the edge, her foot resting on the carpet. He gently entered her, then pushed harder, and Kate gave a gasp of pleasure. He moved slowly in and out, then quickened, and stretched out an arm and pulled her head to the edge of the cushions.

'Come on John, join in,' Eddie said, his voice slightly breathless with excitement.

John knelt on the floor and unzipped his trousers.

'Put it in her mouth,' Eddie said, and watched as his friend pushed his erection against Kate's lips. They slowly parted then opened wide and she thrust her head back and forward taking more and more in her wet mouth.

Two men in her at the şame time. She wasn't doing this for Eddie. This was something *she* wanted.

Kate loved it.

FORTY FOUR

Danny made breakfast the following morning. Jessie didn't eat much, and drank mostly orange juice, but the two men cleared the cooked food from their plates.

'I'm going to show Jack my boat, then go to Horsey and take a walk along the beach. Thought I'd give Maggie a run,' Danny said, referring to Jessie's black and brown mongrel dog.

'Yes, you'll both enjoy that,' Jessie said, starting to clear the table. The two men helped with the washing up and Danny made a large mug of coffee for Jessie.

'Just take it easy,' he said, 'we'll be back in a few hours.'

Danny and Jack put on warm coats and boots, which Danny had insisted his friend bring from London, and minutes later they were driving through country roads towards the river Thurne. When he saw the familiar turning, Danny changed down a gear, and swung off the road on to a gravel track. Then he drove past a couple of large buildings and slowly brought the black Volkswagen Golf to a halt in the parking area of a small boatyard. It was a successful little business, with the main income from repairs to sail and motor vessels, plus the daily hire of small dinghies during the busy summer months.

The two men left the car, Maggie padding behind them, and walked to a glass fronted office in one of the buildings. Danny spoke briefly to a middle-aged man dressed in grease stained overalls, then stuck his head inside the office.

'Just going to take a look at my boat,' Danny said to the young blonde girl sitting behind her paper strewn desk.

'Okay, Mr Buckley,' she said, but before she could continue the telephone rang and Danny left and headed to where his boat was moored, a four berth ex-rental holiday cruiser, which had been renovated and bought as a present by Jessie two years ago. She was half-owner of the boatyard which she'd inherited when her husband drowned after a tragic accident ten years ago.

Danny spent fifteen minutes showing Jack around the boat.

'I've even taken up fishing,' Danny said. 'Great way to relax.'

Jack nodded his head and gave a wry grin.

'I'm seriously thinking of moving out of London,' he said. 'It's so easy to get into trouble there...and I'm fed up doing bird.'

'I've been thinking of selling up in London myself,' Danny said, and chuckled. 'Maybe we should buy a pub down here. Might be a laugh.'

Jack looked at his friend and nodded. Wasn't such a bad idea, at that.

On the day he'd got out of prison he knew he'd have to change otherwise it wouldn't be long before he slipped back into a life of crime. Most of his friends were criminals and the temptation of easy money would always be lurking in the background. And Jack knew if he was ever going to change his lifestyle then it had to be now. He had one hundred thousand pounds stashed away, his share of the security van robbery, which his grateful friends had only been to happy to pay him for keeping his mouth shut. The opportunity might never happen again.

'I see you've called your boat, *Dixie*,' Jack said.

'Yeah,' Danny replied softly. He'd repeated to his friend at the party last night all the details Dixie and Mike had spoken about in the pub.

His friend had listened carefully, and when Danny had finished, said in his steely voice.

'If you need any help, just let me know.'

As Danny carefully locked the rear door of the cabin cruiser, he said, 'There's somewhere else I'd like to show you.'

The two men walked back to the car and drove to Horsey, where Danny parked near the well known windmill landmark, then took a twenty minute walk along a footpath through fields to a cut in the cliffs which led to the North Sea. There hardly ever seemed to be anyone on the pebble and sandy beach which stretched for miles. Too desolate for most people, with only the odd person exercising their dog, but Danny loved it, even in winter. He loved the loneliness, the smell of the sea blowing inland, and had walked there many times, watching the waves break on the shore, often taking Jessie's mongrel with him.

*

Danny had told Jessie about his daughter, Dixie, a long time ago and she'd often said he should try and see her. And after he described Dixie's sudden appearance in his local pub, Jessie said she was happy for him, and stressed he must make sure he stayed in contact.

'Don't lose her now you've found her,' Jessie said.

Danny hadn't given the real reason for the visit, Jessie had enough to cope with. He just said Dixie had decided to find him now that Tom and Margo Fisher were dead.

'I'll be back tomorrow with Jack and stay the weekend,' Danny told her, as he and his friend prepared to leave late morning. He felt guilty about leaving but couldn't break his promise to Dixie.

'You go and see your daughter. It's important,' Jessie said. 'You've got a lot of lost time to make up.'

Danny was relieved that, starting from Monday, Jessie would have help. She was a brave woman, but unfortunately nothing could halt her ravaging illness.

Jessie's doctor had said she should be in hospital but Jessie was determined to spend Christmas at home with Danny. She was in pain and needed daily injections so arrangements had been made for a private nursing agency to give round the clock care. Jessie's cottage had four bedrooms so space wasn't a problem.

'Drive carefully,' Jessie said as the two men left. She watched the black car drive out of sight then went and sat in her favourite chair listening to the radio. Minutes later she was fast asleep.

'She's a nice lady,' Jack said, as Danny drove well within the speed limit. Not that he was obeying Jessie's instruction, the weather was bad. It was snowing, with the wind blowing in great gusts, and it looked as though the weather was going to be a repeat of last year.

'Yes she is,' Danny agreed.

'Pity about...' Jack didn't finish his sentence but the other man knew what he was referring to. Danny had explained the full extent of Jessie's illness when they'd left London on the outward journey. It was eating his heart out but over the months Danny had learned to accept the inevitable. Sometimes he felt cursed and every now and again fate came along and kicked him in the teeth, just to remind him life wasn't a bed of roses. Payback time for being a bastard over the years.

And now Dixie had unexpectedly come back into his life. He was glad - but couldn't help a feeling of unease – and wondered what lay ahead.

The two men sat silent, listening to the car radio, their eyes following the movement of the windscreen wipers. As they neared the capital the snow slowly petered out and by the time they drove through the clogged streets the pavements were dry.

'I'd like you to come with me,' Danny said. It was a last minute thought but knew it made sense.

'That's okay with me,' Jack said, surprised by the late invitation. He'd got the impression Danny was going to meet Dixie and her friends by himself.

'I've been thinking about your offer of help,' Danny said, glancing sideways at his friend, 'and I couldn't think of a better man.'

Jack returned the look.

'Thanks,' he said. 'And don't worry, nobody will get to Dixie. I'll see to that.'

They drove to Jack's mother's flat on a small council estate not far from Kings Cross. He'd been staying with her since he'd got out of prison, rather than getting a place of his own. Jack felt he owed his mother that. She hadn't seen much of him over the years.

A quick cup of tea with the old lady, with Jack assuring her he'd be sleeping in his own bed that night, and then they were driving towards Hampstead.

'Do they know I'm coming?' Jack asked.

'No,' Danny replied. 'But don't worry. Dixie's boyfriend was impressed with you and I know he'll feel happier with you around.'

'Yeah, he seemed a nice bloke. He'll make a good son-in-law.' Jack grinned. 'And you'll make a good grandfather.'

Danny didn't comment. He wasn't used to playing happy families.

FORTY FIVE

It was already dark when the VW drove along the private road just before four pm. The car stopped outside black metal gates and Danny got out and pressed the well lit button under the security camera. The weather had turned icy cold and when he identified himself over the two way speaking system his breath hung like steam in the murky air.

The high electronic gates swung open and Danny drove up the short drive and parked alongside three other cars outside Joey Judd's mansion.

After ringing the bell the oak front door was opened by a man wearing a short grey jacket.

'Come in gentleman,' Stan said, and Danny and Jack entered into the large entrance hall. The manservant took their topcoats, opened a door next to the front entrance, and hung them up.

Another door opened off the hall and Mike walked to where the men were standing.

'I brought Jack along,' Danny said. 'I hope that's all right with you.'

'No problem at all,' Mike replied.

They went into the drawing room where Stan organized drinks while Danny and Jack looked around in silent admiration. To them, it was another world. A world they could only dream about.

They were introduced to Linda, a very pretty woman, and Danny winked as he gave Dixie a warm smile.

The two older men sat on one of the comfortable settees and sipped their drinks. Stan left the room, quietly closing the door behind him, and Mike started the conversation.

'Joey is with his band working on some songs. He's got his own recording studio here and hopes to be with us later.'

'It's certainly a lovely home,' Danny said.

'It's all Mike's work,' Dixie said, and couldn't hide the sound of pride in her voice.'

'So what line of business are you in, Mike?' Danny asked.

And over the next few minutes Mike quickly explained his background and the basics of his company, including his latest venture in Yorkshire.

'I enjoy my work very much,' he concluded.

'Yes, that's always a bonus,' Danny said. 'It must be very rewarding to be able to make a good living out of what you really like doing.'

Danny had never been that fortunate. But that idle remark he'd made to Jack about running a pub in Norfolk had surfaced again in his mind. And the more he thought about it, the more he liked the idea. The trouble being, as usual, a matter of raising the money. Even if he sold his terrace house and business it might not be enough. He owed a fair bit. He always did.

'Now, this meeting. You said it was to do with what we talked about in the Grapes.'

'That's right, Danny,' Mike said, a bit uneasy about what he was going to say next. 'Tom Fisher never adopted Dixie, did he?'

'No,' Danny replied, 'her name was changed by deed poll, but Dixie wasn't adopted.'

'So, you're legally Dixie's father.'

'Yes, I know.'

'Remember we told you about Sandra getting killed in a car crash and we think it was a case of mistaken identity. That Dixie was supposed to die instead.'

'Yes, I remember,' Danny replied, wondering where this was leading.

'And did you realize that if Dixie had died then you, as the next of kin, would have got all Dixie's money? You see, Dixie has never made a will...and Dixie's a very wealthy woman.'

Danny's eyes narrowed as the words sank in.

'I think I understand what you're getting at,' he said slowly, 'and I'm not sure I like it.'

'No, don't get the wrong end of the stick,' Mike said quickly, 'we don't think it's you,' but before he could continue another voice interrupted.

'I've know Danny a long time, Dixie.' It was the first time Jack had opened his mouth since sitting down and the others swivelled their attention towards him. 'And I can assure you he wouldn't want to harm you in any way. Take my word for it.' Jack's voice had a hard tone to it that made his statement a fact, and what he'd just said had better be believed.

'That's the truth, Dixie,' Danny added softly.

His daughter nodded her head, her face serious.

'I believe you,' she said.

'But now I hope you see what I'm getting at,' Mike continued. 'Inheriting Dixie's money would have been the obvious motive if she'd died and you would have been the number one suspect.'

'I'd have been dropped well in it,' Danny agreed. 'But seeing as it *isn't* me, have you come up with anybody else? There must be.'

'Yes,' and Mike carefully repeated their reasons for suspecting Wyatt Peterson and Robert Fisher. 'The trouble is, we're not one hundred per cent sure which one it is,' Mike continued, 'or, to be honest, if it's either of them.'

'And you think I might be able to help?'

'Do you know Wyatt? Have you ever met him?'

'No,' Danny replied. 'But I have heard of the name.'

'Really, that's interesting. What's that about?'

'Oh, it's not important...something personal, from a long time ago,' Danny seemed reluctant in his reply. 'Anyway, I'm sure you've got some more questions.'

'Yes...Robert Fisher, I take it you've met him.'

'Yeah, I've met *him*. That was years ago, and I bet he hasn't changed.' Danny's voice was bitter.

'We know Robert Fisher has an expensive hobby. Have you any idea what it could be?'

Danny shook his head.

'No, no idea at all.'

Mike turned to Dixie.

'Now you *will* have to approach your Aunt Lucy,' he said. 'She's the only other person I can think of.'

'Maybe...we'll see,' Dixie said, obviously still not happy with the idea.

Mike shifted his gaze back to Danny.

'However, there is one thing Dixie's aunt has already told her. That there was a lot of bad blood between you and her brothers. Is that true?'

A brief smile flickered across Danny's face.

'Yes, that's true. Still is as far as I'm concerned.'

'Do you mind telling us what it's about?'

Danny didn't answer straight away.

'No, I don't think I should,' he finally said. 'I don't think Dixie would like to hear it.'

'Me?' Dixie sounded surprised. 'Why's that?'

Danny was slow to answer again, but then clicked his fingers and a look of understanding came over his face.

'Mind you, that could be it,' he said, smiling. 'The reason for you to die and me to get the blame. Robert Fisher thinks he will get all your money, Dixie. Not me. He'll inherit it, well, Lucy will, but he'll be able to control it. Yes, and that was what the trouble was about in the first place, all those years ago.'

'I don't understand,' Dixie said. 'Please tell me.'

Danny stared at the young woman.

'You might not like what you hear, Dixie. But if you really want to hear it, then you'll have to listen to *all* of it. But it will be the truth, I promise you.'

'Yes, I do want to hear what you've got to say.'

Danny drained the remains of his gin and tonic and sat looking at the empty glass, then raised his eyes.

'Your uncle and aunt don't think I'm your father.'

FORTY SIX

A sudden stillness came over the room as Danny's words sank in. Linda was first to break the silence.

'But that's not true,' she blurted out. 'Dixie showed me her birth certificate and your name's on it.'

'That's right,' Danny said, 'and as far as I'm concerned that document is correct in every detail.' He paused. 'But the Fisher family are convinced otherwise.'

'I think you'd better explain,' Dixie said, in a subdued voice.

Mike got up and took Danny's glass.

'Another?' he asked.

Danny nodded and waited until the filled glass was back in his hand before beginning.

'Over the years I seem to have got a reputation as a bit of a ladies man, drinking and always unfaithful,' he said.

'That's my Aunt Lucy's thoughts exactly,' Dixie said.

'Yes, and when I was younger a lot of that was true. I've changed now but...' Danny took a swig of his gin and turned his eyes directly towards Dixie, 'that's not what you're interested in. It's what happened all those years ago you want to hear about.' He took a deep breath as though reluctant to talk about his past. 'Well, when I fell in love with your mother, Margo, I really thought I'd met the woman I wanted to marry. And we did, but after about a year she started to get fed-up with me not having a proper job.' Danny gave a slight laugh. 'I think I was selling second hand cars then...I've always been buying and selling something for as long as I can remember. Anyway, and a lot of this I found out later, Margo was beginning to think perhaps she hadn't married the right man. Probably because we were living in a small flat and the glamour of newly wedded bliss was fading fast.'

Danny took another drink.

'Then she discovered I'd been unfaithful. Nobody special, just a couple of weeks fling with a girl I'd known for years. But Margo found out and there was hell to pay. So I promised her it was the last time and she forgave me. However, I did play around a bit more and, although I was sure Margo had again found out, she never said anything, and me, cockily, thought she accepted me the way I was. I thought as long as I stayed with her she'd put up with me no matter what I got up to. Then Margo met Tom Fisher.'

'When was this?' Dixie asked.

Danny creased his brow in thought.

'It would be in our second year of marriage,' he replied. 'I met him at the same time, it was at some party we'd been invited to. He seemed a nice enough bloke and Margo bumped into him by accident about a month later...and they started seeing each other.'

'When did you find out about this?'

'Margo suddenly told me one day she was leaving me,' Danny said, answering Dixie's question. 'I can't say I was surprised. I had been spending a lot of time in the pub and coming home late. But it still came as a shock, a blow to my pride, to be honest.'

'Did she say why?'

'Yes, she did. Once it was out in the open she told me she was in love with Tom Fisher, and had been for some time. Obviously, they'd been seeing a lot of each other, and I wasn't the sort of person who kept tabs on her. It just never entered my mind she'd be unfaithful to me.'

'It's called taking a woman for granted,' Linda said.

'Yes, you're right,' Danny said, and smiled at her. 'But Margo was full of surprises because she wasn't just walking out on me, she said she was going to the States. Tom Fisher had a job to go to in Boston and she was going with him. He was going to work for a man called Sebastian Peterson, the kind of name that's stuck in my mind all these years. And it's possible he could be some relation of this Wyatt you asked me about.'

'That sounds about right,' Dixie said. 'I know Tom worked in America a long time ago for the Peterson business. Then about ten or eleven years ago Wyatt and his family bought into our company. Anyway, that's easy enough to check out.'

'But something happened when they went to the States,' Danny continued. 'Margo's mother got really sick. She was very close to her mother and then Tom was asked to go and work in San Francisco, another three thousand miles further away from London. So, Margo came back to this country to help look after her mother, who'd had a stroke and was bedridden. Her mother had a large detached house in Harrow and one of our mutual friends contacted me and told me Margo had returned.'

Danny drained his glass again and held it out.

'Same again?' Mike asked, taking the crystal tumbler.

Danny nodded and looked at his friend.

'You too, Jack?'

The hard man knocked back the rest of his scotch and held out his glass.

'Thanks,' he said.

'Please carry on,' Dixie said, who so far hadn't heard anything to upset her, but had to wait until Danny had his gin and tonic back in his hand.

'So I went and saw Margo,' he carried on. 'Now what you've got to remember, is that we were still great friends. What had happened, had happened, but there was no terrible animosity between us. It's probably difficult to understand but there was still a lot of feeling between us, good feelings. And...' Danny paused again...'we ended up in bed with each other. You see, Dixie, and I hope you can understand this, we were great in bed. Sexually we had never had any problems, and Margo was never unhappy in that department.'

'But she'd left you for Tom,' Dixie said. 'It sounds as though you're making my Mother out to be some sort of slut.'

'I know,' Danny said, 'but I'm not trying to give you that impression. It's awkward for me, because I'm trying to tell the truth, without running Margo down. What you've got to realize is that we still fancied each other. After all, we were still legally married, and your mother was lonely.'

Danny smiled.

'You're young, but as you get older and learn more about life, you'll understand these things happen, even to mothers. Margo said she loved the both of us. Me and Tom, but for different reasons.'

'You still haven't explained about Dixie's birth,' Mike said.

'I know, and I'm coming to that now. Margo had been home about two months when Tom Fisher arrived back in this country. He'd taken leave of absence from his job in America and suddenly turned up out of the blue. They had been writing to each other and phoning, but he never told her he was coming back. Maybe he thought something was going on.'

'And he'd have been right,' Dixie said.

'Look, Dixie, I know this is hard on you, and Tom was more of a father to you than I ever was...but this is how it happened. And yes, he did catch your mother and me together, at her mother's house. Thankfully not in bed, but he was no fool, and was suspicious. So, knowing I didn't have a future with Margo, I said I was genuinely concerned about Margo's mother and we'd also been discussing details of our separation. And that was all. Tom believed me. It was easy to get him to trust me because that's what he *wanted* to believe. Anyway, I left and let them get on with it.'

'Then what happened?' Dixie asked.

'Tom stayed about a month then had to go back to the States.'

'And my Mother?'

'She stayed in Harrow looking after your grandmother, who was getting much worse. And I suppose it was about two months later Tom returned for another month. It was then Margo told him she was pregnant. But she wouldn't leave her mother so Tom quit his job and got one in London.'

'How did you find out?'

'Margo phoned me. Tom had to go back to America for a few weeks to sort out some things there.'

'You two weren't still...?'

Danny replied before Dixie got a chance to finish her question.

'No, we weren't sleeping together. Both of us realized that wouldn't help the situation. But it was then I pointed out that her baby must be mine. At first, she wasn't having any of it, but then we worked out the dates together and Margo had to admit I was probably right.'

'*Probably*? So there was some doubt.'

Danny thought for a moment, his eyes looking at the carpet.

'No, not as far as I was concerned, but I think by then Margo had begun to question her own morals. She'd been sleeping with two men, virtually at the same time, and I think she suddenly felt embarrassed. She wanted it to be Tom's and I imagine it was difficult for her to face up to the truth. It couldn't have been easy.'

'But what about Tom?' Mike asked.

'Oh, he thought the baby was his all right, and his first priority was for Margo to get a divorce. But there was one person in the background who was to play a big part in all this. Margo's mother.'

'How was that?' Linda asked.

'Well, Margo had never told her mother about us busting up and her falling in love with another man. Her mother, a widow, was very straight-laced, church going and all that. A bit of a prude.'

'But what about when Margo went to America with Tom?' Mike asked. 'How did she explain that?'

'Margo never told her about Tom. Her mother thought she went to the States by herself to get a job and I was going to follow later. Then Margo was going to tell her I changed my mind and after a period of time she'd say she'd met another man. That's how Tom was going to appear on the scene. But her mother having a stroke had messed up Margo's plans. The one thing she didn't want, was to upset her mother.'

'You mean to say...her mother thought you and Margo were still happily married?'

'Yes, and Margo told Tom she wouldn't divorce me while her mother was so very ill. It would only put extra strain on her mind.'

'That couldn't have pleased him.'

'No, because Margo was living in her mother's house, while Tom had a flat by himself. To make it even more bizarre, whenever I visited, I had to pretend to the old lady over the months that everything was all right between me and Margo.' Danny shook his head. 'But it gets even more strange. When you were born, Dixie, Margo told Tom you were early, a bit premature, which solved that problem. But you were registered in my name to please Margo's mother because she was determined to stay alive until you were christened. Anyway, as far as I was concerned you were my child, and Margo and I were still married so Tom didn't have any say in the matter. To keep Tom happy Margo told him they'd get it sorted after her mother died. Then, six weeks after you were born you were christened in church and your grandmother passed away a month later a happy woman.'

'Then you got divorced,' Dixie said.

'Not straight away because Tom told me as soon as he could marry Margo he wanted to be recognized as Dixie's father. He said if the three of us made a legal declaration that he was the real father then the birth certificate could be altered. Whether or not this was true I don't know but I told him he was wasting his breath. Dixie's birth certificate was staying as it was, or there would be no easy divorce.'

'And you still hadn't told him you'd been sleeping with Margo? That you thought the baby was yours?' Mike asked, his voice sceptical.

'No,' Danny replied, 'I'd promised her I wouldn't, and I kept my word.'

'That's some story,' Dixie said.

'And that's where all the hate crept in because I wouldn't budge. Tom thought I was doing it to spite him for stealing Margo from me, to get even with him. He even wanted to adopt you, if that was the only way he could have you as his daughter. But I told Margo I would go to the Sunday newspapers and tell all. She definitely didn't want that so she persuaded Tom to accept my terms.'

'*Forced*, more like it,' Linda commented.

Dixie opened her mouth but before she could speak the door opened and Joey entered. He looked around at the serious faces.

'Blimey,' he grinned, 'looks like you're having a wake.'

FORTY SEVEN

Dixie stood and made the introductions.

Joey immediately felt at ease with the two men. Danny and Jack were his kind. The type that were part of his upbringing on the streets in the East End where he'd quickly learned how to separate the con artists and bullshitters from people who were telling the truth.

They might be ex-cons but Joey's sixth sense told him they could be trusted. The sort who made good friends - if they allowed you to be. Joey knew only too well that he was lucky to have been gifted with his voice. Otherwise, he'd have probably ended up in the nick himself, like a lot of his old schoolmates.

And Danny was impressed with Joey. He was probably one of the most well known people in the country. His music was often on the radio and television, and was always being written about in the tabloids. Yet, in real life, he seemed like an ordinary bloke with no airs or graces.

'I'll tell you later what's been said,' Mike whispered to Joey as more drinks were poured. 'But it seems there's a mystery as to who Dixie's father is.'

The pop star looked puzzled but didn't say anything and went and sat next to Linda.

'And if you think about what I've told you then that could be the motive you're looking for,' Danny continued.

'You mean, if Tom Fisher was Dixie's father, then the blood line would be on his side, not yours,' Mike said.

'That's right,' Danny agreed.

'So that would mean Dixie's Aunt Lucy would be her next of kin.'

'Yes, and after her, Robert Fisher.'

'But how could this be proved?' Linda asked. 'Especially in a court of law. There's no getting away from Dixie's birth certificate.'

Danny shrugged his shoulders.

'Your guess is as good as mine,' he replied.

'But if there is a way, then that's definitely a motive,' Mike said. 'If something happened to Dixie then all her money would go to her aunt.'

'She doesn't need it,' Dixie said defensively.

'Maybe not, but as Danny said earlier, it's odds on Robert would be controlling it. And don't forget, you also own a third of the company. That's worth a lot.'

'This is bloody upsetting,' Dixie said, and went to refill her glass, brandy this time instead of wine.

'Perhaps there is one thing we're forgetting,' Jack said.

All eyes riveted on the big man.

'What's that?' Mike asked.

'Supposing it does turn out to be Robert Fisher, then why kill Dixie? Why doesn't he just get rid of his sister? Much less complicated. She must be rich and if he's the next of kin all her money goes to him.'

'And he'd be suspected straight away, especially if Lucy's death was a bit iffy,' Danny said. 'That wouldn't be too clever.'

'No it wouldn't,' Dixie agreed. 'Besides, I know my aunt's intentions. And I come out of it better than Uncle Robert does.'

'That's right,' Mike said. 'I remember you telling me.'

'After the burglary Aunt Lucy told me she had made a new will and was leaving her country house to me. And all her other assets, her money and shares, would be divided equally between Robert and myself. She told me she was doing this because her old will left everything to her brothers. And with Tom dead Robert would get the lot.'

'Does your uncle know about the new will?' Linda asked.

'Yes,' Dixie replied, 'and he's also the executor.'

'Do you know how much Lucy's worth?' Danny asked.

'No idea,' Dixie replied, with a shake of her head.

'Well, if something did happen to you, then you'd automatically be out of her will and everything Lucy had would go to Robert when she died,' Linda said, 'no matter who your father is. With you out of the way he'd be the only heir left. And if Tom Fisher is your father he'd get a lot more. Either way he benefits.'

Dixie looked at her friend and shrugged her shoulders.

'It all sounds so horrible,' she said. 'I can't believe we're talking about my death like this...so casually.'

'Don't worry, Dixie, nobody will harm you,' Mike said.

'What's this about Dixie's father?' Joey asked, no longer able to contain his silence.

'Danny's positive he's the father,' Mike replied, 'but apparently the Fisher family think Tom Fisher is the father.'

'So how do you think they were going to prove it?'

'I don't know,' Dixie replied.

'That's easy,' Joey said, smirking, briefly feeling superior to the others in the room. 'DNA.'

'DNA?'

'That's right,' Joey said. 'Blimey, there's enough of us in the music world who get accused of being the father of somebody's kid. And DNA proves if they are, *or not*.'

'Of course,' Mike said. 'I've read about it in the papers. There's been some famous cases.'

'Do you know how it works?' Linda asked.

'Blood tests, I suppose,' Joey answered, 'of all parties concerned.'

'That's me,' Danny said, 'and Dixie...but Tom Fisher's dead.'

'Maybe he'll have to be exhumed.'

Joey's statement briefly silenced the others.

'I'm not sure about that,' Dixie said, and the others felt the emotion in her voice.

'No need to,' Mike said, anxious to ease Dixie's thoughts. 'Just Danny and you should be enough. That'll prove if he's your father or not.'

'Well, *that's* okay with me,' the relief obvious in Dixie's words. 'Does anybody know how to go about it?'

'I'll have a word with my manager,' Joey replied, 'I'm sure he'll know somebody who'll know something about it. The only trouble is, Vic's in the States and won't be back in his office until Monday.'

'That suits me,' Danny said, 'I intended going back to Norfolk tomorrow for the weekend anyway.'

'And we can relax too,' Mike said, turning his eyes towards Dixie. 'Spend the next two days doing nothing...get your mind off things.'

Linda smiled at Joey and squeezed his hand.

'Your manager might think the DNA test is for you.'

'Yeah, probably give him a bloody heart attack.'

*

Joey's prophesy wasn't far out.

'You've got somebody in the club, haven't you?' Vic Ruebens shouted down the phone. 'It'll cost you a fortune.'

'I 'aven't got anyone up the fuckin' spout,' Joey yelled back at his manager, excitedly forgetting his pronunciation. 'I wish you'd listen.'

'Are you sure?'

'Yes, I'm bloody sure. I want the information for a friend of mine.'

Vic Ruebens leaned back in his swivel chair, smiling, his usual cigar clamped in the corner of his mouth, feet on his oversize desk. His office was large, with black leather chairs and black and white carpet. Glass framed photographs and gold and platinum discs hung on the white walls.

'Okay, Joey, how quickly do you want this sorted out?'

'Like yesterday.'

'Okay, I'll speak to you soon.'

'Vic, I'll be in the recording studio the rest of the day, so I'll give you a number to ring. Ask for Mike.'

'Ah, so he's got someone in trouble.'

'Cor, you've got a suspicious mind. And, no. Once again you're wrong.' Joey paused. 'I'm on a mission of mercy.'

'What...you're doing it for the church?'

'If you must know, it's a synagogue. Your lot.'

'Well, if it involves a Jewish woman, that's bad news. They come expensive.'

'Yeah, the only way they can have an orgasm.'

'Don't remind me,' Vic said, swinging his feet to the floor and pulling his chair closer to the desk. 'Okay, I'll get on to it straight away.'

'Thanks, Vic. And don't forget, it might come in handy for you one day. I hear you've been putting it about lately.'

'Bollocks,' Vic retorted, then added. 'You haven't heard anything, have you? You couldn't have...' Vic's voice dropped to a whisper. 'Who told you?'

Joey paused for some time before answering.

'It was the rabbi.'

'Up yours,' Vic shouted into the phone.

'No thanks,' Joey said, laughing, 'I'm not that way inclined.'

The line went dead and Joey hung up, a smile still on his face. Vic sounded guilty, as though he'd been caught out. Nice to know everyone was at it.

Everyone, that is, except him.

Linda...he'd have to do something about their situation pretty soon. Otherwise, he'd go blind.

*

Vic phoned just after noon and Dixie answered the call.

'Hi, how are you?'

'Fine,' Vic replied. 'Joey said I should speak to Mike.'

'I'll put you on to him,' Dixie said, and handed the phone to the young man sitting next to her.

'Have you got a pen and paper?'

'Yes,' Mike replied, and picked up the blue biro laying on a small notepad.

'I've been recommended a place in south London that does these sort of tests, DNA Profiling it's called. Their scientists are government approved and their reports are accepted as evidence in our courts.'

'Sounds impressive,' Mike said, and wrote down the number that came over the line.

'I've been told you should ask for a woman called Wendy Abbott,' Vic continued, 'she's some sort of manager who will explain everything to you.'

'Thanks,' and Mike added the woman's name next to the phone number.

'I hope it works out okay,' Vic said, a trace of amusement in his voice.

Mike clicked off the phone, a grin playing around his lips, knowing what Vic had been thinking.

'Do you want to phone this clinic...or shall I?'

'No, I'll do it,' Dixie replied, and Mike handed her the cordless phone as he stood.

'I'll go and make some coffee,' he said.

Mike took his time and when he returned fifteen minutes later with two mugs Dixie was reading the notes she'd carefully made.

'Everything okay?' he asked, as he put the china mugs on the coffee table.

'Yes, the lady I spoke to was very helpful,' Dixie replied.

'Is it complicated?'

'No, it all seems straightforward. The only thing is, it will take about three weeks before the results are known, which brings it close to Christmas. And the woman said the sooner they have the blood samples the better.'

'In that case, you should try and contact Danny as soon as possible.'

'Yes, I suppose I should,' Dixie said and took from her handbag the business card given to her in the pub.

'Drink your coffee first,' Mike said, sensing a change in Dixie's mood. She took a sip of the hot liquid, and he added, 'does it bother you having to go through with this?'

'No, not really, it's just the uncertainty...'

'You mean, not knowing who your father is?'

'Yes, most people don't have this problem.'

'Well, I don't know who my Father is, and it's never bothered me.'

Dixie stared at Mike.

'The difference here is that I've got two men who have both claimed to be my Father.'

'It is unusual.' Mike put the mug to his mouth and drank, his eyes narrowing as he looked at Dixie over the rim. 'Who do you hope it is? Danny Buckley or Tom Fisher?'

Dixie shook her head slowly.

'I don't know...I really don't know.' She looked deep into Mike's eyes. 'But what I do know is, I wish with all my heart, this wasn't happening to me.'

Mike gave a comforting smile.

'Don't worry, you'll know the answer soon enough.'

'Danny seems a nice man and his name is on my birth certificate, but I don't know him. Maybe in the future, if I see him more often then I'll think different. I like him...,'her voice tailed off.

They'd spent the weekend in bed. Making love, eating, drinking and watching television. Mike had succeeded in taking Dixie's mind off her problems for the last two days. She'd felt safe in his arms and except for showers and going to the loo hadn't wanted to leave their bed.

Joey was still making music with his band and Linda had discreetly stayed with her parents.

But now Vic's phone call had jerked her back to reality.

'I'd phone Danny, if I were you,' Mike said softly.

Dixie nodded.

'Yes,' she agreed, and picked up the phone, looking at Danny Buckley's business card.

FORTY EIGHT

Mandy's voice came over the intercom when Danny pressed the button next to the flashing red light.

'Dixie Fisher on the phone,' his secretary informed him.

'Thanks,' he said, and added, 'hi,' when Dixie came on the line, 'what can I do for you, young lady?'

'I've found out the procedure for the DNA tests.'

'Good, and what's that?'

'Well, it'll take about three weeks for the tests to come through, which means we might get the results just before Christmas. If not, definitely by the first week in January.'

Danny chuckled.

'Make a nice present for me,' he said. 'So what have I got to do?'

'First, I think I'd better tell you what a woman from the clinic told me. She explained what this DNA thing is all about and said everyone in the world is genetically different - except identical twins. And what determines these differences is a substance which is found in all cells of the body and is called...' Dixie broke off for a moment, 'I can't pronounce it so I'd better spell it out for you.'

Danny picked up a pen from his untidy desk and wrote down the letters on a yellow message pad as they came over the line.

Deoxyribonucleic acid.

'I can't pronounce it either,' he said, again chuckling, 'no wonder everyone calls it DNA.'

'Now,' Dixie continued, 'each of us inherits half of our DNA from our father and half from our mother. There are two ways these tests can be done. One way needs just a pin-prick of blood and takes only about ten days to get the result. But in that test blood would need to be taken from my Mother as well as you and me. Then Margo's DNA could be identified leaving the other which would be the father's. However, because my Mother's dead you and I will have to supply ten mills of blood each, which means a syringe in the arm job to get the correct result.'

'And that's why that test takes longer?'

'Yes. Also what we've got to do is sign two sets of forms. The first one is to say that we give our consent to the laboratory to carry out the test and the other requests information like racial origin, medical history, date of birth and...well, whatever else it says.'

'Where do we give blood?' Danny asked.

'We can go to the clinic or get our own doctor to do it and get the sample sent to the laboratory.'

'Where is the clinic?'

'In Teddington.'

'That's way over the other side of London from where I am. And I'm going to be away for a few days.'

'Norfolk again?'

'Yes,' Danny replied, and paused. 'My lady friend isn't very well.'

'Oh, I'm sorry. Nothing serious, I hope.'

'No, no...nothing too serious,' and once again Danny paused.

'What about your own GP?' Dixie asked, sensing an awkward tilt to the conversation, and quickly reverting to their original discussion.

'Yes, I think I could work out something with my doctor. I've known him for years and I'm sure he'd do it for me. But I'd have to phone his surgery to double-check.'

'I was told if either of us use our own doctor we'll also need two passport size photographs...and your GP will have to certify they are a true likeness of you.'

'That's not a problem, I can go to one of those photo booths. They're usually in tube stations or supermarkets. What are you going to do?'

'I was thinking of going to my own doctor as well,' Dixie replied.

'Anything else?'

'Yes. When you find out if your doctor will do it you'll have to give me his name and address so that the clinic can get the forms and a special blood sample kit over to him. I'll tell the clinic to use a motorbike courier service to speed things up, and they can put it on the bill.'

'That's a good idea,' Danny said, 'it shouldn't take me long to get hold of him. I'll speak to you later,' and Danny replaced the receiver. He had a busy afternoon ahead of him if he was going to get everything done. Although he'd only got back from Norfolk late last night, he was in a hurry to return.

Danny had decided to ask Jessie to marry him.

*

It was six thirty by the time Danny left Dr Gray's surgery and headed out of London. Jack was with him because what had started out as an idle remark was now under serious discussion. They were both hooked on the idea of going into business together in Norfolk.

During the journey Danny told his friend what he had in mind for Jessie.

'That's a good thing to do,' Jack said, nodding his head in agreement, and the two men lapsed into silence. Danny turned the radio louder so they could hear the music against the increasing wind noise as the car picked up speed, both men lost in their own private thoughts.

Last week Jessie had told Danny the contents of her will. She was leaving everything to him. Her house, insurance policies, money in the bank and her share in the boatyard. Not a fortune but enough to make his life more comfortable. Pay off all his debts and have some left over.

The two men thought a pub or small hotel would be ideal. They figured they should have enough money between them which would leave only one snag, finding a front man to be the licensee, which was out of the question for them with their criminal convictions. But such a person shouldn't be too hard to find.

When they arrived at the cottage Jessie was asleep in one corner of a large sofa by the roaring open fire, Maggie, her mongrel dozing at the other end. Jessie looked so frail curled up with a blanket covering her, her hair now completely grey. A middle aged nurse in a white uniform sat reading a book in an armchair.

Jack said he'd go into the kitchen and start preparing a fry-up. Both men were hungry after the journey,

'Would you mind helping Jack for a moment?' Danny asked Nurse Coogan. 'I'd like to have a private word with Jessie.'

As the nurse moved out of the room Danny knelt on the floor and gently tickled Jessie's nose with a corner of the blanket. She wrinkled her nostrils and used the back of her hand to rub the annoying itch a couple of times as Danny repeated the process before sleepily opening her eyes to see who her tormentor was.

Danny took both her painfully thin hands in his.

'Jessie, will you marry me as soon as possible?'

She smiled at him, reflected firelight dancing in her eyes, for a brief moment a rush of adrenalin easing the illness from her face.

'Thank you, I'd love to.'

'I've already checked and as long as we get a letter from your doctor the ceremony can take place very quickly.'

Jessie slipped one hand free as Danny laid his head on her lap and stroked his curly hair.

Four days later they were married in the local registry office. Jessie's elderly parents and a few friends attended, with Jack as the best man.

Danny carried his bride into the brightly lit room, lavishly decorated with vases of fresh flowers.

But Jessie stood on her own two feet during the entire ceremony.

FORTY NINE

It was nearly a week since Dixie had given her blood sample and Mike still hadn't gone back to work, except for the odd hour in his London office, and then only when Linda was able to stay with Dixie.

Gerry Dolan griped a bit at first but when Mike had given a full account of the possible danger Dixie was in he'd told Mike to stay away as long as he wanted. As a matter of fact, a few days ago, Gerry had been told about a young architect who had just arrived in London from Edinburgh. Bill Mackenzie had all the qualifications and was a bachelor without any ties.

'If you think he's good enough take him on,' Mike said, who was feeling guilty about not pulling his weight.

'Okay,' Gerry said, 'but I'll stay in Wakefield until you sort out your problem.'

'Thanks,' Mike said, and appreciated Gerry's attitude. The Yorkshire project was special to him and he didn't want a stranger taking over.

*

They were sprawled out watching Saturday evening TV when the phone rang.

It was Joey.

'Still recording?' Mike asked.

'Yeah, be a few more days yet,' Joey replied. 'But I've just spoken to Terry Hayman and he had some news about Wyatt's gambling.'

'Yes,' Mike said interestedly, and moved away from the noisy television, walking into the kitchen. 'What did he say?'

'Well, it looks like our accountant should start going to bloody Gamblers Anonymous.'

'Does he lose much?'

'That's the strange thing. No he doesn't and he's a big time punter. But he's good. And Wyatt is also known in Las Vegas. It would appear that Wyatt's family in the States is mega rich and he gambles big for the kicks. Wyatt's a multi-millionaire in his own right and as far as Terry knows he doesn't have any gambling debts. When he does lose he pays up straight away but most people say he's probably ahead of the game.'

'Doesn't sound as though he'd need to embezzle the accounts,' Mike said.

'No, it doesn't,' the pop star agreed.

'Which brings us back to Dixie's uncle.'

'Anyone found out yet what this expensive hobby of his is?'

'No,' Mike replied. 'Dixie still doesn't want to ask her Aunt Lucy. Feels it might upset the old lady.'

'You've met her, so why don't you ask her?'

'I've thought about that, Joey, but if Dixie found out I'm not sure what her reaction would be.'

'I'd ask her if it was me.'

'Yeah,' Mike said, drawing out the word, then quickly changed the subject. 'Do you want a word with Linda?'

'Of course,' Joey replied.

'Umm, have you two yet...?'

'No, we bloody haven't. Besides, it's none of your business.'

Mike laughed, then added in a quiet voice, 'By the way, it has been noticed the way your speech has improved...keep it up, mate.'

There was silence before Joey gratefully muttered into the phone, 'Thanks,'

'I'll just go back into the lounge,' and Mike returned to the two women, holding out the phone to Linda.

'Joey wants a word,' he said, and plonked himself next to Dixie, his eyes fixed on the TV screen. He'd wait until Linda had finished talking before repeating what his friend had told him.

Joey's words came back to him.

'I'd ask her if it was me.'

Maybe that's what he should do. Talk to Aunt Lucy if he couldn't persuade Dixie.

But everything changed the next day.

*

They'd just finished eating a roast chicken lunch and were drinking coffee when Mike decided to raise the subject with Dixie.

'We can't shut you off from the rest of the world forever,' he said. 'We should either go to the police or hire a private detective. A genuine one this time.'

'I agree,' Linda said. 'Nothing's happened to you, Dixie, because you've hardly left the flat. And when you have you've always had somebody with you. But you can't live the rest of your life like this, always looking over your shoulder. And Mike and I can't keep babysitting you, we've both got jobs to think of.'

'I know,' Dixie said.

'But I don't want you taking any chances,' Mike said. 'So what do you think? The police or a private detective?'

Dixie shrugged her shoulders.

'I'm not sure. What do *you* think?'

'Well, no matter what we do, it will mean someone's got to talk to your Aunt Lucy. It might not be important after all, but I think we should find out what this expensive hobby of your uncle's is, even if only to satisfy our curiosity. And it will probably be better if you speak to her rather than someone she doesn't know.'

Dixie sighed.

'I suppose so,' she said.

'No time like the present,' Linda said, on Mike's side.

'That's right,' Mike agreed, and went and got the phone from its charger in the lounge.

'What do I say if Aunt Lucy wants to know why I want this information?'

'Tell her it's important but you can't tell her the reason. She'll have to trust you, and you will tell her later on. Just stress, it's important you know.'

'Okay,' Dixie said, and pressed the memory button on the phone to connect to her aunt's number.

During the time the call lasted Mike and Linda sat quiet listening to Dixie's side of the conversation, impatient for it to finish so they could find out the other half. Something to do with horses and a stud farm. Half a million, presumably money, was mentioned then Dixie made a writing motion with her hand and Mike went and got a pen and paper.

After writing down an address Dixie said goodbye to her aunt, clicked off the phone and gave it back to Mike.

'So what did your aunt have to say?'

'It's horses,' Dixie replied.

'You mean he gambles on the horses?'

'Not really...no, that's not his problem.'

'I don't understand,' Mike said.

'Well, he doesn't gamble any more than most horse race owners do, according to Aunt Lucy, but some of the horses he's invested in have been duds.'

'I see,' Mike said slowly, 'he owns race horses. I personally don't know much about the sport but from what I've read, buying race horses is expensive, and then there's all the trainer's fees and so forth to be paid for.'

'We heard you mention the figure, half a million,' Linda said. 'Did your aunt mean money?'

Dixie nodded her head.

'Yes,' she replied, 'Aunt Lucy lent my uncle half a million pounds about four or five months ago.'

'Wow,' Mike said, 'that's a lot of money. What was that for?'

'Uncle Robert also has a half share in a stud farm which needed a sudden cash injection. This is the name and address,' Dixie said, motioning to the pad in front of her.

'I thought your uncle was a millionaire, well, wealthy at the least,' Mike said.

'Oh, he is. But Aunt Lucy said a lot of his money is tied up in shares, and it was only a temporary loan. She said Robert has promised she'll have her money back by Christmas at the latest. Anyway, Aunt Lucy isn't bothered and said she could easily have afforded to have given him twice that amount if he'd wanted. Don't forget, they are brother and sister.'

'Putting it bluntly,' Linda said, 'I'd say your uncle is in a pile of financial shit.'

'I agree,' Mike said, 'and that half a million might only be part of it. Who knows what he might have taken out of the company. And there's your motive, Dixie.'

There was silence and Dixie averted her eyes from the piercing looks of the two people sitting facing her.

'It might be a good idea,' Mike continued, 'to tell Wyatt Peterson, or get an independent auditor to go over the books.'

'But what if we're wrong,' Dixie said, lifting her head. 'My uncle would never forgive me...and what would Aunt Lucy say? There has to be trust in a family.'

'We can't ignore it,' Linda said. 'We've got to know the truth.'

'I know...,' but before Dixie could continue the phone rang in Mike's hand. He silently cursed the interruption but managed a polite, 'Hello,' as he held the receiver to his ear, then stood in surprise as the caller identified herself.

'Yes, Miss Smith, Dixie Fisher is here, I'll get her for you.' Mike put his hand over the mouthpiece as he looked down at Dixie. 'It's Kate Smith...she wants to speak to you,' he whispered.

Dixie looked just as astonished as Mike passed over the phone.

'Hello, Miss Smith, I've been wanting to talk to you for some time. Did Mrs Powis pass on my message.'

'Yes she did, but I'm sorry, I've been busy moving house and so on. Anyway, I'm talking to you now.'

There were so many questions running through Dixie's mind she didn't know where to start. But before she had a chance Kate Smith continued.

'I'd like to see you,' she said.

'Exactly what I want,' Dixie said. 'When?'

'Next Wednesday.'

'Why not today? I'd like to meet you as soon as possible.' Dixie knew the woman on the other end held so many answers and was anxious to confront her.

'No, I'm sorry, Miss Fisher, but I can't meet with you until next Wednesday evening.'

'Will your boyfriend be there?' Dixie asked.

'I'm sorry, Miss Fisher, all I can say is that I'll meet you next Wednesday. Please don't ask me any questions now because I won't give any answers.'

'So what time? And where?'

'Eight o'clock in a pub called, The Black Swan.'

'Where's that?' Dixie asked, and once again used the pen and paper in front of her to write down an address as it came over the line.

'Goodbye, Miss Fisher.'

'Don't hang up,' Dixie said desperately, 'I've got things I want to talk to you about.'

'It will have to wait until Wednesday,' Kate Smith repeated emphatically. 'Goodbye.'

'Goodbye,' Dixie echoed dully, then stared at the phone as it went dead. 'That was short and sweet,' she said.

'Did she say anything else besides making a meet?' Mike asked.

Dixie shook her head, her mouth suddenly dry, and took a sip of her nearly cold coffee.

'No,' she replied. 'Kate Smith kept repeating she'd see me Wednesday, and that was it.'

'This is strange,' Mike said, 'to suddenly phone out of the blue and want to see you. There's something behind this, got to be.'

'Like what?' Linda asked.

'Sounds like a trap to me.'

'But I've got to see her,' Dixie said.

'I know,' Mike said, 'but I'm coming with you. And I'm also going to organize some other protection.'

FIFTY

Mike waited until the next day before he called Danny Buckley. No point disturbing everyone's Sunday. There was enough time to sort things out before Dixie's meeting.

Ten minutes past nine Mike picked up the phone but was informed by Danny's secretary he was in Norfolk. 'Maybe for the whole week.'

'That's okay,' Mike said, 'I've got his mobile, I'll call him on that,' and broke the connection, quickly punching in the digits of the other number. A moment later Danny answered and his immediate reaction was the same as Mike's when told about Kate Smith's phone call.

'It's a trap,' he said.

'That's what I think,' Mike said, 'but I don't see how. The meeting's in a public place so it's not going to be easy for whoever's behind this.'

'Maybe not for a so-called accident. But murder can happen in an instant. And somehow I don't think whoever's behind this is going to go to all the trouble of making it look like an accident. Not this time.'

'What makes you say that?'

'Because they must have realized by now that Dixie has put two and two together. They know she's not stupid.'

'So they'll probably think we suspect it's a set-up.'

'Most likely,' Danny replied. 'I'm sure they're not stupid either. The thing is, what are we going to do about it? I take it that's the reason you've phoned me?'

'Yes, but Dixie is determined to keep the meeting. She says she has to because Kate Smith has got the answers to so many questions.'

'I agree,' Danny said, 'and that's what makes it so suspicious. Why should she implicate herself? No, it doesn't make sense.'

'Dixie is going to need protecting, and that's where I thought you'd be able to help.'

'Yes, I can be back in London in a few hours.'

'No, Danny...look I'm not sure how to put this...but Dixie doesn't want you there when she meets Kate Smith.'

'Why's that?'

'Because she's frightened something might go wrong and you could get hurt. She just doesn't want to take a chance of that happening. She's had enough grief with the death of her mother and Tom Fisher and...well, she wants you kept safe, out of the way.'

Danny snorted.

'Mike, I might be getting on a bit, but I can still look after myself. Anyway, Dixie's my daughter, and I feel I should be there.'

'I was thinking of your friend, Jack. Him and maybe someone else and, of course, I'll be around as well.'

There was silence before Danny continued.

'You certainly couldn't get a better man than Jack and I know he'd do it,' he said. Danny hadn't told Mike or Dixie about his recent marriage or how ill Jessie was and he'd asked Jack to keep quiet about it too. There was no point adding anymore complications to the young couple's problems at the moment. But Jessie was much worse and he did want to spend as much time with her as possible. He knew he'd be lucky if she lasted to Christmas. However, he didn't want Mike to think he was ducking out of his responsibility.

'You're sure you and Dixie don't want me to come to this meeting? You're absolutely positive?'

'Yes,' Mike replied. 'Dixie doesn't want to take the risk of anything happening to you.'

'All right then, if it'll keep her happy, but I want you to keep me informed of everything that goes on. And as it happens, okay?'

'Yes, of course.'

'So, do you want me to get hold of Jack and arrange for him to contact you? I think it would be better for you both to meet as soon as possible.'

'Yes, you're right. Give him Dixie's telephone number and then I'll get him to come here, to Dixie's flat. We can take it from there.'

'Okay, Mike, I can't say I'm pleased, but if that's what you want me to do then I'll stay here. Just make sure you look after my daughter,' Danny paused for a moment, 'and tell Dixie I appreciate her concern for my safety.'

Danny clicked off his mobile and looked through the small square bedroom window panes. It was snowing, thick and heavy, with hardly any wind. Big white flakes dropped relentlessly from the sky - and settled. The lawn had already disappeared under a blanket of white.

Under different circumstances Danny would have loved it.

He turned his head and gazed at Jessie propped up against the puffy lace pillows in the large bed. She was dozing, a paperback novel loosely clasped in one hand. So pale, so ill, so sad.

Danny had erected a large Christmas tree in the room, brightly decorated and positioned so that Jessie saw it as soon as she opened her eyes.

As the dejected looking man gently sat on the bed a slight shudder ran through him and he involuntary sighed. Danny seemed surrounded by death.

*

The heavy flakes reached the capital just after lunch. Snow for the second winter running - unheard of for years in

London - well, certainly the amount that was falling now. But it seemed the weather was changing all over the world.

Jack had arrived half an hour ago and immediately assured the young couple they had nothing to worry about. He said he wanted to go the Black Swan pub to look around the area and Mike insisted on going with him.

'Of course,' Jack said. 'I've got two men waiting downstairs. They'll be coming with us.'

'You should have invited them up,' Dixie said, 'it must be cold outside.'

'No, they'll be okay, they're in a car.'

They were waiting for Linda to arrive and when she did, about fifteen minutes later, the two men left the flat.

Outside a sharp wind whipped snow into their faces, stinging their skin, nearly two inches already covering the pavement and road. A black Jaguar saloon car parked fifty yards away flashed its headlights and swept smoothly forward to where Jack and Mike were standing. They got in the back and the thick set man sitting in the front passenger seat turned his head and gave a brave attempt at smiling, which did little to soften the hard look in his eyes.

'This is George,' Jack said, and the man stuck his arm over the back of the front seat. Mike shook the massive hand extended to him and felt the strength of the other man. Christ, Mike thought, it would take a tank to stop him.

George grunted in greeting and Mike smiled back.

'Nice to meet you,' he said, retrieving his hand and patting the driver lightly on the shoulder as the car drew away. 'You too,' he added.

'That's Tony,' Jack said, and the driver took one hand off the steering wheel and raised it towards the back of the car in salute, his eyes never leaving the windscreen. He too was large with the same menacing air about him. Both men were in their late thirties with close cropped hair and smartly dressed in dark suits.

Jack gave the address of the pub and the four lapsed into silence as the car cautiously maneuvered through the snow. Mike knew the men he was travelling with were the type that let their actions do their speaking and remembered a phrase from his teenage years.

You don't *talk* a good fight.

Mike felt a lot more confident knowing these men would be looking out for Dixie.

The Jaguar passed Marble Arch into Edgware Road and a couple of intersections later turned left, through a set of lights then slowed to a stop. Tony kept the engine running so the wipers could do their work. It was still snowing heavily and didn't look like easing up.

'It's the next street in front of us,' the driver said.

'Right,' Jack said. 'Mike and I will go into the pub together and you two arrive separately. Give us a good twenty minutes 'cos I want to suss out the area first.'

'Okay,' Tony said, as the back seat passengers got out, careful not to slip.

The snow crunched under their feet and Mike and Jack bowed their heads against the flurries as they approached the road. The two men stopped on the corner carefully taking everything in.

The street was a mixture of private houses and shops about one hundred and fifty yards long bordered by T-junctions at either end. It was one way only and narrow with no parking meters. The Black Swan pub was in the middle flanked by several shops, now closed after the day's business. Jack looked at his watch. It was six thirty. A few more shops were opposite and these too were closed.

The men walked along the road and Jack noticed one of the premises, a Chinese restaurant, had ceased trading. *A To Let* sign was above the front.

The men reached the opposite T-junction and saw the adjoining road was much wider and busier.

'Let's go to the pub,' Jack said, and Mike nodded in agreement, glad to get out of the cold.

There was only one door leading into the Black Swan. Inside the walls were wood panelled with a low beamed ceiling and the soft lighting gave a snug cosy feeling. There was just one bar with booths against the walls and a few tables and chairs in the middle. Colourful Christmas decorations were a reminder that the festive season was here. It wasn't a big pub and there were about a dozen people inside.

Jack ordered a pint of bitter from the middle aged barman and Mike had a large scotch and water.

'I don't suppose you'll be busy on a night like this,' Jack said to the barman.

'Doesn't make much difference,' the man replied. 'Our main trade is usually during the lunchtime. Packed to the rafters we are. But in the evening it's mainly the locals who come in here and, of course, we get quite a few tourists in the summer.'

'Nice pub,' Mike observed, and looked around.

'Yes, there's been a pub on this site for over a hundred years.' The barman broke off and moved to serve another customer who'd just arrived, his dark grey overcoat flecked with white flakes. It was George and another five minutes later Tony entered looking just as windswept. One stayed at the bar and the other sat in a corner booth.

Jack and Mike reordered. Ten minutes later Jack went to the toilet and after he returned the two men finished their drinks, said cheerio to the barman and left.

'There's a fire exit in the toilets,' Jack said, as they trudged back to the car. 'It opens into a fair sized back yard with a high brick wall and there's a gate to the street which is padlocked on the inside. So it looks like the only way in and out is through the front entrance we used.'

They arrived back at the Jaguar and minutes later Tony arrived, opened the doors and the men gratefully slid inside.

Then the front passenger door opened and George lowered his bulk on to the seat before the saloon car moved off and carefully retraced its path back the way it had come. Tony was a good driver and handled the car well in the hazardous conditions.

It was another quiet journey but when the car stopped and Mike moved to open the rear door Jack gripped his arm.

'The three of us will be back at the pub tomorrow lunchtime and in the evening,' he said. 'I'll phone you Wednesday morning and then we'll make arrangements for later on in the day.' Jack stared intensely at Mike. 'And don't worry about Dixie. We'll look after her.'

Mike pushed open the door and stood on the pavement looking down at the man with the broken nose.

'Thanks,' he said, 'I know you will.'

FIFTY ONE

They left the apartment block early. Mike was driving his Range Rover with Linda and Dixie in the back. Linda had insisted on going and wouldn't listen to any of her friend's arguments.

'I'm coming with you and that's final,' she said.

Mike stayed out of it, frankly not sure if it was a good idea or not. Jack just shrugged his shoulders when told.

'Whatever,' was his only comment.

The snow had stayed and the weather forecast showed no change for the next week. Another fall earlier in the day had continued for over an hour but grit on the main roads kept risks down to a minimum. However, it was still bitterly cold.

Jack, with George behind the wheel, were following in a grey Volvo estate. Tony was already parked near the Black Swan, with everyone keeping in contact via their mobile telephones.

They arrived forty five minutes before eight o'clock and Mike stopped his car in near enough the identical place the Jaguar had occupied two evenings previous. Tony was sitting in that same vehicle a few yards away.

Mike checked on his mobile everyone was in place and a moment later George came into view and walked towards the Range Rover. Linda got out and was quickly escorted round the corner to the pub. Five minutes later George reappeared and Mike and Dixie alighted and were also accompanied into the side street.

Jack had hoped to have the Volvo parked directly outside the Black Swan's entrance but this space had already been taken up by a dirty white van. A piece of paper under a wiper said it had broken down and the police had been informed. The inside of the van could clearly be seen from the windows in the back and, except for a few boxes, it was empty. It appeared genuine but it meant that the Volvo had to park either in front, or behind the van. Jack had opted to go behind, but not too close. The only inconvenience was that the estate car was further from the pub entrance than had been anticipated.

Jack stood directly outside the Black Swan in his long overcoat watching the young couple as they approached.

The side street hadn't been touched by the gritters and the snow on the road was packed down tight and slippery. The pavement wasn't much better. Parts, by the shops and outside the pub had been cleared, but the rest was treacherous. The earlier fall had added another inch and yellowy light from the street lamps reflected off the snow.

The sudden change in the weather hadn't happened until after Kate Smith's phone call and Jack wondered if that would make any difference to the plans of whoever was organizing this meeting.

After Mike and Dixie safely entered the pub Tony came hurrying along the street, dressed in strong leather boots, jeans, a heavy thick sweater and hooded parka. He took a set of keys from Jack, walked to the other side of the car and slipped into the driving seat of the Volvo. He would stay in the car while the others were in the Black Swan. Except for the van it was the only vehicle parked in the road.

When Dixie and her friends left the pub they would be driven home in the estate car. George and Jack would follow in the Jaguar and Mike's car would be returned later after it had been thoroughly checked over to see it hadn't been tampered with. Nothing was being left to chance.

Jack pushed open the door and entered the warmth of the pub. The three young people were sitting at a table and Jack went and sat on the vacant chair awaiting him where he had a good view of the front entrance.

George was sitting by himself in a booth. He'd taken off his topcoat and placed it on the bench seat on the other side of the table, hoping to put off anyone sitting there. Not that the pub was busy. There were even less customers than there had been when they'd first visited the Black Swan. It seemed the weather had become a deterrent after all, even affecting the locals.

'I bought you a pint of bitter,' Mike said, as Jack unbuttoned his overcoat.

The big man nodded.

'Yeah, thanks,' and Jack took a sip. 'But I'd better check out the toilets,' he said, moving away from the table. A minute later he was back. 'Everything seems okay,' he informed the others.

The four sipped their drinks slowly and made small talk, their eyes returning every few minutes to a brass ship's clock behind the bar. There was a feeling of tension at the table.

Eight o'clock came and no sign of Kate Smith. Mike bought a third round of drinks and placed them on the table. Quarter past the hour and everyone was looking at their own watches seemingly not trusting the pub clock anymore.

Half past eight Mike voiced the question on everyone's mind.

'How long do we wait?'

'I don't know,' Dixie replied, deeply disappointed because Tom Fisher's former private secretary hadn't shown. But she was still hopeful. 'The weather's pretty bad and maybe that's held her up.' The young woman paused then focused her attention on Jack. 'What do you think?'

'Give it till nine and then we'll leave,' he replied. Jack wasn't concerned about the time because as it had become more apparent that the appointment wasn't going to be kept he now figured the danger would be outside the pub, when they left. The promise of a meeting with Kate Smith had just been bait to lure them there. He was sure of it, but kept this thought to himself.

'Perhaps she changed her mind,' Linda said, and added optimistically, 'maybe she'll phone you later, Dixie.'

'Maybe,' Mike muttered, and the group once again fell silent.

Ten minutes to nine Jack stood and put on his overcoat.

'I'm going to have a look outside,' he said. 'Won't be long.'

Since they'd been in the pub it had started snowing again, not heavy, but the blustery wind whipped powdery flakes into Jack's eyes making him blink. He looked around. The street was quiet, even the two main roads at the T-junctions hardly had any traffic. It was a night for being indoors.

Jack walked into the road and the window on the driver's side of the Volvo slid down.

'What's happening?' Tony asked.

'The woman hasn't shown. Doesn't look like she's going to either,' Jack replied. 'Seen anything suspicious?'

The driver shook his head.

'No, but I've had to have the motor running some of the time to heat the car. It's fucking freezing sitting out here.'

'Yeah, well, we'll be leaving soon. I just want to check around a bit,' and Jack started walking. The few shops on either side of the road were shut with Xmas lights glimmering through the glass fronts, except for the closed-down Chinese restaurant. Some of the private residences had been converted into flats, judging by the extra doorbells in the porches, and nearly all these had their curtains drawn tight.

It all seemed peaceful - too peaceful - and that bothered Jack.

He reached one end of the street and stood on the corner. There were quite a few cars parked in the main road, most of them with some form of snow covering, making it hard to judge how long they'd been there. The Jaguar he'd be riding in later was just yards away.

Jack walked back along the street to the other T-junction. There were more cars parked in this main road too. He looked back up the side street. The Volvo estate and van were still the only vehicles visible.

Jack wiped his eyes and returned to the Black Swan, pushed open the door and sat down.

'Are we ready to leave?' Mike asked.

'In a minute, so you'd better get your coats on,' Jack replied, and glanced over at George, who was now in his topcoat. A look passed between the two men, and Jack took out his mobile phone, quickly pressing the small buttons. It was answered by Tony.

'Get ready,' Jack said, 'we're coming out now.'

FIFTY TWO

The figure in black motorcycle leathers carefully unlatched the front door of the Chinese restaurant. He'd been there for hours keeping warm in the empty eating place with the help of two paraffin heaters and a large flask of coffee.

A powerful dark red Suzuki motorcycle was parked in the middle of the room pointing towards the entrance.

The Volvo estate was about thirty yards away on the opposite side of the street with its lights on and the motor ticking over. The driver had turned on the engine several times before but this time he'd leant over and pushed open the front and rear passenger doors nearest the pavement. He was expecting company.

And John knew the moment was at hand.

'Any minute now,' he whispered into his mobile phone and immediately received confirmation from Eddie that he understood. John slipped on his crash helmet and silently opened the restaurant door inwards on hinges he'd made sure were well oiled. Then he picked up a glass bottle nearly full of liquid from the floor, swung his leg over the sleek motorbike and eased it off its rest, pushing himself forward until the bike's front wheel was nearly on the pavement.

John was wearing wool mittens with no fingers and he flicked open the top of a Zippo lighter ready to light the petrol soaked piece of cloth protruding from the neck of the large bottle. The butt of a twin barreled sawn-off shotgun stuck out from the front of his leather jacket.

The door of the Black Swan opened and the man with the broken nose appeared followed by Dixie Fisher and Linda. Mike and another man followed close behind.

The group walked past the dirty van until they reached the Volvo, the two women quickly slipping into the back seats. Mike got in the front next to the driver and the doors slammed. Then the two big men started walking away from the estate car heading towards the end of the street.

It was as though the sound of the closing doors had been a signal and in one fluid movement, John started the Suzuki, lit the wick of the petrol bomb and was out into the street struggling to keep the powerful machine under control on the slippery surface.

The Volvo had moved only inches from the kerb when the glass bottle went hurtling through the air and exploded against the car's windscreen, covering the vehicle in flaming liquid. The motorcyclist now able to use both hands steadied his machine and just before he reached the end of the street slid into a neat U-turn. He grabbed the shotgun from his jacket, cocked the twin hammers and started back towards the burning estate car.

Immediately the bottle had smashed against the windscreen Tony hit the brake but couldn't prevent the heavy vehicle sliding forward until it crashed into the van. As soon as the Volvo came to a halt Tony burst open the driver's door and flung himself into the road, then hurled himself into a shop doorway, struggling to extract an automatic pistol from the inside pocket of his parka.

The reflexes of the others in the car had been just as quick and they instinctively threw open their doors and plunged out of the car, rolling on the snow. It only took seconds but time appeared to go into slow motion and everything seemed dream-like. However, the main thing was, no-one was hurt and Mike grabbed hold of Dixie, shoving her away from the burning Volvo.

'Get over here in case the petrol tank blows,' he shouted to Linda. As the three moved further from the burning vehicle Mike saw Jack and George running towards them who'd been stunned by the abrupt turn of events. Then George darted into the road just as the motorcyclist drew nearly level, his shotgun aimed towards Mike and the girls. Without hesitation, the large man launched himself through the air at the red Suzuki hoping to knock the barrel of the gun sideways. Just as it looked as though he might succeed John pulled both triggers and the blast caught George high in his left shoulder, the pellets spinning him in mid-air, causing one of his feet to connect with the bike's rear wheel. The heavily built man thudded on to the icy snow as John wobbled and tried to control his machine, but couldn't help going into a skid and slid sideways across the road only stopping when he hit the front of a flower shop.

'Stay there,' Jack barked to Mike, and swiftly covered the distance to where the leather clad motorcyclist was struggling to rise. Jack grabbed hold of the man and rammed his head forcefully into the wall at the side of the shop window. A loud crack was heard as the crash helmet thumped against the solid brickwork, then Jack gripped the black helmet with both hands and twisted viciously with all his strength. There was a slight popping sound as the biker's neck snapped and John dropped lifeless to the snow covered pavement.

For a brief moment there was an eerie stillness, then the momentary silence was unexpectedly broken by the deep throated roar of a sports car quickly going through the gears. Jack looked round and saw a green MG hurtling along the pavement on the pub side directly towards Mike and the two women. But before Jack could do anything, Tony, now in a crouching position with a Browning automatic clasped in both hands, took careful aim and squeezed the trigger several times. The side window of the sports car shattered and the curly haired driver felt a sudden pain in his chest. But Eddie kept his foot jammed hard on the accelerator tearing towards his target. One thought only in mind.

It took several seconds for the danger to register with Mike. Events of the last couple of minutes had happened so fast the startling sight of the MG racing over the pavement towards them in the opposite direction of the one way street took him completely by surprise. But his instinctive feeling to protect Dixie kicked in and he immediately lunged forward giving both women a powerful shove in their backs. The force sent Dixie and Linda flying forward on to the road but, before Mike had a chance to leap clear, the sports car clipped him hard sending him crashing chest first into the sharp corner of a concrete porch. The impact bent his body forward and his head smashed against the wall with a sickening thud.

Dixie picked herself up from the road and saw the crumpled figure of her boyfriend lying on the pavement.

'Mike,' she screamed out, and a moment later was by his side anxiously staring down into his face. He was unconscious, his breathing barely audible. There was a nasty cut on his forehead which was already beginning to swell. But, more worrying, a small trickle of blood oozed out of one corner of his mouth. Linda joined her friends, standing over them, feeling helpless. Everything had happened so fast it was difficult to take in.

Tony, still crouched, his eyes following the green MG loosed off several more shots. The .32 calibre bullets ripping into the boot of the sports car before it skidded wildly round the corner of the T-junction and disappeared.

Jack saw the middle aged barman standing in the doorway of the pub and shouted to him, 'Call an ambulance.'

The man vanished back inside the Black Swan and Tony and Jack immediately went to help George who was groaning through gritted teeth. But he had managed to hoist himself to his knees and his friends put their hands under his arms and lifted him into a standing position.

'Is it bad?' Jack asked.

'Not sure,' George replied. 'I think it's just my shoulder.'

Tony undid a couple of buttons of his friend's topcoat, ripped open his shirt and looked at the wound.

'I've seen worse,' he grinned. 'You'll live, you big ape.'

'Do you want to wait for the ambulance?' Jack asked. 'Or will you go to our usual man?'

'We'll go and see the usual doc,' Tony replied, 'or otherwise we'll get involved with the old bill.'

'Yeah, that's best,' Jack agreed, as the two men started to move away. 'Let me know how much it costs. Speak to you later,' then he spotted the sawn-off shotgun laying in the snow, 'hang on a minute, you'd better take this.' Jack picked up the gun and handed it to Tony.

'I'll add it to my collection,' he said, and stuffed it down the front of his coat.

Jack kicked snow over George's bloodstains hiding the telltale red marks and wondered what he'd tell the police when they arrived. He knew the barman wouldn't have just called for an ambulance and, as though he'd been reading Jack's mind, the publican came out again. This time clutching a large fire extinguisher.

'I called the police as well,' he said, as he started to spray the Volvo.

'Good thinking,' Jack smiled.

'Any idea what happened? I thought I heard shots...and where are those other two men?'

Jack shrugged his shoulders.

'They did a runner...I don't know what it's all about. But that bloke over there looks as though he's had a bad accident,' and Jack pointed over to where the motorcyclist was stretched out by the red Suzuki.

'Blimey, he looks dead.'

Jack didn't say anything else and moved away from the man. He took off his overcoat, rolled it up and placed it gently under Mike's head, then squatted by the side of Dixie. Mike didn't look good at all. He'd lost a lot of colour in his face.

'The ambulance is on its way,' he said.

Dixie looked at the hard man, tears in her eyes.

'Good,' she said. 'He won't die, will he?'

'No, of course not,' Jack replied, and hoped his voice sounded convincing. 'He's young and strong. Don't worry, he'll be all right.'

'How are Tony and George?' Linda asked, and her voice dropped to a whisper. 'George got shot, didn't he?'

'He's okay,' then Jack paused. He felt awkward knowing he had to talk cold and rational, but it was crucial they got their story right. 'Look,' he said, addressing both women, 'let me do most of the talking to the police. That's important. And if they do push too hard, go hysterical, or whatever. But don't forget, the old bill weren't here and they don't know what went on. So if we all stick to the same story then they'll have to believe us.'

'Okay,' Linda said. 'What do you want us to say?'

'You were never in the Volvo, all right? A man by himself was in the car when everything happened. And George wasn't with us either. It was just a coincidence he came out of the pub after us. Now forget their names. You don't know any names, and you didn't hear any shots because all you wanted to do was get away from the burning car. You don't know how the car caught fire and you haven't any idea what happened to the man in the Volvo or the man who came out after us. Everything happened so fast it seemed like a blur.' Jack stopped for a moment racking his brains. 'Oh, yes,' he continued, 'and as far as you can remember, it looked like the man in the sports car was trying to escape from the man on the motorcycle and he hit Mike. The bike went into a skid and went into the wall.'

'How is the man who was on the bike?' Linda asked.

'I think maybe he's dead.'

'Do you know who he is?'

'No I don't. He's still got his crash helmet on and I didn't see his face. But I'm sure he'll be known to the police.' Jack paused, then added. 'And there's one other thing you and Dixie must remember.'

'What's that?'

'You two women, Mike and me arrived in Mike's Range Rover and we were going home in it. We just happened to be in the wrong pub at the wrong time.'

'Okay,' Linda said, 'but what were we doing here in the first place?'

'Simple. Mike and I were here a couple of days ago, liked it and thought we'd bring you out for a drink. Dixie, this is something you've got to remember. Danny Buckley and I are thinking of buying a pub together in Norfolk and you were going to help out Danny with finances. So we've been looking at various pubs to get a rough idea of what decor we'd like. That's why we were here.'

'Sounds a bit weak,' Linda said. 'I can't imagine anyone wanting to go out on a night like tonight just to look at pub decor.'

'Yes, I know, but that's all I can think of at the moment. Unless you've got a better idea.'

'Where's the bloody ambulance,' Dixie said, desperately squeezing one of Mike's hands.

'It'll be here soon,' Linda said, putting an arm around her friend.

'The thing is,' Jack continued, 'it all depends on whether you want to tell the police everything. And I mean *everything*. But that would mean a lot of publicity. And I think...' Jack's voice tailed off.

'Yes, what do you think?' Dixie asked.

'I don't think you'll be bothered anymore. I don't think anyone will try and get to you again. Not after tonight.'

'You mean I'll be safe?'

'Yes,' Jack replied. 'I do.'

'But I still want to find out the truth, and who's been behind this.'

'I'm sure Danny and I will be able to do that for you.'

'Dixie, don't let's say too much to the police. I think Jack's right,' Linda said.

Just then an ambulance with a flashing light turned into the street, closely followed by a police car and fire engine. There'd been no need for sirens, the roads had been clear.

'Okay,' Dixie said. 'I don't care about anything anymore,' and she moved out of the way as a medic bent down and looked at the young man on the pavement. 'Just as long as Mike's okay. He's got to be.'

Linda gave Dixie a supportive arm as they watched Mike being attended to, and wondered if Jack had only said Dixie would be safe now, to make her feel better, or whether it would turn out to be true.

But one thing was for sure. Her friend had been right.

Somebody *was* trying to kill Dixie.

FIFTY THREE

Coming out of the skid the driver of the MG slowed down. He was hurt...bad. Although the pain in his chest had settled into a dull ache, he felt light headed, there was a taste of blood in his mouth and his breathing sounded hoarse. Eddie knew a bullet had punctured one of his lungs.

It had all gone badly wrong.

Dixie had arrived with her boyfriend but when it become apparent they were going to leave in another car Eddie and John had to quickly change their plan.

The Range Rover's four tyres had been punctured and that should have delayed them long enough for the job to be properly finished. But leaving in the Volvo screwed things up. Also, the snow hadn't helped and though he'd figured the young woman would have some protection it never crossed his mind they'd be tooled up and start shooting back. Eddie glanced at the dull grey of the automatic pistol laying on the passenger seat. He'd never had a chance to use it.

And what had happened to John? He was could be dead or in police custody. But Eddie knew his friend wouldn't talk. The same as he wouldn't if the circumstances had been reversed.

He coughed and it hurt. Eddie knew he needed medical attention but also knew if he went to a hospital the police would be called. Fuck the old bill.

That's where John would have come in handy. His friend knew a bent doctor who'd have helped. John had mentioned him several times in the past but it was the kind of detail Eddie had pushed to the back of his mind because he didn't think he'd ever need it. And if he did, he'd have got John to arrange it.

But John wasn't here. And it was no use contacting his employer. He'd run a mile.

Eddie was pissed off because in the back of his mind he knew the truth. He slipped one hand inside his raincoat and felt his shirt. It was sticky. He withdrew his hand and wiped the blood on his dark blue coat. He wouldn't be around to spend his money.

The job had fucked up tonight...so why not fuck the man responsible for getting him in this mess? Why should he get away with it? But he wouldn't drop Kate in it. Let her enjoy the money. He knew he'd lied to her in the past, only telling her what he thought she should know, but now it was time Kate knew the truth. She probably wouldn't like it, but that didn't bother him, not now.

Kate had given him more love and devotion than anybody else he'd known and deserved a break. But fuck his employer...and he could do it.

Eddie suddenly felt very cold. Sweat glistened on his forehead and the smashed side window didn't help. Fortunately, it had stopped snowing and the main roads were fairly clear, just slushy. He kept an eye on the speedometer making sure he stayed within the limit. It would be just his luck to get a tug from a speed cop.

He drove carefully but felt sick and nearly passed out ten minutes before his destination. He was now in the East End not far from home and pulled into the side of the road. He rested his head on his hands gripping the steering wheel until the nausea passed, then continued his journey, automatically going through the gears. Everything seemed an effort but his senses were still sharp enough to park the MG in another road about a hundred yards from his house.

He shoved the gun into a side pocket of his raincoat, hoisted himself from the sports car and literally staggered to his front door holding on to garden walls and hedges, the snow covered pavement not helping. Anyone seeing him would have thought him drunk. Eddie wished he was, but the ache in his chest was getting worse, reminding him it was much more serious.

Eddie didn't even try to get out his door key and hung on the doorbell until Kate answered, falling into her arms when she opened the door.

'Oh my god, Eddie, what's happened?' she gasped, as she took the weight of his body.

'Close the door,' Eddie said, and Kate kicked it shut. 'Take me upstairs.' The words came out as a croak and Kate knew something was very wrong.

They slowly managed the stairs and in the bedroom Kate helped Eddie off with his raincoat and leather jacket.

'Oh, Eddie, what's happened,' Kate repeated, when she saw his blood soaked shirt.

'Get me on the bed,' Eddie said in reply, 'and let me sit up.'

Kate adjusted the pillows, pulled back the duvet and helped the injured man into a sitting position, then took off his shoes and perched herself on the edge of the bed. She slowly undid his shirt buttons and saw the bullet hole in his chest, blood oozing from the wound.

'You've been shot,' Kate said, her voice almost a whisper.

Eddie nodded.

'Yes, everything screwed up tonight.'

'But you said you were only going to talk to Dixie Fisher.'

'That's right,' Eddie sighed. 'But I don't trust anyone. And that's why I didn't want you to come with me, just in case something like this happened. I walked into a trap.'

'You mean, Dixie was responsible for this?'

'No, not her...*our mutual friend.* He's the one who got me shot,' Eddie said.

'The bastard,' Kate said, 'what happened?'

'Don't let's worry about that now, but take my word for it, he is the one who's to blame.'

Kate had a sudden thought.

'Where's John?'

'I don't know.' Eddie gripped Kate's arm. 'Get me a scotch.'

'You should be in hospital, Eddie. Let me call an ambulance.'

'No, no ambulance. They'll call the police. No, just get me a drink and there's a first aid box in the kitchen. In one of the cupboards. Please...'

A few minutes later Kate was back in the bedroom with a glass, bottle of whisky and a small green plastic box with a white cross on the lid. She immediately set about cleaning the wound as best she could, using antiseptic lotion and finally stuck a large plaster patch over the hole.

'You'll die if you don't go to hospital,' Kate said bluntly, fighting back tears.

'I know, but it's too late now anyway.' Eddie coughed and it sounded like a rasping gurgle. A small trickle of blood oozed out the corner of his mouth. 'I'm not going to make it but I want you to promise to do something for me.'

'Oh, Eddie,' and Kate clasped one of Eddie's hands, 'let me get help, please.'

'No. No help. Just do as I ask.' He finished the scotch in his glass and held it out for a refill. 'In that drawer, under my shirts you'll find an address book. Bring it here.'

When Kate had done that Eddie pointed to his raincoat.

'There's a gun in a side pocket. Get that as well.'

'A gun?' There was shock in the woman's voice.

'Yes, just do as I say...please.'

Kate once again did as she was told and took the automatic pistol from the raincoat. The gun felt heavy in her hand and she laid it on the bed next to the black leather book.

'Go and get your money next week,' Eddie continued.

'But you won't be with me. What I've got already is enough.'

Eddie coughed again several times. It was hurting worse and his eyes glazed over.

'You'll get your money without any problem if you do exactly what I tell you,' he continued in a weak voice, and picked up the small book. 'Then I want you to phone this person, but not until you're safely out the country. You'll make contact on one of these numbers.'

Kate looked at the name and telephone numbers Eddie pointed to in the address book and a surprised look came over her face.

'You mean, he's involved in this too?' disbelief in her voice.

'Yes,' Eddie replied, his voice weaker. 'And it's about time you knew the truth about what you got yourself into. Then I'll tell you what to do.'

Kate was shocked by some of the things Eddie told her but lowered her head close to him and listened intently to every word he said.

FIFTY FOUR

Linda phoned Joey from the hospital and he arrived in less than an hour.

'How's Mike?' was his first question.

'Not good,' Linda replied, 'and there's been no change since we arrived here.'

'Where is he?'

'He's still being examined. One of the doctors told us it looks like he's got internal bleeding and he's still unconscious. Mike's head is also hurt pretty bad and he's got to have scans and X-rays, that sort of thing. We're waiting to hear more.'

Dixie was sitting on a padded bench seat in the brightly coloured waiting area. Jack was ensconced in an armchair just a few feet away.

Joey knelt in front of Dixie and she put her arms around his neck holding him tight. The pop star could feel her tears wet on his face.

'Oh, Joey,' she said. 'Mike's been badly injured...I'm afraid he's going to die.'

Joey gently pulled apart from Dixie and looked straight into her eyes.

'No he won't, Dixie,' he said. 'Mike's going to be all right. He's a fighter, he won't give in. So don't worry. He's going to be okay. You've got to believe that.'

Joey lifted himself up and sat next to Dixie. He took one of her hands in his, held it tight and Linda sat on the other side of her friend.

'What happened?' Joey asked.

Linda looked at the singer knowing she didn't want to repeat the evening's events in front of Dixie, it would only upset her more.

'I think it would be better if Jack told you,' she answered in a soft voice.

Joey immediately twigged what she meant, patted Dixie's hand and stood.

'Of course,' he said, and turned to the big man. 'Let's go somewhere else.'

Jack nodded, and the two men walked slowly from the waiting room into an empty corridor, their footsteps noisy on the lino tiled floor.

'What happened, Jack?'

Over the next few minutes the big man explained the earlier events of the evening and a solitary nurse rounding a corner did a double-take when she recognized the younger of the two serious looking men engrossed deep in conversation.

'I want to have a word with my driver,' Joey said, and the two men went out the hospital front entrance where Stan was sitting in the Rolls. He got out of the car when he saw Joey.

'How's Mr Saxby?' Stan asked.

'It seems it's serious,' Joey replied. 'Look, Stan, why don't you go home. I don't know how long I'll be and I can always get a cab.'

'No, Mr Judd, I'm staying. But I'm not supposed to stop in the front here, so I'll go to the car park at the rear.'

'Okay, thanks. And come and join us in the waiting room. Dixie and Linda are inside.' Joey looked at Jack. 'The pubs are closed but there's a coffee bar over there. Stan, tell the girls I'll bring back some drinks.'

'I will, Mr Judd,' and Stan got back in the limousine and drove off.

Jack and Joey crossed the road to the brightly lit coffee bar where Jack finished his story. The police had been a bit of a problem and it was obvious they were sceptical, to say the least, about Jack's version. But there were no other witnesses, except for the two women who seemed confused and upset, so what could the police do? The barman hadn't seen much, or wasn't saying much. Probably thought there might be some sort of retaliation against the pub if he made too much of a song and dance about things.

True, someone had thrown a Molotov cocktail and there was a dead man at the scene, but it had to be odds on the motorcyclist was a criminal. So let the old bill chase that angle.

'One other thing I never told the police was that Mike's car had been got at,' Jack continued. 'Dixie went in the ambulance so I borrowed the keys from his pocket for me and Linda to get to the hospital. Then I found all the tyres had been slashed. I didn't want the old bill to find the Range Rover like that so I managed to drive it to a few streets away and Linda and I got a cab.'

'Where's Mike's car now?' Joey asked.

'Don't worry, I arranged for it to be picked up, and by now it'll have a new set of tyres and should be parked outside Dixie's block of flats.'

Jack grinned.

'The police said they'd get back to me. I wonder what they'll think when they find out about my past.'

Joey stared at the broken nosed man and couldn't help thinking that sitting opposite him was a bloke who'd killed another human being just hours ago. But then, it *had* been self-defence. And Jack *had* promised to look after Dixie.

The pop star wondered if he or Mike would have had the balls to have done the same.

Mike...his best mate. Mike...he had to come through this. Joey had never felt so down in all his life.

Come on God, give us a break.

*

A surgeon removed Mike's spleen in the early hours of the morning. Being hurled against the concrete corner of the porch had done the damage. Several ribs had been broken, and there was heavy bruising to the chest and abdomen, but there was no serious internal bleeding after all. However, the young man was still unconscious.

There were no clots on the brain but he had sustained a skull fracture and the doctors couldn't be sure if there would be any permanent damage. Head injuries could be dangerous. The brain was the major organ of the nervous system so until Mike regained consciousness, and doctors could do further tests, nothing was certain.

Dixie refused to leave the hospital so Linda went back to the flat and brought her friend a change of clothing.

Joey returned to his mansion and, although there was only one more day's recording, the singer told his band it would have to wait. They understood and so did Joey's manager.

'Don't worry,' Vic said, 'that can be sorted out later. You just look after Mike. I'm sure he'll be all right...and my wife sends her love. Anything you want, just let me know.'

Joey had a few hours sleep and Stan drove him back to the hospital but there was no change in Mike's condition. He was still unconscious.

Jack left with the promise he would be contacted as soon as there was any news, and Danny Buckley had arrived by the time Joey returned.

Danny felt terrible, blaming himself because he hadn't been at the Black Swan.

'You couldn't have done any more than Jack did,' Linda assured him. 'He and his friends saved our lives...that is, except for...' Linda paused, 'and what happened to Mike...nobody could have helped. I just hope he comes through this okay.'

'So do I,' Danny said, 'It's just that I feel so helpless,'

'So do we all,' Linda said. 'But we can only wait and hope.'

Dixie decided against telling her Aunt Lucy or Uncle Robert about this recent attempt on her life, nor the tragic consequences.

Something inside her told her not to. Not yet.

*

Mike had been transferred to a single room but only one person at a time was allowed to sit by the side of his bed. Dixie insisted it was her and only left to use the bathroom, determined to be there in case he suddenly came to. So she sat there praying and staring at his pale and swollen face, his head bandaged. His body and arms hooked up to various drips and wires leading to monitors.

The others put their heads round the door from time to time but most of the afternoon they spent in the waiting room, drinking coffee and making brave attempts at small talk. Stan brought in sandwiches but nobody had much of an appetite.

So far the press hadn't been alerted to Joey's presence, but he knew it was only a matter of time.

It had snowed again, the flakes finally petering out in the early evening.

'Let's get some fresh air,' Joey said, and pulled Linda up from her chair.

'I'll get the car,' Stan said, 'it's not very nice out there.'

'Yeah,' Joey sighed. 'We can have the windows open instead.'

Danny said he'd stay just in case Dixie needed something and Linda and Joey went out into the darkness.

They got into the Rolls and settled back against the soft leather seats as the limousine glided along the streets near Paddington Station. It was still early, not yet nine o'clock, but the pavements were nearly empty. They were slippery and dangerous to walk on.

But not for a group of children who'd found a strip of ice several yards long and were running up then seeing how far they could slide before falling over. Choir practice at the

Sacred Heart church hadn't long finished and some parents were late in picking up their offspring, who were being watched over by Father Ignatius, huddled in a long black overcoat.

'Stop,' Joey suddenly said, and as the car came to a halt grabbed his thick suede coat and opened the door. 'I won't be a minute,' and he walked over to the small space in front of the church where the priest was blowing into his hands trying to warm them.

'Evening, Father.'

The mild mannered priest, in his forties, with wispy black hair, peered through his glasses at Joey.

'Good evening,' he smiled.

'Are you open for business?' Joey asked.

'Pardon?'

Joey hesitated before continuing.

'Well, I was thinking...I'd like to say a prayer in there,' and the singer nodded in the direction of the large wood and metal studded church door. 'It's for a friend of mine...he needs all the help he can get.'

'We're not really open,' Father Ignatius said. 'We've just finished choir practice. If it's possible to come back tomorrow...,' and his voice tailed off awkwardly.

Joey nodded but his attention was focused on a big notice board in front of the church.

'Are you a Catholic?'

'Huh?' and Joey switched his gaze back to the priest, not sure how to reply. The closest he'd been to religion in recent years was when he'd been in the *godvan*.

'I don't know what I am,' was his honest answer. He looked once again at the notice board and a big smile spread across his face. 'Wait here, I'll be straight back.'

As Joey went over to the Rolls one of the boys, about twelve with bright red rosy cheeks, broke away from his friends and spoke to the priest.

'Do you know who that is, Father?'

'No,' and the priest shook his head.

'That's Joey Judd, the famous pop star.' The boy's voice held a trace of awe. 'He's the best.'

Father Ignatius took in the information and stared at the back of the famous person, now leaning into the expensive motor car.

'Pass me my cheque book and pen, Stan,' Joey said, and the chauffeur opened the glove compartment.

'What are you doing?' Linda asked.

Joey kissed his forefinger and placed it on her lips.

'Never you mind. I won't be long.'

When Joey stood once again in front of the priest he pointed at the notice board.

'It says you're trying to raise money for Christmas presents and a party for old age pensioners. The target's a thousand pounds. How much short are you?'

Father Ignatius thought carefully before answering.

'About half, unfortunately,' he replied.

Joey opened the book in his hand, quickly scrawled in it and tore out a cheque, which he handed to the priest.

'Now you're not short any more,' he said.

Father Ignatius looked at the piece of paper in his hand and gave a little gasp.

'But this is for *two thousand* five hundred pounds,' he said, amazed, and looked again at the writing to make sure he hadn't made a mistake.

'Well, you can have a New Year's party as well,' Joey grinned. 'Now, please, do you think I could spend five or ten minutes in your church?'

'Of course, of course,' the priest replied, nearly shouting out the words in excitement. He gave a beaming smile and looked at the young choirboy standing by his side. 'Anthony, please show Mr Judd into the church and make sure all the lights are on.'

The boy, hardly able to believe being so close to one of his idols, was lost for words and silently turned towards the church.

'God bless you, God bless you,' Father Ignatius called out as Joey followed the choirboy up the steps, still partially covered with snow.

The heavy door swung open surprisingly easy on well oiled hinges and Joey entered into a small vestibule where Anthony pushed open one of two smaller swing doors leading to the interior of the church. It was dimly lit by electric wall lights and at each end of the altar several large candles were burning brightly. A slight smell of incense hung in the air.

'Do you want the big lights on?' the choirboy asked, finding his voice.

'No, this is fine,' Joey replied, and walked towards the altar.

Anthony moved to his right and walked up the stairs leading to a small gallery where the choir sang and looked down as the pop star sank to his knees in the front pew.

Joey felt awkward. He didn't clasp his hands in front of him but desperately wanted to say a prayer. The trouble was - this was the first time. He knew he'd been christened, because he'd been told so by his mum, but such a long time ago he couldn't remember. And going to church hadn't been top of the family's priorities.

When he'd seen the priest outside he hadn't been sure what to call him, and had only addressed him as, *Father*, because he'd remembered it from some film.

He was so caught up with his thoughts he didn't hear the door at the back of the church open as Linda stepped through, careful not to make a noise. She stood, half obscured by a large stone pillar, and gazed at the kneeling figure of Joey illuminated by the flickering candles.

'God, I'd like you to help my friend, Mike,' Joey said out loud, his words carrying clearly up to the cavernous beamed ceiling. 'He's been hurt bad...and I want him better. With your help, if possible...,' and he paused, struggling to find the right words. 'I'm not very good at this prayer thing...but I do mean it. I'm not the best with words...,' and a smile suddenly broke out over his face. 'But I can sing. Maybe that will help me get through to you.'

And Joey held his head up high, stared at the large cross suspended above the altar and opened his mouth.

'*Amazing grace,*
How sweet the sound,
That saved a wretch like me,
I once was lost but now am found,
Was blind, but now I see...'

As Joey's voice resounded through the church it was joined by another. Hesitantly at first, but then the soprano gained in confidence, until the two voices were united in perfect harmony.

Joey turned, surprised, then gave a thumb's up sign to the lone choirboy singing in the gallery.

'*...When we've been there ten thousand years,*
Bright shining as the sun,
We've no less days to sing God's praise,
Than when we first begun.'

It was in that moment Linda knew, without any doubt, how much she loved Joey, and blew a silent kiss in his direction before slipping quietly out of the church.

FIFTY FIVE

Eddie died in the early hours of Saturday morning. He was delirious a lot towards the end but Kate stayed loyally by his side. She did panic slightly when he gasped his final breath, and only because she'd never witnessed death before. But then her common sense took over. Her calm orderly mind that had made her such a good secretary.

There was nothing to be afraid of. Eddie had loved her and she'd loved him. They'd been lovers and he'd never hurt her. What she had to remember were all the good times they'd had together.

And the promise she'd made to Eddie on his deathbed.

Kate tidied the bedroom, took the glass and, by now, two empty bottles of whisky and the first aid box back to the kitchen. Then she returned to Eddie, smoothed the duvet cover and sat next to the bed.

*

Dixie was asleep, sitting in a chair with her head resting on the bed, when she felt a hand gently stroke her hair. She looked up and saw Mike's eyes open. She blinked her own, not sure if she was dreaming, then realization set in.

'Mike...you're awake,' she said, tears running down her cheeks with relief, the days of waiting and built-up tension finding a release. She wanted to hug and kiss the man lying in the bed but instead, gave him a peck lightly on the cheek, as though frightened he might break in two.

'Hi,' Mike said, in a weak voice, then smiled. 'Love you.'

'Oh, you too, darling,' and Dixie grabbed hold of his hand, smothering it with kisses, careful to avoid the plaster securing the needle of the drip.

Then she remembered what the doctors had told her to do if there was any change in Mike's condition. She rang the bell for a nurse, but didn't wait.

'Back in a minute,' she said, and dashed out of the room. It was four am and Linda, Joey and Stan were asleep in the waiting area, uncomfortably sprawled out.

'Wake up, wake up,' Dixie said excitedly, and shook her friends arms.

They were immediately awake and didn't have to ask, they could tell by the smile on Dixie's face.

'Mike's okay...he's okay,' the pop star said.

'Yes, Joey, he's okay,' Dixie repeated.

'Well, let's go and see him.'

When they arrived at the room a nurse was there.

'A doctor's on his way,' she said, 'so be quick, Mr Saxby mustn't have too much excitement.'

Joey laughed.

'Not too much excitement? I don't know about him but I'm going to get pissed.'

*

At six thirty am the time came to leave. Kate bent over and kissed Eddie on his forehead, already cold, and ran a hand through his lovely grey, curly hair for the last time. Then she left the house in the early morning darkness to walk to the nearest tube station. Eddie had told her not to order a minicab in case she was remembered.

As she neared the end of the snow covered, deserted street she couldn't resist turning to have one last look at the house and wondered how long it would be before someone discovered the body.

'Goodbye Eddie,' she whispered, and carried on with her journey. She had business to attend to.

But Kate also needed sleep. So when she arrived at her small apartment she took off her clothes and got into bed, remembering to set the alarm, and fours hours later woke to the insistent bleeping of the small clock.

A quick bath, then dressed and a couple cups of coffee inside her, she felt fit again to face the world.

Although deeply emotional about the death of her lover she'd had over two days to adjust to the inevitable, and revenge now was the emotion that would take her mind off her loss. Her thoughts kept going over the instructions Eddie had given her. She could hear his voice inside her, and knew she would carry out his wishes to the very last, whatever the outcome. That thought somehow keeping him close to her.

She lifted down a Yellow Pages directory from a shelf and sat next to the telephone. Then she began phoning. But, as she'd expected, being so near Christmas all of the hotels she called were fully booked. The other problem was that she wanted a good hotel, not some cheap place.

Then one hotel said they had a cancellation. Yes, it was for the day she wanted. A company had booked it for one night but the hotel had just, literally minutes ago, been informed there had been a change of plan. And it was free.

But, it was a small suite, not a room.

'That's okay' Kate said, thinking that was even better, 'I'll be there within an hour to pay for it. Make sure you keep it for me.' And gave a completely fictitious name.

She quickly put on her warm, long coat, left the apartment building and hailed a taxi. The hotel was in a fairly quiet street not far from Green Park and not as large as some of the big name hotels in the West End. It was exclusive and expensive - and just what Kate wanted.

'It's for my boss, but put in my name,' Kate said, confirming the false name she'd given over the phone, and smiled at the smartly dressed, young Spanish man behind the reception desk, 'so his wife can't find out.' Then added, as she said she'd pay cash, and not by cheque or credit card, 'My boss doesn't want it to go through his company books.'

'Ah, I see,' and the young man grinned back at Kate. 'I think maybe your boss won't be alone, eh?'

After she'd put the receipt in her handbag Kate looked around the lobby. It was perfect. She walked over to one of the lifts and saw the indicator went as high as seven, the floor her suite was on.

Then she walked to a telephone booth in one corner of the thick green and gold carpeted lobby, opened the door, put a couple of coins in the box and pressed the buttons. Kate tapped her fingers as she waited. Her call wasn't expected and if he wasn't in she'd keep trying. Then the receiver was lifted the other end.

Kate kept her voice calm although she held this man responsible for Eddie's death.

The man was surprised by her call because he didn't think they'd be speaking again until they met. He was worried Kate wanted to call off the meeting but was assured it was still for the same day and time, just a different hotel, that was all. When he queried the change of venue Kate told him it suited her purpose better, and she made him write down the name of the different hotel, so there would be no mistake.

Kate replaced the receiver, adjusted her glasses and looked up another number in her address book.

This time an answer machine turned on and the woman left a message.

'This is Kate Smith and the message is for Dixie Fisher. I hear there was trouble outside the Black Swan the other evening but I assure you it had nothing to do with me. I was told I wouldn't be needed at our meeting, that someone else was taking my place, and a certain matter would be explained to you. This person was going to give you a letter explaining the death of your parents. However, I have since found out that this didn't happen, and I want to make another arrangement to meet with you. But this time I am prepared to go much further. I will give you documented proof and also deliver to you personally, the man behind this. I will keep phoning you till we speak. Sorry, but I can't give you a number where you can contact me. Goodbye.'

*

When Danny Buckley received a phone call and heard the good news about Mike he was thankful for two reasons. One, for Dixie's sake, and two, he wanted to get back to Norfolk. He'd spoken to the nurse and Jessie was worse. There wasn't much time left.

But he knew he had to go to the hospital first before he left London. And Jack was coming with him. They really were interested in going into business together.

There had been some other good news. George was well on the road to recovery. His thick clothes had lessened the penetration of the shotgun pellets and there was no permanent damage.

When Danny and Jack arrived at the hospital they were greeted with happy faces.

'I'm pleased it's worked out okay,' Danny said, as he hugged Dixie.

'Oh, so am I,' she smiled. 'I couldn't have had a better Christmas present.'

Joey was well on target to keeping his promise. He and Stan had arrived back at the hospital with two dozen bottles of champagne for the nurses and doctors, and was doing a great job helping them drink it.

Danny and Jack spent just a few minutes with Mike. He was going to get better, and that was the main thing. Mike had been checked over and all the tests were fine. His vision was perfect, there was no loss of feeling and his reflexes and co-ordination were in first class order. And there was no loss of memory, as there sometimes is with a serious head injury.

Definitely good news.

'Thanks for everything,' Mike said, and shook hands with both men. Dixie hadn't been hurt and that's all he cared about. 'Will we see you before Christmas?' he asked.

'I'm not sure, Mike,' Danny replied, and he and Jack left the room.

Jack was still concerned about Dixie's safety and had a word with the others in the waiting area. Although they tended to agree with his theory that there probably wouldn't be any more attempts on Dixie's life, nobody was taking any chances.

Jack thought the best thing to do was for Tony to move into Dixie's flat as a bodyguard tomorrow and accompany her wherever she went, just as a temporary measure until Mike was fully fit. Linda agreed. It was a busy period for her father's business and she was needed to help out. And it didn't take any persuading to convince Dixie what was best for her. Now that Mike was going to recover she would agree to anything.

'And after Christmas I'll make sure I find out who's behind this so you won't ever have to worry again,' Danny said.

'Thanks,' Dixie said.

'But we will be speaking before then anyway,' Danny said, a slight smile playing across his face.

They both knew what he meant. The DNA tests should, hopefully, be through by the end of next week.

Danny gave her a kiss on her cheek then he and Jack left the hospital.

FIFTY SIX

At nine thirty Nurse Coogan changed from her white uniform into pyjamas and a yellow candlewick dressing gown, went downstairs and made a cup of hot chocolate in the kitchen. She'd spent most of the evening with Jessie, reading and watching her patient slip in and out of sleep. Even when Danny had arrived Jessie couldn't do much more than smile then drift off again.

'I'm going to bed to finish my book,' she said.

'Okay nurse, goodnight,' Danny said, and Jack nodded his head. She was a kindly woman, well suited for her job, with an abundance of energy.

Both men were dressed in jeans and sweaters, comfortable in armchairs watching a film which had just started on television when the phone rang in the lounge. Danny had unplugged the one in the bedroom he and Jessie shared so she wouldn't be disturbed, and would reconnect it when he joined her later. He still slept with her and was determined to do so until the end. He wanted Jessie to know she wasn't alone when she woke and that her illness didn't make one iota of difference to him.

Danny went over to the small writing desk, picked up the phone and frowned when he recognized the voice.

'Is there anything wrong?' he asked. 'Is Mike okay?'

'Yes, it's nothing like that. Mike's fine, it's just that, 'Dixie paused, 'when I got home there was a message for me on my answer machine,' she paused again. 'It was Kate Smith.'

'What the hell did she want?' Danny exploded into the phone, causing Jack to shift his eyes from the screen and look at his friend.

'She wants to make another meeting with me.'

'Is she crazy? After what happened at the last one...she must be mad.'

'She said she had nothing to do with that,' and Dixie went on to explain the rest of the message.

'Well, if what she says is true then all your problems will be over. But can you trust her? I wouldn't. Anyway, until you speak to her personally, you don't know where this meeting will take place.'

'No, I'll have to wait. The only trouble is, I intend being at the hospital as much as I can.'

'Dixie, on your answer machine, is it your voice that tells people you're not at home?'

'Yes.'

'So you could record another greeting, is that right?'

'Yes.'

'Well, why not do that, and leave your mobile number. So if Kate Smith calls again and you're not in, she can get hold of you on your mobile.'

'People aren't supposed to have them switched on in the hospital,' Dixie said.

'So break a rule. This is important.'

'Okay, I will. You're right, it is important.'

'But don't go anywhere without letting me know first.'

'Of course.'

'Has Tony contacted you yet?' Danny asked. 'Jack gave him your number.'

'He left a message for me too, and left his number, but I haven't spoken to him yet.'

'Phone him as soon as we've finished talking. Tell him to be at your place early tomorrow morning. About seven o'clock.'

'Okay, I'll do that.'

'I take it, Linda is with you now?'

'Yes, she's making us something to eat. I've got my appetite back.'

'Okay, Dixie, have a good night's sleep, and let me know the moment you hear from this Kate Smith. Speak to you soon.'

Danny put down the receiver deep in thought.

'Trouble?' Jack asked.

'Could be,' Danny replied, just as a sudden gust of wind rattled the window panes. He leant across the writing desk and pulled back the curtains of the small window. The moon was bright and it looked like a blizzard outside, a strong wind swirling heavy snow against the cottage. 'Could be,' Danny repeated.

*

As it turned out it wasn't necessary for Dixie to record another message for telephone callers because Kate Smith rang early, at seven thirty, half an hour after Tony arrived.

'Yes, what do you want?' Dixie's voice was icy cold.

Kate immediately noted the tone in the other woman's voice but tried to keep pleasant.

'Did you understand my message?' she asked.

'Yes, but I'm not happy arranging another meeting with you.'

'Why's that?' Kate was intrigued to hear Dixie's version of events because Eddie hadn't elaborated about what had happened at the pub, and she hadn't pushed because of his injury.

'You mean, you really don't know?' Dixie asked.

'No. I told you I wasn't there because of a change in plan.'

'My boyfriend was nearly killed. In fact, he's still in hospital. He was unconscious for two days.'

The news stunned Kate.

'I'm sorry,' and she paused. 'Will he be all right?'

'Yes, fortunately, but it's no thanks to you.'

'I really didn't know,' Kate said in a low voice.

'Two men tried to kill me,' Dixie said bluntly. 'One got away but the other man is dead.'

Now Kate knew what had happened to John, but she felt confused. Eddie had told her he'd walked into a trap set up by his employer but hadn't gone into detail. She'd believed Eddie then and still did. She reasoned in her mind she felt muddled because she didn't know all the facts.

And she would keep to Eddie's plan, no matter what.

'Well, nobody is going to try and kill you when we meet.'

'I haven't agreed to meet you yet,' Dixie said, her voice still hard.

'Let's see if I can change your mind,' and Kate told the younger woman what she had in mind for Monday, plus the time and name of the hotel.

'What's to stop me bringing along the police?'

'Nothing,' Kate replied.

'And then you'd be arrested for concealing evidence of a crime...and I suppose blackmail. I take it you are bleeding someone dry.'

'Perhaps, but do you want all the publicity a case like this would get? Your family name and parents plastered all over the tabloids. I can't change what has happened but what I'm offering you is justice...a chance to get even.'

What Kate Smith said was true. Even more so if Joey Judd, pop star, was involved. Then the press *would* have a field day.

Reporters had finally found out about Joey's visits to the hospital and several photographers were still outside the front entrance.

'I suppose you're right,' Dixie reluctantly agreed. 'But I'm not making up my mind now. I want to discuss it with someone first. Can you give me a number I can get you on?'

'No, I'm sorry, but I'm not going to,' Kate replied. 'When do you think you'll know and I'll call you back?'

'Sometime later today,' Dixie answered, then remembered, 'oh, and I'd better give you the number of my mobile as well.'

'I'll phone you this evening,' Kate said pleasantly, after she'd entered the number in her address book, 'goodbye.'

Dixie didn't bother answering and just hung up.

FIFTY SEVEN

It was decided Dixie should meet Kate Smith at the hotel but there would have to be a concession.

'I'm going with you,' Danny said, 'don't tell her my name, just say a male friend. And if Kate Smith doesn't agree to that then you don't see her.'

'That's fine by me,' Dixie said, whose resilience was starting to wilt. She was happy about Mike but the worry and stress was still there.

She had to get her life back to normal.

'Today's Sunday,' Danny said, 'and I can be back in London tomorrow lunch-time if that woman agrees someone can be with you.'

'Okay, I'll phone you as soon as she's called me back.'

Dixie left for the hospital mid-morning with Tony sharing her taxi. He said he'd prefer not be stuck behind a steering wheel, even if it did mean relying on other transport.

Linda said she had a lot of washing to do and would see Dixie later. She was meeting Joey at the hospital in the afternoon.

When Dixie arrived she saw a great improvement in Mike. The swelling on his face had gone down a lot, though he did still have a quite a bit of purple and yellow bruising on his forehead and eye area. The bandage had been taken off and replaced with a large plaster.

'I've been told I'll be able to leave by the end of the week,' he said.

Joey had handled the press very well and hadn't tried to hide from them. He'd posed for pictures and explained that his best friend had been injured in a car accident but was now getting better.

Satisfied, they'd gone away, except for a few freelance photographers who always hung around looking for anything they could flog to the tabloids.

Joey and Linda arrived at two thirty and as soon as the pop star heard when Mike was going home reminded the others about their Christmas plans,

They agreed there was no need to change anything and they'd spend it at Joey's as arranged.

'Any idea what you'd like for Christmas,' Joey asked, when he and Linda were drinking coffee in the waiting room.

'I don't know, surprise me,' Linda replied.

'Are you getting me anything?'

'Joey, it's rude to ask, just wait and see.' Linda pushed her face close to him. 'Why, is there something special you'd like?'

'Could be...but I'll let you surprise me too.'

'Maybe I will,' and Linda gave a wicked grin.

Dixie came and joined them and then told Joey about Kate Smith's phone calls. He was just as shocked as the rest of them had been.

'You haven't told Mike, have you?' he asked.

'Of course not,' Dixie replied.

'Are you going to see her?'

'She said she'll phone me later. I'll know then. Danny wants to come with me and if she says yes, we'll go.'

'What about him?' and Joey indicated in the direction of Tony.

'I don't know,' Dixie replied. 'I'll leave everything to Danny.'

Joey nodded and looked at the tough looking individual sitting quietly in an armchair browsing through a magazine.

Tony was dressed in a smart business suit and Joey wondered if he was carrying a gun, like the other night. Most likely.

Kate Smith got Dixie in her flat about an hour after she returned from the hospital and had no hesitation in agreeing to the young woman's request.

Dixie immediately phoned Norfolk.

'It's on,' she told Danny. 'She had no objection to someone coming with me.'

'Good,' he said. 'At last we'll find out what this is all about. And who's behind it.'

*

Linda conveyed Dixie's plans to Joey. The singer had insisted on that.

'Mike's in hospital and I'm going to make sure I help this time,' he said.

'What are you going to do?' Linda asked.

'Not sure yet, but I'll let you know when I've worked things out,' Joey replied.

Once again the pop star enlisted the help of his manager, who wasn't at all enamoured by Joey's request.

'Why do you stick me with all the shitty jobs?' Vic Ruebens asked. 'And this one I'd say is near enough impossible. I know what it's like trying to get rooms this time of the year, especially for one specific night.'

'Vic, I'm sure if anyone can do it, you'll be able to,' Joey said. 'Bribe someone...get somebody kicked out of the place...I don't care how you go about it, or how much it costs. But I must have a room in that hotel for tomorrow.'

'Okay,' Vic growled, 'I'll see what I can do.'

'And one other thing. Put the room in a woman's name. Linda will be picking up the key, but don't use her's.'

*

The moon shone bright over the West End of London. Still plenty of snow and there'd been no respite from the cold wind over the last couple of days. Under a week to Christmas and the stores and shops were staying open late to keep pace with the hectic shopping. The weather, though cursed by some, had guaranteed a true festive spirit.

Snow, Santa Claus, children and bright window displays were a bewitching combination. People could feel it in the air. And it showed on their faces.

And the lobby of the hotel was bustling as Joey pushed through the swing doors. He had a long scarf wrapped high around his neck and matching dark blue wool ski hat plonked on his head, covering his ears. A white handkerchief held to his nose made him unrecognizable. He swivelled his eyes around and saw the large frame of Tony sitting in one of the comfortable armchairs as though waiting for someone. Then he made straight for the lifts, coughing and snivelling into the white covering over his face, until he reached the sixth floor. He got out, turned right and half way down the corridor rapped his knuckles on the wood panelled door of room sixty four. Linda opened up and Joey walked in, gratefully taking the handkerchief from his face.

He looked at his watch. Exactly six thirty.

*

Kate Smith had been on tenterhooks for the last couple of hours, ever since she'd checked into the hotel. She'd turned the television on and off several times and drained the large pot of coffee she'd ordered from room service as soon as she'd arrived in the luxuriously furnished suite. No alcohol today. Although she felt she needed a stiff drink - keeping a clear head was more important.

Kate paced up and down the thick carpet of the lounge, continually glancing at her wristwatch, and felt a sense of relief when she heard someone knock firmly on the door.

Dead on eight o'clock.

She crossed the room, opened the door, and a surprised look briefly fluttered across her face. Dixie she recognized immediately but it was the person standing next to her who made her feel uneasy. His grey, curly hair, just like Eddie's. This had to be Danny Buckley.

'Come in,' Kate said, and stood to one side as they entered, before closing the door.

'Now what?' Dixie asked, her face nearly as frosty as the weather outside.

'Who's your friend?' Kate enquired amiably.

'Never mind,' Dixie replied.

'I'm here to see that nothing happens to Dixie,' Danny said. 'That there's no repetition of the other night.'

'I see,' Kate said matter-of-factly, her voice dropping any pretense of friendliness. 'Someone made me promise that you should know the truth behind your parents deaths and everything else that has happened over the last year. Tonight I will keep my promise.'

'Who is this someone?' Dixie asked.

'It doesn't matter,' Kate replied, picking up her shoulder bag from a chair. 'But there is something I want you to do,' and she walked across the lounge and opened the bedroom door. 'I think it would be better if you waited in here,' and Kate entered the room. 'I'm going down to meet somebody in the lobby. Then I'll bring him up here and you'll be able to listen if you keep this door slightly open. You can take off your coats if you like.'

'How long will you be?' Danny asked.

'My meeting is for eight thirty,' Kate replied, and looked at her watch. 'I should be back here within fifteen minutes. Just make sure you keep quiet.'

Tom Fisher's former secretary smiled, slung the bag over her shoulder, then left the suite.

As soon as she'd gone Danny picked up the cream coloured phone by the side of the bed and dialled an internal number.

'Joey? It's me Danny. I'm in the suite with Dixie, and Kate Smith has just left to go down to the lobby. She said she'd be back here in about fifteen minutes, so this is what I want you to do. You're just below us so go to the emergency fire stairs next to the lifts, come up one floor, and wait on the stairs where you can't be seen.'

'Okay,' Joey said, 'then what?'

'As soon as the Smith woman gets back I'll contact you on your mobile. I'll let you know what's going on, but it's important you mustn't be spotted.'

'What about Tony?'

'I'm going to phone him on his mobile now. But I think it'll be best if he stays there on the ground floor, to cover the front entrance.'

'Okay,' Joey said, and Danny replaced the hotel phone, then took his mobile from his inside pocket. Both he and Dixie had declined Kate's offer and remained in their heavy outdoor coats.

After Danny had given Tony his instructions he quickly began searching the drawers in the bedroom, then the lounge, and found what he was looking for when he pulled open the doors under a bookshelf cabinet. A brown leather briefcase. It wasn't locked and inside were two large brown foolscap size envelopes. They were both sealed and Danny carefully replaced the briefcase, then went back and joined Dixie in the bedroom.

FIFTY EIGHT

The lift stopped at the ground floor and Kate and several other hotel guests emerged into the foyer. It was busy and a group of Japanese tourists had congregated close to the swing doors waiting for a porter to organize taxis for them.

Kate walked to a gold velvet covered two seater settee positioned near an eight foot high Christmas tree and sat down. She kept her attention intently fixed on the entrance, every now and again flicking her eyes downward to her watch, never once suspecting she was under observation herself.

Tony had recognized her instantly from the description given over his mobile, and Danny's instructions were explicit. The woman was meeting a man and after they'd met his only interest would be making sure the man never left the hotel, unless Danny was with him. Forget about the female unless he was told different.

A couple of minutes after eight thirty Kate glimpsed the man she was waiting for push through the doors and politely thread his way through the tourists. He looked around, his alert eyes taking in everything, until he spotted Kate. He smiled and made his way to where she was sitting. Just before he reached her she stood and matched his intense gaze.

'Good evening,' Robert Fisher said in his courteous voice, looking immaculate in a dark blue cashmere overcoat. 'We've spoken on the phone but I haven't seen you for some time. You look well.'

Kate ignored the compliment. Instead she felt like screaming in his face that he was responsible for her lover's death. But she didn't. She kept calm, just like Eddie had told her to.

'Is that the money?' she asked, indicating towards the black briefcase held in his right hand.

'Yes,' he replied, 'and I take it you've got the documents. Both sets, as promised?'

'I have,' Kate said, 'but they're upstairs. I have a small suite here.'

'Umm,' Robert mused. 'Not exactly what I had in mind. I thought we were going to do the exchange in public. Why don't you go and get them? I'll wait here.'

'No,' Kate said, keeping her voice soft. 'I thought it would be more discreet for you to check out what you're paying for. And I could count my money.'

'Don't you trust me, Miss Smith? I trust you.'

The silver haired man looked at his former employee, studying her face. He'd wanted Eddie at this meeting, somewhere in the background, so he could follow Kate Smith and get rid of her. But he hadn't spoken to Eddie for over a week and knew something must be drastically wrong. Dixie should have been taken care of by now but Robert Fisher hadn't heard anything to that effect. And he didn't want to phone his niece or sister and ask questions.

All he could surmise was that Eddie's plan hadn't worked. The trouble was, Eddie was his only link to the criminal world, so he'd had to keep this meeting by himself.

He nodded to Kate's request, knowing he had no choice but to comply.

'Okay,' he said, 'we will go to your suite.'

The woman brushed past him and Robert followed her to the lift. They rode upwards with other guests, neither speaking, and when they reached the seventh floor were the only two people remaining. Kate stepped out of the elevator with her companion close behind, the key ready in her hand as they reached the door of the suite.

'I see you can afford the good things in life now,' Robert commented as they entered. Kate didn't answer and left the man to close the door.

'Take a seat and I'll get you a drink,' she said, as Robert unbuttoned his coat and sat down on the small sofa Kate had pointed to, his back to the bedroom. 'What would you like?'

'Scotch and soda, please.'

Kate mixed the drink from the small, but well stocked bar, and placed the glass tumbler on the ornate coffee table in front of Robert. Then she went to the cupboard under the bookshelves and took out a brown leather briefcase.

Robert's eyes had followed every movement and when she stood looking down at him he smiled.

'A fair swap, eh?' and held up his own case. They exchanged and Robert immediately opened the one Kate had given him. He extracted two brown envelopes and quickly tore both open before taking out the contents of one of them, ten pages of typed foolscap paper.

The accountant took a pair of gold rimmed glasses from his coat and rapidly flicked through the pages, stopping every now and again, as though double-checking something. His lips tightened and relaxed several times, a smile of relief finally settling on Robert's face, as he put back the documents in the envelope.

He picked up his drink and drained it in a couple of gulps.

'Another?' and Kate took the empty glass before Robert had a chance to reply, pouring just the one drink even though she felt like one herself.

One hundred thousand pounds. The figure kept floating through her mind and she knew her heartbeat had risen.

She'd also opened the case given to her and, although she hadn't counted it, saw the inside was crammed full with neatly stacked fifty pound notes.

Kate placed the refilled glass in front of Robert just as he took off his spectacles and returned them to his inside pocket. Then she sat in a chair facing him, her shoulder bag on her lap.

'There's enough information here to destroy my life,' he said.

'I know,' Kate said. 'Otherwise you wouldn't be paying me all this money.'

Robert picked up the tumbler and took a sip.

'And there are no other copies?'

'No,' Kate replied, 'and after tonight you'll never hear from me again. So don't send anybody looking for me.'

The silver haired man narrowed his eyes and stared hard at the prim looking woman.

'You don't think I'd try and harm you, do you?'

'Yes I do. You had your own sister's house burgled trying to find these documents and she got hurt.'

'That was a mistake.' Robert was quick in his reply. 'She's very precious to me.'

'Your brother wasn't,' Kate swiftly countered.

The man paused, his gaze once again hardening, as he looked at the woman sitting opposite him.

'What do you know about that?'

'It was obvious.' Kate was calm as she unobtrusively slipped the catch on her shoulder bag. 'As soon as I read those papers your brother asked me to look after I knew his death hadn't been an accident.' Kate paused. 'But why kill his wife too?'

Robert once again quickly knocked back his drink before replacing the empty glass on the coffee table.

'Margo...that *was* a tragic accident.' The accountant's voice sounded strained and he stood. 'That was never meant to happen. She was just in the wrong place at the wrong time.'

Kate rose from her chair and the man and woman stood looking at each other, but not speaking their thoughts.

'The same as me the other night, Uncle Robert?'

Dixie's voice cut clearly through the silence causing the man to spin around in astonishment, his eyes gaping. And when Robert saw the person standing before him he visibly paled and felt physically sick in his stomach.

Dixie took a couple of steps toward him, the sofa separating them.

'However, I wasn't, was I?' Dixie continued 'I wasn't in the wrong place at the wrong time. You intended me to get killed but your man failed.' Dixie's voice rose in anger. 'Mike saved me and nearly died instead. He's still in hospital, you bastard.'

Robert stood looking at the beautiful young woman unable to speak, his shoulders drooped.

'You killed your own brother so it wouldn't be found out what you're up to, whatever that is. My Mother died too. You murdered the two people I loved more than anything in the world.' Dixie was fighting to keep her voice under control, her face full of hatred. 'Nick, my boyfriend at the time, also died. And don't forget Sandra, the mother of a small child. That's four deaths on your hands. All innocent people.' Dixie paused and took a deep breath. 'What kind of man are you?'

Robert didn't answer, his eyes now staring down at the carpet.

'And what is the reason you want me dead? My money?'

Again there was no reply. Then a different voice broke the stillness of the room. A man's voice.

'Yes, why don't you explain to my daughter why you tried to have her killed.'

FIFTY NINE

Robert Fisher's head jerked up as he heard the other voice. And his eyes opened wide as Danny Buckley stepped from the bedroom into view.

'*You*,' he hissed.

'Yes, me. The person you tried to set-up to take the blame. And I think I know what your plans were. But you were wrong. Tom Fisher wasn't Dixie's father. I am.'

'No, you're not.' The words spat like venom from Robert's mouth. 'My brother told me the truth. Tom was Dixie's father. You were jealous and tried to screw up Margo's divorce. Screw up their lives.'

'And you thought you'd get control of my money if I died,' Dixie said, her voice now lowered to little more than a whisper. 'You're unbelievable.'

Kate had quietly slipped on her outdoor coat and picked up the black briefcase while the others had been talking. But she had one more thing to say before leaving.

'It never started out that way, did it Mr Fisher?'

The silver haired man looked at Kate in surprise.

'So you do know everything?'

'Yes, Eddie told me.'

Robert looked astonished.

'You mean, you two were working together?'

'Yes.'

'So where is Eddie?'

'He's dead.'

Kate didn't elaborate and before the accountant could speak again, Danny asked a question of his own.

'Is this Eddie...is he the person who impersonated me? I'm Danny Buckley.'

'Yes,' the woman replied.

'What did you mean by, *it never started out that way*?' Dixie asked.

'Miss Smith's right,' and Robert turned towards his niece. 'It was never my original intention for you to be harmed in any way. And if you hadn't gone looking for this person,' Robert glared at Danny, 'the situation would have been entirely different.' He paused, searching in his mind to find the correct words, but knew whatever he said, wouldn't come out right. 'But things just seemed to happen.'

'Why go after Dixie?' Danny asked. 'Why not your sister? She's rich.'

'I could never kill Lucy,' Fisher replied, in a strained voice. Then he glared and turned his words to Kate Smith.

'It's all your fault,' he snarled. 'Your demands made me desperate for money.'

Danny Buckley gave a sarcastic laugh.

'And *I'm* supposed to be a louse.'

'Well, I'm going to leave you three to sort things out,' Kate said.

'You're not going anywhere,' and Danny moved forward. 'What's in that briefcase? Money?'

'You don't need me here,' Kate replied, slipping her free hand in the bag hanging from her shoulder. 'Somehow I don't think you're going to get the police involved because of your family business. So what you do with your uncle is entirely up to you. I know what I'd do.'

'I said you're not leaving,' Danny repeated, then stiffened as Kate Smith suddenly withdrew a lethal looking automatic pistol from her shoulder bag. It looked heavy and awkward in her hand.

'I know how to use this, I was shown,' Kate said confidently. 'The safety's off and all I've got to do is point and pull the trigger.'

'There's a hundred thousand pounds in that case,' Robert said. 'And she's had more than that already. Company money.'

Danny slowly started to edge towards the woman holding the gun, the small sofa still between them.

'I mean it,' Kate said. 'I don't want to kill anybody but I will shoot whoever tries to stop me.'

Kate had swivelled the gun in Danny's direction, her attention focused on him, as she moved toward the door of the suite leading to the hotel corridor.

It was this movement that took Kate within an arm's length of Robert and he reacted with hardly any thought. Survival, instinct, a chance to get out of this room, he wasn't sure. But he knew he had nothing to lose and grabbed Kate's wrist with one hand and yanked the gun from her with his other. Then he pushed her violently away from him, sending her crashing to the floor, still clutching the black briefcase.

'Stop,' he snarled at Danny, 'and you know I won't hesitate in shooting *you*.'

'No, don't,' Dixie cried out. 'Don't shoot. Just go.'

'Dixie, he's going to have to kill the three of us, if he's going to get away with this. He can't leave any witnesses.'

The young woman looked at Danny realizing he was right and stood rooted as he suddenly pulled his mobile phone from an inside pocket and hurled it at Robert Fisher. The accountant instinctively ducked and pulled the trigger as Danny flung himself behind the sofa then pushed upwards hoping to push the piece of furniture over the coffee table against the man holding the gun.

Robert looked at the gun in his hand and pulled the trigger again as Danny's head came into view. But nothing happened.

'There aren't any bullets in the clip. I took them out, just in case I accidentally shot someone.'

Everyone stared at Kate, now back on her feet, the black case clasped in her arms held in front of her.

Danny was the first to react as the information sank in and used the back of the sofa to pull himself up. He lunged at Robert who threw the useless automatic at the man coming for him. It hit Danny on the side of the forehead, splitting the skin, sending blood trickling down the side of his face. The blow stunned him for a moment and he shook his head to clear the pain.

Robert grabbed hold of the brown leather case containing the documents and ran to the door. Pulling it open he looked both ways along the corridor, then set off hurriedly in the direction of the lift.

'Keep hold of that woman,' Danny shouted as he started after the accountant.

Dixie moved towards Kate who began backing off. Then the older woman switched the briefcase from her arms to one hand and swung it upwards. One corner of the case hit Dixie smack in the stomach and she doubled up.

'Sorry about that,' Kate said, and fled.

*

Robert Fisher reached the lift and banged a fist against it in frustration. The indicator showed it was on the third floor and going down. He looked back along the corridor and saw Danny charge out of the suite. The fire exit door was set back in a recess just feet away and Fisher barged through the door, then stopped in amazement when he saw the person in front of him.

'So it was you after all,' Joey growled, just as surprised himself. 'You two faced scumbag.'

The accountant tried to push past the young man but Joey grabbed hold of the front of the expensive cashmere overcoat preventing him. However, Fisher had a height advantage because he was standing on the small landing and Joey was below him on the stairs. Realizing this the older man frantically kicked out hard against the pop star's legs and when the grip loosened on him lifted one foot high and pushed firmly against Joey's stomach. The singer, letting go of the coat, lost his balance and fell backwards down the carpeted stairwell his arms flailing. Fortunately he managed to grab the banister and clung on tight.

Fisher seeing his path was blocked downwards spun on his heels, still clutching the briefcase, and charged in the other direction up the stairs just as Danny pushed open the fire door.

'You okay?' Danny called out, then went and helped pull Joey upright.

'Yeah, I'm fine, let's get after him.'

Both men followed in the direction the accountant had taken, running up two flights of stairs, coming to a different type of fire door. Danny pushed up the bar and the heavy door swung open into the cold moonlight. They were on the flat roof of the hotel.

Cautiously the men walked through the door into the biting wind and looked around. Joey had left his topcoat in Linda's room and immediately regretted it.

A lot of the area was covered in ice and snow, with clear patches where warm air vents protruded from the roof. A hum of machinery could be heard from behind large padlocked doors of a lift shaft. There were plenty of places to hide.

'I wonder if there's another way down,' Danny said in a whisper. 'You stay here and I'll do a circle of the roof. If you see him, shout. And don't let the door slam shut, there's no handle this side.'

Joey nodded his head as Danny moved away, treading carefully, so as not to slip. Gusts ruffled his grey curly hair and the wind turned his cheeks to marble. It was freezing cold. The area was much larger than Danny thought it would be and halfway across came to metal stairs leading to a lower roof. He still hadn't seen any other exit.

Danny eased his way gingerly down the treads gripping tight both rails and looked around again. The moon was bright, casting long shadows. Danny heard the hum of a different lift shaft and moved in that direction, then spotted another fire exit door nearby firmly shut. And there was no way it could be opened from the outside. Another door adjacent to it was locked and would need a key to gain entry.

So Robert Fisher still had to be somewhere on the roof.

Danny moved towards the parapet about twenty yards away and rested his hands on the tubular metal handrail that ran along top of the low concrete wall, looking down into the street. It was one hell of a drop.

Danny took his hands from the rail and blew some warmth into them. His teeth were nearly chattering with the chill wind and his feet were beginning to lose their feeling. He slowly moved his eyes around trying to work out what the man he was after would have done and came to the conclusion there was only one thing he'd have wanted. To get off the roof somehow and back into the hotel. The accountant couldn't stay out in this weather much longer.

The grey curly haired man walked slowly back to the metal stairs and had just placed a foot on the bottom tread when he thought he heard a noise. But before he could turn around felt himself being dragged backwards. Robert Fisher had seemingly appeared from nowhere.

Then Fisher swung the brown leather briefcase in an arc with all his force and caught Danny on the side of the head, knocking him down on to the hard cold roof. He hit a patch of ice and slithered on his back several yards as Fisher hauled himself up the stairs.

The accountant made it to the top and paused, trying to remember where the fire exit door he'd used was. He figured his pursuers would have kept it open and had just started to move again when he heard a shout behind him.

'Joey,' Danny called out, 'look out, Fisher's coming.'

The silver haired man quickened his pace, cursing the icy conditions, when suddenly Joey appeared from behind the wooden outbuilding covering the top of a lift shaft.

The pop star immediately launched himself at Fisher, hitting him waist high, and both men went sprawling, the briefcase slipping from the accountant's hand. All feeling of cold disappeared from the young man as he felt the adrenalin surge through his body.

'Over here,' Joey shouted, and as Fisher tried to push himself up, the singer threw a punch catching the older man on the side of his chin. Fisher fell back and then rolled away from Joey before leaping to his feet.

'There's no escape, Robert.'

Danny Buckley's voice was calm, sinisterly so. Joey looked at Danny, who'd come into view, and followed his lead as he began to walk slowly towards the accountant.

Fisher seeing both men coming at him moved backwards. He wasn't a fighter - and he was scared. He'd been caught out. He wasn't in charge. He couldn't give orders and make people toe the line. He was trapped and had a terrible sinking feeling in his guts.

'Please let me go,' he said. 'Just give me a head start and I promise I'll leave the country and you'll never hear from me again. Please.'

'You're whining, Robert.' Danny smiled. 'What's the matter? Don't you like being found out for the little shit you are? You've made a lot of people unhappy, and now you want mercy? What do you say Joey?'

The singer didn't answer and kept moving forward.

'Please let me go.' Fisher sounded almost childlike in his plea. 'I'm sorry...I'm sorry for all those things I did.' Then the heel of his shoe hit against the concrete parapet and he looked around. He tried to move away quickly, but in doing so, slipped on a patch of ice and fell against the low metal handrail. He started to topple over and Joey and Danny darted forward as Fisher managed to grab the rail with both hands, gripping tight as his body hung, suspended in space.

'Help me, for God's sake help me,' Fisher's voice sounded frightened and desperate.

Joey and Danny each grabbed one of the man's wrists, taking the strain of his weight.

'Pull me up,' Fisher begged the two men, looking wildly up at their faces above him.

'What do you say, Joey?'

The pop star stared at Danny.

'He nearly killed my best mate.'

The older man stared back.

'I know,' he said.

'So fuck 'im,' and Joey let go of the accountant's wrist. The sudden weight on Danny's grip was too much for him to hold and couldn't help the dangling man being ripped from his grasp.

'Baaastards,' Robert Fisher cried out as he fell, his eyes glaring fixedly at the two men, his arms flapping like useless wings.

Seconds later there was a scream from the street a long way below.

'I didn't think he'd have the guts to commit suicide,' Danny said.

'Yeah,' Joey breathed out. 'At least it saved a fuckin' trial.'

'Let's go.'

Danny moved away from the parapet, pausing to pick up the brown leather briefcase, then headed for the fire exit they'd used to get on to the roof.

Joey followed with one thought only in mind.

He'd got even for Mike.

SIXTY

Danny rapped gently a couple of times on the door of the suite.

'Who's there?' a woman's muffled voice asked.

'It's me and Joey.'

Dixie opened the door and the two men entered and walked into the lounge.

'Where's Kate Smith?' Danny asked, looking around the room.

'She got away,' Dixie replied, sounding embarrassed. 'I tried stopping her, but I couldn't.'

'Don't worry about it,' Joey said.

'No,' Danny agreed, and held out the brown leather briefcase to the young woman. 'This is what's important.'

Dixie took the briefcase.

'What happened to...' The young woman hesitated before managing her question, 'Where's Uncle Robert?'

Both men looked at her with blank faces, then Danny spoke.

'I'm sorry, but he's dead.'

Dixie seemed to sag and Joey grabbed an arm to steady her.

'No, no, I'm fine,' she said, taking a deep breath and gently loosening Joey's grip. 'What happened?'

'He jumped off the roof,' Danny replied. 'We chased him up there, got him cornered, and then he jumped.'

'That's right,' Joey said. 'There was nothing we could do about it.'

'Did he say anything?'

'Yes he did,' Danny answered. 'He said to tell you and his sister he was sorry. He said the best way out of it was for him to end his life and he was sorry if his death caused any more problems. But he couldn't face the humiliation for what he'd done.'

There was silence as Dixie digested the words.

'Yes, maybe it's for the best,' she said in a hushed voice. 'I'll have to tell Aunt Lucy.'

'No,' Danny said. 'Don't do that, well, not yet anyway, because I can see a way out of this. A way which might prevent most of this mess becoming public knowledge. You'd prefer that, wouldn't you?'

'Yes, of course,' Dixie replied, 'And besides, I really don't know how much more I can take.'

'What have you got in mind?' Joey asked.

'Let's get rid of this first,' Danny said, picking up the automatic pistol and stuffing it in his overcoat pocket. Then he located his mobile phone which he'd hurled at Robert Fisher. 'It's still working,' he muttered, surprised, as he pressed the small buttons and spoke to the man sitting in the hotel lobby. 'Tony, we don't need you anymore. Leave the hotel and I'll speak to you later.' Danny kept the phone pressed to his ear as the other man spoke, then pressed the off button, looking thoughtful.

'Everything okay?' Joey asked.

'The police and an ambulance have arrived outside the hotel.'

'So what do we do?'

'Let's go to your room,' Danny answered. 'I'll tell you what I've got in mind then.'

'What about this mess...and the glass and coffee cup?' Joey asked. 'Fisher and the Smith woman drank out of them.'

Danny looked at them lying on the floor, knocked off the coffee table, when Danny had upended the sofa.

'Leave everything as it is,' he replied.

'There will be fingerprints.'

'Exactly,' the older man said. 'So just let's worry about mine.' And over the next few minutes Danny wiped everything he thought he might have touched. 'My prints are on record,' he informed the others, 'but you don't have to worry about yours.'

When he was satisfied Danny told Joey to go back to Linda, using the stairs, and he and Dixie would follow in five minutes.

*

Dixie and Danny left the exclusive hotel together an hour later. They were picked up by Stan in the next street and fifteen minutes later Joey and Linda joined them, the pop star heavily disguised in his ski hat and long wool scarf. None of them had noticed any police presence in the hotel foyer and the ambulance had long gone.

Stan dropped off Danny first, at his small terrace house in Holloway, then carried on to Joey's mansion where the three young people would say they'd been all evening if anyone asked.

Mid-morning, the next day, Stan drove the two women to Dixie's flat and she discovered two messages on her answering machine. One from Wyatt Peterson and the other from her Aunt Lucy.

Dixie called her aunt first.

'Robert's dead,' Lucy sobbed tearfully over the phone.

The young woman's reaction was one of appropriate surprise and shock. Dixie felt two-faced but it had been discussed and the decision reached that it would be better if the elderly lady didn't know the complete truth.

Dixie had studied the documents Kate Smith had used to blackmail her uncle and it soon became apparent that a lot of money had been siphoned off into private bank accounts here, in this country, and several in Switzerland.

Knowledge of Robert Fisher's embezzlement from the company would have to be revealed to his sister at some stage, but no way would Dixie tell Lucy about the involvement Robert had in his brother's death, or any of the other murders. It would break the poor woman's heart. Possibly even kill her.

No, some secrets had to be taken to the grave.

'Have you spoken to Wyatt yet?' her aunt asked.

'No, I haven't,' Dixie replied, 'but he's left a message for me to call him.'

'He said Robert committed suicide last night. Jumped off the roof of a hotel.'

Again Dixie expressed shock and horror.

'Why would he do such a thing?' Lucy asked, still sobbing.

'I don't know, but I'll speak to Wyatt and try to find out.' Dixie paused. 'Could I have a word with Mrs Hayes for a moment?' And a moment later Dixie was talking to her aunt's housekeeper telling her to make sure Lucy had plenty of rest and that she'd try and visit her as soon as possible. 'If there's anything she wants let me know straight away.'

The housekeeper assured Lucy's niece she would and the two women said their goodbyes.

Dixie immediately phoned Wyatt Peterson.

'Have you heard the news?' The accountant's voice one of disbelief.

'Yes I have,' Dixie replied. 'I've just spoken to Aunt Lucy. She told me.'

'How is she?'

'She's taking it pretty badly.'

'The police got hold of me about two o'clock this morning but I didn't phone your aunt until about eight. Didn't think it necessary to wake her early. I left you a message.'

'Yes, I got it, thanks.'

'The police said Robert jumped from the room of a hotel. The police asked me if I knew why, but I told them I didn't.'

Wyatt paused. 'I still can't believe it. Robert dead...have you any idea why your uncle would want to commit suicide? He didn't seem the type.'

'Yes, I know why,' Dixie replied.

There was a stunned silence before Wyatt could speak again. When he'd asked the question he'd fully expected a negative reply and was amazed by Dixie's answer.

'What was the reason?' the accountant asked in a strained voice.

'I'm afraid my uncle has stolen a lot of money from our company.'

There was a tense silence before Wyatt managed to speak again.

'Robert a thief? It doesn't seem possible.' There was another pause before the accountant continued. 'How much? And how do you know?'

'I've got proof,' Dixie replied, 'documentation that will explain everything...look, I think it's best if I come to your office now, and bring what I've got.'

'Is it much money?'

'I'd say over a million, and he owes Aunt Lucy another half million. But I'm not an expert so I can't be one hundred per cent sure.'

'Oh, my God,' Wyatt groaned.

'I'm leaving now,' Dixie said. 'And don't worry, I'm sure we can get out of this mess. I'll help.'

Dixie ended the conversation and ten minutes later she and Linda were in the street hailing a taxi.

*

Wyatt Peterson finished going through the papers and stared across his desk at the two women. He hadn't questioned Linda's presence because he knew Dixie wouldn't have brought her along if she didn't want her friend to know what was going on. The accountant knew how close the two women had become.

'I'd say your estimate wasn't too far off the mark,' he said. 'We'll have to get independent auditors to go over the books to find out the exact amount, and obviously, everything will be done as discreetly as possible.' Wyatt paused, and looked curiously at Dixie. 'How did you obtain these documents?'

'I really do think it best if you don't know,' she replied.

Wyatt nodded his head.

'I see,' he said, 'but this information would be a powerful tool in the wrong hands. Was Robert being blackmailed?'

'Yes.'

'Do you know by who?'

'Again I think it best if you don't know. That way you can't let anything accidentally slip out to the police.'

'Talking about the police, they phoned me again just before you arrived,' Wyatt said.

'Yes, and what did they have to say?' Dixie asked interestedly.

'They think Robert met some woman in a suite in the hotel and they had an argument. Apparently, some young Spanish receptionist at the hotel remembers this woman booking the suite and saying it was for her boss. I've checked with Robert's secretary but she doesn't know anything about it.' Wyatt looked Dixie straight in the eye. 'Was it this mysterious woman in the hotel who was blackmailing Robert?'

Dixie ignored the question.

'Let the police think what they like about her,' she said, 'but I want you to inform the authorities of the results of our audit as soon as possible. The stolen money will be the reason Robert committed suicide. And let's see if we can stop that becoming public knowledge because it won't do our company any good at all. I'm sure there's someone here who will have some pull with the police.'

'Yes, I see what you mean,' Wyatt said. 'As long the police and the coroner are satisfied that was the reason for Robert's death then it should be all right. No point in pillorying us for his mistakes.' Wyatt paused. 'The police did tell me there would have to be an inquest but that's a matter of procedure.'

'However, there is one thing you'll have to do,' Dixie continued. 'We can't tell the police about these papers because, and you'll have to trust me on this, it would be disastrous for the police to think blackmail is involved.'

'So what is it you want me to do?' Wyatt asked.

'You'll have to come up with a good reason for suddenly having our books checked over. You see, Wyatt, we will be telling the truth about Robert and the reason he killed himself. It's just that,' and Dixie shrugged her shoulders, 'it's not the *whole* truth.'

The accountant couldn't help giving a slight smile.

'The difference is young lady, *you* appear to know *everything*, whereas I seem to be in the dark.'

'Yes,' Dixie said, 'and I think it's best it stays that way. Believe me, it will better for the company.'

'If you say so.'

'There was another copy of these documents,' Dixie said, 'but I destroyed them. I suggest you do the same with these.'

'Agreed,' Wyatt said, then paused, looking thoughtful. 'However, there is one more disturbing point here, and I don't know if you've thought of it.'

'What's that?' Dixie asked.

'Judging by the dates on some of these documents this information is eighteen months old.'

There was silence in the accountant's office as his words sank in.

'You mean there could be more money missing?'

Wyatt looked at Dixie and nodded.

'A year and a half is a long time,' he said.

SIXTY ONE

It transpired Wyatt was right and the final total of Robert's embezzlement was just over two and a half million on top of the money he'd borrowed from his sister, Lucy.

It hadn't been easy for Wyatt to get in a team of independent auditors to go over the company accounts. It was just days before Christmas - and there was a lot of work involved.

However, the old pals act in the money world worked wonders, plus the agreement of a large bonus because of such short notice. It meant a team working round the clock but the job was finished by the end of Thursday. Wyatt immediately phoned Dixie.

'Obviously I couldn't give them the information I had from those documents,' he told her. 'I gave a few hints but had to let them find out for themselves.'

'So when will you tell the police?' Dixie asked.

'Tomorrow,' the accountant replied. 'It'll be Christmas Eve so I don't expect there will be a lot of reaction until after the holiday period.'

'Have you thought of a good reason to tell the police why you had the books looked over?'

'Yes, and I'm going to keep it plain and simple. I'm going to say I had a hunch.' Wyatt chuckled. 'We Americans are well known for our hunches and I was just covering my back. I'd had no suspicion in the past but I was as interested as them why Robert committed suicide. Now the reason is apparent.

Robert was an embezzler and must have know he'd be found out sometime in the near future. He couldn't have got away with it for much longer.'

'That sounds reasonable,' Dixie said, 'and there is one other thing. I'd appreciate it if you didn't tell them about the money Robert borrowed from my aunt,' Dixie said. 'I really don't want the old girl bothered by the police. I would prefer it kept between us.'

'Yes, that was purely a family matter and I don't think there's much point in the police being made aware of that.' Wyatt paused. 'But will you tell your aunt about the money Robert took from the company?'

'Yes,' Dixie replied, 'she's got to know the reason why her brother killed himself, if only to put her mind at rest. I think she'll be able to come to terms with that explanation.'

'Why? Is there another explanation?'

'Wyatt, please don't pry. I trust you and we all like you. But it is best if you never ask me any more questions about my uncle's death. Let's treat the matter as closed.'

There was a brief silence.

'Okay, Dixie, you've my word on it. By the way, what about Robert's funeral?'

'I'm handling the arrangements,' Dixie replied. 'Aunt Lucy is the next of kin but I've told the police she's not strong enough to be worried about things like that. They seemed perfectly happy with my suggestion and I'm making arrangements for the funeral. I've been in touch with my uncle's solicitors to see if there were any special instructions in his will as to his funeral. And there weren't. So I'm trying to make arrangements for the cremation to take place next Wednesday. I know it's in between Christmas and New Year's Eve, but that can't be helped. I take it you will be there?'

'Yes, of course,' Wyatt replied. 'Robert wasn't such a bad person, besides, it was only money. As a matter of fact, I really liked him.'

Dixie kept her face blank and didn't react to the accountant's statement.

If only Wyatt knew the truth.

*

Christmas Eve and Mike was leaving the hospital. Dixie was busy packing a case to take to Joey's and Linda was doing likewise. Linda's intention of helping her father in his business had gone out the window with the death of Robert Fisher. Although both women knew Dixie was no longer in danger it somehow seemed natural for them to stick together. And there was still the funeral to come.

'I'll wait until after the New Year before I start back to work,' Linda said. 'Mind you, my Dad said he'd believe that when it happens.' She laughed. 'I'd have been fired by now if I worked for someone else.'

'Yes,' Dixie said, 'your parents have been wonderful.'

Linda nodded her head and smiled, then moved her head as she heard a sound in the hall.

'Sounds like the post has come,' she said, and walked out the room, returning a moment later with a bundle of letters and cards in her hand. Linda quickly shuffled through them and handed most to Dixie.

'I think there's a special one there,' she said.

Dixie looked quizzically at Linda then down at the mail in her hand. She fanned open the envelopes and saw *Private & Confidential* boldly typed on one. Putting the others on a table she tore open the flap of the white envelope and pulled out two foolscap pages.

One, a covering letter - the other, technical jargon relating to the laboratory DNA profiling tests.

Dixie began reading the letter, heart thudding, her top teeth biting into her bottom lip.

Dear Miss Fisher...her eyes scanned, searching...and then she found it...*Mr Danny J. Buckley is excluded one hundred per cent of being your father...*

Dixie brought a hand to her mouth, and began rubbing her lips slowly.

'What's the matter?' Linda asked, immediately seeing there was something wrong.

Instead of replying Dixie thrust the letter towards her friend then turned and walked to the kitchen where she busied herself making coffee. Linda followed several minutes later.

'I really don't know what to say.'

Dixie looked at Linda.

'Nor do I,' she said.

'Should I ask, is it what you expected? Is it what you wanted? Are you happy? Disappointed?'

Again Dixie stared at her friend and silently opened her mouth a couple of times before making a sound.

'I really don't know, I have to think,' she finally managed, and picked up the two mugs of coffee. Both women sat at the kitchen table looking at each other before Dixie took the letter from Linda's hand and once again read it. 'It's Danny I'm thinking of,' she continued, 'he seemed so positive he is my Father. I wonder if he knows yet?'

'Are you going to phone him?' Linda asked.

'I'm not sure what to do. I'll leave it for a bit and see if he contacts me. I don't want to disappoint him...I don't know how he's going to take it.'

'There's no doubt now that Danny isn't your father,' Linda said. 'But does it make any difference to you?'

Dixie shook her head.

'No,' she replied, 'to be honest, not really. It's just straightened things out as far as I'm concerned, and now they're the same as they were at the beginning. I loved Tom Fisher as a Father. Danny was a stranger. I've met him now - and I like him. But he's not my Father. Simple as that. And it's made me feel a lot easier in my mind.'

'Did you think Danny was your father before this DNA test?'

Dixie shrugged her shoulders.

'Yes, I suppose I did...but it's less complicated now.'

'However, there is one other thing we mustn't forget,' Linda said.

'What's that?'

'Well,' and Linda hesitated. 'Genetically it's been proved that Danny isn't your father but...'

'Go on,' Dixie prompted.

'Well, on the other hand, it's not been proved that Tom Fisher is your father.'

'Oh, come on, Linda. You make it sound as though everyone was sleeping with my Mother. Tom *is* my Father.'

'Yes, but you've got the wrong end of the stick. *We* know Tom is your father but...I was thinking of your birth certificate. It still says Danny is your father on it.'

'Ah, yes, I see what you mean.'

'So, will you get it changed?'

'No,' Dixie replied. 'I'm going to leave things the way they are, and not meddle anymore. I'm going to live a normal life from now on and try and forget everything that's happened.'

'Good,' and Linda smiled. 'You're out of danger now and deserve some happiness. Mind you,' Linda's face became serious, 'and this is the only time I'll mention it. It does prove that the theory about your uncle was right. He would have got control of your money.'

*

The women were ready to leave about fifteen minutes before Stan arrived to pick them up in the Rolls. They were going first to the hospital to pick up Mike and then on to Joey's.

Last minute Christmas shopping had been hectic trying to squeeze in time here and there with their busy schedule. Joey had been a great help, also organizing everything for Mike, even to the extent of buying him a load of clothes to wear when he left the hospital. A lot of his stuff was still in Wakefield.

Presents bought were hopefully the right ones.

'Right, let's get out of here,' Dixie said chirpily, as Stan helped them with their cases. 'Let's go and pick up the love of my life.'

The phone rang just as Dixie was about to shut the front door. She looked at Linda and frowned.

'Shall I?'

Linda nodded.

'You'd better...you never know. I'll see you in the car downstairs.'

Dixie went back inside, picked up the ringing phone, and was glad she'd bothered. It was Danny.

'Hello,' he said. 'I suppose you received the result from the clinic today.' He sounded down.

'Yes,' Dixie replied.

'I feel gutted. This has come as quite a shock to me. I was sure I was right.'

'It's not the end of the world,' Dixie said gently, feeling slightly embarrassed.

'But I was wrong...after all these years. I can't believe it...but those tests don't lie. I'm sorry, Dixie. I really did think you were my kid.'

'I know,' Dixie replied, keeping her voice soft, 'but let's look on the bright side. We've got to know each other now and all of us are friends. You, me, Mike, Joey, Linda...and of course, Jack. We've got a lot to build on. Let's face it, we might never have met.'

'You're just trying to cheer me up,' Danny said. 'But I do appreciate it.'

'And I do want you to cheer up. Tomorrow's Christmas. This is not a time to be feeling unhappy.'

'Yes, your right.'

'Are you in London or Norfolk?'

'Jack and I are in Norfolk. We'll be staying here until after the New Year.'

'Well, have a nice time and I'll speak to you soon. I've got a present for you but it will have to wait until we next meet. Wish Jack a Merry Christmas for me...and you as well, Danny.'

'Thanks, you and Mike have a good Christmas too. The same to Joey and Linda.'

Danny put the phone down his end and looked at his friend sitting comfortably in an armchair..

'How has she taken it?' Jack asked.

Danny shrugged.

'Okay, I guess. And she wishes you a Merry Christmas.'

Jack nodded and went and sat down near the fire as Danny headed upstairs to Jessie in the bedroom. Nurse Coogan was still with them but was out doing some last minute shopping. She said she'd be back for lunch. Jack took a sip of his can of lager and looked at his watch. Nearly one o'clock.

He put down the beer, folded his arms across his chest and closed his eyes.

The police had been to see him again - several times. They'd discovered his criminal background and were more than suspicious of his version of events for that evening the motorcyclist died. Door to door inquiries had revealed that several people in the flats above the street thought they heard shots fired. And several bullet cases from an automatic pistol had been found in the snow during a thorough daylight search.

But Jack maintained there were no shots fired when he left the pub. Well, not that he could remember hearing. The sports car and the bike rider was all he saw. He didn't even see who threw the petrol bomb.

Ask Dixie, Linda or Mike.

Which is what the old bill did. And that didn't get them very far. The girls were still vague about the events of that evening and when the police spoke to Mike in hospital he had even less to add. After all, he'd been knocked unconscious.

The dead motorcyclist had a criminal record but there was nothing to associate him with Jack. So the police were stymied.

Dixie, Linda and Mike were, without a doubt, impeccable witnesses, exemplary citizens without a stain on their characters. They were well off and had no known connection with any criminal activity.

Except for Jack.

'I'm not satisfied,' the police inspector in charge of the case had told the ex-con. 'But so long as those young friends of yours back up your story there's nothing I can do.'

'That's because it's true,' Jack had told the policeman.

A smile flashed across the hard man's chiselled features as he relaxed in the armchair.

Well, some of it was.

SIXTY TWO

Joey had offered Stan and Marie the holiday period off, saying that he and his friends were quite capable of looking after themselves. But they'd declined, preferring to stay in Hampstead.

'That's fine by me,' Joey told them, 'if you're sure that's what you want. But I don't want you waiting hand and foot on us. You just behave like you're part of the family and enjoy yourselves.'

'Well, that's how we already feel, Mr Judd, and that's the reason we'd like to stay. We couldn't think of a nicer place to be.'

That really touched Joey.

A thought shared by the others when Mike, Dixie and Linda arrived.

'But *I'll* need a lot of waiting on,' Mike said, grinning. 'Don't forget I've just come out of hospital.'

'There's nothing wrong with you, mate,' Joey said. Which was true. Mike had made a remarkable recovery. He still needed to take things easy but the doctors had told him there wouldn't be any permanent damage from his injuries. It was only a matter of convalescing and he'd be as good as new.

It had been snowing again during the day, a good four inches covering the ground, and when they all retired for the night couldn't resist standing at their bedroom windows gazing at the white landscape, seemingly all the more luminous under a bright moonlit sky.

Something peaceful about snow, Joey thought, as he turned off his bedside light and snuggled under the duvet in his four poster bed. The radio was softly playing Christmas carols as he dozed, peacefully drifting off to sleep.

He wasn't sure what time it was when he heard someone call his name, only that it must have been early morning. And it was quiet. The radio had been turned off.

'Joey,' a voice called softly, and then repeated his name. The pop star struggled to open his heavy eyelids and slowly raised his body, resting on one elbow.

'Joey,' then he recognized Linda's voice, and his eyes shot open.

Moonlight was streaming through the windows illuminating the bedroom and Joey saw Linda standing on stiletto high-heeled shoes several feet from him wearing a red Santa Claus coat reaching half way down her thighs. Taking hold of the front corners she stretched her arms wide, the movement pulling the coat open like wings. Underneath Linda was wearing only a brief black bra, matching colour panties, black suspenders and stockings. Around her waist she'd tied a big red bow.

'Merry Christmas,' she said, and let the coat slip off her shoulders and drop behind her on to the carpet. 'Your present has arrived.'

*

Mike noticed the difference in Joey on Christmas morning, and soon learned the reason why, when Dixie told him Linda had moved her things into Joey's bedroom.

Everyone had got up early, eager to open their presents, which took over an hour and several dustbin bags were filled with torn wrapping paper.

Breakfast was on a help-yourself basis with everybody mucking in. Eggs, bacon, mushrooms, tomatoes, baked beans...with mounds of toast or fried bread.

They were excited and their adrenaline was flowing.

And then the young people joined forces with Marie and Stan in helping prepare the giant turkey and all the trimmings for lunch.

Friends came and went during the afternoon and evening, including a brief appearance of Vic Ruebens and the rest of Joey's band. And Gerry Dolan arrived driving a mini-bus with all Mike's London based staff on board to wish him a speedy recovery.

The next day was special for Dixie and Mike and they went for a walk on the snow covered Hampstead Heath. Exactly a year from when they'd first met - all down to a little dog.

On Monday the celebrations started to wind down and by Tuesday the household was solemnly awaiting the arrival of Aunt Lucy for her brother's funeral the next day. She was being driven down in a hired limousine, with her housekeeper, and Stan had graciously offered to take them back to Elm Hall on Thursday. She was welcome to stay longer, Dixie told her, but Lucy said she'd be happier in her own home.

She would be taking Robert's ashes with her.

*

The day after the funeral Dixie informed her aunt about the money Robert had embezzled from the company. Lucy listened quietly, every now and again nodding her head, but hardly saying anything. Never once did she express an opinion or condemn her brother's crime.

'Wyatt says he thinks he's worked out a way to pay back the money to the company so no clients suffer a financial loss,' Dixie said. 'But he'll need your co-operation to finalize all the details. It's to do with Robert's shares in the company. Everything has been left to you.'

'I know,' Lucy said, 'my brother's solicitors have already explained the contents of his will. Tell Wyatt I'll agree to whatever is best for the company and our family name. It's the least I can do.'

'But Wyatt's not sure what he can do about the money Robert borrowed from you.'

The elderly woman waved a hand dismissively.

'It doesn't matter,' she said.

Dixie said goodbye to her aunt and Mrs Hayes as they sat in the back of the Rolls.

'I promise I'll come and see you very soon,' she said, holding Lucy's hand tightly.

'I know, dear,' her aunt said. 'And I hope I'll be better company by then.' She stared at Dixie. 'I loved my brothers...and now they've both gone.'

The young woman leant forward and kissed Lucy on the cheek.

'But I've still got you,' her aunt said.

Dixie smiled.

'Of course.'

*

The next day was New Year's Eve and not the rave-up they'd envisioned months ago. They'd had a wonderful Christmas, but what with the funeral and Mike's recuperation, decided to see in the beginning of January quietly.

Joey insisted Stan and Marie join them for the evening and to hear the chimes of Big Ben strike midnight. Then everyone downed champagne and began making calls to their families and close friends, using mobiles and the house phone.

Half past twelve and Linda whispered to Dixie.

'What about Danny?'

Dixie looked thoughtful.

'Yes, you're right, I should,' and moments later the phone was ringing in the cottage in Norfolk. Jack answered.

'Happy New Year,' Dixie said.

'And to you as well,' Jack's voice full of enthusiasm. 'Did you want Danny?'

'Yes please.'

'Won't be a minute, I'll get him.'

Jack put down the phone and quickly went upstairs and poked his head into the main bedroom.

'Dixie's on the phone,' he said quietly, 'wants to wish you a Happy New Year.'

Danny rose from his chair and looked across at Nurse Coogan, seated on the other side of the bed. She looked tired. The nurse was a caring woman and the last few nights had given up much of her own sleep to sit with Jessie. She knew there wasn't much time left.

'Won't be a moment,' Danny said, not wishing to use the extension in the bedroom. He went downstairs and picked up the phone. 'Happy New Year.'

'Happy New Year,' Dixie echoed. 'When will I be seeing you again?'

'I'll be up here for another week or two yet, but as soon as I'm back in London I'll call you.'

'Well, don't make it too long...goodbye.'

'Goodbye,' Danny said, and returned upstairs.

*

Jessie died at six in the morning. Danny had sat by her side all night holding her hand. He'd dozed with his head on the edge of the bed, every now and again waking for a few minutes, but now woke to find Jessie had slipped away from him, free of pain at last. Danny cradled his wife's head in his arms and grieved for his loss.

Five days later Jessie was buried.

The funeral took place in a church over eight hundred years old and a lot of people came. Jessie had been loved by many and Danny had also become part of the community. As the people left the church following the coffin bearers Danny untied Maggie, and the mongrel trotted obediently by his side in the deep snow.

Jack stood next to his friend as the coffin was lowered into the hole dug out of the ice-cold ground. Jessie's elderly parents stood with them. They knew how much Danny had loved their daughter and were proud to have him as a son-in-law.

After the service finished the mourners made their way to their cars. There was food and drinks waiting for them at the cottage and they were eager to get out of the cold.

Jack stopped by the church gate and looked back through the snow covered graveyard, the ancient headstones standing like frozen sentries guarding their loved ones.

Danny was crouched down by the side of Maggie at the edge of the open grave, both of them saying their last silent goodbyes to the woman who'd meant so much to them.

SIXTY THREE

His secretary, Mandy, was complaining, good-naturedly, but Danny had to admit she had a point. More and more work had fallen on her shoulders over the last couple of months because of the time her boss had spent in Norfolk. Fortunately, a lot of his deals could be done over the phone so he hadn't lost too much business. The marvel of mobiles.

But Danny had to make a decision.

It was two weeks since Jessie had been buried and he had to decide whether to sell up in London and settle in Norfolk where Jack was still interested in them going into business together. Or should he stay in London and only use the cottage for holidays and weekends?

Danny had been back to London for a few days and was now returning to the cottage with Jack, for the weekend, to think things over. He'd discussed his dilemma with his secretary and his friend, promising them he'd have made up his mind by Monday morning. They both said there wasn't any hurry, knowing how much he was still upset by Jessie's death, but Danny had said, no. He had to try and get his thoughts straightened out, depressed or not.

However, Danny did feel guilty about one thing. During the time he'd been back in London he hadn't contacted Dixie, as he'd promised.

But, he told himself, he would. Next week for sure.

Jessie's dog had travelled with him to the capital and as the black VW drew up outside the cottage Maggie began scratching at the car window with excitement. And as soon as she was out of the car bounded up the snow covered path to the front door.

The central heating was on a time switch, so the cottage wasn't cold, but Danny still lit the logs piled in the open fire, just as Jessie had always done. Half an hour later the dog was stretched out in front of it fast asleep.

After sandwiches and beer for lunch Danny went out into the shed in the back garden for more logs.

Jack was about to follow when the phone rang and went over to the small writing desk and picked up the receiver instead. Then, as he listened to the voice at the other end, an astonished look came over his face.

'He's outside at the moment,' he muttered into the phone, 'but he'll be back any moment.'

And as he said that Danny came into the room with several logs in his arms but came to an abrupt halt as he saw the look on Jack's face.

'It's for you,' Jack said, holding out the receiver. 'It's a lousy connection...but it's Kate Smith.'

'Kate Smith?' Danny repeated, a look of amazement sweeping across his features. 'What the hell can she want?' He dropped the logs on to the stone surround of the fire and walked towards the stairs. 'I'll take it in the bedroom,' he said, and a moment later Danny's voice came over the extension. 'You can hang up now, Jack. I've got it.'

'Okay,' his friend growled, and replaced the receiver, but immediately picked it up again, clamping a hand tightly over the mouthpiece, just in time to hear a woman's voice come over the earpiece asking, 'Is that Danny Buckley?'

'Yes, it is...did you just hear a click?' Danny's voice sounded anxious as he put the question.

'No, but this is a terrible line,' the woman replied. 'I'm calling from a small island in the Mediterranean. Did your friend who answered give you my name?'

'Yes, Miss Smith, and the last time I saw you was in that hotel suite. Where exactly are you now?'

'Never mind. But I have a message for you...from Eddie. Before he died he made me promise to contact you.'

'Eddie? Who's Eddie?'

'Don't play games with me, Mr Buckley,' and the woman paused for a moment as loud crackling exploded over the phone. 'Eddie told me all about your deal. He told me to tell you he was sorry he didn't pull it off. Well, he's no longer with us now, so I don't suppose it matters.' Another pause for noise on the line. 'But I'd like to say a few things myself,' Kate continued. 'You see, if Eddie had succeeded it was you who would have got all Dixie Fisher's money. I know you weren't in on it from the beginning, but I think you're worse than Robert Fisher wanting that poor young girl killed because Eddie told me the reason why. You're Dixie's father...not Tom Fisher.' The noise on the line had nearly faded to nothing which only seemed to emphasize Kate Smith's next words. 'Do you still want her dead?'

Jack listened as the woman repeated everything Eddie had told her. When the line went dead he hung up, his face like stone.

*

'What did she want?' Jack asked, comfortably relaxed in an armchair, when Danny returned downstairs.

'Just to say it's all over. There was another man involved in this but he's also dead. And to say she's sorry if she hurt Dixie when she escaped from the hotel in London.' Danny smiled. 'She said Dixie's safe now.'

'Good,' and Jack returned the smile, 'I wonder how she got this phone number?'

Danny shrugged his shoulders.

'No idea,' he replied.

During the afternoon both men fell asleep and when Danny woke it was pitch black outside. Shaking Jack from his slumber Danny fed the dog then let her out into the back garden.

It was six o'clock and the men were hungry. The freezer was well stocked and it took only a moment for them to agree on large sirloin steaks and chips.

'But I think I'll have a bath first,' Jack said.

'Yeah, okay,' Danny said. 'I'll get this meat thawed out and do the rest. Your turn tomorrow,' he added, with a grin.

'Yeah, sure,' Jack said, and went upstairs to the bathroom. Turning on the taps he opened the mirrored medicine cabinet and looked inside. Shoving several small bottles into his pocket he then went into the main bedroom. Looking through the bedside drawers he put more bottles of Jessie's into his pocket. Pain killers and sleeping pills. Danny had assured Nurse Coogan he'd dispose of them but hadn't yet got around to it.

Jack turned off the bath water then went into his own bedroom and put the bottles in a drawer. Then he bathed and went downstairs into the large kitchen to eat.

'I'll do the washing up,' Jack said, after they'd cleared their plates. Danny didn't need any persuading.

'Okay,' and he rose from his chair, 'I'll go and turn on the television.'

'I feel like tying one on tonight,' Jack said. 'Haven't been pissed for a long time.'

'Yeah, well there's plenty of booze here.' Danny's voice dropped. 'They didn't drink much after the funeral.' Then his tone immediately lightened. 'Yeah, that's not a bad idea. I'll join you.'

After Jack finished drying up he shoved two spoons into his jeans back pocket, tore off some kitchen paper from a roll, and went upstairs to his room. There he quickly took half a dozen tablets from one of the bottles, crushed them individually between the spoons, and emptied the powder into a piece of kitchen paper.

Going downstairs into the lounge he sniffed loudly several times.

'I had to go upstairs and get a handkerchief,' he explained as he wiped his nose. 'Hope I'm not getting a bloody cold.'

After a couple more beers the men graduated on to spirits. Danny drinking gin and tonic, and Jack whisky and water.

'And get some more ice,' Danny called out as Jack went back into the kitchen to refill his small water jug.

Jack went to the freezer compartment of the fridge, extracted an ice-tray and emptied the frozen cubes into a beer glass. Then he took the crushed white powder from his pocket and carefully mixed it in hot water in another small jug until dissolved. Finally Jack poured the water mixture slowly into two of the indentations for ice cubes and returned the tray to the small freezer compartment.

A couple of hours later both men were well on their way to being drunk. Slurring their words, laughing inanely at out-of-date dirty jokes and talking of crooked strokes they'd pulled in the past.

It was still only ten thirty when Jack went into the kitchen, took out the doctored ice cubes and slipped them into Danny's drink. An hour later Danny stretched, yawned and said he was sleepy.

'Don't be a wimp,' Jack slurred, 'have another one.' And topped up the other man's glass.

Another fifteen minutes and Danny tried to lever himself out of his armchair, but flopped back.

'Gotta get to bed,' he said, his words running together, 'Christ, I can hardly keep my eyes open.' He peered through slit eyes at Jack. 'Give us a hand, mate.'

Instead Jack stared straight at the other man, his face hardening, and held out his right fist in front of him, the index finger pointing straight at Danny, his thumb sticking upright. Jack pulled his finger back and forth several times as though pulling a trigger.

'You're dead,' he said softly, his voice perfectly normal. He'd made sure there had always been more water than whisky in his glass all evening - and was far from drunk.

Danny looked at him through watery eyes, stunned, as comprehension filtered through to his brain.

'You listened...you bastard,' he gasped, but was no longer in control of his senses, and his head dropped forward unconscious.

Jack immediately went upstairs, put on a pair of leather gloves, and returned to the lounge with all the medicine bottles. He dumped them on the coffee table in front of Danny then went into the kitchen, returning with two tea towels and a small metal meat hammer.

First, he emptied the contents of the bottles into one of the cloths, purposely letting some of the pills fall on the carpet. Then Jack wiped all the bottles clean with the other tea towel and placed the bottles one at time in Danny's hand.

Next, using the metal hammer, he pounded the tablets wrapped in cloth into tiny pieces. Then he emptied the contents of the cloth into Danny's glass, adding more gin and tonic, all the time stirring the concoction with the slim shaft of the hammer. Finally he wiped clean the hammer and returned it to the kitchen.

Then he took a plastic funnel from a cupboard and once again returned to the man fast asleep. Jack wrapped one of the towels under Danny's chin and, pulling back his head, inserted the narrow end of the funnel into his mouth and very slowly poured into the other end the slushy contents of Danny's glass.

The sleeping man gagged several times and some of the mixture dribbled down his chin on to the towel. But Jack was patient and twenty minutes later most of the lethal liquid was inside the inert figure in the chair. Plus more gin and tonic.

Jack turned off the television, which had been playing to itself most of the evening, and returned the tea towels he'd used, to where he'd got them from. He washed the plastic funnel but left the other stuff on the coffee table. Then went upstairs to bed and slept peacefully.

Next morning he came downstairs, fully dressed, at seven o'clock and found Maggie whining pitifully on the carpet by the still figure in the armchair.

Jack checked for a pulse - but there was none.

Danny Buckley was dead.

The hard looking man with a broken nose bent down and ruffled the dog's ears.

'Don't worry, I'll look after you.'

Then he went to the phone and called for an ambulance and the police.

SIXTY FOUR

The meeting in Wyatt's office didn't take long. But it was important. Wyatt had resolved the matter for replacing the stolen money and wanted to explain the details to Dixie.

'It's nowhere near as bad as we first thought,' he told the beautiful young woman sitting opposite him. 'It would have been worse if Robert was still alive but his death released his assets. And, surprisingly, he wasn't mortgaged up to the hilt.'

'Well, that sound's good,' Dixie said. 'But there was something I meant to ask you. Aren't we insured against losses like these?'

'Yes, we do have Personal Indemnity Insurance,' the accountant answered, 'but that's really to cover small losses and to do with junior partners. But Robert was a senior partner and, well, the amount he stole was a very large sum. This was theft on a grand scale. We might have got something back if I'd pushed it but that would have meant insurance investigators probing into our affairs. And...'

'And that's something I didn't want,' Dixie interrupted. 'Yes, you did the right thing, and I'm grateful.

'No, I wanted it too. It wasn't just this mysterious blackmail situation I'm not supposed to know about, but there is the company name to guard. We have a fantastic business here and I hope no-one is going to be any the wiser. Anyway,' and Wyatt smiled, 'let me tell you what I think we should do. Because of the buoyant property market the sale of Robert's penthouse apartment brings the debt down very considerably.

And then there's his shares.' Wyatt paused, 'I'm going to buy them.'

'You are?'

'Yes, Dixie. I know the shares now belong to your aunt and by rights she should get the money. However, she's agreed that the cash is to be used to pay back what her brother took. But she will get back the half million she lent Robert after all.'

'She should have got the profit from the penthouse too,' Dixie said.

'I know. Your aunt has been very generous.'

'Was there any money in those secret bank accounts Robert had?'

Wyatt smiled.

'Yes, just over two hundred thousand pounds. And that I offered to your Aunt Lucy, to help compensate her for all the aggravation she's had. But she didn't want it. Said it was dirty money and wouldn't want it on her conscience. I told her it could be paid into the company and then one of our cheques sent to her. Make it clean, so to speak.'

'What did she say?'

'Still didn't want it. Said you could have it if you wanted. Do you?'

'No,' Dixie was emphatic, 'I agree with her...it'd be tainted.' But then she paused as a sudden thought flashed into her mind. 'Could it be put into a trust?'

'Yes. Yes, of course,' Wyatt replied. 'But who for?'

'A little boy called Connor. His mother was killed in a car crash. Yes, that would be putting the money to a proper use.'

Wyatt stared at the young woman but didn't bother to ask any questions. Somehow he knew he wouldn't get any answers.

*

Linda had moved in with Joey so Mike and Dixie had the flat to themselves. Mike had gone back to work a couple of days a week in London but was itching to get back to Wakefield.

The snow was finally thawing and the doctor had said give it another week and Mike would be fully fit.

Also, Gerry Dolan's life would return to normal.

The couple had just finished eating their evening meal when the buzzer on the internal phone rang. It was the duty porter in the lobby.

'There's a gentleman here who wants to see you. Says he's a friend,' a voice informed Dixie. And then Jack's voice came on the line.

'All right if I come up?' he asked.

'Of course.' Dixie hung up the phone on the wall and looked at Mike. 'It's Jack.'

'By himself?'

'He didn't say,' Dixie replied.

'I'll go to the front door,' Mike said. 'You sit down.'

For some reason they couldn't explain they both felt uneasy.

Dixie was perched on the edge of her chair when the two men entered the lounge and could tell by their faces something was wrong.

'Jack's just told me something,' Mike said, a slight quaver in his voice. Pulling Dixie to her feet he held her arms and took a deep breath. 'It's Danny...he's dead.'

The impact of the words on Dixie was immediate and her face screwed up in pain, her eyes bulging. She moaned and threw her arms around Mike sobbing.

'No, no, this can't be happening. I thought it was all over. No, no...'

Dixie cried uncontrollably for a long moment hanging on to Mike so tight it began to hurt. Then she loosened her grip and looked at Jack.

'What happened?'

Jack sat down in an armchair but before he could speak Mike asked if he wanted a drink.

'Yes,' Jack said gratefully, 'a scotch, please.'

Dixie sat back in her chair and didn't want anything except a box of tissues from the bedroom. But Mike joined Jack, pouring them both large ones.

'Danny committed suicide,' Jack continued.

'When?' Mike asked.

'Early this morning. We had a heavy session last night. Drank a lot of booze. I went to bed about midnight but Danny stayed downstairs. Said he had a lot of thinking to do. I came back downstairs about seven and found him dead in a chair. He'd taken a load of pills. Pain killers and sleeping tablets.'

'He didn't...,' Dixie hesitated, before completing her question,'...do this because of the DNA tests, did he?'

'No, I'm sure that wasn't the reason.' Jack took a drink. 'He was very depressed because his wife died on New Year's Day.'

'He was married?' Surprise in Dixie's voice.

Jack looked at her.

'Yes, very recently. Jessie had incurable cancer and he wanted to marry her before she died.'

'He never told us.'

Jack shrugged his shoulders.

'He figured you had enough on your plate without having to hear about his problems.'

'I knew about his lady in Norfolk,' Dixie said, 'and he *did* say she wasn't very well. But he said it wasn't serious. Oh, he should have told me...I suppose that's why he spent so much time with her.'

She looked at Jack for confirmation.

'Yes, that's right,' he replied. 'He knew she didn't have long to live and tried to be with her as much as possible. They'd been in love a long time.'

Dixie snivelled and tried hard to stop herself crying again.

'Another suicide...another funeral...when will it end? Oh, it's so sad. After everything all of us have been through...,' her voice tailed off.

'Yes,' Mike agreed. 'And he must have been depressed because I wouldn't have thought Danny was the kind of man who would commit suicide. That's surprised me.'

'He was depressed, for sure,' Jack said. 'I'd never seen him like that before. He was really broken up about losing his wife…and the booze didn't help...I just wished I'd have stayed drinking with him and not gone to bed.'

'It's not your fault,' Mike said. 'Unfortunately, these things happen. What did the police say?'

'There will be an inquest and then...a funeral. I'll arrange it if you like.'

Mike looked at Dixie before speaking.

'Well, Jack, I know the DNA tests proved that Danny wasn't Dixie's father, but legally, on paper, because of Dixie's birth certificate...she is his daughter. And, I believe, his next of kin.'

Jack nodded his head in agreement.

'Yes, you're right. Danny didn't have anyone else. Not anybody I can think of.'

'So, shall we make arrangements for the funeral?'

'What about if we do it together?'

Dixie looked at the big man and managed a smile.

'Yes, that's a good idea.'

*

The inquest was straightforward and the verdict reached that Danny had taken his own life while the balance of his mind was disturbed after the death of his wife.

It was decided Danny should be cremated and the service held in Norfolk rather than the body taken to London.

'I think that is where his heart really was,' Jack said, and Dixie was quite happy to go along with that.

There was only one hitch. Joey had to be in Los Angeles for a week and couldn't attend the funeral.

'It's something I can't break,' the pop star said. 'It's been arranged for some time now, and I've just got to go.'

But then Jack came up with an idea. The weekend after Joey returned from the States they could scatter Danny's ashes in the place he loved best.

'Where's that?' Dixie asked, and listened attentively as Jack explained about Danny's frequent walks on the beach by the North Sea.

'He told me it was the most peaceful place he'd ever known,' Jack said.

So it was agreed.

And Maggie, Jessie's mongrel dog wasn't forgotten either. Jack kept his word and she travelled with him wherever he went. In London Maggie was looked after by Jack's mother, but most of the time he was in Norfolk anyway, staying in the cottage, so the dog never felt too unsettled.

It was strange the way things had worked out.

When Jessie had died her will was straightforward. Everything was left to Danny. But it had never been put in her will, as it is with some, that if he died within twenty eight days of her death, then her estate would go to someone else nominated by her.

So when Danny died without leaving a will - everything went to his next of kin.

Which was Dixie, according to the law.

'This has come as a surprise to me and I want you to stay on in the cottage,' Dixie told Jack. 'That's if you want to.'

'Yes, I'd like that.'

'You were thinking of going into business with Danny,' Mike added. 'So maybe we can work something out. A pub wasn't it?'

'Yes, that's right,' Jack replied.

He'd been driving Danny's car on his trips to London and Dixie said he might as well keep it. A present.

'No, thanks,' Jack said, 'but I wouldn't mind trading it in and getting something else. I don't think black VW's have been lucky for us.'

'And we'll pay the difference, so make sure you get a new one,' Mike said, looking at Dixie, who nodded her head in agreement. 'We owe you a hell of a lot.'

SIXTY FIVE

Jack led the group of people across the fields. Dixie, Mike, Linda, Joey and Stan, with Maggie trotting in the rear.

The snow had melted and the ground was wet and heavy. Jack had warned the others to make sure they wore proper footwear and were well wrapped up against the cold, and the driving wind that always seemed to blow in off the sea. They had taken his advice - and were glad of it.

It took about twenty minutes before the group came to a concrete lined cut in the cliffs leading to their destination, the North Sea. They heard the roar of the water crashing on to the shore as they walked up a slight incline long before they saw it. Then the dark grey sea and white capped waves came into view, spray swirling in the wind, and they slowly and carefully descended halfway down the other side of the slippery ramp.

The group stood looking at the bleak desolate scene. The pounding waves and beach stretching empty in each direction as far as the eye could see. Then Jack, carrying a small plastic urn, walked on to the sandy, pebbled beach heading for the shoreline and the others followed.

'This is as good a place as any,' Jack said, stopping close to the foamy water running up the beach, some of it washing over his leather boots. He held up the urn about to remove the top.

'Before you do that,' Dixie said, raising her voice against the wind. 'Let's all have a thought for Danny.'

And the group of people bowed their heads.

Jack was the first to move after about a minute and slipped the lid off the urn. Then, sensibly, didn't try to hurl the ashes into the air, but waded out until the cold water reached just under his knees, and scattered Danny's remains on the water. He turned, walked back to the beach and saw Dixie crying softly on Mike's shoulder.

'Let's go,' Joey said, deeply affected by the occasion. He'd thought a lot of Danny.

'Mike, I'd like a word,' Jack said.

The young man looked at Jack and gently pushed Dixie towards Linda.

'I won't be long,' he said. 'Look after her,' he added, as Joey put a comforting arm around Dixie.

Then the group, led by Stan, moved away leaving Jack and Mike by themselves, the harsh, cold wind gusting against them.

'I want to tell you the truth about Danny's death,' Jack said, giving Mike a penetrating look.

Mike looked puzzled but didn't speak.

'Danny didn't commit suicide,' Jack continued. 'I killed him.'

A look of sheer astonishment swept across Mike's face as the shock of the older man's blunt statement hit him and it took a strong effort for him to form his words.

'I don't believe it.'

'It's true, Mike.'

'But why? You two were such good friends.'

'I know, and I really liked Danny, but I've never been more wrong about a bloke in all my life.' Jack's voice was bitter. 'He conned all of us.'

'You didn't answer my question. Why?'

'Because Danny wanted Dixie dead too.'

'He what?' Mike paused for a moment, disbelief in his voice. 'How do you know?'

'Kate Smith phoned Danny at the cottage and I listened in on the extension. It was her boyfriend, his name was Eddie, who was the person trying to kill Dixie all along, on Robert Fisher's instructions. Fisher wanted control of her money, but this Eddie, wondering why it was so important Danny had to be blamed contacted him. Then Danny told him he was really Dixie's father, not Tom Fisher. So Eddie had nothing to lose. If he killed Dixie then he would have got paid by at least one of them. It would have been up to Danny and Fisher to have sorted out who Dixie's father was.'

'And you think Danny agreed to have Dixie killed?' Amazement on Mike's features.

'Yes, and if you'd heard Kate Smith's conversation, you would too,' the big man replied stonily.

'For chrisake, Jack, Danny thought Dixie was his daughter at that time. His own flesh and blood.'

Jack paused for a moment knowing he had to pick his words carefully.

'I think for many years Danny was in love with a dream, a dream that he had a daughter somewhere. That he might find her one day. But the reality is, when Eddie told him that Dixie was going to die whatever happened, Danny went along with it. Remember, Danny hadn't seen Dixie since she was a baby over twenty years ago. That's a long time, and I think it was then he realized that for all his daydreaming, he and Dixie were nothing more than strangers. He didn't know her. She was just a name and didn't think he'd ever see her again. So he went for the chance of big money. Danny was often short of cash.'

'Dixie told me this Eddie character is dead,' Mike said.

'So Kate Smith said,' Jack replied. 'He was the one driving the sports car...the one that slammed into you. I know Tony fired off several shots...so he must have hit him.'

'But I don't understand,' Mike said. 'Even if what you say is true, it still doesn't make sense, because those DNA results established that Danny wasn't Dixie's father after all. He wouldn't have got any money...he didn't have a motive.'

Jack turned his head, looking at the raging sea for some time, before swivelling his gaze back to the young man.

'Did you ever have a conversation with Danny about Dixie's happiness? Did you tell him if he hadn't come on the scene Dixie would have been happy to always think of Tom Fisher as her father?'

'No,' Mike replied.

'He told me that's what you said. He said you and him had talked about it. That Dixie's life would have been less complicated if he hadn't reappeared in her life.'

'I don't know what you're talking about,' Mike said. 'Danny and I never had any conversation like that.'

'He told me he was only interested in Dixie being happy and after hearing from you how she felt didn't mind making a sacrifice. And so that's why we did what we did.'

'And what was that?'

'It was *my* blood that was sent off for those DNA tests. Not Danny's. He said it would be better for Dixie if it was determined he wasn't her father. And I like a fool believed him.' Jack snorted. 'Now I know he lied. And why.'

'But the doctor...'

'Dr Gray is well known by people like me and Danny and will do anything if the money is right. You see, all he had to do at a later date was say he'd made a mistake and got the samples mixed up.'

'And if Dixie had been killed,' Mike said, haltingly, 'Danny would have supplied a real blood sample.'

'Yes. Dixie's DNA test is now a matter of record and it would have been easy to prove the match.'

'So Danny was right in thinking he was Dixie's father all along,' Mike said.

Jack nodded.

'Yes. He knew.'

Mike stood there, leaning into the buffeting wind, his mind trying to make sense of everything.

'All this...what you've told me...seems too incredible. Mind you, we'll never really know the truth, will we?'

'What do you mean?' Jack looked enquiringly at the younger man.

'Danny's dead. As a matter of fact, all that's left of him is here.' And Mike indicated towards the sea. 'So we're not going to get any more blood.'

'Yes we can,' Jack said. 'Dr Gray did take a sample from Danny as well. It's in his surgery now. I can get it if you want.'

The answer surprised Mike, making him think harder.

'No,' and he shook his head, 'I suppose it's best to leave things as they are.'

'You believe Danny was Dixie's father, don't you?'

Jack's question was direct and Mike stared hard at the other man before replying.

'Yes I do. I don't know why, but I always did.' Mike paused. 'But there is one other thing I don't understand.'

'What's that?'

'Jessie, his wife who died. She left him the cottage, money and part ownership of a business. Surely he wouldn't have needed Dixie's money now.'

'Perhaps, but don't forget,' Jack reminded the younger man, 'Danny was already involved before Jessie died. He was already committed, and if Dixie had died in that car crash, he would never have met her. And you must also remember, Danny might have prevented that if he'd contacted Dixie.'

'That's for sure,' Mike said. 'He should have warned Dixie as soon as this man told Danny she was going to die. Or, at the very least, he should have said something as soon as he met his daughter.'

'Of course,' Jack agreed. 'But what could he say? At first I thought it was okay for you to be murdered but now I've met you I've changed my mind. No, he had to keep quiet, and hope nobody found out. So, Danny was as guilty as the murderer.'

'You're right,' Mike said slowly. 'But this man, Eddie, is dead now. So...would Danny have got someone else to go after Dixie?'

'It wouldn't be a problem,' Jack replied, 'I can think of half a dozen people right now...off the top of my head. And Danny knew them as well.'

'Maybe he wouldn't have tried.'

Jack gave a harsh laugh.

'You could be right, but would *you* have been prepared to take that kind of chance with Dixie's life? Even the smallest chance?'

Mike shook his head and his reply was so soft the wind nearly drowned out the words.

'No...I wouldn't take that chance,' he admitted. 'Not with Dixie's life.'

'And if Danny was going to do anything he would have made his move very soon.' Jack's tone was emphatic.

'Why do you say that?'

Jack smiled at the man standing before him.

'I take it you will be marrying Dixie?'

'Yes, without a doubt. As a matter of fact we've agreed on a date. This Easter, but we haven't made it public yet.'

'There you are. Once you and Dixie were married then you would become her next of kin, not Danny. I don't suppose Dixie's made a will yet.'

'No, not to my knowledge.'

'So if Danny was going to do anything he would have had to done it before Easter. I'm sure Dixie would have told him about your wedding plans.'

'Yes, I suppose she would have.'

Jack turned his head out to sea again for a long moment before turning back and looking at Mike.

'I promised Danny, and you, nobody would hurt Dixie. *And I've kept that promise.*'

Jack turned his head away again and Mike knew the conversation was over. He started to move but then paused and placed a hand on the big man's shoulder.

'Thanks,' he said, 'and *I* promise I'll never repeat this conversation to anyone else.'

Jack didn't say anything, just nodded his head, and Mike hurried in the direction Dixie and his friends had taken, leaving the older man with Maggie faithfully crouched by his side. Both looking out to sea, the man's wet feet icy cold.

Jack felt moistness in his eyes and blinked his lids several times as he stared at the water, Danny's ashes now vanished with the violent waves and flying spray. His gaze lifted towards the distant horizon. Must be the wind.

Bastards don't cry.

Do they?

Also in print by the same author:

We'll Meet Again

Order on the internet
www.antra.co.uk
or buy in bookshops

Antra Publishing

About the author:

Ray Chapman was born in London's East End in 1937. A wartime kid he was bombed out twice during the blitz.
'*Hitler was beginning to give me the hump.*'
Ray always wanted to be a writer and at the age of seventeen sent a film script to Hollywood.
'*My first rejection.*'
Ray started his working life as a ladies and gents hairdresser and worked in Canada and America in the late 1950's. Then he did a couple of years as a deck hand on an American oil tanker before returning to England and another stint in hairdressing.
But Ray still had a burning ambition to write and became a freelance journalist selling stories to all the national newspapers.
'*And learning how to be a Fleet Street drunk.*'
Ray joined the News of the World where he worked as a reporter for over thirty years and is now in semi-retirement.
He has three daughters and one son and lives with his third wife, Judi, in north London.
Only As A Stranger is Ray Chapman's second book.
'*A best seller...well, that's what my dear old Mum and Dad would have said, if they were still alive. God bless 'em.*'